Silent Symphonies

SALLY CHIWUZIE

My J.C,
Thank you so
much for your
support
xx
Sally

ISBN: 978-1-4834-2038-7 (sc)
ISBN: 978-1-4834-2039-4 (hc)
ISBN: 978-1-4834-2037-0 (e)

Lulu Publishing Services rev. date: 1/19/2015

I dedicate this to the members of my inner circle, who require no introduction. Thank you for being the anchor to the woman who feels safe enough to be nobody but who she is. Because of you, I am simply Sally ☺

Acknowledgement

Silent Symphonies has been a long journey and will feel incomplete without mentioning a few people who pushed this dream with me.

I would like to recognise my Chief Editors—Aaron Oteze and Ruth Lunn and my Reviewers/Consultants—Malaika Mazise, Tracey Chiwuzie, Dee Castro-Uwajeh, Ifueko Yayi, Tiyan Alile, Deirdre Lowe, Yvonne Harrison, Michelle Van Otten and Aaron Oteze. Thank you for taking the time to read endless chapters of Silent Symphonies repeatedly until we were content.

Thank you to Charlie 'Tuns' Okpaise for the inspiration behind the book cover.

Thank you to Jasper Chiwuzie, Nonny Azike and Thelma Chiwuzie for consultation on the Ibo Language and Culture.

Thank you to Gaurav Verma, Anirban Ghosh and Kailash Sahoo for consultation on the Hindu Language and Culture.

Thank you to my fantastic crew for the creation of the Book Trailer:

Production and Direction—David Innes Edwards, Richard Pailin, Amaka Jackson

Crew/Support/Consultancy—Tracey Chiwuzie, Malaika Mazise, Jasper Jnr. Chiwuzie, and Amaka Jackson

Make up by Jessica Summer Buckley, thank you

Music by Aitua Ogiamen, thank you

Acting Crew—Tristan Smith Morris, Marco Biagioli, Penelope Read and Emmira Obayuwana

During the course of preparing Silent Symphonies for the market, www.sallychiwuzie.com was born. The introductory video would not have been possible without the input of the following people:

Consultancy/Production—Michelle Van Otten, Fantasia Studios—Watford, and Ric Pailin

Music by Aitua Ogiamen, thank you

Thank you to the following people for taking time out to aid my research and open up in interviews—Amaka Jackson, Aisha Alli, Penelope Read, Lem Nwabueze, Yvonne Harrison, Shirin Kousari, Souzana Papadopoulou, Ranjini Argawal-James, Surekha Patel, Michelle Van Otten, Charlotte Myring, Thelma Azike

Thank you to the members of the Together We Are Unshakable Movement on Facebook for love and inspiration.

There are a few people who have taken on multiple roles through this journey that I would like to give special recognition to, especially for the emotional/mental support provided, sometimes at the most inconvenient times. Thank you for your honesty, patience, dedication and limitless support at varying points through this process, in some cases, throughout.

Malaika, Tracey, Jasper Jnr., Thelma (Mum), Jasper (Dad), Aaron, Fola, Tiyan, Ifueko, Chioma, Yvonne, Dee, Amaete, Ekpen, Cornell, Simba, Tuns and Jania.

Finally—thank you to Immi and Khare—the two people who call me Mummy, and added depth to the emotive language required during the creation of Silent Symphonies.

I am grateful and remain indebted to you…

Prologue

Her bright red rocking chair.

'In life there are no guarantees. There could be dust or rain, gold or gain, cold moments of pain. You just never know. It is only certain that you will laugh, you will cry, you will die!'.

One could tell that Mother Nature had once upon a time been generous to her. The telltale signs of stunning beauty still lurked underneath the shadows of a wrinkle or two.

From the haven of her shed, Leila gazed reflectively at the sky, her eyes dancing about like Ping-Pong balls, observing. Before her was a dark, angry night. It was typical: nature at work. The sky roared with thunder but in its viciousness still was the most beautiful sight to behold. Its boldness and authority overlooked the whole beach for at least a thousand miles and faded to the beyond. The trees swayed naturally according to the rhythm of the wind; the water was restless with tempestuous ripples, coloured black, grey and silver by the reflection of the sky; the clouds seemingly divided in two dark orange shades of confusion. It was evident that somewhere, somehow, a storm was craving liberation. It longed to wet the firmaments with its tears. It was unusual. She immersed herself in its beauty, relishing this rare picture. It also brought back memories.

She stroked the tattoo on her right foot very gently. Lost in a trance, her mind wandered, her toes curled, her fingers gently caressed the embroidered slits on either side of a beautiful black maxi dress. She allowed herself to traverse without sift, backwards down memory lane. The past was recaptured in detail as moment-by-moment flashbacks caused tears to trickle down her cheeks.

'Please don't close your eyes.'

Chapter Two

A miserable Leila sat outside the café just across the road from work. It was small and dingy, and smelt of stale coffee but she loved that café for no other reason than the disconnection it offered. She found herself there most afternoons and was even on first name terms with the attendants. She went there not for lack of choice, but simply because it was time out from crossing t's, dotting i's, looking important. She was comfortable enough to lose herself to her subconscious and her mind often travelled miles as she took tiny sips of coffee. For the last two years she had visited the café at least every other day and had never managed to finish that cup of grande soya Americano she ordered each time. It was simply a large coffee with soya milk, which always turned cold way before she awoke from her thoughts. It was also the only thing that didn't have to be in pairs. Perhaps the fact that she drank half the cup offered a compromise to her random idiosyncrasy.

That afternoon she had been there an hour that felt like five minutes, mulling over the events of the night before one more time. In the last few months Akash had become a stranger - inconsiderate, self absorbed and selfish. He was usually predictable but there seemed to be something unsettlingly different about her husband's behavioural pattern that totally rattled her ability to manipulate his heart. So much so that she, once ebullient, had suddenly turned into this meek, languid person with insecurities, totally uncharacteristic of her personality.

It was a rude awakening from what she imagined a marriage – *her marriage* – would be. Tears crawled down her cheeks.

'I told you, Leila, sometimes, I just need to be by myself to sort my head out.'

'This is so unlike you, Kash. Normally, you would call to let me know you would be late.'

'Leila, your paranoia will be the death of this marriage!' They both watched his mobile phone ring endlessly. If he were going to just watch it ring, one would think he would be subtle about his ringtone choice. Something so 'animated' was bound to attract her attention surely. The *'You can't touch this'* song by MC Hammer always lingered on, like a hammer hitting nails emphatically hard in her brain for hours after, and it was always on repeat.

'Aren't you going to answer that?' she asked him after the seventh or eighth ring and she reached out for the phone.

'It's my phone, Leila. Not yours!' He rushed forward and snatched it, walking into the bedroom. She stood in the kitchen confused as she heard him tell the caller that he was in the middle of a 'discussion' and would call back at his earliest convenience. Only he didn't go back into the kitchen to appease her, to tell her it would be okay and that he still loved her the same way he did when they had exchanged those vows on their wedding day. He rushed into the shower in a flash. Within twenty minutes, he was dressed and out the door, the scent of his perfume mixed with a potent amount of his masculinity lingering on way after his rather rude departure.

'But you only just got back home,' she called helplessly after him, and then added pathetically, 'where are you going?'

At least he peered through the kitchen window. 'Something requires my urgent attention,' he said, not looking her in the face. No kiss goodbye. No second look. No second thought.

'Back soon!' he called out hurriedly as he picked up his phone, dialing a number.

She spent most of the night in bed staring at the ceiling. It was way past midnight when she heard the sound of his engine; she turned over, rolled herself to the edge of the bed facing the wall, and shut her eyes. He silently slipped into bed without an explanation, without a kiss and without his customary, cheesy, 'I love you, wifey. Didn't you stay up for me?'

'It happens all over the world… to most couples,' Olga had said.

'It really ought to be a lot simpler!' she mused.

She still managed to love him so much that the thought of losing him was like a knife through her heart. She hated herself for feeling so vulnerable, so helpless, and so dependent on him for her happiness. He hadn't even sung for her in yonks! She wished he would sit with her on one of those benches in the park and sing to her. He had a beautiful voice. She smiled sadly.

Often Leila denied herself any feelings of uncertainty that everyone felt every now and then (she hoped) but this night was different. It had come over her in a sudden rush. She sat there in the café and recalled how she had just about managed noiselessly to cry herself to sleep. She foresaw more tears in the future…if she did not sort this out with him. She was scared. The foundations of her marriage were rocky and she sat there feeling the strong vibrations, unable to stop their once solid foundation from falling apart. She stared blankly at the words on the page she was writing:

Dear Diary,
I swung open the doors of my nature-loving mind's eye
That it may once again embrace the perfect moment as it went by
The scene opened with the brightest blue lacy sky
Overlooking a perfect world that would never die
The perfect lawn, green, screaming delight, bathed in rain
The singing naked child, ever so joyful, not a care, no pain
The happy couple, so in love, so delightful, walking down the lane
Never had two perfect scenarios of love's beauty looked exactly the same
The mystery lonely bird on the tree, chirping the melody on my mind
Aching desperately for me to feel the moment I couldn't find
You'd hurt me, my heart so broken, numb and oblivious; pain: the worst of its kind

For though those doors were swung open, even my nature-loving mind was sad, its eye, momentarily blind.

She signed it with a stray, telltale tear, oblivious to the world and its chirping birds (Okay so it was London City - hardly any chirping birds but there was one which appeared and disappeared intermittently). Someone close invaded her space and broke her reverie. She looked up. A man towered above her table, afraid to interrupt, patiently waiting to attract her attention.

'Sorry to bother you… can I sit here? It's just that it's so busy in… in…inside the ca… ca…café, there are no… no…no… uno…ccupied seats and I would really love to sit and… and… and… drink my coffee.' He stuttered all the way through his sentence.

She had been wallowing in self-pity and needed a moment to recover from her flounder. She hoped he hadn't noticed her tear stained face

'Sorry, be my guest,' she offered, surreptitiously brushing across her right cheek with her finger.

He had dark hair, very dark hair, she noticed. When he did catch her gaze he gaped at first like he had just seen a ghost. He looked confused, with his mouth torn ajar slightly, but he got over it swiftly and regained his composure. She wondered if she had lipstick blots on her teeth or ink stains on her cheeks or something. She concluded that her mind was playing tricks on her. Akash was obviously driving her crazier than she thought.

'Is everything ok?' Her question was lost in the explosive sound of drilling. Construction workers outside the cafe had started work.

'I'm just on…on… a quick lunch break,' he said.

'What?' She had not heard a word. He came closer and spoke directly into her right ear.

She nodded and flashed a swift decorous smile.

'Where do you work?' she shouted back into his ear.

'O…o...over there,' he managed to say eventually pointing across the road.

'Excuse my speech impediment, it's intermittent,' he apologised. Leila furrowed her brow slightly, amazed at how he could use words like 'impediment' and 'intermittent' without his stutter and yet struggle with the simplest monosyllables. She smiled. The construction workers had wandered off, thank goodness.

'At the hospital?' she asked, somewhat shocked. He looked far too casual, she thought, with no disrespect whatsoever intended.

It was his turn to nod and smile.

'Casual Friday,' he said.

'But it's Tuesday.'

'Well it's still Friday, otherwise I would have been home and back at least four times.'

'You mean you have been at work since Friday?' she asked horrified.

'Only joking,' and then he laughed subtly. 'But it was worth it to get that expression from you,' he added.

Leila softened. 'What do you do?' she questioned.

'I mend broken hearts,' he replied, flashing the most gorgeous, genuine smile she had seen in a long time. 'And I mean that li..li... literally,' he added enjoying the puzzled look on her face.

Ok, whatever the 'obvious' joke was, it flew over her head. She just stared blankly. He seemed to have a suppressed grin on his face.

'I'm a cardiologist,' and again, he managed that particularly 'baritone' line without a stutter. Leila smiled. It was perhaps the cheesiest line she had ever heard, but it intrigued her. It was her first heart-felt smile all day, but he did not know that. (It turns out he sensed it, but she found that out later.)

'Maybe I've met the right person then,' she thought aloud without meaning to.

'Maybe,' he replied thoughtfully matching his words with a conflicting nonchalance, his expression screaming, and 'I am not chatting you up!' She took note of the word and the expression and decided on balance of probabilities that it was better not to seek clarification. He asked no further questions, she offered no explanations and they made no more courteous conversation. They sat, silently sipping coffee and staring at that random bird chirping on the tree. Each made a conscious effort not to look in the other's direction. Finally polite goodbyes were said with both wishing the other a good day.

He crossed the road to the hospital and she went back to her desk to write her next article. It got published in the popular magazine – Silent

Symphonies. For no apparent reason, it was bigger in Switzerland – than in the UK, despite the language barrier. Gaurav Verma, the big boss, paid someone to translate the magazine into Swiss-German and the people loved it. Her PA thought it had something to do with her matter-of-fact, blatant, and occasionally bordering on rude representation of matters of the heart. She had found the people in Switzerland quite impolite but had been told that they were 'honest', unlike the Brits. The magazine was also affiliated to a book-publishing firm, one that had been trying to inveigle her into publishing her collection of articles and short stories for two years and counting. It had never felt like the right time to do this though.

Anyway, following on from her fascinating day, the evening came and her husband seemed less inconsiderate and self-absorbed, less selfish, or if he was, she didn't notice. Her thoughts were dominated by 'interesting conversations' – what she should have said, what she shouldn't have and why. For some bizarre reason and curiously so, a tall stranger with very dark hair was on her mind. These were the kind of 'not-particularly-guilty' thoughts that carelessly flirted in the minds of perhaps single, bored, or emotionally neglected women. In this case, it was a shame to note which category or categories Leila fell into. It had been a while since her husband had 'noticed' her, but that night, she did not bother with lingerie – not one out of her Rosamosario collection that Akash loved but had not contributed to in seven months and counting – or the red one he could hardly resist. No, she went to bed in an old, creased tee shirt that she had only just rescued from the washing machine – and yet, Leila felt incredibly sexy. Her thoughts were dominated by 'interesting conversations' – what she should have said, what she shouldn't have and why (to a tall stranger with very dark hair). These were the kind of 'not-particularly-guilty' thoughts that carelessly flirted in the minds of perhaps single, bored, or emotionally neglected women. In this case, it was a shame to note which category or categories Leila fell into. Her husband still did not notice her; she did not care – she slept peacefully. She even managed to get through the night without chanting Karyn White's '*Superwoman*'!

The next morning, Leila was first at the breakfast table.

'You look pretty this morning,' he said. She met his eye over the teacup he had raised to his lips, hiding behind it to observe her. He did not look too bad to the eye either. That morning he wore his Pal Zileri suit – the grey pinstriped one with the gloss. The detailed trousers with its peak lapels, ticket pocket and flat front pants. It gripped his bum in the right places. He dressed it up with a polka-dotted grey and pink tie. He wore that over a shirt that was so softly pink it made his eyes sparkle.

'Flattery will get you nowhere, Mr Yoganathan,' she joked light-heartedly.

He was in a good mood, she noticed. They had obviously both forgotten the awkward conversation in the kitchen. It was typical of their relationship, a fatally dangerous coping mechanism. They were too cowardly to confront their fears head on, preferring instead to let it build over weeks and months. Every day they patched together the torn fabric of their marriage hoping that one day it would stop ripping. Why was it ripping? Were their stitches not strong enough? Would it therefore be a tangled mess of thread one day? One day… too late?

'That's a lovely top,' he said, then added, 'Karen Millen?'

She paused from drinking her coffee. 'You bought it, Kash.'

'I know!' he said casually through squinted eyes.

She half smiled. That morning, she plucked her eyebrows, wore mascara and slid on her 'all-day-long guarantee' cherry red lipstick. She also stared intently at herself in the mirror, still in self-denial when even the application of her Caron's Poivre was somewhat sensual. She told herself that the humming and adornment was in anticipation of the 'important clients' that were due in the office at 10 o'clock. Nothing to do with the chance encounter she was hoping for. Nope, that would be absurd, she said pouting nonchalantly.

'Listen, about yesterday or was it the day before…'

'Kash, just leave it, OK,' she interrupted not wanting to re-live the awful moment. She had heard it all before any way.

'But…' he attempted. She cut him short.

'You are going to say to me that we are not joined at the hip, you need to live your own life independent of our marriage, we are separate individuals and that you don't need to answer to me because I am not your mother, aren't you?'

'No, I am not.'

'Then you are lying,' she added matter-of-factly and sipped more coffee, bracing herself for the explosion. Accusing Akash of dishonesty was like baiting a wounded lion.

'Do not fucking call me a liar!' he snapped, slamming his fist on the breakfast table.

She jumped.

'It is glass, AKASH. A fucking expensive glass table too!' She had tired of absorbing his excesses. Time to give back.

'I bought it! I know what it is made of; I know how much it cost too. And don't call me Akash!'

They stared coldly at each other for a few seconds.

He took a deep breath.

'All I am trying to say, darling…' He took another deep breath; she raised an eyebrow in sarcasm and exasperation. He continued, '… is that just because you don't know every time I sneeze does not mean I don't love you. I love you. That's why I married you. You preach to me every day that a relationship built on a strong foundation of love can never be rocked by the storms of life, and we have that…we have love, right?'

'Do we?'

'You taught me that love is patient, love is kind.' He parried her rhetoric, quoting her favourite Bible verse. Once upon a time, she had melted each time he quoted a Bible verse. These days he used it as a manipulative tactic, and it belittled her. She was Christian and he, Hindu, and as much as it had never been an issue for them, his parents had taken a while to come round to the idea even though, hypocritically, his mothers heritage was a mix of Muslim and Hindu. In the course of getting to know each other, they had taught each other about their respective religious beliefs and somehow in her passion for her Christian beliefs, she had managed to turn Akash into some sort of mini apostate, taking him to church with her and observing all major Christian events together.

'Love also encompasses compromise, self-sacrifice and understanding because these are all elements of unselfishness as well, Akash,' she interrupted.

'Don't call me Akash, Leila.'

Leila looked away.

'Love covers a multitude of sins,' he continued. She detected a hint of sarcasm.

'Oh shut up!' she snapped with as much control as she could muster. 'Stop quoting Bible verses that you care nothing about!'

'Leila, you are a selfish little diva. At least I picked up your Bible verses because they were important to you. I have gone from referring to your crucifix as your *plus sign necklace* to learning numerous Bible verses for you. What Hindi stuff do you know out of the Bhagavad Gita? Can you speak or write Hindi? What have you learnt?' Leila wanted to vomit her irritation. She straightened and fired back a salvo.

'In sāat qadmoon kē baad āap mērē dōst ban ga'ē hain. Mein aasha karti hun k mein aap ki dōstī kē lāyak hō sakoon aur mērī dōstī mujhē aur aap ko ēk banā day' - With seven steps you have become my friend. I hope that I deserve your friendship and that our friendship makes me and you one'

'And this is a Sanskrit, holy words known by a learned few. How do I know? I am interested and I listen to everything you tell me. Anything important to you is important to me!'

'Is this a competition then? Who knows more? More so, do I enforce it on you? Do you have to know it? Practise it?' he asked her. It was a weak comeback and she saw it in his eyes. He had been taken completely unawares. 'The words? Or Hindu? I don't ask you to be Christian, do I? As for the words, I live them, don't I?'

There was that hurt look on her face again. The one that sent him apologising even for crimes he had never committed. He softened.

'You're not asking me to change are you? Night can never be morning or vice versa and just because Queen Leila is inconvenienced by it, Monday will never come after Tuesday. That's just the way it is,' he said softly, but firmly – licking his lips and slicking his hair. This was characteristic. That morning he looked delicious. She wished she could peek around to see his taut bum again. When he licked his lips, he raised his right eyebrow and squinted, looking down at Leila. Her sisters had always commented that he was the tallest Asian man they knew. Well, he was from a town called *Punjab,* which had unconfirmed rumours that the men from this town were tall and hunky, broad and brave (especially the clan of them who had migrated in hundreds to Canada, referring to themselves as 'brown'). This town had a reputation for successful agricultural economies, import and export of farm produce so they were hard working physically which accounted for their build – apparently.

Leila fought the impulse to spit at him and jump astride him, the latter comprising tearing the shirt to shreds whilst playing tonsils wrestling and moving onto other games that involved pretend horse-riding. Both impulses came in at the same time.

'Such arrogance!' she thought angrily. 'Fucking sexy beast!' She sighed. He knew how to get to her, but every now and again – such as moments like this – he overstepped his boundaries, so much so that where she ought to see a harmless, beautifully tamed puppy, she saw a hyena – a dangerous one. He also had a bad temper and chose the wrong times to exhibit this bad habit. Leila was secretly scared of his outbursts but would be damned before she let him see her fear. So far, she was confident that he would not dare lay a finger on her.

She understood he would never change, but she had only realised yesterday that every day another little piece of her heart got broken and slowly she was losing her faith in what she had always known as and believed in – love, good old fashioned love.

'You will never know everything, Leila, but I will never do anything to hurt you and that should be good enough for you,' he said softly, with an undertone of something. Leila was not sure if she had imagined that smirk, but these days, the grey shades were blatant. She did not know what to think any more.

'Not consciously you won't,' she said shaking her head at the helplessness of the situation.

'I do love you, though,' His words did not match the arrogant expression on his face. She stared blankly, although her betraying heart agreed that even with his frailties, sales pitches, and pompous words, she still loved him. She was attracted to the air of authority around him. When he spoke, people listened. This turned her on. Not to mention his good looks and suaveness. He was proud, but she knew somehow that she could press his buttons. She was his weakness. They made the perfect magazine cover couple. The problem with this of course was that in a relationship one could not rely solely on love. One had to make an effort as well, because most times, as people tend to find out a little too late, love without its many accompaniments simply is not enough to make a relationship work. What about honesty, respect, compromise, self-sacrifice?

'And I love you too…' she replied sincerely, then kissed him on the lips and added, 'but sometimes, love is not enough.' Akash slid his left hand out of his pocket and glided it in her direction, reaching out to her right arm as she walked away. She slipped out of his grasp and walked out. She felt like she was on the edge of a cliff. At some point She knew she would step off it. What she could not

predict was what would happen next.

'Do I fly or fall?'

He took a couple of steps towards the door and then froze. He slid his hands back into his pocket. Why did he have to prove anything? He raised an eyebrow and made his way to the kitchen window. He stared on after her with a squint. She was a far cry from the vulnerable woman he had met in the park some six or so years ago. She had grown, found a voice.. She no longer melted in his arms. He had thought then that he had the perfect spell over her and all his immigration worries were over. Falling head over heels in love with this female fatale had not been part of the deal for him. She did anger him to the point where he wanted to walk away, but he did not. She knew she held him in the palm of her hand like a stress ball, and boy, did she squeeze! Subconsciously, she knew it was all about the papers. She must have done. Did she not think the wooing a bit OTT? Sometimes he found it comical; he smiled, thinking about the flowers and poetry. He had loved playing the game. She, in return, had to admit that she was the envy of the town. He lavished her with 'good boyfriend' stuff. But then, his love for her began to radiate in his eyes. It showed in her gentle confidence, in those stringy knickers she wore round the house, the pole in the middle of the bedroom and the impossible positions she assumed hanging upside down from it, her hair – especially in an untidy mess – her beautifully mixed blood. It was the way she called his name. Yes he fell, but he always kept his eye on the prize. He had the prize with a genuine marriage to her as a bonus. Now what? Now he could not live without her, yet, in a million years, he would never have chosen someone so stubborn. He would be damned if he would show any weakness to make her feel good about herself, not after all the effort he had put in. Yes, he had paid his dues. She would be a good little wife for him. His eyes narrowed. After all, he had chosen her when a submissive, humble Hindi chick would have sufficed. Who needs love and its complications? Yet here he was staring out of the window. He shook his head.

'Arrrggghhhhh!' he fumed as he slicked his hair…and licked his lips.

As she drove through the City traffic, her mind pondered on many 'what ifs' and 'maybes', doubts and hopes, dreams and realities. She thought about what it was; what it is now, what it ought to be and worried because she searched her future and she just could not find Akash in her vision. Once upon a time, they shared everything. He was her partner, her life. The sun rose and set in his eyes and for every minute away from him, she found it harder to breathe. She missed the flowers and the chocolate and the cards, the attempt at poetry and the adoration. She craved his attention, being the centre of his universe. These days, she felt like she did not exist. He waltzed in and out of their home as he pleased, offering no explanation and was cagey about his whereabouts. They had become two strangers living two separate lives, sharing a house, not a home. It was all the things they had promised never to make each other feel. It was the smallest, but yet the biggest things; the things that kept the fire burning. Leila felt betrayed. Before she married Akash Yoganathan, her relationship history was hardly worthy of reminiscent thought. It consisted of a couple of dead-end relationships. When he found her, she was picking up the gazillion pieces of her one-too-many-a-time broken heart. He had rescued her from her relationship land loping and nursed her back to believing in love at the point when she had just about given up. She, on the other hand, had picked him up from a low point in his life when he was considering going back to India. She had convinced him to stay, and drawn a beautiful picture of his achievements and all the heights she knew he would achieve in the future.

'But my visa will run out. I have no status in this country,' he had said after one of their endless love making sessions.

'Status? You have me. That's all the status you need.' He had held her tight that night and promised the moon, stars, heaven and earth. He even chucked in a rainbow for good measure. Then he lay back, switched on the TV and watched Formula One. That night, Leila watched him pick his nose excitedly as he watched Michael Schumacher race down the tracks. She knew he was comfortable with her at that point. Disgusting as the habit was, the fact that she could lie there almost amused put her at ease. His flaws did not bother her. That night, she knew she had found a husband. She would marry him ASAP. She was not letting him go back to India. Leila pressed hard on her brakes.

'BASTARD! He married me for his papers?' It had never even occurred to her. She shook her head. That would render her whole marriage a lie. But he had sung to her, made love to her, wined and dined her. Leila was confused. How cruel! She shrugged her shoulders as she gave up. She switched on her radio for her daily torture of dedications and love songs played repeatedly for the lucky few. She listened to one of Gloria Estefan's numbers, and instead of wallowing in self-pity, the lyrics whispered on her lips amidst a distant wishful smile on her face; reminiscing, imagining slow dancing whilst feeling the gratification that only true love can bring. In her mind, she slow-danced in the dark with the perfect man… more specifically, a tall man with thick dark hair and perhaps a speech impediment because, at the moment, Akash did not fit in with the picture, and she could not dance alone. No, that would make the most unnatural daydream. This stuttering man would have to do for the purpose of this particular daydream. Leila thoroughly enjoyed her daydream, and wondered what with all the shower head episodes whether this new found DIY attitude was healthy. Despite the traffic, she got to work earlier than usual. She had a detoxing green tea and then a coffee (oh, the weird things she did when her mind was in a state of disarray!).

Leila got on with her morning. The one thing she had going for her was her career. She was not exactly Bill Gates, but compared to the average woman, she ranked pretty highly. She was located right in the heart of London city, and was accorded the automatic prestige that accompanied her geographical location. *Silent Symphonies* was reputable and generous, and she took home a very healthy pay package every month. It couldn't compare with Akash's, but still it could sustain her needs comfortably and even leave her a little extra for her worldly requirements – Hermes Birkin bags and Prada loafers inclusive. Five years ago, she would never have dreamt that all this would happen so soon, but here she was.

Her thoughts were interrupted when she saw her 'to do' list. She had taken up more responsibilities with Silent Symphonies and it was no longer simply about the weekly articles. She had built her own clientele within the magazine. There were contracts to sign, articles to finish and clients to deal with at 10 o'clock. She did all that and still there was a whole hour to go before her accustomed noon lunch break. Even with the resistance put up by the photocopying machine, she still seemed to be working in fast-forward. Someone somewhere had conspired to stop the clock! Surely, it was time for a break. She convinced herself that she was starving. All these thoughts were leaving her in dire need of some carbs! The Atkins Diet was doing her no good! She gaped curiously out of the window. It had absolutely nothing to do with the tall dark man making his way to the café… after all, despite her husband's shortcomings, she was still madly in love with him. Still, she stared on and something in her stomach did a double somersault.

'Bianca,' she called out, still staring out of the window. 'I'm off to lunch early, I'm starving.' It was 11.45am and being such a creature of habit, the sudden craving for carbs (or something) was questionable, but she ignored her reasonable gremlins, powdered her nose and literally power walked to the café.

'Hi,' she said shyly. He smiled warmly. He tried to look calm and blasé, but she suspected he was nervous and probably pleased to see her too.

'Please...' he said, pulling out a seat opposite his, indicative of an invitation.

'Can I g...ge...get you a... drink? Lunch?' He did sound a bit nervous.

'A grande soya Americano would be great, thanks,' Leila said. Of course a double brandy would have been the preferred option – something to sedate her unruly nerves, but she decided to behave herself. He nodded and signalled across to the waiter.

'I'm Kaobimdi, shortened to Kaobi, with a silent 'a' in be...be... between the 'K' a...a...and the 'O-O-O', so pronounced Kobi. My middle name is Kevin. Colleagues and the bank and the immigration guys–' (he winked, Leila blushed) –'call me Kevin. But to complicate it that bit further, everyone calls me 'Prince'. By everyone, of course, I mean friends an...an...and family.' He offered a handshake.

'Not another one with immigration problems,' she thought, but gave nothing away.

'Leila,' she said politely, shaking his hand. There was a mystery behind this man, she sensed. His thoughts were ditto about her. An hour and a half later, she had learnt that he was originally Nigerian (although his mother was quarter Indian, but all things Nigerian), 38 years old, been married to a Nigerian woman, Ada, for 11 years and had twin boys aged one. He had graduated from University of Leeds Medical School, been on the 'highly skilled' visa initially, but had now naturalised and was permanently resident in the UK with no intention just yet of relocating back home.

Not that it made a blind bit of difference, but Leila breathed a sigh of relief, almost audibly.

And by way of an exchange, he found out that Leila was partly English and partly something else black and/or Asian that she did not know. The parts were too numerous and inconsequential to mention, but the blood flowing through her veins was a random cocktail. She was Christian (practising, not fanatical, but would love to be a bit more passionate), 33 and had been married to Akash who was originally Hindu and a quarter Sierra-Leonean on his mother's side for a little over five years. She also did not like odd numbers. He had raised his eyebrow at that one, but said nothing.

'So, a product of some multi racial engagement then?' he teased.

'Not unlike yourself,' she said.

'Mine is quite diluted now. It is hardly apparent on a f..f..first look. But you…' he said, referring to her curious mix.

'I like to call it mixed blessings, yes. My friend Olga calls me Mulatto…with good reason I suppose,' she rambled on awkwardly, swallowing nervously, chuckling (or something), and then asked, 'So… is "Prince" just a nickname or are you affiliated to some sort of Nigerian sovereign?'

He looked at her intently for a couple of seconds.

'Now that's a…a… very long story. All shall be…be… be revealed in due course,' was his reply. They talked about their careers, about how he ended up being a cardiologist. He had been involved in the bionic heart operation that had made the news earlier that year. There had been the public uproar about the National Lottery, but some of the people had found peace when the battery-operated heart was advertised. She could not believe he had been part of that medical team. How amazing! Akash had followed the story fanatically for some reason, but then Akash did all sorts of strange things and if he could sit giggling hysterically over Tom and Jerry (– a cartoon Leila found worryingly sadistic), then she could not really say that she could gauge his hobbies with confidence.

He found out that she, a writer, ran a successful weekly blog with the magazine '*Silent Symphonies*' and her column was called 's*mile – your heart's on camera*'. She had also recently inherited other duties within the magazine. They talked more intimately about how they were both searching for something they had lost somewhere traversing through life.

'So did you know straight away that he was Mr Right?' he asked.

'Back then, I thought I was sure,' she replied.

'Back then? …Was?' he questioned.

'What I meant was… what I mean is…' Leila didn't know what to say. If she were to tell the story, where would she begin? But at that moment, her heart reflected in her eyes and he was looking into them so he stole her thoughts and read them. In those eyes, he saw untold confusion, longing, and maybe even unhappiness – but he was not sure.

'Listen Kaobi…' she began.

'Prince...' he interrupted.

'KK,' and she froze because she did not know where that came from. 'Prince…' she said quickly, but said nothing else.

He smiled. 'KK. I love it!' and it was slightly awkward for a few more seconds because he said it in an almost inaudible whisper, trying to peer in her face. Leila sat with her head down and eyes widened. He cleared his throat.

'Leila, I know what you mean.'

'How can you tell?'

'It's in your smile.'

'You can tell my life story by my smile?'

'There is no such thing as an ambiguous smile when the smiler has eyes. Eyes don't lie, they don't know how to.'

He said that so eloquently, she wanted to write the words down quickly for further investigation and possible blogging. She wanted to give him a round of applause, she also wanted to kiss him, and/or tell him how cheesy and rehearsed it was, whilst rolling her eyes imperturbably. Once again, she was attacked by impulses. She wanted to do all of these simultaneously. As usual, she froze and did none of the crazy five. Instead for 11 seconds they had a stare out; and they both held the intense gaze. In his gaze, she detected the same shocked look as the day before. He probed thoroughly like it was a medical examination or like he was putting a puzzle together and the clues lay in her eyes. She was about to question the intense scrutiny, but then, typical moment spoiler, her mobile phone rang.

'Bianca? Yeah, I erm…had to…I'll be back shortly. Tell them to wait. Serve them some coffee and biscuits or something'.

'It was interesting talking to you… err… KK….Kaobi…I mean, Prince… but duty calls,' she said in the calmest voice she could muster. He smiled again.

'You look o…o…oddly fa…familiar,' he said to her in a rather distant tone, squinting slightly, and then added more consciously, 'per…per… perhaps for everything in life, Leila, there is in...in…indeed a reason.'

'I know, I believe that too,' she replied and leaving him with that, she walked away, slowly, alarmingly conscious of his gaze burning her back… 'I hope my bum doesn't look too big in this.' She adjusted her waistline nervously, and walked on, head held high.

Leila sat at her desk almost ashamed of her thoughts. There was something flirtatious about their meeting but on the other hand, it seemed so innocent. Something about him made her want to reach out to her inner self, hold on to her belief in true love, in soul mates and romance, but the pressures of present day society left her so confused. 'What is love?' She knew the answer, but she had forgotten. Then just to add a bit more confusion to her thoughts, she was overcome by a sudden surge of guilt and indignation.

'It was just coffee for fucksake!' she berated herself. He was perfect because he shared her views on just about everything. His last few words rang repeatedly in her head… 'For everything there is a reason…' It was not just the words though; it was the underlying tone, the expression on his face, the look in his eyes. She wandered back to the first meeting. She admitted that she had wished the construction workers would keep going, just so he could keep speaking into her ear. She remembered his breath on her skin. It traced its way all down her nervous system. It travelled from the nape of her neck, and then down south, his obvious masculine tone, his Nigerian accent. She had recognised the accent even before he had told her. Her friend Lala had the same accent. She remembered particularly because even though anyone would have to get that close to hold a conversation with the racket the construction workers were making, her senses were alert, she was aware that he was… a man!

She picked up her phone and called Olga. Olga was the one person who she knew would give her an honest opinion. Despite Olga's closeness to Akash, she could bare her soul without fear, and if she had done anything stupid, Olga would tell her. She was her best friend. It would never get back to Akash. Olga had an amazing business/causal friendship with Akash, and they shared thoughts, but ultimately, her loyalty was to her best friend.

'Olga? How are you babe? I had a coffee with a man. I told him my innermost thoughts consciously. Am I cheating on Kash?' she lunged in straight away without pleasantries.

'What the potatoes are you on about now, Mulatto?' Olga was taken aback so Leila unfolded the events of her whole week including her increasingly worrying arguments with Akash and how lonely she felt these days.

'Listen babe…' Olga began. 'Sometimes a woman needs to be loved, appreciated, and understood. Love is strong. Love is not enough. I can bet my last penny on the fact that Akash loves you, but only you can answer the question as to whether or not his interpretation of his love will keep you satisfied for the rest of your life, because that may be the only thing you may have to hold on to. You need to search yourself and…' And as Olga preached, Leila's mind travelled. She visited the Bible book of Corinthians and the meaning of love. She recited: Love is patient, love is kind... etc, but surely, some sort of reciprocation was expected if one was expected to follow God's words without backsliding every now and again! Did all the expectations of that Bible verse still apply to unrequited love?

'Nobody said it would be easy. You know this, Leila,' Olga concluded.

'Indeed,' Leila said and then they moved on to talk about traffic, work, holidays, joining the mile high club and Olga's new kitchen – anything but the state of Leila's marriage.

As she drove home, Leila thought about the unbelievable metamorphosis her husband had undergone and then thought of Kaobi and their lovely, revealing chat. She made up her mind that the grass always looked greener on the other side of the fence. Kaobi was probably a secret serial killer or something and Akash…well, Akash was the devil she knew… and loved. Tonight though, she would speak to him, explain how she felt more clearly and he would understand. They would make love passionately and it would be the start of a brand new relationship. This was her plan. After all, she thought to herself, she loved her husband and she always would and the beautiful thing was, she thought, he loved her too and nothing could convince her otherwise. She just sort of knew! The underlying question had been whether love was enough. However, tonight, she would put all that aside and concentrate on the two of them. Tonight they would celebrate their love. She planned it all excitedly. Then she burst into laughter when she remembered his comment about the crucifix. It had taken months of constant correcting to get him to stop calling it the 'plus sign necklace'. Akash made her laugh. She smiled for about ten seconds and then suddenly went straight faced. He was so clever. She did not know when he was acting and when he was being genuinely stupid.

'Plus sign necklace my arse!' *sigh*

It was 8 o'clock that night when she sat down to dinner alone. She stared at the food for a few minutes. Akash was not yet home. Her mind was constantly flirting with thoughts of Akash and intermittently moving on to mini visions of Kaobi. He had said that eyes don't lie. If her confusion was that obvious, then why couldn't Akash see it? She sighed and reached over for her very best friend… her diary. She needed to understand how to undertake this new mission of hers. How do you love without expecting love in equal measure as remuneration? How?

Not every sky will be blue and not every day is springtime. So on the spiritual path a person learns to find this kind of happiness without needing nice things to happen on the outside. Rather, you find happiness by being who you really are. This isn't mystical. Young children are happy being who they are. The trick is to regain such a stage when you are grown and have seen the light and dark sides of life.

Deepak Chopra

Chapter Four

Fallen Front Man and a Rainbow

My comrades and I stand shoulder-to-shoulder fighting a tough war – the war for the rainbow, wielding shields, deflecting blows. We search in unity for the brightest colours. Ironically, we are a colourful army; different kinds of people, strong individuals in our own rights. We have different dreams, aspirations and hopes. Different backgrounds and ideas that make us cross swords within our ranks but we stick together still because we are a fierce team with a war to finish and in our search, we share moments of gold and gain, cold moments of intense pain!

Sometimes the battle has been ferocious and I have been almost overwhelmed but I have looked to a select few and something about the wild passion in their eyes, the sincerity of their hearts, their commitment to the cause, would give me renewed energy to carry on.

There was one – a front liner, a leader. The one, who occasionally stood on the pedestal, reached out to the rainbow with his fingertips and named the colours one by one. He whispered when the colours were dull and none matched his thunderous roar when colours were vivacious. He was one of those who would find food if people went hungry, share a joke if spirits needed uplifting, lend an ear, give a hug. He had the most amazing, charming smile. He smelt of the sexiest perfume, his hair was perpetually tidy; his eyes mirrored his heart – his beautiful heart. In his company I found a haven.

He joined the Chorleywood ranks in the 80s, when I was learning to use the sword. He featured more prominently because he was too. We learned side by side and looked to each other to point out mistakes and learn new techniques. He became a front liner – one of the really good ones. Sitting in his company, the colours always appeared bolder and the rainbow seemed within reach somewhat. I trusted him – infinitely. There was a special category of people who I grew up to understand were intrinsically linked to me for life because we grew up in parallel. So even when we flew the nest, it was not unusual for paths to cross and there was always the feeling that we had seen each other only minutes ago, not weeks or months or in some cases, years, because our lives were so solidly interlinked that oceans would never divide us. We still had the same view of the rainbow – understood which of us would bring out the best in every featured colour, we would name the rainbow, colour by colour.

I wish, before they fall, I could reach out to every soldier and tell him or her how special they are, how I love who they became, how I understand the path they chose and why fundamentally they are who they are – how I look in their eyes and I do see the colours of the rainbow. For those who were generous with the ear and the hugs, I wish I could thank them. If they offered company, I wish I could tell them those hours passed in laughter and reminiscing, hours that felt like minutes, because we all carried each other's hearts along our individual journeys – sometimes, constant reminders were neither necessary nor relevant. It is what it is! (It truly is as simple as that!) I wish I could tell them that they have flown the nest and become strong and that I don't see them every day but I cherish the phone calls, the catch ups, that the reunions are the best! I wish I could stand up on a stage and gather them together and scream at the top of my lungs with a microphone – remind them that we are one people and one heritage, one history and that we will always share one common goal, that we shall always be one nudge away from each other until we attain that final goal. I want to peek in all their eyes to show them. Regardless of where we stand on Earth, we look through the same eyes and in that horizon, we can see our beautiful rainbow.

I write because I realise that I have described all of the above in the hope that he was certain about his place within 'the family'. He was the ultimate front liner!

Dear Comrades, like I always say, there could be moments of gold and gain, cold moments of pain. It is a dark day in our army. Even the effervescent rainbow that stands out like a twinkling star out far in the horizon loses its glory. Today it tells our story. In the distance it shares our stance. It mourns; it churns naught colour, bar this dark, dark shade of insane pain. We know why. We sigh. We cry. Yet destiny and fate heed not our plea that death shall from our midst flee. It overrides rainbow's glow.

Comrades, we are a man down…

Leila ☹

Chapter Six

She put the diary underneath her cup coaster with a mental note to post to the website later. She fetched another bottle of red wine from the wine-holder. Whenever Leila wrote, she let rip, literally. She could put her thoughts into coherent order fearlessly. Her words played devil's advocate. Heck, she even swore every now and again. Her grandmother would not be impressed. She smiled at the thought of grandma sitting with her laptop reading Leila's articles with shock and horror. Nah! She bet grandma had a few choice words in her time herself!

She had barely had her first sip of Sancerre when the phone rang. It's probably Akash working late and calling to say he would be home soon, she thought to herself as she made her way to the phone. But it wasn't.

'Hello, Kash?'

'Leila, no, it's Toks.'

'Hi Toks.' Toks was one of her childhood friends. She was married with three sons and a successful career, so a phone call from her these days was a rare surprise.

'Toks, are you alright?' Leila asked because all she could hear was sobs and mumbled speech.

'It's not good news, I'm afraid…' the mumbling weeping voice managed… 'Yardua died in a car crash last night.'

Yardua was also a childhood friend who, as it happened was Toks's ex-boyfriend and her first true love. He was a strong-minded person, who had, despite life's cruelty, succeeded in reaching his own goals. He was a doctor. It felt like only yesterday when Leila, Toks, Ifi, Tia, Jennifer, Yvonne and Joy (five other close childhood friends) had hired a mini-bus to attend Yardua's mother's funeral together. The particularly sad thing about that day was that his father had passed away a few months before that. He had greeted them with a genuine smile and a warm heart filled with hope for a better tomorrow. 'I love them and I miss them both terribly at this time, but I'll see them again someday, because God has promised, and God's promise for tomorrow never lies,' Yardua had said in his farewell speech that night; tear stained, but brave.

'I'll be there in 40 minutes,' Leila said and she put…no… threw the phone down. She put her shoes on; she fetched her car keys and then sank into the sofa. She tried to stop it but her lachrymal glands gave way; fifteen minutes it was, she sobbed. Her heart was so worn, so broken. A significant part of her wanted to rush to Toks and give her a big hug, yet another part of her really needed Akash to put his arms around her and kiss her own tears and fears away. Phone glued to her ear, she listened to his phone ring ceaselessly as she scribbled a note. She declined the option to leave a voice message. The note reminded him that she loved him; it said she needed him and that she would try to make it home before midnight because all she wanted to do was fall asleep in his arms and that nothing else would do. Cuddly teddy bear would not suffice tonight (neither would showerhead. She smiled for a second, but then decided it inappropriate, and therefore best not to include! She wondered if he would think it humorous. They had shared all sorts of jokes – some rude. They did not laugh any more). She would rekindle the laughter. Tonight it would be him, her husband - the love of her life. Simples.

A swollen-eyed Toks greeted Leila at the door and they hugged. Joy, Jennifer, Yvonne, Tia and Ifi were there already. Toks's husband had never met Yardua and owing to the awkwardness of the situation, he left the girls to it and hid himself and their sons in the bedroom. The heart-broken girls hugged, cried and cried some more as they shared fond memories of 'Onyechi' as Yardua was fondly called.

'It seems like only yesterday that we went for his mother's funeral,' Joy began. The others nodded.

'I don't understand sometimes how this all works. He had endless trials throughout his life and had only just reached the point in his life where he could get over all the hurt and confidently start to count his blessings,' Joy lamented.

'Joy…' Leila began, 'let's not even begin to ask questions we cannot find answers to. God knows best, right?!'

'Can you remember when he walked into that party and all the girls stood obviously drooling at the sight of him?' a tear stained Toks asked, smiling and sniffing.

The girls reminisced endlessly about their encounters with Yardua and all the fun they had had back in their university days.

'And look at us now – all successfully doing this, this and that and running our own lives,' Jennifer remarked proudly, looking at her friends.

Each nodded. Each thought about the 'successfully' bit. Each breathed deeply. Each agreed nonetheless.

They had all been contemporaries and friends from birth really, raised within semi-strict Christian homes, in the cult of a five-mile radius – posh, little neighbourhood somewhere in the heart of Chorleywood. They were all the same age, give or take a few months; they all went to the same school, so it had been no surprise that birthday parties, parents' meetings and social gatherings brought their families together. At college their bond grew as they ushered in adulthood together. They stood that night, each with a mental picture of their salad days when they were all impressionable young women, making big plans for life ahead. They had tackled important issues – boys, menstruation, changes to physiological appearances, and parties. They laughed hard thinking how grave those issues were at the time. Now it was time to face the real life issues. They weren't all married yet (if ever), and Toks, Ifi and Jennifer had children, and Joy was pregnant (or so Toks and Leila suspected, gossiping in the kitchen while waiting for the kettle to boil). Leila took a step back and marvelled at how each girl had been carved into a woman she almost did not recognise. They were all on the same path initially, then life happened and at the maze of a crossroads, they took different paths – a couple going down the same road, but ultimately, they had made totally different decisions and even their thought processes were no longer the same. They were no longer best friends, but there was a bond, which consisted of irreplaceable memories and respect.

In recognition of their upbringing, they joined hands, formed a circle and said a prayer. It was a simple prayer, each adding their bits when one of them choked on their tears, stumbled, or was lost for words. They prayed for a better tomorrow, for good news, for love, for happiness, for health, for their families, for better understanding of life and most importantly for Yardua's soul and his grieving family.

'And as our faces differ, so do our needs. Dear Lord, look in our hearts, please take away our trials and tribulations, and make our dreams come true,' Joy said conclusively. The girls hugged, cried a bit more and promised to keep in touch.

Leila was aware of Yvonne and Tia's probing eyes. Both had always had the uncanny ability to decode her moods. She longed to tell of her emotional lows and unanswered questions, but somehow it seemed inappropriate and besides, truly, she would not know where to start. She kept peering in her mobile phone for missed calls or voice messages. There were none.

It was quarter to midnight when an anguished Leila got home. The note she scribbled was still on the table. She ripped it in two, grabbed her diary from beneath her cup coaster and crawled into bed. According to Ecclesiastes – a book in the Bible – there was a time to laugh, a time to mourn, and so on and so forth. This was their time to mourn and perhaps the right season for Yardua to die. God had his reasons. Despite her sudden hatred for her Akash, she included him in the prayer she said. After all, she thought, everyone had their flaws and no one was short of human weaknesses as mere mortals. She wrote:

And for everything in life, there's a time, a place, a season
Sometimes there isn't, but sometimes there's a reason
And even as in the pain of death no one understands
We can share the memories, laugh, cry, hug or hold hands
There are faces we see rather rare or every day

To these faces, if we may, can we just say
How we care, let's just share, how beautiful these faces are
For souls forever near could without warning be someday
somewhat far
Even as human beings we are subject to frailty
If at this moment we could set aside negativity
And look in the eyes of even those at whom we've once raved
and ranted
And appreciate faces we often take for granted
And if for this second our hearts are pure, space only for love
We can open wide the eyes of our hearts and look above
In both their eyes and their smiles we can hear his thoughts
Side by side, The Lord and 'Onyechi', both smiling down on us

Having written her valediction to Yardua alias 'Onyechi', Leila closed her diary and stared at the ceiling. She spoke to Yardua's heart. 'I wonder if you can see me…' she said… 'I wonder if you can hear me. Maybe you can. I never really knew you as well as I could have, but I am actually truly very fond of you. You seemed like you were just another friendly, familiar face, but so well known to Toks's broken heart. I must have underestimated the power of your importance, silly me, because for some reason, the fact that I will never see you again makes me feel like we all cheat ourselves out of love in living life. I feel this because somehow, I realise that I do love you. I loved the fact that you existed, that you made my friend happy, that you shared life with me, that we both breathed the same air and that you were just there, living alongside me. I recognised your presence and never for one second thought of a world without 'Onyechi' in it. I cannot believe that I will never get the chance to tell you that I loved the man you were because I took it for granted that you would always be there, so it didn't matter. But I realise now that it does matter. People always need to know these things because no one knows what tomorrow will bring. And so, if I promise to appreciate people more and I promise that I will forgive more easily and I will love more, then perhaps there will be more value to your memory. What I have learnt today is that to live for today and love for tomorrow is the wisdom of a fool; tomorrow is promised to no-one. Yardua, rest in perfect peace.' Having said that she looked all around her; it was all well and good, and easy, promising to love unconditionally at all times, but in terms of the kind of love shared between husband and wife, she still came back to the question of what happens when it is unreciprocated? How do we handle that? How simple is it to love until you feel like an idiot? Do we go on believing that one day that will change? Do we accept it as it is and settle for less than we deserve? Or are we allowed not to sell ourselves short and fight for what we believe in? What if it is a hopeless situation? Do we walk away and cut our losses, or will God then frown down on us? There was no Akash to appreciate, no one to call, no one to share her grief with and even no one to take for granted. Everyone was busy living their own life and she felt non-existent to the world at that precise moment. It seemed that in marrying Akash, she had lost her life. She felt so lonely. At 3.30 am, a mentally exhausted, emotionally drained Leila felt more alone than she had ever done before and subsequently cried herself to sleep.

Meanwhile, many miles and a heartbeat away, Kaobi stood overlooking a beach, staring into the night. He had been awakened by a strange dream. He watched teardrops fall from a beautiful pair of eyes in slow motion, hitting the floor with such impact, they could easily have been rocks. He felt a cold wind blow across his face. It was very familiar. It was the chill he felt when the cold hands of death had snatched someone away. He was so uneasy just thinking about what that person's family would be going through at that moment. He had never been wrong about this chill. He prayed that whoever was crying over this loss would be comforted. He prayed that the person's soul would rest in peace and then he prayed that the soul that was once his twin sister and best friend found eternal rest wherever she was and he whispered into the night that he loved her and he missed her. He knew she heard him; he could feel her wipe the tear that trickled down his cheek and so he smiled. Kaobi had never actually managed to get over his sister's death. That night in particular when he eventually managed to tear himself away from the still waters and get himself into bed, he had found it impossible to sleep. It was the wee hours of the morning and yet he lay in bed staring at the ceiling, the awkward feeling all around him never ceasing for even a second. It was more than just the chill that caused his insomnia. The chill had only reminded him of the pain he felt at his own loss and the sadness he felt that someone somewhere was feeling as empty as he had felt back then. He lay there because he had seen the face of his beloved sister in a woman only earlier on that day. He had only met this woman and yet he loved her instantly. He loved her because of the memory she brought back to him but also because in those eyes he saw tears, tears that he longed to kiss away. Despite the differences in perhaps culture and distinct physical features, this woman bore a striking resemblance to his sister and could pass for a reincarnation for those who believed in that sort of thing. He was Christian but sometimes his mind wandered at a thousand miles a second. It was not just her look. It was in her expressions, in her gestures, in her eyes and her heart. It was the same kind of pain he saw in his sister's eyes whenever she was heartbroken. This woman who bore this striking resemblance was of course…'what's her name again?' he questioned himself for a second and then he smiled. 'Leila!'

'Leila…' he muttered thoughtfully as he fell asleep and he managed to wake up with her name still lingering on his lips.

She woke up abruptly, she had blood-shot eyes which were not quite open – or open, yet vacant! She had been crying most of the night. Her body was awake, but her mind was still in that languid, half-asleep state. She was startled because she could have sworn she heard her name in a weird distant whisper so she looked around. Still there was no one next to her or anywhere in the room. Leila had a headache and very sore eyes. She also felt angry. She managed to successfully pull herself out despite the bitter disappointment of rolling out of bed through Akash's empty side. Akash hadn't been home that night. It was the first time. Could he have chosen a worse night to introduce new bad habits? Yet she wasn't going to drown herself in grief or self-pity or even be consumed by the anger she felt. It was Thursday morning and like every other Thursday, she was going to work. She noticed a Bible passage her mum had stuck on her mirror last visit: Psalm 69, verse 17… *'I am thy servant; do not hide thy face from me. Make haste to answer me, for I am in distress…'* Overwhelmed by sorrow and many conflicting emotions, she said a prayer for Yardua's family, for her sisters, for her friends and her only brother and parents for she loved them and missed living with them as a nuclear family unit (where of course there was hardly any responsibility. In fact, most times all she had to do was make her bed and turn up at the dinning table at meal times). Leila forbade that any harm should ever befall her family and then lastly, she said a special prayer for her troubled soul and prayed to God that if ever he was going to take Akash away from her for any reason, be it divorce, death, etc, that He make it as painless as possible, because she couldn't bear the pain of the loss that once was the blessing she would count twice, thrice even and four times fondly (so it would not end in an odd number). Was it also the stigma she feared? Her family was perfect. She therefore had to follow suit. Till death do us part was what it ought to be – what it would be. At this point, Akash leisurely walked – nope! – swaggered in.

'Ignore him, stay calm,' she repeated under her breath as he made his way across the room to her.

'I tried to call you last night, but…' He stopped and peered in her face. She sipped on her green tea, determined not to explode.

'Have you been crying? It's not like I died in a car crash last night or something. I am here. Besides, you called me twice. If I were dead, how would you have felt when you found out that I had died and you had only tried to hunt me down twice?' Leila glanced up because she was curious to see his facial expression at that moment. As soon as she spotted that he was serious, her eyes widened with animal rage (it was no domesticated animal either. It was a hungry, untamed, un-named species from the dinosaur ages). Her look said it all. 'Ok, my fault. I am sorry, but…'

'Seriously?' Leila's could feel her heart palpitating. And it began:

'Not everything in my life is about you, you clueless, selfish, self absorbed bastard…' she yelled at the top of her lungs, but then the words trailed off as she took a deep breath. She was so livid, she had lost it momentarily and even squirted saliva in the process of that rather unlady-like bark. She shocked herself sometimes, she did. He shook his head, and took his left hand out of his pocket. 'Don't call me names, woman!' he said pointing.

'Yardua died in a car crash and I…' Then suddenly, she whispered, 'It doesn't matter.'

'What?' he whispered in disbelief. She could hear the genuine shock in his voice. Akash had known Yardua because during his relationship with Toks, he met Leila and there were endless double dates. Leila and Toks would hide in the kitchen gossiping while the men rattled on about football, the political situation in Zimbabwe with President Mugabe, and how Simbarashe's (a family friend) views were extreme, or whatever else was news. She could have done with the hugs last night and as much as she wanted to reach over and kiss his crying eyes, she could not see past the hurt he was causing her, and at that time, his very presence irritated her and so did the feminine perfume he stunk of.

He reached out to her; she shrugged him off hysterically.

'Get off me,' she said hastily and tore out of the house, burning hot tears streaming endlessly down the aisles of her beautiful face.

As Leila drove off, Akash stood by the kitchen window staring out after his wife. He loved her insufficiently – he knew. He could see the pain in her eyes. Anyone could! If he had told Leila five years ago that he was mentally unprepared for the commitment of marriage, she probably would have walked away from him concluding that he did not love her. He would have lost her then. There was also the other issue – the forbidden conversation – his immigration status. It was all well and good deciding to marry for love, it was quite another to add the pressure of imminent deportation as a consequence of not marrying her. He needed that marriage certificate. He had built too solid a foundation in the UK to start from scratch in India. Where would be begin? So everything Leila asked for, Leila got, regardless of rationale or lack of thereof. She blatantly refused a Hindu wedding. He nearly choked when she said it was her final word. He knew his parents would hate her for it. What kind of man born and bred Hindu got married in a church? But he had no choice. He was also too ashamed to tell his parents that he had been in the UK for eight years and was always borderline illegal immigrant the whole time. They assumed it was sorted because Akash made things happen. Therefore, Leila had shackles on his feet. 'Whatever you say, your highness,' he had replied and even managed a smile – a smile so fake that even a blind man would have seen through it. A blind man would have spotted the fury behind it. It lurked right there in the back. But to little Miss Perfect, it was all good. Personally he would have waited another couple of years, but this way, he got his papers and she got the fairy tale church wedding with a dress so beautiful, no Disney Princess would outdo her. Full stop! He would have even considered having two weddings just for peace, but Leila was headstrong, and, in matters of utmost importance to her, inflexible. Despite winning no awards for being saint of the century, her Christian background meant a lot to her – sometimes her perceptible hypocrisy infuriated him. He had spent a lot of time convincing his parents that he was no hen-pecked husband. That added to the resentment of the whole marriage thing. Leila was a loving woman, but she was also a tough cookie. Marriage was about compromise, right? It felt like a small sacrifice. He had defied his parents' wishes and given up on the idea of a Hindu wedding. He remembered watching her walk down the aisle in that magnificent dress. His heart had melted and nothing mattered in those few seconds. The feeling was only ever temporary. She infuriated him. His feelings of inadequacy when it came to playing the good husband mentally and emotionally often took its toll. He was doing the most stupid things. He really did not want to hurt her and there was no other woman in the world that he would rather spend his life with. He was successful enough to the eyes of the world (and Leila), but secretly, he had huge financial problems stemming from some terrible financial decisions. It was worrying and he knew that if the economic climate did not miraculously hit a sunny spell, his stockbroking business would definitely hit rock bottom. He had even seen a lawyer. No, bankruptcy would never be an option! He could tell Leila. She might be able to help. She would help if he asked. He knew that Leila's love for him was limitless. He knew people were right to refer to him as an arrogant bastard. What kind of weakling of a man would accept a woman's money? He had the penis, not her! Additionally, Akash had emotional problems and being an only child, he had never had to depend on or consult with anyone. Characteristically, he was a lone ranger. He did his things his way, himself. So far, he had always managed impressively well. He had even bagged himself the sobriquet, 'Cash Kash'! He smiled as he remembered several instances when he would walk into a crowd of his boys and they would all hail, 'Cash Kash!', and he would prove this by popping a seven hundred pound bottle of champagne or something. There would be cheers all round. Now, he had a wife to cater for financially and emotionally. This was hard work for him. He wondered if perhaps his marriage to her had caused him to derail from his genius financial track. On some subconscious level he blamed her for his setbacks. Bizarrely so, for in his more rational moments, he could not justify these thoughts to himself. He had secretly tried to speak to a counsellor. She had advised him to speak to his wife and even bring her in but every time he thought might be the perfect moment to tell her, he would look at her beautiful smile and think how hurt she would be to hear that he wasn't happy and he would therefore defer it to a 'more suitable' time. As a result, every day it got worse and he found himself sinking more and more into alcohol, gambling, the odd episode of womanising, pornography, but worse – depression. He washed his tablets down the kitchen sink. He looked up and watched her drive away. He knew that one day she would be driving away for good. He felt powerless by this thought. 'Don't judge me!' he said to nobody in particular.

'Fuck!' he exclaimed running his hands through his hair.

'She is going to end up in the arms of another man and you will lose our Mulatto Princess for good,' Olga had commented to him the other night. He had nodded and said that everything was under control.

'She loves me,' he had said to Olga. Stroking his wedding ring, he made a vow to himself. That night, he would undertake some damage control. He would talk to her, he would explain. It was not Leila's fault that he had so much going on in his life. She should not have to pay for it. He would tell her the truth. She would not think any less of him.

Then he chanted his mantra – *'Mani jeetai jagjeet – he who conquers the mind, conquers the world'*, but rather unfortunately, he made his way across to the cupboard where his various brands of brandy lived, even though it was still only quite early on in the day. He also logged on to his laptop and hit the casino site. He was conscious of the gambling warnings on TV stemming from the introduction of the National Lottery. Some thought it a genius idea, others with high moral standards (like his parents) thought it despicable that the UK would encourage gambling. He thought they needed to get off their high horses. The first winning went to a good cause – the first man to have a battery-operated heart – a bionic heart. He thought that was amazing. Then he thought what he would do with the millions if he won. He had played his lottery for the week – he felt into his back pocket to make sure the slip was still there. It was. Then back the casino site he went, spending unforgiveable amounts of money each time. Akash was obsessed with Formula One, so he had the Grand Prix from the weekend before on in the background for inspiration. Michael Schumacher had won by an astronomical 3.9 seconds. It would be a good week. Michael's luck would extend to him. As Akash's losses grew, he took bigger gulps of brandy too. For good measure, he lit a cigar. Then his thoughts drifted back to Leila. He dedicated a moment to sink himself in the bombshell she had dropped on him before she left. Yardua had been a decent kind, a bloke with a decent heart and a decent word or two to say always.

'Yardua…' he said aloud as he took yet another big gulp. 'Yardua, you don't approve of me, do ya?' He looked up at the ceiling. 'What happened to you, Yard? Were you alone? Did it hurt? I'm so sorry, mate,' he lamented. He picked up his phone and dialled a number.

'Yeah, hi, I need to speak to you as soon as possible… Listen, this cannot go on any more. I love her. You know I love her. I am sorry but I need to speak to you tonight. Dinner? Tomorrow night? No tonight…' The person on the other end of the line obviously did not agree to this arrangement so Akash ended up having to settle anyway.

'Tomorrow night it is then, but don't think you can put it off forever. OK sure, whatever. It would have to be a quick one because tonight, I want to sort things out with her…' He listened to the voice grumble bitterly. Akash sighed and added in a husky whisper: 'I am actually really sorry,' and with that, he gently put the phone down.

'What kind of man are you? How could you let her go to work in that state?' he asked himself. For long minutes after that, Akash just stared stroking his wedding ring; depression was kicking in, in new depths. He fought – '*Mani jeetai jagjeet – He who conquers the mind, conquers the world.* I am Cash Kash!' he chanted, rocking back and forth.

Interestingly, Leila did not go to work. She was momentarily taken over by madness; rationale flew out the window as she helplessly drove straight to the hospital across the road from her office. Leila had family and friends who could support her but at that moment; it was not what she needed. What she needed had no semblance to anything she had felt before, so how would she explain her feelings to anyone? Ostracised from the world of happiness, she was in dire need of comfort and somehow she knew she would get this from Kaobi. He had told her the day before to come to him if she wanted to offload. She hoped it was not like one of those official letter endings – *if you have any further enquiries, please do not hesitate to contact us.* No, it wasn't. He meant it. He had spoken with his eyes.

'You know what they… they… they… say? A problem sh… sh… sh…shared is… is…is…a prob…prob…problem halved,' he had said somewhere in that hour and half long conversation they had shared only the previous afternoon. Therefore, here she was taking him up on his offer. 'I bet he didn't think it would be so soon.' She sighed and pressed the buzzer. The receptionist let her in.

'I'm here to see Dr Kaobi Kevin Chetachi-Uba,' she said to the receptionist struggling with the tongue twister. She had only ever read it off his business card. There had yet to be a reason to say it out loud, to a listening ear.

'Do you have an appointment?' the receptionist asked.

'No, but I was just…'

'Leila?' He appeared. 'Are you ok?' he asked. Leila had expected a bit more shock at seeing her. She got a concerned expression instead.

'I… I…' For a moment roles were reversed and she was the one with the stutter.

'Come thr…through.' He led her to his office.

In the privacy of his office, she hysterically threw her arms around him.

'Oh, it's been a nightmare,' she began.

'Shh…' he whispered… 'Tell… tell me all about it.'

And so she did. She blubbered on and poured her heart out to this familiar stranger and as she did, he stroked her hair soothingly, pacifying her. It didn't feel odd at all. It felt natural to be in his arms.

'What did you say you called him?' Kaobi asked.

'Onyechi!' she replied.

'It means *no one is God,*' he whispered sweetly. 'He's Ibo – from Eastern Nigeria, just like me.'

'Really?' Leila asked, momentarily distracted. 'What are the chances of that?'

'Well, these days, we are everywhere!' he said.

'The Ibo tribe?'

'No, Nigerians. We a…a…are all o…o…over the world.'

'Is Nigeria no good?'

'Nigeria is fine. I…I…I will tell you all about the place.' He was glad to offer a momentary distraction.

Kaobi smiled. 'No-one is God, Leila. Sometimes we…we…we just have to trust that God knows what he is doing, ok?'

Leila agreed but cried a few more tears still.

'Are you Christian?' she asked.

'No, I'm Kaobi Kevin, or Prince, or as you called me the other day, KK.'

She gave him that exasperated 'please stop joking for one second' look and he rolled his eyes.

'Very Chri…chri…Christian s…s…sometimes, very confused sometimes,' he replied, sighing.

'I understand.' She smiled softly.

'I know you do; I ca…ca…can tell!'

'I'm sorry,' she said softly when she had finally regained her composure.

'What for?' he asked.

'Seeking solace in your arms.'

He ignored her and just stroked her hair. Grief was exposed blatantly all over her face and he knew that the wind that came to him the night before at the beach was the harbinger sent heraldically in advance of this heart-breaking moment.

'You can't go to work today. You need to… to… rest for… for a little while o… o…ok,' he whispered softly. She attempted to protest.

'Doctor's orders,' he whispered gently. She hesitated.

'It's best,' he whispered, luring her.

Leila who lived for her job was fed up, too tired, too emotionally ill to argue. She did not want to either. She picked up her phone.

'Bianca? There's been a bereavement in my family. I will not be in today and probably tomorrow as well, but I leave it all in your capable hands … yeah… ok, thanks… I probably just need the weekend to recuperate. I'm on the mobile. Ring if you need me. Thanks, hon. Take care, bye.'

'Good girl...' Kaobi commended.

'I'll get you a ho…ho…hot drink, you ju…ju…just lie here… everything will be right as rain.' He was still half whispering as he led her to the settee in the office.

'Promise?' she asked as though all the pain would go away if he answered in the affirmative.

'Promise…' he whispered. She believed him so she lay on the settee, no questions asked. With this man, she felt safe! Something in the way he said 'good girl...' and … 'promise…' made her feel like a little girl would in the arms of her father or older brother, like he would protect her. Confused by the power of the many emotions she felt, yet calm and relaxed like a sedative had been administered, Leila succumbed to mandatory slumber. Her body had not had a proper night's rest for a while now and at this point, not even the strongest cup of coffee or can of 'red-bull' - the mind and body stimulant – could save her. Slumber caught up with a normally excessively ebullient Leila.

He tiptoed out of the office for a few minutes to get some flowers to cheer her up. At the flower shop, he came across a selection of seeds. He thought for a while and picked a few up. He closed his eyes for a few seconds.

'Are you alright, sir?' the shop assistant asked, having watched him for a good few seconds. He nodded.

He looked at the pre-written note, attempted to take it off, but was unable to without upsetting the beautiful arrangement of the bouquet. They had only just met… kind of. He shrugged his shoulders. 'Oh well.'

Upon his return, he sat at his desk opposite the settee desperate to get some work done to make up for the hour he had spent taking care of this stranger. He looked up at her and smiled.

'O-M-G, she is so beautiful,' he whispered under his breath and then wrinkled his brow in amazement.

'Oh my God, she looks so much like Kamsi,' he added, unable to take his eyes of her. He brought out the photo of his deceased sister, which lived in his wallet and compared their features. He wondered if this was just his imagination. He was tempted to ask his PA to compare just for his sanity. There was something about Leila. He felt this compulsion to protect her in a way that was very brotherly but by the same insane token, he was drawn to her... sexually. How bizarrely sick! How could she remind him of his sister, and yet be sexually attracted to her? Besides, he was married, and although he had not been romantically acquainted with Ada and therefore had not married for love, his eyes had never strayed. He was scared of going against God's will, scared of the implications of adultery, but also, equally importantly, Kaobi had never really been attracted to anyone sexually. He had sexual relations with his wife almost because he was duty bound. It was the natural course of events, wasn't it? Then he sat back to wonder if he was in love with her. He shook his head vehemently to shake off his crazy thoughts. He often wondered if this was because he had never met his perfect woman, if it was because marriage had automatically blinded his eyes to other women. He wondered at the uneasy feeling in his stomach! He asked himself again, but this time out loud slowly.

'If this woman is so much like my sister, how could I possibly be attracted to her sexually?' He wasn't imagining it either. The sudden bulge in his crotch area at the sight of her fingers running through her hair in her sleep was enough proof.

'Oh my God,' he whispered, running his hands through his dark, subtle Afro. Looking up at the ceiling in prayer, he added,

'*...and lead us not into temptation...*'

She slowly stirred and so Kaobi's mind drifted back to reality. He had been lost in confused thoughts for an hour. He shook his head and urged himself to regain his composure.

'So much for getting any work done,' he muttered quickly, glancing at the pile on his desk before looking up to the most beautiful smile. He smiled softly.

She awoke to find a beautiful bouquet of a dozen subtle pink lilies by her side. The note attached read:

My day is made when thoughts of your beautiful smile
Crystallise into a joyful tear…so please don't cry.

It was a pre-written note so she did not think too much of a romantic connotation. Not for about half a minute anyway, and then she panicked. She had just met him! Yet, bizarrely, a part of her was almost disappointed that it was pre-written. It would have been an interesting complication to her life if he had written it himself. She suddenly felt like a bored housewife and dismissed her thoughts with finality. 'He probably hadn't read the note. Typical man,' she thought. That was the end of that! Only the thoughts did not go away. 'He probably just grabbed the first bouquet he saw in the shop.' She was making excuses for him as she shook her head lamenting about how useless men were at this sort of thing. Perhaps in Leila's mind it was easier to think this way... for now anyway!

'Thank you,' she whispered as a tear trickled down her cheek. He just smiled gently.

'Do you fee…fee…feel better?' he asked. She nodded. 'Let's go then,' he said, getting up from his desk.

'Let's go where?'

'You'll see, it's a surprise,' he replied excitedly.

She took note of how in truth his speech impairment was only intermittent. With some sentences, he would struggle, while at other times, the whole conversation would flow un-hitched. Excitement didn't seem to bother his speech like the average typical stutterer. She thought this was really interesting and made a mental note to research it later and find out what she could on the subject. He was her first friend with a speech problem and she was very intrigued by the impediment. Actually, she was intrigued by him, full stop!

Two hours and a bit, it was they drove through the busy city and out of London and yet he never gave any clues as to their possible destination. Many hills later, the road signs said they were heading towards Kewstoke. There was a sharp bend in the road and they suddenly drove through some archaic but timelessly beautiful gates and before her eyes was the most amazing Victorian age, castle-like building she had ever seen. She had often daydreamed about retiring in one of these. It was divine. Leila could not quite keep her mouth closed. She gasped.

'We are here…' he announced excitedly, holding the door ajar.

'Your parents don't live here, do they?' she asked.

'My parents?' he asked, perplexed.

'Who lives here then?' she asked.

'No-one… I come here whenever I seek the serenity and strength to face lingering ambivalent thoughts,' he said rather solemnly.

'Who talks like that?' she wondered. Sometimes he sounded like a walking dictionary.

They traversed straight through the front door to the back. There were similar neighbouring houses, Leila noted, but none for at least half a mile. The opening was communal, but with enough privacy to feel like the beach belonged to this one house. She didn't think these existed in this part of the country, but judging by the cattle, poultry and tractors she had seen as they drove through the most unsafe narrow roads, she could hardly be surprised. There had to be at least a dozen Road Safety rules broken. It did not get more country than this though, and she loved the freshness in the air. It was unpolluted, plus it felt great to get away from those construction workers. More than one bird chirped happily away and Leila took it all in with scintillating eyes. The house overlooked the beach and the scenery was captivating. About a quarter mile off in the distance were huge rocks sparsely decorated by the wildest, most beautiful seaweeds Leila had ever come across. It was the best one could ever get out of nature in terms of the natural picturesque look.

He watched her. Only a select few would appreciate the beauty the way she did. Having said that, Kamsi had been, but everyone else was aware of its existence. It was his little sanctuary. He, of course, kept this information to himself for fear of frightening her. He did notice the look of confusion when she saw that pre-written note on the bouquet. He should have abandoned that bouquet and gone for one that did not have a note pre-empting the buyer's state of mind.

'You own this?' she asked, mouth partly ajar in awe.

He nodded. He reached into his bag and fetched a red picnic cloth and a basket with bread, orange juice, sausages, and hard-boiled eggs – necessary condiments for the perfect picnic. Bag in hand, he ran towards the rocks, but not too far away from the waters so that they could still appreciate its reflective ripples. He laid the cloth, lowered himself onto it, and then signalled an invitation for her to join him. She followed enthusiastically, clearly thrilled to be a part of it all. It was the scenery, the birds, the sky, the water, the rocks; it was the most romantic view ever. At that moment, the sun shone brightly up in the skies. Once again, they shared thoughts, listened to each other's ideas about love, about life, about everything. She could talk to him about just about anything. With him, she felt this inexpressible feeling of being safe, neither having to weigh thoughts nor measure words, but pouring them right out, certain that he would understand. If her views differed from his, this would trigger a healthy debate, and if they were the same, they would talk at length about it just the same.

'You are not happy really, are you, Leila?' he asked, genuine concern written all over his face and in his eyes.

'Not that there's anything you or anyone can do about it,' she replied.

'You know, somehow, I think I understand how you feel and I am helpless that truly there may not be much I can do about it. But if for today, you would just let me take care of you…' he said, wrapping his right arm around her and with his left, he dug into his pocket and rooted out a few seeds.

'Oh yeah…I nearly forgot…' he said, opening his hands and showing Leila.

'What are those?' Leila asked, puzzled.

'S…s…seeds,' he replied.

'I can see that,' she said sarcastically, rolling her eyes and then added, 'What are they for?'

'Come, I will show you,' he said lifting himself up and pulling her up to join him. He rushed her breathlessly across the beach right to the left corner of the house and he chose a favourably earthed spot and then stopped and said, 'Let's plant these!'

Odd as it seemed, Leila got busy with this crazy man digging a little hole in the soil by the corner of the house.

'Man of many talents!' she teased, as he lectured her about choosing the most suitably earthed spot.

He smiled.

'Medicine, horticulture, what next?' she teased playfully.

'Voodoo?' he suggested, and then smiled. 'You are really goo…goo… good at this yourself,' he replied, thoroughly enjoying the moment.

'What have we planted?' she asked.

'A future flower.'

'What future flower?'

'You'll see. I'm actually not sure,' he replied smiling thoughtfully adding, 'It's a sur…sur…sur…surprise!'

'When? When will we see?'

'In t…t…time, Leila, in time, it will all be revealed. Let's not be too hasty.' She chose not to question any further but to take particular note of this moment. With that done, he squeezed her hand in his and ushered her back to their abandoned picnic.

Once again, they stared into each other's eyes for 12 intense seconds. Most bizarrely, Leila must have fallen into some sort of mini-trance. It was the most unnatural moment she had never experienced. She saw a very strange unconnected story in his eyes. It was a moment of hypnosis for her or at least this was the only way she could explain it logically to herself (not that it made sense still). She saw a little girl pointing at the sun and smiling at her, saying 'mum' over and over again; and then she witnessed a wedding with hazy clouds forming words spoken by the man. 'This time, I promise you, it's for ever,' the man whispered. From total shock and lack of comprehension, Leila withdrew her gaze and shook her head, blinking millions of times. She would ponder about that later on, she said to herself. It was the excitement. It had all been a bit too much for her to handle, or maybe it was a dream in a flash. She hadn't had any alcohol or she would have put it down to that. Usually, the combination of alcohol and emotional distress did weird things to her mind, but – 'nope, not a drop,' she said in a whisper.

'Drop of what? Are you ok?' he asked concerned. She nodded and just like that, she forgot about it.

'Just a little dizzy… I am fine now,' she replied, brushing it all aside. He looked at her thoughtfully for a second remembering his dizzy spell when he had picked up the seeds but the combination of her not talking about it and him not wanting to scare her, he let it pass as well.

She took his hands in hers and smiled. He had a birth mark on his right cheek, somewhere in-between his nose and his lips. His lips… she thought to herself and then she scolded herself, 'Stop it!' She stole one last quick glance at the birthmark on his cheek and then his lips, and then they both stared on, but this time, in the same direction over and across the beach. It was the most infrequent, most awesome sight. Suddenly, the sky and the clouds appeared to reflect a curious shade of rusty orange and then slowly metamorphosed into an equally bizarre hue that was definitely unclassified and undiscovered. It then divided into two dark shades, the one above darker than the one below. The water was coloured burnished gold by the reflection of the sky and the ripples were more and more frantic as the seconds went by.

'I've never seen the sky look like that,' she whispered.

'It's rare for me too. The last time I saw that, my sister was swimming and suddenly I could not find her. We had just had an argument you see.'

'You didn't tell me you had a sister?' she accused subtly.

'I do, my twin sister lives in my heart forever because her memory can never die.'

'I'm so sorry,' Leila whispered, realising what he meant. His twin sister had died about 11 years ago. She had drowned. How awful that must have been.

'And I never got the chance to say sorry,' he said.

'I tried my best to save her,' he added.

'I'm sure she understood, KK. I am pretty sure there is nothing you could have done. There was probably nothing to forgive,' Leila said, reaching out to him.

'She was my best friend, Leila. Some people say it was the bond of twins, but it was more than that. I adored her. She knew me, she understood me. She knew what I was thinking because most of the time, she was thinking the same thing too. I would have done anything for her. That night there was nothing I could do…' He accepted the comfort she offered in her outstretched arms.

They stared at each other for a few seconds and then back at the sky before them and then at each other again. As the seconds went by, it was harder and harder for Leila to resist the temptation that beguiled her. The voice inside her was screaming 'KISS HIM!' She peered into his face and into his eyes. The desire she sensed was so strong that it choked her. Lips to eyes, eyes to lips, their gazes wandered both luring, both seeking. It felt so good; she clung to him to convince herself the moment was real. Two minutes later, they both succumbed to fervour. They hesitated slightly, which heightened the passion, but then resistance failed woefully. They locked lips. They locked lips softly, then passionately, wildly, hungrily and then gently, then sweetly. The combination was perfect. It lasted only about 20 seconds, but, to Leila, it was the most pleasurable, most satiating 20 seconds she had felt in a long time, and the taste lingered for a long while still. She was weak to the knees and felt intoxicated by the strength of her desires. Her body had ached for those stormy hands and musky odours and stubble to scrape her cheek for a long time now. Akash had fed her hunger every now and again, but these days, it had lacked lustre and passion, and more recently, she almost had to be inveigled into any such act in the first place because it often felt unnatural and mechanical. It felt like an automated service, like the voice mail on his phone. Having listened to it so many times (because she could never get hold of him), she could recite the apology for being unavailable, exact breath pace, pause and all! Their recent indulgencies did nothing for her body parts which tingled hysterically long after each episode of love they shared. With Kaobi, it had been but a kiss, yet Leila closed her eyes and breathed a sigh of satisfaction. Her eyes opened to the most gorgeous smile, and his eyes were a lighter shade of brown than normal. They were gorgeous!

'This is rare. The sky, looking like this, that is. Whenever you see this, remember me. Remember our kiss; what we shared today.'

'I will; but only if you promise me something in return. Promise that you will remember me too and that you will smile at your sister's memory.' In months to come they would cherish these words, but also would find humour in how much it sounded like some sort of rehearsed speech at a wedding reception.

'Tha..tha..thank you.'

'In your own time,' she teased.

'Cheeky!' He pushed her gently and then pulled her into a hug.

'Thank you,' she whispered back to him.

In years to come, she would appreciate just how rarely the sky looked exactly like this.

'You are a married woman, Leila,' he said.

She nodded. '…And you, a married man, Prince KK,' she said patting him on the shoulder to lighten the moment.

Nothing more needed saying, so nothing else was said. That was that! They understood that it was the beginning; it was also the end! It was wrong, and it would never happen again. Then of course, perfect timing – the typical British summer weather kicked in and the rain poured down aggressively, so like first time teenage lovers, they raced indoors hand in hand, giggling endlessly about nothing in particular.

It was about 7 pm when Leila got home that night. Like the day before, Akash wasn't home. She hummed a love song as she cleaned the kitchen, the bedrooms and the front room. Every now and again, she would reminisce about those sweet 20 seconds and she would get the feeling that somewhere in her stomach a million butterflies were playing 'catch'. Satisfied that the house was immaculate, she sat down to dinner with her unfinished, open bottle of chardonnay from the night before. She sat and she wrote:

They whisper loudly, unconcealed my eyes do
The truth concerning wonders so new
When eyes met eyes, did soul meet soul?
For that briefest, shortest,
Sweetest, craziest moment in time
When eternity was a second
a minute was but a lifetime
The slightest, faintest hint of
The echo of a whisper
And steady rhythm of normal heartbeat
Was my soul's most joyous,
Loudest, bestest song…

My heart lounged in perfect bliss
My soul felt the harmony of peace
I remembered...
The pleasures of a happy heart
So light, so beautiful to sight
And in my natural struggle of everyday life,
I laugh, I joke, I wine and I dine
Yet awakened within are the once forgotten cravings of a lonely heart
That could bravely do without
When eyes met eyes, did soul meet soul?
For look hard in my face,
Beyond that big, broad smile
They whisper loudly, my eyes do
And eyes don't lie

Leila hastily shut her diary and out of the blue came the waterworks. She cried because she was aware that she was sending her soul singing songs of approbation, rejoicing in the wrong. He was not her husband, no; worse, he was someone else's husband. She cried because, yet there her heart was, feeling hardly any indignity or remorse for its actions. She felt liberated from bondage. She was free from the torture of unanswered questions. Kaobi had answered those questions. He had reminded her of what a happy heart felt like, for at the moment they kissed, nothing and no one existed but the moment before them. The world had been excluded from that time-stopping 20 seconds. She was going to face her fears. She decided she was leaving Akash – not for Kaobi, nope, that would be even more stupid than staying with Akash, but for herself and her sanity. After all, she said to herself, she would rather be alone, than be unhappy. Kaobi had a family to cater for and she would not be responsible for breaking up a happy home. Even if he gave her the option to do so, the way she felt about adultery, she would strongly disagree.

'What God has put together, let no man put asunder' she reminded herself of the biblical words she had heard countless times at weddings, reciting them under her breath. Still, it had taken Kaobi to make her realise that her dream of perfect love had ended and she would always be grateful to him for that. God was right about love. It was unselfish, it was kind, it was gentle, it was beautiful, and it was caring. Neither of those adjectives could describe her marriage but somehow they featured in every vibe she got from Kaobi. She had to let him stay happily married. For her, it was too late. It was time to end her marriage while she still had one or two happy memories left – that way, she would still have those to last her the rest of her life without bitterness. After the way they had parted earlier this morning, if Akash still had any feelings for her whatsoever he would have at least called to see how she was doing. He was not home and he had not called. These thoughts circled round and round in her head.

In his beautiful office, Akash sat with his clients, staring at his watch.

'Listen, errrrr, Sir,' he hesitated, hands in pockets as he slowly rose out of his chair, choosing his words carefully. 'This is far too unsociable an hour. Can't we go over this tomorrow morning?' He slicked his hair. It bounced back to its original position with the amount of hair gel he had in it.

'Do you want to close this deal or not, Mr Yoganathan?' one of the men asked, irritated. Akash sighed and sunk in his seat. He wanted to catch Leila awake tonight.

'I have to tell her the way I feel tonight. I don't want to lose her and I can feel her slipping away from me.' His eyes squinted as he zoned out of the meeting. Did he close the deal? When he eventually tried to recollect, he could not.

Whilst she tucked herself in bed, Leila bravely recalled the weird seeds and then even more courageously questioned 'the twelve seconds'. For lack of explanation, she convinced herself that it was her imagination. It was something that would nag at her psyche from time to time, but absolutely nothing worth further consideration. That was that! She thought, though, that it was worth writing about – a mental note if you like:

In twelve seconds I saw a vision
A little girl called me 'mum'
She looked up and pointed and said 'sun'
And the rainbow smiled at me

In those twelve seconds with unnatural intuition
A couple vowed eternity
Blessed by a priest and blessed by love's unity
My whispering inner voice said, 'that's me!'

In these twelve seconds I stood still
I moved not, I travelled not, I breathed not
The world moved, the world travelled, the world breathed on
I conquered in love; it was my rise, my happiness, my rise
And in those twelve seconds I only stared in this stranger's eyes.

And almost as soon as she recreated the moment according to her own interpretation of events, she forgot about it. Rebuking the thoughts to the back of her mind, she shut her eyes and fell asleep.

It was 2 am when Akash snuck into bed beside her. Prior to that, she had long since given up on being perturbed by the fact that he was not home. Talk about some roller coaster emotions! One minute she was angry with him, the next she was indifferent. She was probably fed up, she concluded. She thought he reeked of the same cheap (probably was not cheap, but it made her feel better to think it was) feminine fragrance that did not belong to her, but tonight she was not sure. It could have been paranoia; making up things that suspicious wives looked out for. The mind was a powerful thing; it could also be brutally irrational as well. Besides, for the first time ever, she was no epitome of righteousness herself. Yet when he put his arms around her and began to nibble at her neck, he did it all in vain because for the first time since they had been married, she blatantly denied him his privilege as a husband.

'I have a headache,' she said coldly pushing him away from her.

'Why?' he asked edgily.

'*Yeh* mērā adhikāra hai *Leila! Main tumhārā pati hūm̐ – It is my right, Leila, you are my wife,'* he grumbled bitterly.

'Yeh aap ko sagiikat gaum kejub near farz nahi – *it is your privilege, not my obligation,*' and with that, she crawled out of bed and into the guest room. She slept there instead.

'Leila…' she heard him call out to her.

She ignored him.

'Leila, I need to talk to you…'

'Not good enough,' she thought to herself.

'He was either too drunk or not desperate enough, because he never came after her. This was the least of Leila's problems. She slept with a smile on her face. In her slumber, she indulged in fantasy. She was reunited with her Prince and those 20 seconds played over and over again, sometimes in slow motion so that it lasted the whole night.

'KK…' she called out gently in her sleep.

Across town, Kaobi heard his name and woke up. It had been but a whisper. He looked around, but there was no one there, so he went back to sleep with a curious smile flirting on his lips. He should know better, but no feelings of guilt were forthcoming. He had never cheated on his wife in all the time they had been married, and that night, Ada, his wife, was ostensibly irritated by his presence, so she slept with the twins in their room.

On Friday morning, Akash was up before Leila.

'I need to speak to you,' he said.

'Kash, I can't deal with this so early in the morning.'

'Can we talk tonight?' he asked. Leila shrugged her shoulders. Exasperated, he stormed out of the house. Leila called Olga.

'I've done a terrible thing.' she said nervously down the telephone. 'I know you're going to think I'm mad, but right now, I don't care.'

But Olga didn't tell her she was mad.

'Listen babe, I need to tell you something.' Despite the fact that she had more or less done the same thing the night before, Leila's world came crashing down on her as Olga confirmed what she had thought all along.

'Are you sure?' she asked.

'Well I think so.'

'Does he love her?'

'Is that the only thing that would bother you?'

'I don't know. It makes a difference, doesn't it? Not that it's the main problem really. Oh I don't know…'

'You want to hang out?'

'I had just decided last night to leave him anyway, Olga.' That was Leila's best shot at nonchalance. Olga who knew her way too well unveiled the act.

'This is me you are talking to, Mulatto,' she said gently. The outburst came only seconds later.

'I should have fucked him, shouldn't I? I should have fucked Kaobi!' she said angrily.

'Leila???'

'Oh what now, you can speak French and I fucking can't, Miss Goody Two Shoes?' she spat.

Olga ignored the urge to tell her off for being so insolent.

'I have been so lonely, Olga. I just do not understand why. The truth is, I don't condone it but a fling is not the problem with our marriage. The problem is with Akash and me. Everything else is secondary. But it still hurts,' Leila said in a whisper.

'Leila, I'll get off work early. I'll be at yours about two.'

'OK. Bye…' she said and she put the phone down.

'Is this the end?' she asked herself. She loved him. She had gone on about how she was definitely leaving him but the truth was she did not want to lose him. He was her husband, the one she had chosen to be with. She loved him. She wasn't without fault. If only she knew what she was doing wrong, she would fix it. 'Marriage is for life, damnit!' she said out loud through gritted teeth.

She crawled back into bed. Maybe she had caused it; she might have done something wrong. But he should have told her. She had been willing to change, to sacrifice anything to please him. She had even changed so much to suit him that sometimes she did not recognise herself. Leila opened her Bible and read with scrutiny from 1 Corinthians 13 over again: …*'love is patient; love is kind and envies no one. Love is never boastful, nor conceited, nor rude; nor selfish, not quick to take offence. Love keeps no score of wrongs; does not gloat over sins, but delights in the truth. There is nothing love cannot face; there is no limit to its faith, its hope, and its endurance. Love will never come to an end. Are there prophets? Their work will be over. Are there tongues of ecstasy? They will cease. Is there knowledge? It will vanish away… in a word, there are three things that last forever: faith, hope and love; but the greatest of them all is love.'*

'Dear Lord, I am sorry if I am failing you right now, but please in your infinite mercy, look upon me, look at the state of my heart and forgive me. These words ought to be enough consolation for me, right? I feel empty. I feel a void. I feel angry and helpless. Lord, the path you have paved for me has some happiness in it, right? If I continue along this path, there is no happiness in sight. I have tried and no longer feel any hope. As you made me in your likeness, you understand my imperfections. I love Akash and feel failed by him. I don't want to lose my faith, but please, let me leave him, that my soul may find the strength to serve you once more like I used to. I know I have not been fully committed to you recently, and I am sorry. Please let me rectify my mind so that it will regain sanity.' She took off her wedding ring and placed it underneath her pillow and then she got out of bed and went about her normal home life business until there was a knock on the door.

'Olga…' She greeted her.

'Mulatto!' They hugged.

'Let's talk about pleasant things. If I wallow in self-pity, I haul you into depression too, Olga,' Leila commented, and they both agreed. She attempted instead to tell Olga about her experiences with Kaobi. Leila found that, surprisingly, she couldn't explain it all to her friend. She did not know what to say so she gave her friend an inadvertently sketchy run down of the recent events and together they got on the internet and downloaded endless pieces of information about speech impediments, therapies available and possible cures. Olga smiled as she watched Leila. Leila was a strange woman indeed.

'Apparently, most times, it's psychological as opposed to physiological, Olga,' Leila explained excitedly, educating her friend from a print out on the issue. As Leila did so, her eyes sparkled at the prospect of making a positive impact in Kaobi's life. She wondered what could possibly have gone wrong between Akash and Leila. They watched a re-run of the previous night's EastEnders, and then a movie and then Olga and Leila decided to go out to dinner instead of moping around in the house pondering upon the effect of men on women. They journeyed endlessly through London town until they arrived at Petrus. Petrus was perfect. It was a tranquil environment, perfect for calming nerves, candle-lit with a live band playing old, slow, soul jams, music that, at that moment, brought out the sore spot in a very vulnerable Leila.

'Kash brought me here a couple of times,' Leila said thoughtfully.

'Table for two please,' Olga said to the waiter who greeted them at the door.

'Do you have a reservation?' the waiter asked politely.

'No, but…' Leila began.

'Yes we do!' Olga said, smiling at her friend. Leila flashed an appreciative smile. They sat in the far corner by the window with Olga facing the door. Settled in and glancing through the menu, the women chatted about Yardua's memorial service amongst many other things. They spoke a lot on the phone but, like typical Londoners, it was almost impossible to meet on a regular basis. When they did meet, they touched base on everything. Leila could see that Olga was treading carefully. She did not want to upset her, but she did not want to pretend the problem did not exist either.

'Have you thought about what you are going to do?' Olga asked.

'I am leaving him,' Leila said and then sighed. 'But let's not talk about it, Olga, not tonight.'

Olga nodded and added, 'Just for the record, babe, I think you deserve a lot more. At least there are no kids involved.' Leila nodded impatiently and moved on.

'To friendship and better times ahead,' Olga toasted, raising her glass.

'To friendship and better times ahead,' Leila repeated. They clinked glasses and sighed.

'Do you want to tell me more about this cardiologist then?'

'No,' Leila said whilst pouting mischievously. 'Well, he is a strange man, Olga,' was all she could say, smiling.

'Strange, good? Or strange bad?' Olga quizzed.

'Good, I think, and he's a very good kisser,' she added even more mischievously.

'You didn't!' Olga said hands over mouth.

'I did!' Leila said although she knew she was telling Olga because she was trying to rescue her bruised ego. Olga indulged her.

'So you had to rush over to Toks's house,' Olga was saying.

'I bet she didn't take it too well. Why did they break up again? They remained good friends, right?' Olga asked. Leila nodded.

Olga continued, 'He was such a nice…' Olga paused abruptly staring straight ahead.

'You look like you've just seen a ghost,' Leila said and curiosity got the better of her and she turned round. It was her Akash hand in hand with this beautiful blonde stranger who she was unacquainted with. As he secured their table, he lightly brushed her lips with his. She knew his kisses, she knew that one did not mean much, and then became furious with herself for persistently making excuses for him! A kiss was a kiss, and it was a kiss…on the fucking lips! Leila had no time to think up an appropriate reaction to this sudden twist to her unfortunate tale. Discombobulated and angry, she went momentarily insane.

'Let's leave…' she said to Olga. Olga did not argue.

On their way out, Akash's eyes caught hers and he froze.

'Hello Kash, I forgot to leave you a note saying I would be out with Olga tonight.'

'Leila, this is… errrr…not quite what you think it is,' he began.

She flicked at his wine glass, tipping it onto his shirt and trousers.

'Oops,' she said. They locked gazes.

'How dare you?' the lady challenged.

'I'm his wife…' Leila said icily, and then continued, '… and you better fucking stand back. I will cause a scene. I have nothing else to lose right now you see.' Then she paused and turned to Akash. 'I have just lost my husband!' (And she watched Akash's face drop at the announcement.) 'I am therefore happy to create an entertained audience right here!' She spat viciously in an enraged whisper. The woman looked just as disoriented as Akash. Leaving them with that, Leila held her head up high and cat walked out of Petrus, despite the fact that internally she was petrified. All eyes were on her and she knew it. She breathed heavily as soon as she walked out.

'Breathe, Leila, breathe!' Olga was whispering to her.

Leila's thoughts were extreme. She hated him and loved him still. She was bitter, but helpless. Leila was scared and confused, but the main emotion present was anger, deep anger. Leila thought a thought that she would never tell a soul, a thought that was so extreme and evil that it shocked her to her bones. Leila wished death upon this cruel husband of hers. 'Let me understand the reason, Lord, why I cannot have him completely, why I cannot live happily ever after with the man that my heart has chosen to love, the man that I thought you chose for me.' As they got into the car, Akash begged her to stop, but Leila sped off without a second thought or a glance across at him. She saw him through the corner of her eye and she sensed his pain, but she rebuked any desire to let him 'explain' to the farthest back of her mind! That was that: over.

Akash just stared after the car for many moments after.

'You deserve that,' the voice in his head was saying. 'You left it too late. Love cannot wait.'

'But I was breaking it off with this woman tonight. I guess I will learn the hard way.'

The exasperated woman came up to him.

'There is no reason why we cannot be together now, Kash.' The woman treaded carefully.

'Don't call me that!' he spat, shaking his head without looking at her.

When her tears went unnoticed, she placed her well-manicured, bright red fingernails on his shoulder and he shrugged it off. He preferred the less dramatic pink shades Leila wore, not that it mattered. She called him Kash? He shivered. That was for close friends and family. Actually, no. That was for Leila and Olga, not even his mother called him that.

'Take a cab home,' he advised her, totally detached.

'But…' she attempted to protest.

'TAKE A FUCKING CAB HOME, WOMAN,' Akash repeated flinging some money her way. She just stared at him in disbelief.

'Listen, I am sorry. You were never under any illusions!' He strolled off into the dead night leaving the woman astounded by his insolence. The worst thing was deep down he knew Leila leaving him had nothing (much) to do with having an affair. This was the final straw that broke the camel's back, this was Leila's perfect opportunity to walk away blameless.

Still…

'What appears to be the end of the road
simply may be a bend in the road'
Robert H Sculler

Chapter Eight

And the caged bird sings…

So when the moment came, the world stood still, and naught could be seen nor heard through her mind but the sound of silence and random pop-up thoughts, curiously so was the one other sound that drowned not with the rest of the world. It was the singing bird in the cage. Symphony respected not private thoughts and often intruded with song. So while the caged bird sang only in her subconscious, today the melody pierced through, particularly loud, and even became her contemplation.

She walked up to the cage and peered in her eyes. 'Symphony, what do you sing about?' and she was further lost in a world where Symphony answered. Symphony was happy to be there, nourished and embellished with all that she needed…or so it seemed.

'How is it then that I have wings and pretty colours, the heart to entertain all day long and nothing to complain about, and yet beyond this cage is a life I shall never know. For though I understand the concept of the world being a cruel, cruel place and this a haven, perhaps somewhere in the distance beyond the rainbow is something that ought to be mine. Perhaps I ought to sing of something dissimilar to this, but all I know is within this cage… but something in the beyond beckons upon my heart to reach out and sing a song which will be revealed to me, but only upon my release, a song which it appears I may never know. I am a caged bird with the basic necessities but am I ungrateful to desire the sustenance that only an uncaged world can provide?

There is more to life than whom I reveal to the world and I sing as normal, but within my melody is sadness but joy, satisfaction but hunger, water but still….thirst.

So she reached forth and opened the cage. Symphony flew through with aggressive desperation and her melody sounded more liberated. Excited at the prospect of doing her some justice she opened the window. 'Go Symphony, go!' and she did.

So she sat in her chair and re-drowned in her thoughts wondering if to walk out the door and never come back to the life that was all she knew. Symphony was her inspiration. She looked up. Puzzled, she noted that Symphony was back of her own free will, into her cage she flew. The cage door remained open. So Symphony was neither in the cage nor out and what a confused melody she sang.

'I understand,' she said to Symphony. 'A little taster once in a while perhaps, but of what consequence is that? Does it nourish your soul, inspire you to explore or does the fear of the unknown signal your return? For all you know, Symphony, is that little cage and even when now the choice is yours, it's not that easy a decision to make, is it? The world neither labels you a trespasser, nor welcomes you with open arms.'

She stared at the door to the world she knew and even ventured to peek outside, and though she felt caged like Symphony, she understood then that should she take one step out in the cold, she wouldn't know whether to turn left or right. If she wished hard enough, she thought enthusiastically, a voice would lead her to the warm embrace of comfort. Disappointment awaited her though, for each time she tried, she was greeted by an ambiguous silence. Back into the familiar she went and like Symphony's cage, she left the door to the world unlocked but sat within it and while Symphony sang her song, she wept trapped tears that never escaped through her eyes as she stared at the open door. Once again she drowned in the thoughts that were of all of the above. The end!

It really ought to be simpler!

Leila x

Chapter Ten

'Let's go to a bar… I need a drink,' she said to Olga, panting heavily.

They drove in silence but Leila's viciously pulsating heart was almost audible. She cursed the day she met Akash Yoganathan. She cursed love; she cursed life. At that moment, the untactful radio played a love song – it was Whitney Houston's *'one moment in time'*, and on a normal day when she hadn't just dumped her husband, she liked the song very much. But for that moment, it was inappropriate. The screaming and cursing and general profanity in Leila's head became alarmingly loud and clear to her but still was not a good enough expression of the anger and hurt she felt. She went mad.

'For fuck's sake…' she blurted out without warning. Completely consumed in a fit of rage, she attacked the radio and nearly lost control of the car. Eventually, a genuinely frightened Olga, who was at that time frantically praying for their lives, managed to coerce her into parking. Leila hit the radio repeatedly with her purse, and then she threw the purse in the back seat. With her hands, she hysterically ripped at the cables while Olga struggled to switch it off and calm her down.

'I hate him, I hate myself…' she screamed manically. Olga tried to hold her friend, but she was lost in emotion that was almost animal; it was physically impossible for Olga or anyone else to restrain her.

'Why?' Leila screamed.

'I have given him everything I have.'

'Leila, what did you give him?'

'My heart, my soul, my time, gave up my name – me!'

'He broke your heart. Your heart will heal…'

'I cannot get over this. How dare he? He loves me. I am Leila. His Leila.'

'It will pass, babe.'

'This cannot happen to me. I married him. Marriage is for life.'

'But you said you were leaving him.'

'Saying it is one thing…I can't believe I will form part of the statistics of failed marriages! I just can't believe it.'

'What hurts? Your heart or your pride?' Olga asked, suddenly quite perplexed.

'Both! He cannot do this to me!' Leila screamed.

'It will pass! It will pass. I promise,' Olga said screaming to drown out Leila's hysteria. In one last mad fit of rage, Leila tore out the photo of her husband in her wallet, ripped in into bits, stuffed it into a little empty bottle that lay littered in the car and threw it out of the window smashing it against the pavement into a thousand unrecoverable pieces. Olga reached over and hugged her friend but Leila resisted the hug. Difficult as it was, Olga did not let go, and Leila was forced to accept the comfort. In Olga's arms, Leila sobbed uncontrollably.

'I have cried him a river, he will cry me an ocean,' Leila vowed still weeping.

'He will cry me an ocean,' she repeated.

'He will cry you an ocean babe,' Olga said stroking her hair thoughtfully.

'Feel better?' Olga asked gently but sarcastically and they both burst into laughter amidst tears. Olga cried because, having been down this road before, she understood it perfectly. It brought back bad memories for her because although she was now married, it was her second time lucky. Her first marriage had been a total disaster. It had lasted four years. Four happy years! One day he upped and left. There had been no sign. (OK, Olga had ignored the subtle hints.) His reason? He never meant to fall in love with the other woman. It just happened whilst he was working abroad for a few months. What could one do? These things happened apparently. You pledge love for life and one day you wake up and it's all gone. They pledge it to someone else. Olga shook her head at the thought.

'Life is a fucking bitch!' Olga said in a half whisper.

Then, it had hurt like hell, but now, she was happy with Chris who she believed to be her soul mate. It was also particularly heart breaking for Olga because through her pain, Leila had been the only constant thing in her life, so even though she never showed it, she clung to their friendship. When Olga had gone home to Russia, determined to 'get away from it all', Leila had paid a surprise visit, because they both needed to find Olga's 'closure' together.

'These things happen, right?' Leila asked her friend.

'You will love again,' was Olga's response.

'Promise?'

'Promise,' Olga assured her, nodding softly.

Leila and Olga switched the half-broken radio back on but chose a station that stuck to up-tempo beats. Right there, in Leila's drop-top Mercedes, parked half blocking the kerb in a side street, they sang for 20 minutes at the top of their voices. People walked past staring, some joined in, and others shook their heads and walked on. It was a policeman who eventually urged them to move on threatening to arrest them for disorderly behaviour and disturbing the peace (after routinely checking that they were neither intoxicated nor in possession of drugs or dangerous weapons). Quite happily blowing kisses at the police officer, they sped off. Olga had an unruly mane of neck-length curly hair. The wind took it in all directions, but as she desperately tried to restrain the voluminous strands, she was more worried about Leila who broke speed limits without fear of consequences.

'It will be a good night!' Leila said, smiling at Olga. Olga reciprocated her smile albeit nervously. Leila's smile did not light her eyes up. It was no smile!

They parked in a side street and walked, arms linked, through the streets of Soho until they came across a row of fortune-tellers.

'Twenty pounds. I will tell you all you need to know,' a wrinkly old lady lured.

'What have we got to lose?' Leila asked.

'A fortune-teller, Mulatto? Really? You've lost your marbles.'

'Oh come on, live a little,' Leila said handing the woman two twenty-pound notes and dragging Olga into her little shrine. Her chiffon curtains were red with gold streaks, which circled the five by five foot shrine. There were two stools within it. She asked Leila to step outside for a second while she spoke to Olga. Leila's protests fell on deaf ears; eventually she gave up and left. Less than five minutes later, Olga stepped out and asked Leila to go in.

'What did she say?' Leila asked.

'Nothing that makes much sense,' Olga said nonchalantly. 'Now you go find out your destiny so we can toast to the future.'

'Sure thing!' Leila said, parting the curtains and stepping into the fortune-teller's world.

'Sit. It's you! I have something for you,' the lady said and her shaky hands handed over a piece of paper with a drawing on it. It was a picture of a tangled mesh of some sort, Arabic writing enclosed within it. The fortune-teller's scrawny fingers caressed the piece of paper for a few seconds.

'What's this then?' Leila asked staring at the picture; it teased the wheels in her head.

'This is your destiny.'

Leila stared at the drawing. It looked roughly sketched, but the talent behind it shone through as the drawing spoke to her. Although she could hear its voice, it was impossible to make out what it was saying. In listening intently, Leila lost nearly ten minutes of conversation with this crazy, incoherent lady. She spoke in weird cryptic Victorian-age English anyway, so Leila reckoned she would not have understood much of it, to be honest.

'OK, thank you,' Leila said as she walked off with the drawing. She folded it neatly and slipped it into the left pocket of her jeans.

'What did that crazy chick say about you?' Olga asked curiously.

'She mumbled a bunch of random stuff and gave me this drawing,' she said pulling it out of her pocket. She handed it over to Olga who stared at it, puzzled.

'Isn't it the most captivating drawing you have ever seen?' Leila asked.

Olga furrowed her brow. 'Erm…not really…' she said, her eyes darting around as if to say Leila had certainly gone mad.

'Personally, I think you have–' (she whistled and crossed her eyes) –'lost it!'

Leila locked arms with her and pulled her along.

'Let's go into that vintage shop,' Leila suggested and so off they went, shopping in strange places. Soon, they came up to a body piercing shop. Leila stopped outside.

'Now what, Mulatto? You are going to pierce your belly button, are you?' Olga asked sarcastically.

'Precisely!' Leila said.

'Oh no, you are not!' Olga said, pointing her forefinger at Leila.

'OK. I am not. We are rebellious tonight. Let's go get tattoos,' Leila said thoughtfully.

'You have lost your marbles!' Olga exclaimed.

'That's the second time you have said that, Olga,' Leila responded in fits of laughter.

'What happened to getting a tattoo when you were eighteen?' Olga asked, horrified at the thought.

'I never felt the impulse to.'

'Let's have a drink and discuss this,' Olga said.

'OK. Find out what time they close though,' she said checking out the opening times.

'OK, we have enough time. Let's have a drink.'

They sat in a bar and ordered. Twenty minutes later, Olga was on her second cocktail. Leila, on the other hand was on her third double Courvoisier.

'You wanna pace yourself. What are you doing?' Olga asked, alarmed.

'OK, drink over. Let's go.' Leila said.

'Go where?'

'To that tattoo place…and you are getting one too. I am not doing this alone,' Leila informed her.

Olga rolled her eyes.

They sat in the tattoo parlour looking through endless designs. Olga chose a little gold butterfly with a sparkle effect. It was the smallest, most inconspicuous she could find.

'You chicken. That's like a dot!' Leila said. Olga ignored her.

'Have you chosen yet?' Olga asked Leila. Leila nodded. 'I am going to have this tattooed!' she said, retrieving the drawing from her back pocket.

'What? Why?' Olga was horrified.

'I don't know, but I am!' Leila said dismissively. And Leila did. On her left ankle. It ran all the way from her middle toe, to the joint that connected her foot to her leg. It ran down the side of her foot as well. It sat majestically, occupying almost half her foot, but worse still, it took hours!

'Did that not hurt?' Olga asked. 'Not much,' she responded.

'That is the weirdest tattoo I have ever seen' Olga said. Leila beamed from ear to ear.

'I know!' she said as she bought a pair of slippers and swapped her Louboutins.

'OK, now let's go to the bar,' Leila said.

'It is well past midnight!' Olga sighed. That night, Leila was impossible!

Ever has it been that love knows not its own
depth until the hour of separation.
Khalil Jibran

Chapter Twelve!

Four or five double Courvoisier's and 'sex on the beach' cocktails later, Olga was exasperated with Leila. 'Don't you think you should go home?'

'Home? What home? I am coming back to yours, babe! Let's celebrate, I am a liberated woman,' Leila replied signalling to the waiter to bring them more drinks. That was the last conversation Leila would remember for a while.

It seemed like an hour or so later in Leila's mind. She could hear muffled voices; she could especially make out Olga's voice in the haze – what she could not make out was what they were saying. Actually, she could not see them. Instead she saw clear skies as she travelled through what she later described as an endless hollow white tunnel. The part she never told anyone about was the moment when once again, she was sat before the wrinkly old fortune-teller with the scrawny fingers. The woman had tears in her eyes and spoke with great difficulty. Her eyes were closed and only opened intermittently. She also had her right hand on Leila's shoulder and she was shivering. This time, she heard the conversation with the lady.

What are you on about, crazy lady?' Leila slurred through her words in her half drunken stupor.

'Precisely. You know. On that day she will testify. From then you die!'

'Who? Tell me what? Who? Who?' Leila asked over and over again, as the vision slowly faded.

'Who?' Leila asked as her eyes finally opened.

'Who?' From the muffled din, Olga's voice crept out. Reality returned then. She learnt that it was it was 2 pm on Saturday afternoon (not an hour later, as her mind had wrongly predicted) – in a hospital bed hooked up to equipment she saw only in ER and the BBC medical dramas.

'Why am I here?' she asked in a whisper, the pain in her head so excruciating she could barely speak.

'Leila, I've been so worried... how are you feeling?' It was Olga.

'What happened?' Leila asked feeling her forehead with her fingers.

'The doctor said that you had some drugs in your bloodstream.'

'And alcohol poisoning,' the nurse pointed out sternly, looking condescendingly at Leila who glanced over at her briefly but ignored the comment, dealing instead with more pressing issues.

'Drugs? What drugs? I don't do drugs!' Leila was confused.

'Shh… I know… don't get upset… remember the young men you were talking to in the bar?' Olga asked hastily.

'No…' Leila shook her head.

'One of your gentleman friends made a pass at you. You were having none of it. He got a little upset. I guess the rest is history. I guess they put something in your drink to make you less erm…tense.'

'People do that even in the City? Where did we go?'

'City, yes.' Olga said nodding distractedly. She added in a worried whisper, 'Leila, Kash is here to see you as well.'

'Akash? I don't want to see him,' Leila said frowning and flashing Olga her best 'you-have-betrayed-me' look.

'He is your next of kin, silly!' Olga said rather annoyed. 'Perhaps you ought to change your medical records before you go on a self-destructive mission with alcohol.'

Leila kissed her teeth and rolled her eyes. Olga did the same.

'Leila, baby, I am so sorry, I know I have a lot of explaining to do. This is probably not the best time, but I know I am responsible for all this. I just want to take you home and we can talk about it later.' It was Akash speaking.

'Yeah, brush it all under the carpet as usual,' she muttered bitterly under her breath, refusing even a glance in his direction.

'I will make it all better.'

'It's too damn late,' she thought stubbornly to herself.

'We can get through this.'

Leila turned her head in the opposite direction. Akash just stared helplessly at her, and just as he was going to give one more shot at the conversation, the doctor came in. He confirmed that she was not in the habit of taking class A (or any type of) drugs, slipped a few leaflets on drug and alcohol abuse into Akash's hands with some advice and tablets, and discharged her. She was still very drowsy, but she heard Akash thank Olga for her assistance and promise to get Leila to call her when she was feeling much better. Olga whispered in her ear – something about being sorry for ringing Akash, but that she had panicked and did not know what else to do, and besides the hospital were going to ring him as per her records anyway. Leila nodded nonchalantly. She got in the car and they drove home in silence. Upon arrival at their once happy home, Akash attempted to make polite conversation, but due to the pain in her head and the disgust she felt at even the sound of his voice, she remained silent and curled herself into a ball underneath her favourite red blanket, on the settee. She fell asleep.

When she awoke again, it was Sunday afternoon. It took a few minutes to remember where she was and then the events of the last two days unfolded before her in a flash. A tear threatened to let loose, but she fogged it off. 'No more tears,' she told herself.

'Leila?' It was Akash. She did not respond.

'Why won't you just talk to me?' he enquired. Nothing!

'I know that things have been horrible, but I can explain. It's not what you think…' She glared at him.

'Listen, we can make this work, you don't have to…'

Leila was not interested. She got up mid-sentence, and headed straight for the shower. She had not had a shower in 48 hours and considering all the alcohol and smoke she had been exposed to, she felt filthy! Whilst in the bathroom, she heard some sort of explanation about clients and a meeting. It was all waffle to Leila.

'I don't give a shit if I never see you again in my life!' she muttered under her breath. She had gone cold…numb.

She called Olga.

'I'm so sorry about it all… no, I don't want to hear the gory details. I am fine now…' she said. Then there was a pause for a few seconds.

'Yes, yes I am. I am leaving him. I will call you later, babe. I have a few things to do.'

During their telephone conversation, Olga gave Leila details of the long talk she had had with Akash while she lay in that hospital bed. Apparently, he was sorry but had no logical explanation for his erratic behaviour, and he would rather die than watch Leila walk away from him.

'Well, he has gone out,' Leila said with a tone so sharp, it sliced the air of conversation into pieces. She hesitated then added, 'You know what, Olga, I will be fine. I just need to be clear my mind, by myself, on where to go from here.'

Leila put the phone down and thought long and hard about what she was about to do. The truth was she could forgive infidelity. She could forgive it if she tried hard enough. What she was finding difficult to understand was the abuse. There she had said it. She had suffered emotional abuse with this man. Whatever was going on with him, she was not sure but did not think his behaviour was permissible. She, on the other hand, had not covered herself in glory either. She had met a man and kissed him. The justification for this was the emotional abuse she had experienced with Akash. She knew she was not blameless. She also knew that she deserved more. She knew that with a decently behaved Akash, her eyes would not stray. Or would they? She had never met a man like Kaobi, but that was beside the point. She concluded that he deserved something or someone else – someone that was not her. It was obvious that she was unable to please him. She simply was not good enough. She thought about his immigration status, the fact that he was now British by virtue of his marriage to her. She had heard gory stories of people who did this exact thing. They got married, secured their papers and buggered off. Was this what this was all about? Leila found that hard to believe. Something had gone wrong with Akash. She did not know what it was, but she thought that she was neither strong enough, nor patient enough to stick around to find out. It would definitely lead her to an early grave. At that point, she felt like a failure.

This could not possibly be happening to her. What would people think? She sighed.

Leila sat before the mirror and dug out her make-up bag. She took her time. She lined and then highlighted her eyes, lashed on layers of mascara and wore a subtle shade of pink for lipstick. Then she wore a little skirt and took it off.

'Too slutty and tacky.' She threw on a longer version. 'Too work day-ish'. The Karen Millen skirt she finally settled for had a lovely lycra feel to it with a subtle shimmer. It was just below the knee, and hugged her skin elegantly, accentuating a figure that many women would kill for. Leila had beautiful legs and knew it.

'If you've got it, flaunt it!' she said mischievously to herself as she admired the slit down the side. Every step she took showed her legs off deliberately. There was then the other issue. What shoes does one wear a day after getting a rather conspicuous tattoo on one's foot? She looked down and stroked it gently as it still stung. She found a pair of sandals so stringy, they had hardly any impact. Her sister had once likened the Christian Dior sandals to thongs. She giggled at the thought.

She thought to herself that she loved the way she looked, that she was a beautiful woman. She got compliments all the time in the streets, and Kaobi had said so as well. She believed in the beauty of the inside as well as the external and tried her best to stay clean and positive inside. She thought about her Christian background and how she had done things she had never imagined she would. She could almost step out of her body and look upon her life as someone else's. Still she tried to convince herself that it was not so bad. She was in perfect health, she was in a good place financially, she had family and friends who would love and support her regardless. At that point, Leila could not help it. She felt alone and unattractive! Leila had glassy looking eyes as she stared at her mobile phone. She picked it up. She dialled Kaobi's number, she hesitated and cancelled the call, and then seconds later she redialled. On the phone to him, she summarised the events of the last two days and arranged to meet him for dinner and 'cheering up'.

As Akash tore wildly down the M25 to his meeting somewhere in the heart of the City, he had a feeling he had lost her this time. There was this numbness in her eyes, where love normally shone through, even when she was at her angriest with him.

'You fool!' he kept on saying to himself, hitting his forehead with his hands repeatedly.

'How do I salvage this?' he wondered.

'I love her. I have never loved anyone the way I love her. She is the one for me. I cannot lose her. I am nothing without her!' He feared the worst.

He rushed through the impromptu meeting. His body was present; his mind? Well, his mind was travelling at a thousand miles an hour. At the end of the meeting, he made his excuses for being unavailable for drinks at their usual spot.

'But we are celebrating,' a colleague said.

'Have one for me,' Akash said patting him on the shoulder.

He was getting back on his feet. The financial pressure was easing off. It had taken a lot of hard work on his part, a lot of networking, engaging in social habits he ordinarily would not care for. This was the beginning of getting himself back on track. Leila would be proud. Leila did not know of any difficulty to begin with though. He shook her head at the deception – omission, he corrected himself. If he pulled off these deals, he would be in better financial standing than he had been previously. Was it worth it? A little voice in his head informed him that he had attended this particular meeting at the expense of his marriage. The thought caused him to go into migraine mode. The other voice in his head reminded him that Leila was a diva, a spoilt brat, used to getting her own way – a princess, and totally weird. I mean, what was that tattoo she had indelibly marked her foot with? He shook his head. He disapproved strongly. Tattoos, in his opinion, were for labelling cattle! He had failed to comment at the hospital because it shocked him that she would indulge in such juvenile activities. He had his immigration papers; it was time to cut his losses and move on. He measured his achievements so far. He had riches, he had his British Citizenship, but there was the possibility that he no longer had Leila. These three things were of utmost importance to him. Which was priority though? Leila? He had not showed that. Would he hand back his British Passport and financial success to reclaim her love if it ever came to that? Akash was baffled. He was unable to answer the question.

Off home he sped, but not before stopping by at the flower shop. He bought her three-dozen mixed yellow and red roses, some chocolate (it had to be Amelie Chocolate, her favourite), and a bottle of Romanee-Conti. Leila always said lavishness and cash did not impress her, but he was pulling out all the tricks in his hat tonight. He made a mental note to manipulate her with her favourite love songs – he would sing to her like he used to. She loved that. She would stare into his eyes with unashamed adoration. He would remind her of all the reasons why she fell in love with him and hoped that this would stir some sort of emotion in his numb wife. He decided to have some faith in his suaveness. He was well above the speed limit on the motorway – it had a bit to do with his nerves, but he felt this strange rush of adrenalin at the challenge before him.

'*You and me, having sex after an argument, that shit's the best*,' he sang along to the R Kelly song on the radio. He sure was looking forward to it. He had a mischievous smile on his face just thinking of what he would do with her. Oral sex was obviously on the cards. Leila loved that. He was aware that sex had been a bit mechanical recently. He would spice that right up.

However, every now and again reality would kick in. All this could be months, weeks, or even days too late! He shuddered at the thought. What an idiot he had been.

Well, across town, Leila was satisfied that she looked good. She knew exactly what she was about to do. She opened her little purse. Credit Card. Debit Card. Diary. Passport. Driver's Licence (she changed her mind and flung that on the dressing table. No driving tonight). She swayed all the way to the front door and froze. She turned around and made her way into the kitchen, all the while staring between the door and the kitchen window. Would Akash's Mercedes pull up any second? She rushed to Akash's alcohol cupboard and quickly scanned through. She found an open bottle of brandy and gulped down a shot, and then another. She was a woman on a mission, in search of happiness. If it were out there, she would find it. *Any* kind of happiness would do, she would even settle for the temporary version. She got to the door and hesitated. This was her final chance to change her mind. The unfortunate thing about life, perhaps, is that human foresight only goes that far. There is a good chance that if at that point Leila could read Akash's mind, she would have slipped into her pyjamas and fluffy slippers. That would be too easy. Therefore, still wallowing in self-pity, Leila rolled her eyes briefly in deep deliberation, her heart stiffened; she slammed the door shut, walking into the night in search of happiness…and the definition of love…and some magic.

'Do I fly or fall?' she asked herself as the mental image of Akash and the blonde stranger tortured her psyche; that image rotated with the image of him signing their marriage certificate with a smirk on his face. Did she imagine the smirk? She had never noticed it, not until the mental image showed up that night. Was this justification for her intended actions? She had not even called Olga back. That was usually a sign of guilt. If she could not tell Olga, then it was pretty bad. She tried to convince herself that she was fine and that her anger had ceased. She said to herself that she was eager to move on and start afresh. In reality, Leila was bitter and hurt, confused.

'Two wrongs don't make a right,' she thought to herself as the taxi driver ushered her in.

'Heck! He's probably up to no good anyway!' and she got in, popping two mints in her mouth during the two-way conversation with herself. 'His loss...' she muttered and added, 'it's too late!' Life. If Leila had not reached for the mints in her purse at that second, if she had only settled for one instead of deciding she could not live with odd numbers even with mints and reach for the second one; if Leila had not bent down even further to make sure her tattoo sat comfortably and infection-free within the 'thong sandals', she would have noticed Akash wildly tearing down the street, towards their home… but life plays these tricks sometimes. If Leila had seen him, what turn would that night have taken?

Akash walked into the empty house whistling.

'Leila! Leila! Leila!' he called out, frantically making his way round the house. He shook his head in annoyance. He rang her mobile phone multiple times, each time just redialling the number. She was obviously ignoring his calls. He dumped the wine, flowers and the chocolate on the table in the kitchen and with a double shot of brandy drank in one gulp, he sank into the settee in the living room.

'She'll be back soon,' he said glancing at his watch, reassuring himself. He gulped down another double shot. He gulped down another. Then he poured a double shot into a glass...and then another!

'You look gor...gor...gorgeous for s...s...someone who has been in... in...in hospital,' he said as he took her coat at The Lane Bar, somewhere off Brick Lane. Was he stuttering because his speech impediment just got worse, or because his tongue was hanging out of his mouth at seeing Leila dressed up?

'Adolescent thoughts,' she muttered under her breath, almost ashamed of herself.

'You too...too...took a taxi?' he asked, concerned.

She nodded and added, 'Doctor said not to drive until I feel a hundred percent.' He nodded his approval.

Initially amongst other things, they discussed his speech impediment.

'Have you always had this problem?' she probed.

'Like I said to you the last time, sweetheart, it's intermittent. Sometimes the words overwhelm me and I find it difficult to express myself eloquently and coherently, but unlike the majority of the cases, it's not subject to emotions such as anger, etc,' he explained.

He continued, 'It got progressively worse over the years and especially when Kamsi passed on, but somehow, I think it has generally gotten slightly better every day – more recently anyway.' He smiled.

'And you said that without any hesitation you know, KK,' she said, hungrily tucking into her chicken Caesar salad. He smiled again.

Leila told him about all the research she had discovered and how he could undertake therapy to drastically reduce or in fact annihilate the problem totally. Kaobi marvelled at how much time she had put into her enquiries, and the ease with which she offered her assistance.

'I will be happy to help you practise if you like. I would really love for you to overcome it completely,' she said. He nodded.

'Ok, I will look into it with you.' He smiled once more. At that point, they shared a very comfortable silence and then went on to discuss so many other things.

'I'm so sorry to burden you with my problems,' Leila sighed. 'I just wanted to talk.' He nodded. And as per usual, she told him all about it. He lent his ear, his shoulder, his heart, and his soul. He was sympathetic and understanding. He promised her that tomorrow would be a better day for her. Somehow, Kaobi always seemed to understand and share her pain. 'Would you like to dance?' he asked. She smiled. Therefore, in that little bar with the red scented candles and the crazy epileptic lights doing funny things to her senses, and the man with the crazy piano singing crazy ballads, stories of love and passion, they slow danced. That night, she convinced herself, was the night when she would remember what it felt like to be adored by a man. She did not want to be reasonable. She did not care to decipher right from wrong, she did not want a declaration of undying love either – all she wanted was to remember tenderness and intimacy. She was on a mission. She would remember love; she would remember what she was worth, someone to appreciate all she had to give. His breath on the lobe of her ear and his impressive sized manhood pressed against her thighs and tingling part; Leila's senses temporarily took leave of her. She clung to him and suggestively whispered in his ear how she loved him. Leila *did* love him, for the way he made her feel about herself; she had misplaced her belief in what love ought to be, and now she had found it again; she loved him for the sense he made every time he spoke to her, for his sincerity and for the light brown colour of his eyes (she would always wonder what that shade was called. It was in-between light and dark brown). Pre-Kaobi, she had been convinced that her marital problems were her fault, and that she obviously was not trying hard enough. Even when she could not identify the problem, she just sulked. At some point, she accepted that all relationships suffered the same fate. Now she knew better. Yes, relationships were hard, but hers was fatally defective. Somewhere out there, there was love for real; she just had not found it just yet. When the epileptic light got a little less crazy, but dimmer and the song was a favourite Kenny G number, she pulled him closer and co-ordinated her perfectly endowed hips to the rhythm of the song. She wriggled her little waist repeatedly. He asked her what she was doing, in an obviously rattled whisper. Her response: 'just dancing'. He could not help himself. He told her that he was inching closer to insanity by the second. Leila knew about the powers women had, and gloated inwardly at how she weakened this man – a man who could be easily be described as the epitome of high moral standing.

'Kiss her,' she whispered, referring to herself in the third person as she often did. Naturally, right there in the restaurant, she let her lips reunite with his. She had longed to recapture those blissful 20 seconds that they had shared only the previous Thursday. This time though, she let herself participate fully and deliberately. She explored every bit of his lips and his tongue, stroked every inch of his dark African hair, teasing him more boldly as the seconds went by. At every move she made, he gasped with sexual pleasure, driving her more insane than she was moments before. Almost midnight it was when they finally left the restaurant and headed for the car. He drove to a deserted open spot somewhere just off Leicester Square and turned the ignition off. He stared at her and she stared back at him as well but consciously not too intensely for fear of seeing things such as the weird '12 second moment' back on the beach. Suddenly, the tears she could hold back no longer came flooding down by the dozen.

'It's OK, sweetheart…' he whispered, pulling her close. He turned the car ignition back on and increased the heat as she shivered hysterically. She was scared, confused, miserable and nervous all at the same time. She chuckled and almost choked on her tears all because she loved the way he said 'sweetheart'. His Nigerian/English intonation was prominent when he said this one word and he never stuttered on it. 'Isn't it funny how I can find humour in just about any situation?' she wondered to herself. Earlier on, she had willed her mind to stop crying. She told herself that if he made her cry, then he wasn't worth it; she had cried rivers of tears for this unworthy cause already. Yet still the unruly tears rebelliously flooded down by the gazillion tracing jagged paths down her cheeks. He wiped them away, he kissed them tenderly, he stroked them, and then he got out of the car and urged her out as well.

Underneath the iridescent trillion stars glittering above, he held her in his arms for endless minutes and consoled her. He whispered in her ear how beautiful she was, how he loved her from the very second his eyes had met hers. In that magic moment, he somehow managed to seduce her senses. They kissed endlessly as he caressed her softly. Hardly any fraction of her remained un-investigated by his lips and strong restless hands – her hair, her eyes, her lips, her neck; he tore open her buttons with his teeth. His experienced fingers unclasped her bra, explored her breasts. He gently caressed the sides close to her nipples. His member hardened as he bent close and blew ever so gently, teasing her nipples. His eyes narrowed as he felt stronger and stronger waves of aggressive sexual euphoria whilst he watched her areolas and nipples swell and then harden. Next, his hands wandered to her stomach, her inner thighs, her legs, her feet, her toes. In mutual consent, she reciprocated with just as much passion, kissing him fiercely, grabbing at his shirt buttons, and stroking his thighs with the inside of hers gently, but not without illuminating her constrained yearning. With no one but those trillion stars watching, he tenderly lifted her onto the warm hat. With her name on his lips, he penetrated her tingling part. An easy task it was with her skirt lasciviously slit down its left side. His thrusts were powerful yet gentle; repeatedly he pleasured her gripping her around her waist and lightly tapping her buttocks, eyes hardened and flaming with passion boring into her. She was insatiable; he was up to the task. The more she let out little gasps and yelps of pleasure, the harder he thrust, the deeper his plunges and the more animal-like he was in manipulating her body. When she screamed aloud in sheer delight he covered her lips with his and decreased the speed of his rhythm, nourishing her with more of a grind than pace. He seemed to go deeper by the second, exploring her bared flesh with his hands simultaneously.

'Shhh,' he whispered in her ear, but she never stopped screaming or gasping and he never for one second paused to let her either. His dedication, naturally heightened by passion drove Leila to a mental state that was the closest she had been to orgasmic insanity and she absolutely loved it. Her gasps encouraged his desire to please her. He gave, and then some! He set her soul alight as he fuelled, and then extinguished her starvation, until she thought she saw the glittering trillion stars all smiling. Well the part of her soul that manipulated her sexual desires certainly was smiling. It had found what it had subconsciously sought without fulfilment for a long, long time. For the first time in unforgivably long, the aftermath of the incident left Leila feeling like a real woman should; well and truly sexually gratified! It was at this moment that reality sunk in and Leila realised they had made love. Physical evidence that he also had reached some sort of culmination was all over her skirt and her thighs. Somehow, due to their sudden movements, he hadn't managed to 'finish off' inside of her, not completely. She looked at her thighs; little squirts maybe. She expected to see buckets of the creamy stuff, but it did not always work that way apparently. In any case, a river of evidence would have been a tad inconvenient taking into account the inappropriateness of their geographical location. Leila was ecstatic! In fact, once the first few minutes of shock were over, they both giggled endlessly. Their heart-felt laughter was a mixture of embarrassment, shyness and the shocking sheer impulse of it all. Wrong as it was, it had been gratifying.

'Should I drive you home?' he asked. Leila shook her head.

'I don't want to go home! I want to have a selfish night. I want what I want.'

'What do you want?'

SILENCE

'What do you want?' He tipped her head up to meet his eyes.

'Magic,' she replied. There was a brief pause before he nodded. 'Your wish is my command. Sit in here where it's nice and warm, while I make a few phone calls to see if I can order you some of that.' She smiled nervously, but obeyed.

Ten minutes later, he got back into the car and started the ignition.

'Does he know you are out on a mission?' he asked. 'Does she?' she responded with the same question. He drove. She never asked where.

They got to Stansted Airport. They checked in; they flew business class to Paris. He drove her to the Four Seasons Hotel George V.

At the hotel, Leila collapsed into her bed inviting Kaobi to join her.

'Did you marry the girl of your dreams?' Leila asked, unexpectedly. Kaobi thought for a few seconds before responding.

'She saw me through a lot and n…n…not many people can understand me the w…w…way she does,' was his reply.

'Is that a yes then?' Leila asked.

'If I say yes, then wh…wh…what am I doing here? There are questions that can never be…be…be answered, sweetheart, but I am content with her.'

'Why did you wait seven years to have children?' Leila quizzed gently. He paused for a few seconds.

'We couldn't have kids! We had to go through IVF and the whole rigmarole it…it…it involves. It was particularly hard in our case be…be…because with IVF, there are still particularly slim chances of fertilisation with men with low sperm counts. Most clinics will consider doing IVF only for men with at least 3 million motile sperm in the ejaculate. If the sperm counts are lower than this, then ICSI or microinjection is a better option,' he said smiling at the bamboozled look on Leila's face. He broke down the medical jargon. Leila nodded attentively and asked questions where necessary. 'Ob…ob…obviously. It took seven years because we didn't seek any help in the first three years,' he replied.

'I am sorry to hear that,' Leila said sympathetically.

'We have two lovely boys now so it's ok. I don't think I want to have any more kids any way.'

He explained to her the torture and humiliation he had experienced when the doctor informed him that his semen was more or less futile and that the chances of him ever being able to father a child naturally were, honestly speaking, next to nothing. The summary of it in fact was that his sperm were too lazy to swim, her eggs – not too enthusiastic about being fertilised anyway so couldn't be bothered much to ripen, or whatever apt medical description would be appropriate.

'She was desperate for kids, but she never for one…one…one second placed that priority over our marriage and I…I…I…really appreciated that considering the fact that back home in Nigeria, the cul…cul… culture expects the fruit of the womb nine months after the wedding. It would not matter what the doctors say. A fa…fa…family like mine ignorantly conclude that any childbearing problem is…is…is the woman's.' Leila listened fascinated by the stories of how his family had on more than one occasion turned up with a beautiful virgin for him to take as a second wife.

'They can do that?' she asked in bewilderment.

'Yes, they can. I would have been well within my rights to take another woman home, but I don't believe in all that,' he replied.

Leila was full of compassion, but reminded him of how lucky he was to have the boys – Armani and Adrian; he had nothing to worry about unless he wanted more kids. Leila could not believe how such a powerful, controlling organ like his (and her vaginal muscles tensed as an involuntary reaction to the thought) could be incompetent. He should be able to produce triplets or quads, she thought mischievously. In most cases she had heard of, the man was usually unable to perform the act in the first place, much less fertilise an egg in the process. There was a pause for many minutes as both replayed the events of the night. They shared shy glances.

'What's that on your foot?' he asked.

Leila hesitated. 'Something silly I did,' she said as her face thoroughly flushed. She remembered the look of shock and some expression that resembled disgust on Akash's face.

He did not want to touch the sore tattoo so he bent over and stared at it through severely squinted eyes. He said nothing. She offered no explanation. For a second, she thought back to the wrinkly old fortune-teller with the scrawny fingers, but she rebuked her words to the back of her mind. Gibberish!

'Is it ok if I have a quick shower?' She had to get away from the tension. It threatened to choke her. He nodded.

She stepped off the bed conscious of his trailing gaze. She would never be able to confirm her reason for not completely shutting the door behind her; nor the reason why she undid the zip of her skirt as she walked towards the bathroom, never bothered with a towel when she walked across the room right past the railings which housed them. She made her way to the bathroom stark naked! If he was peering through the slightly ajar door he would see everything. What was she doing? She fought the temptation to turn around to check if he was. At full blast, the hot water was soothing, the power shower rather noisy, the sound of a door shutting had to be her imagination. She wiped some water from her face and stopped short. Through the blurry panes was the silhouette of a naked man. She fought for breath looking at Kaobi holding the shower door open and smiling.

'May I?'

She could not answer and he did not wait. At close proximity, with the water running over their bodies, many things happened, things that Leila put into a box and locked away. From the minute she met him at Brick Lane to ending up in a shower at the Four Seasons in Paris, Leila experienced many things. Maybe one day she would open that box!

'Sometimes feelings just get mixed up. I am fighting my demons, and you have your issues as well, he said gently.

'Let's just forget it,' she whispered back. She gave him a hug, a smile and in true British style, she also gave him a pat on the back and called him a 'mate' to loosen up the tense atmosphere. They both smiled.

They decided they would beg God for forgiveness and move on. As no lightning had struck them dead, they agreed that God had made his peace with it and they had gotten away with not even a slap on the wrist, probably due to extenuating circumstances.

'Do you think he handles cases on individual merit?' Leila asked. Kaobi smiled. 'Well my Nan always used to say that,' she said. Feeling a bit lighter, with that load taken off their shoulders, they made a pact – they would always be friends because there was an obvious bond between them. They would be careful from then on not to cross the boundary. They were sure it would never happen again. They both came to the conclusion that there was a wide void in both their lives which somehow they filled for each other, but that they would look to God to fill it and doing that did not in any way involve sex, regardless of how explosive, natural and powerfully right it felt. Leila was still half expecting lightning to strike them both dead (or at least some sort of metaphoric equivalent) when Kaobi pointed out that they needed to let it go. They both were quiet for a few minutes, each with their own thoughts, conscience and wonders about the potency of the morrow.

'Tell me about Nigeria,' Leila said breaking the silence, her eyes lighting up with excitement at the prospect. He always told her tales about back home and what life was like over there. She particularly fancied the idea of being able to walk into the garden, bare feet perhaps and definitely without a winter coat, to pluck an orange or pear straight off the tree. He also told legendary stories about his history, his royal heritage (hence the soubriquet 'Prince' apparently), and her favourite fable was how she would be treated like the true princess that he thought she was. He told her tales about the 'Obi' (king) and the yam festivals they had during their great annual harvests; the funny (sometimes scary) faced men all masqueraded in their fancy outfits, doing their funny dances (she had even seen videos of these amazing dances), the animals they reared, walking miles to the stream to fetch buckets of bath and even drinking water in the remote parts of the little villages, etc. These stories were like bedtime tales to Leila. Although he had showed her a couple of videos of the ceremonies, she often wondered about their authenticity. One day, Kaobi promised, she would find out.

As he told her tales of Nigeria, of himself, of his innermost thoughts, Leila smiled. With this man, she felt at ease. Her heart was at home. She felt no defensive impulsion to weigh thoughts nor measure words but pouring all out, bare as they were, confident that he could do little or perhaps no harm at all. And even if for that moment only, she willed her soul to be happy to the exclusion of the world. Whilst in his arms, she closed her eyes and with a semblance to the nap she had earlier in the week in his office, she surrendered herself to much needed peaceful slumber with mostly pleasant thoughts. He snored loudly; it did not bother her. The only slightly uncomfortable thought was the wrinkly old fortune-teller with the scrawny fingers who kept making an on and off appearance. 'Go away' – she shooed! Although she felt no desires to kiss, snug or make love to him, her thoughts consisted mostly of slow dancing in darkness to one of Kenny G's records – particularly, *By the time this night is over.* The shelter she felt just lying with his arms wrapped around her was just as good a feeling as those she experienced when he had made love to her, only this time, it was a different feeling, peaceful, serene, real, protective.

They got the first flight back to London and by special arrangement, Kaobi waved a magic wand and they were at the Four Seasons in London.

'What time is it?' she questioned, yawning lazily.

'10 am,' he replied as he planted a kiss on her forehead. 'I ha…have to go…' he explained.

'I know… you have to go back to her.'

'And work…' he added, a bit uncomfortable with the conversation obviously.

'Last night, I had an indescribable time. I thank you for that, and I know it will not be happening again. We know that now, don't we?' he asked still searching her eyes for reassurance that things would be alright between them.

She whispered, 'You belong to her.'

'Are you upset about that?' he asked.

'No. No, I'm not. I love you KK, but I cannot rejoice in the wrong. Forget what I want. I want you to be happy. You are the best friend ever, nothing more.'

'If things could be different, Leila…' he began and then paused and then he added thoughtfully, 'Could they?' he asked giving her the opportunity to declare her love or intention to keep him for herself if she so desired.

'I don't think so; I don't want to ever lose your friendship. To me, that's more important than any feelings we may think we have for each other.' She looked at him through sincerely unselfish eyes.

'It's not just her. It's the kids. My family. Your family. There is too much at stake. Boats will rock. Boats the size of the ti…ti…titanic.'

She nodded.

'It's strange, but I love you in a way I cannot explain, Leila… maybe one day, I will shed more light on this, but not until I figure it all out completely myself.'

She nodded again. 'I'll be fine. Just go,' she added gently.

He smiled at her, reached out and hugged her, planted a protective kiss on her forehead, but he didn't leave. They had breakfast, played Scrabble, had lunch, watched a movie, stared out of the window and talked endlessly. At 8.30 pm, Leila knew it was time.

'I'll be fine… just go!' she said to him once more reassuring him that she was alright. He smiled at her, and then once again reached out and hugged her, planted a kiss on her forehead but this time, he left…but as he stood at the door, he turned and said to her: 'Something happened last night, Leila. Something that will follow us for the rest of our lives.' Leila nodded. This line would haunt her!

As much as Leila had been dreading this moment, she felt no regret, no bitterness, and no resentment at all. She knew it would never happen again, he had somehow won her eternal friendship. She was grateful to him for the experience. All she wanted was the reassurance that sparks, real sparks exist and she was not insane to want a bit of a spark in her dull life. She knelt down and spoke to God. She reminded Him that she was human and never in her right mind would she want to upset Him. Sometimes feelings shared between a man and woman could get very confusing. He loved her a lot, she knew, but it was more a case of caring for her and feeling protective and concerned for her wellbeing. Somewhere along the line, they had been misguided perhaps. She would not beat herself up about it; sometimes in life, things happened for a reason. After dinner, she fell asleep. She looked peaceful. Once again, she was slow dancing in the dark to Kenny G. It was an amazing night!

Love is the answer, but while you are waiting for
the answer, sex raises some pretty good questions
Woody Allen

Chapter Fourteen

Relationships: The Diamond Ring On The 4th Finger Of My Left Hand

At the risk of sounding arrogant, I will tell you that I wear a beautiful eternity ring on the 4th finger of my left hand. It comprises little diamond studs worth the equivalent of a deposit for a huge mansion – and not in a diminutive suburban village in the middle of nowhere, no! I, recipient and eternal beneficiary of said ring, am for the most part, grateful – most days! I tend to sashay around in my little bubble reminding myself repeatedly about the day it was given to me. He pledged his love all over again. He sang along as he played the guitar. He sang 'when God made you' (Google it in one of your soppy moments, it's a potently beautiful tear jerker). So that's what I do 80% of the time; 20% of the time, I feel like 'bleh' (total crap – excuse my language), and today, I am going to write about it.

I love my rock! Most of my friends want it. If they understood what wearing it entailed, perhaps they would be less enthusiastic in their blatant envy and sometimes resentment. So I sit on the train this Thursday morning in May and as the spring/summer sun causes it to sparkle conspicuously, erratically, wildly and brightly, so equally matched are the thoughts in my head, which scream out violently, deafeningly and just as erratic.

Giver of said ring, aka Husband, tends to think that money can buy him everything he wants. In most cases, it does. I think expecting to be treated like royalty when you have an abundant supply of money is perhaps understandable, maybe subconscious. BUT (– and here comes the rant):

I am not your slave. I do not have to be everything you want me to be, especially someone I am not. I will tell you how wonderful a person you are, but I refuse to massage your ego if it means that you and/or I will have to put myself down in the process. I will cook your meals and even do you a three course on the odd occasion, but I will reserve the right to order you a take-out in the event that I have chicken pox...or like when the cat died or I couldn't fit into my size 0 jeans and sunk into depression as a result. While we are on that subject, I relish your constructive criticism, but I would like you to love me just as I am – size 0 or 24. Should it matter? Didn't you preach your love to me? Come to bed with me regardless of my size.

I need, for my own sanity, to have my own opinions. If the BBC News is a sad movie and makes me cry, don't give me that 'you are pathetic' look in disgust, appreciate that I am who I am; after all, I think Spiderman is a stupid, pointless movie, but I will enjoy the story line for your sake. These are the things that matter, babe. If you buy me daisies every now and again, well that's a bonus, if you don't, that's fine too... I promise. It really does not matter as long as you respect the person that I am. In return for this, I will give you everything within my power to, and if I cannot, I will give the best compromise – you won't even know the difference. This is my eternal promise.

*While some of these are just my metaphor for some of the despicable things that happen within a marriage, I will recap by saying: I am my own individual in my own right. I want to look in the mirror and be your eternity woman, but I also want to be who I am and be OK about it. Once again, I thank you for my beautiful ring, but the moment life persistently feels like less of a compromise and more like a *$"%&^* lifelong custodial sentence, or like a knife stabbing at my heart over and over again, or like a brain tumour, or some kind of spiritual bondage, or...*breathe*, I will chuck your damned eternity ring into the River Thames. Babe, because I am the mother of your (unborn) kids and your wife (proudly so), but before any of all that, my name is Leila and that is who I will be until the day I die, and even then it will be engraved on my tombstone – 'Proudly Leila'. Any attempt to muck about with this reality or rock the foundation of my being will be treated like a terrorist attack and you know how seriously such offences are taken, especially in light of recent global events.*

I love you much more than the eternity ring. And yes, I am a diva – fact! But here is another fact – I am the only diva in this world that can love you the way you want and need to be loved. I tick all your boxes and do the all-rounder thing. That's why you married me. Yet another fact – the demise of our marriage will be most unfortunate, but we will live through it. At the risk of sounding like a broken record, I am grateful for my ring, but it means nothing, absolutely diddlysquat, if you do not love me the right way!

Note to reader: For the purpose of this article, I wrote in first person because it was easier to express my thoughts this way. It is hardly relevant to my own personal circumstances, but if it's easier, please construe as you wish – that's fine. This is on one condition though – take the message contained within along with you on your journey. The message? Whoever you are, you are made to perfection. Your uniqueness was stamped and authorised by God himself. Look in the mirror every day and recognise yourself. If today you do not, think carefully. You were never born to be a slave!

Until next time, let's dig deep!

Leila x

Chapter Sixteen

On Tuesday afternoon, Leila sat contemplating her future. She had wasted enough time. It was hopeless. Maybe he was going through a phase but he had to make his mistakes on his own time. She had to get on with her life.

'Where do I start?' she wondered to herself.

Something inside her consciously made the decision to begin a new era! In that moment, she left him. The whole week she had been threatening to do so, but her heart still clung to him. Now she would attempt to free herself of him – body and soul alike. She owed it to herself, to him and to what they had shared in the days of their relationship when love was all they knew. 'I walk away from you today, Kash,' she said to herself as she opened up her diary.

The second I walk away
And I tell you; I say I may
My eyes that sought yours may shut down
My smile for you will wear a frown
I may cry, I may sigh, but many a tissue in my hand
For my mind's eye must go blind, thoughts of you worthless
and banned

The minute I walk away
Hear me pray, this day, I say

I will drop this surging burden that is you
Embrace this cursed blessed day that's brand new
Walk on air, fly the skies, kick a fuss if I must
I love you, you decide, you are boss, it's your loss

The hour I walk away from you
In this sour hour I will wave goodbye through and through
I will wipe my sore eye
I will cry, I will sigh, I won't die
Whatever it takes even as my poor heart breaks
I will learn from mistakes even as my love is at stake

And this day I walk away
I walk away from all I know, loves seed I once sowed
I sowed to reap; I lived to believe, so the story goes, I was told
I am woebegone, distraught but the pain won't stay
A new day today, I did right by heart so I say
Today, no looking back, I have walked away.

She read back through her scribbling again and the strength of the anger in her words pierced her heart right through and she felt it bleed profusely. She remembered the last time they had had a huge argument. She has warned him that she had no energy left in her because her love for him was running on batteries.

'I am warning you, Kash, if I walk away from you, I will never look back,' she had said to him that day.

'Is that a threat, Leila?' he had asked.

'No, baby, it's a warning,' she had said calmly walking away from him. Snapping back to reality, she said aloud to herself, 'yesterday's sorrow, today's incomprehension, tomorrow's blessing' and she shut her diary, making the necessary arrangements to check out of the hotel. That saying had stemmed from Kaobi and if he believed it, it was good enough for her.

'Silver lining, I patiently await you…' she said, and then added, 'but what I want to know is...do I fly or fall?'

Meanwhile as Leila was making big decisions, unbeknownst to her, a frantic Akash paced up and down the kitchen like a spoilt child who had been denied a toy. He had cancelled all his meetings for the afternoon because he was finding it hard to concentrate on anything but his wife who had mysteriously disappeared. He knew it was his fault but was unsure of what steps to take to rectify the situation.

'What have I done?' he asked himself repeatedly, letting the burnt off ash from his cigarette fall to the floor. Seventeen of 20 cigarettes in his pack had suffered the same fate. He had a bottle of brandy with three quarters of its content already consumed in his other hand. A full bottle lay in wait on the table.

His gaze drifted to the dying roses and melted chocolate nestled next to the bottle on the table. He raised the bottle to his lips and gulped the rest if its contents. The tears pushed out of his eyes before the last drop of brandy entered his mouth. He stared out of the window and threw the brandy bottle at his reflection. It hit the window, bounced on to the kitchen sink and then on to the floor into a thousand irreparable pieces. He took in the shattered glass in one glance; ironically, this was their marriage! * Sighs*

Leila was on her way to pick up some of her things from the house. She went less reluctantly because she thought it unlikely Akash would be home. She chose Tuesday afternoon because, in her subconscious, she didn't want to face him. On a typical Tuesday, Akash would be inundated with back to back meetings which were usually compulsory face to face; some would be business lunches, others workshops. Tuesdays were her worst days. It was not the first day of the week; it was far from the end of the week. It was not even the middle of the week. It was the second day and even though she ought to tolerate it if only because two was an even number, she just did not like the day. She walked through the door only slightly nervous but was taken aback. Akash stood before her looking angrier than thunder. If she had come through the kitchen door, she would have noticed his car and would have cowered and run away – or at least she would have been prepared. He looked like he had steam coming out of his ears. The steam must have done something funny to his hair because it looked almost frizzy, yet Akash's hair usually was dead straight. He also smelt like he had been running back and forth between a farm and a brewery.

'Where the fuck have you been?' he spat furiously. The first thing Leila noticed was the thousand pieces of the broken brandy bottle on the floor. Confused, she asked, 'What happened here?' pointing. She glanced at the empty bottle of wine, the dead flowers and melted chocolate as well but ignored those, although she took a deep breath recognising that this moment was a potentially difficult one.

'Kash?' she called out again in a concerned whisper when she got no response.

'I said where the fuck have you been?' he screamed again, this time, slowly. He was still scratching his head intermittently.

'That's none of your business, Kash. I don't have the right to question your whereabouts, so what gives you the right to question mine?' she spat right back at him. She was at a loss as to what to think or do. She was actually intimidated by him at that moment. She covered it up quite impressively though. She glared at him. She hated him so much, and yet somewhere deep down, she still loved him. How did their relationship become this?

'I just came to get as much of my stuff as possible!' She sighed deeply and shook her head. She waved her hands in front of him surrendering.

'I don't understand what you are trying to do to us,' he screamed at the top of his voice. Leila shook her head, fighting back her tears of hurt and frustration.

'Can you not see that I am trying?' he asked.

'Was this man blind?' she wondered. Sometimes it was better to ignore him, but she just couldn't help herself at the moment. She was the victim in this case and here he was attacking her and accusing her of causing him pain. How confused he must be.

'You are not going anywhere,' he said looking vicious through squinted eyes. Her husband had a tempestuous temper, which surfaced only when he reached the peak of anger. She had never seen him in this state though, she admitted to herself. He looked rough and unkempt. Curiously, there was a packet of cigarettes on the table and a bottle of brandy. As far as Leila knew, Akash hated the smell of cigarettes and never indulged in excessive drinking. He only did the odd pint or two socially. He stank of alcohol and tobacco and he clearly had not shaved in days. She felt that a tiny bit of her feared for what he might do to her or indeed himself, but she would not give him the satisfaction of sniffing fear, not today or ever. She boldly walked to their room, head held high, and packed as much as possible as quickly as she could. She lifted her pillow and her wedding ring was still there. She picked it up for a moment and then on second thoughts put it back underneath the pillow, ignoring the ache in her heart. She looked around the room mentally saying her goodbyes as she made her way to the door. Akash stood in the kitchen waiting for her, obstructing her exit.

'I said you are not going anywhere, Leila… Didn't you hear me?' he bellowed.

'Kash, I don't want to do this… I… I…I don't want an argument, and... I don't want to be with you anymore. Please step away from the door. Let me go.' Her head was lowered, avoiding his eyes. She didn't want to read his eyes. She didn't know what she would see in them. She was petrified of what she foresaw would happen in the next few minutes. Leila sensed his animal rage!

'You can't leave me,' he screamed. One of us will have to die for that to happen. Leila, you promised for better, for worse – remember? Till death do us part? Or didn't that mean anything to you at the time?' He rushed forward and violently snatched the suitcase from her hand.

'Kash, let's be civil. Our marriage is over. I cannot do this anymore. It hurts too much,' she explained almost in a desperate whisper.

'I don't want to hear it, Leila; I can't let you go. I won't let you go,' he replied.

'Please Kash, let me go,' she screamed, trying to reach her suitcase. He threw the suitcase against the wall with such animal strength that made Leila jump. She rushed to the suitcase, hands on knees and began to retrieve the contents frantically. He pushed her; she pushed him. He pushed her harder; she fell to the floor. She was up in a flash. He approached her. She slapped him hard across the face.

'Behave yourself!' she screamed at him. She was petrified at that point and her premonition of the next couple of minutes was not looking good at all. He stared at her in disbelief for about ten seconds and then he attacked like a bull with a red cloth before its eyes. He missed a couple of times obviously due to alcohol intoxication, but when he did finally get hold of her, the southpaw raised his left hand and gave his wife a slap across her left cheek, a punch in the eye and a kick in the stomach. She fought back as hard as she could, but she was obviously no match for his strength. She fell to the floor and what was worse was she fell onto the broken brandy bottle. She was in shock, but for the fear of what she sensed he was about to do, she jerked herself up in a flash supporting her bleeding body with her bleeding palms. She made her way to the door. He pulled her back by her hair.

'Kash, you are hurting me,' she screamed.

'You bitch, you are hurting me too…' he barked, greeting her with yet another slap across the face. Even as she fell to the floor for a second time, he didn't feel enough remorse or self-control to let her be.

'Kash, the glass… the glass, Kash,' she reminded him frantically. He ignored her. He launched forward, and began to rip at her clothes. She aimed for his groin, but only managed to kick him in the stomach and scratch hard at his face. Her nails drew a long line across from his cheek, down to his neck. For a second, he stopped and put his hand over his cheek. He stared at the blood on his trembling left hand, but still in a flicker, he managed to unzip his trousers. There was nothing she could do. She cried. He pinned her hands over her head and kicked her legs apart.

'Don't make me hurt you even more,' he barked at her as he forced her legs apart. Leila resisted tossing left and right hysterically. She re-crossed her legs each time he pulled them apart.

'Do you want me to break your legs?' he asked her in a cold whisper.

'No, Kash, I don't want you to break my legs,' she said over and over, shaking her head, pleading for his eyes to meet hers. He couldn't do this to her, could he?

'Just wait, Leila, you should want this; you do! You know you do!' he sounded like he was trying to convince himself more than Leila.

'Mein tuatara pati hoon, yeh mera haq hai aur yeh tumhara farz hai – I am your husband. This is my right. This is your duty!'

'Kash, no…Kash please, no…!' she screamed. Then added: *'Kr̥payā mērī rakṣā karō- please protect me,'* in a desperate whisper. It fell on Akash's deaf ears. Leila fought and cried but he was a very strong man and she, strong though she was on the inside was rather frail physically especially when matched against Akash – a fit man! In a flash, he was in! Thoughtlessly, he brutally thrust without her consent for ten endless minutes.

'You used to enjoy this once,' he said over and over again, panting.

'Pleeeeease Kaaaassssssssshhhhhhh!' she cried.

'Shut up, bitch! You know you want more. You love this; don't pretend you don't. I will die before I see the day you leave me.' Akash carried on and on, harder and harder, more brutal as the minutes went by. As he did so, he pulled at her hair for support occasionally letting go to toss her hand out of the way or pull her leg further apart.

Leila screamed, Leila fought, Leila begged. Leila was in shock so for the last few minutes she lay there motionless and numb looking in her husband's eyes, imploring his heart to have mercy. For a second, he did look at her. In his eyes, in that flash, she saw a mixture of pain and resentment and even the hint of a teardrop or two building up, but he got over that quickly enough and just as hastily kept on at his business.

'Nothing to say?' he asked.

She was silent.

'Oh, you like it now?'

Leila shook her head. That must have angered him because he took his penis out and inserted it in her mouth. He held her jaw between his thumb and his other fingers. Perhaps he feared she might bite! She did think about it, but it all happened too quickly and she was traumatised to freeze point. He shoved it in until she nearly choked, then he withdrew.

'I am Cash Kash! It's me! I'm still Kash. That's your lollipop baby, remember?!' he said spitefully. Leila spat! He went back down and promptly re-inserted himself. He quickened his angry violent plunges to achieve his height sooner than he would have done under more pleasant circumstances. As he climaxed, he let out a scream of perhaps frustration, perhaps anger, perhaps incomprehension of his actions. His helpless sounding cry was incessant, yet his eyes reflected this dark coldness still.

'You are my wife. It is my right…' he cried out, panting heavily and when he got up, he tugged at his hair as he spat on her half-conscious body.

'Look what you made me do, Leila – how could you turn me into this? Look what you made me do…' he whispered still pulling at his hair but glaring at her in shock. He stood for a few seconds still breathing heavily and watching her writhe on the floor. He paced the kitchen looking confused. He shook his head. He burst into tears and as though possessed, he approached her on the floor.

'No. No, Kash, leave me alone,' she said weakly.

'I just want to hold you,' he said weeping.

'No, please Kash, leave me alone!'

And that triggered him off!

'I will fuck you if I want!' he said, but this time quietly. He undid his zip again and went in. Leila had no strength to fight. She just lay there.

There had never been any previous instance of domestic violence. She felt physically and mentally weak. Akash looked down at her. She was surprised at just how unkempt he looked. He could pass for a rough sleeper in the streets. There was the scratch all the way down his cheek, but when Leila stole a glance at him, she also sensed the same long scratch existed in his heart. How would he turn this one around? There was no going back now. He had made sure of that. As Leila stole this glance at Akash she felt like she had let him down. This man needed help – her help – but she had not noticed he was ill. Still, rape? He had obviously been dissatisfied with the marriage – but rape? She was furious at him, but also felt sorry for him. Rape? It was not the coldness in his eyes that spoke to Leila; it was the emotion behind the coldness in his eyes. Insane as it was, Leila's emotions were mixed up. She, the victim, felt sorry for him, the attacker – her husband. The wildest fit of typical Akash-type lalochezia, Leila could have tolerated, but rape? Physical abuse? Leila felt liberated. She remembered the biblical words… '*These three things abound, love, faith and hope; but the greatest of these is love…*' and because of the strength of what these words represented to Leila, how she lived to exemplify them as one of the most powerful emotions in the scriptures, plus the love she once felt for him,

Leila chose to archive this moment. No police. Leila lay bruised and battered, but breathed a heavy sigh of relief. For some reason, all she could see in her mind's eye was the day Akash sat with her in the park and sang George Benson's *'Nothing's gonna change my love for you'* to her. It was an indiscriminate flashback, totally inappropriate considering the present circumstance, but that is what her mind chose to play.

'This is what closure really feels like. It's over,' she whispered as she shut her eyes.

Fifteen minutes later, she had just about managed to reach the phone and dial Olga's number.

'I can't speak...' she mumbled. 'Please come... Please... now... Please...' and she left the receiver hanging off the hook, not intentionally, but because she couldn't reach to replace it. She was in agony.

'Leila?' the voice on the other end said a few times before hanging up with a final, 'Oh my God! What the fuck has happened at the Yoganathan's?'

Although she thought she heard her husband's voice in a loud echo outside, the scene Leila missed happened the moment Akash walked out of the house and into his car. His hands were shaking, his body felt alien to him.

'What kind of animal am I?' His shriek of disbelief and disgust echoed through the empty night. In his car, hands over his face, he shivered, screaming and weeping bitterly. He asked the God that Leila served to take him out of this stranger's body. He wanted to go back in on bended knees and comfort her until all her hurt went away. His hands trembled. He had blood in his palms. He had glass on his shirt and on his shoulder. Heck, he picked a piece off his cheek. He felt a stinging sensation and touched his cheek. The blood was everywhere on his face. Leila had dug her nails so deep into his skin, it felt like he had had a brush with a bladed object. That was nothing compared to what he had done to her, he was quick to remind himself.

Perhaps he had gone through an insane phase of confusion; he knew he had not been mentally ready for the commitment of marriage. There were times he felt like a bird in a cage. But now, he was OK. He was ready to start afresh. He was ready to bare all. He wanted her to know about the shrink, about the gambling, the potential bankruptcy, his fears, everything. Well, now it was too late.

'I don't deserve another chance,' he muttered. The part of him that wanted to run back into the house got out of the car and stood staring at his once happy home altogether dumbfounded. He could not bring himself to do it. He drove off, but parked close by, well hidden in the dark night. He didn't leave until he saw Olga's car pull up in his driveway. Satisfied that she would be okay, he got into his car. When he heard Olga scream (probably at the sight of Leila), a terribly mortified Akash shivered thoroughly; his heart felt like it had been physically ripped out! He drove off with a screech into the cursed night with one thing only on his mind… suicide!

'What more could there be to live for? What the fuck is left? Look what I did! Take your fucking British Citizenship, Leila. I choose you. I love you. You have killed me. *Aaj mein mar gaya hoon kyun k tum mujh say pyaar nahi karti*. Today I have died because you no longer love me!'

'Where are you, Leila? What happened?' Olga asked hurriedly bursting into the house in search of her friend. Her voice had sounded terribly distressed on the phone and Olga had prayed all the way there. She was suddenly stopped in her tracks when she got into the kitchen.

'Leila?' she shrieked in horror when she saw her friend. She ran to the window for a second as she heard a loud screech outside, then back to Leila's side. Leila had bruises on her face, scratches all over her body and her clothes were torn…no, her clothes were in shreds with bloodstains on the floor and all over her body. The worst ones were on the palms of her hands because they looked like they had been pierced with glass.

'Hang on a minute, there…there…is fucking glass all over the fucking floor,' Olga screamed at the top of her voice outraged.

'What happened?' Olga hysterically clung to her friend and cried.

'Stop it, Olga. You are frightening me. Take me away from here. Closure.' Leila begged with all the energy she had.

'Closure? My goodness, you are so weird. I need to call you an ambulance…' Olga said trembling.

Leila shook her head.

'Burglars? The police will need fingerprints,' she said.

Leila sobbed weakly.

'Did...did Kash do this, Leila? Did he?' Olga asked hoping Leila would tell her a wild tale about how burglars or someone... anyone, but Akash had just attacked her. Leila shook her head denying the obvious, or maybe not so obvious.

'No... no.... no police, no ambulance, Olga, let's go'. Leila begged. That was all the confirmation Olga needed as she cursed Akash aloud.

'That fucking bastard!' she screamed as she ran into Leila's bathroom, manically. She found a towel, wet it and gently wiped her friend's injured face, seeing the pain etched there.

'I have to...I have to, babe...' she whispered softly to her holding her head in her lap.

'OK... but it hurts,' Leila whispered back. Olga stared in her friend's face for a few seconds and it took all the strength in her not to burst into tears then. She could see that Leila had taken a beating. As she took stray pieces of glass out of her friend's hair, she examined her from head to toe. She did not look at her thighs. She just wiped the bruises, weeping silently on the inside. With great difficulty, she managed to get Leila settled into the back seat of her car, lying down; this time, she came face to face with what she feared most. When Leila's eyes followed Olga's gaze down to her bruised thighs, instinctively, protectively, she shielded the reality of her experience from the world with her blanket. The two exchanged wounded glances, but nothing was said.

Safely at Olga's, Leila lay on the couch and fell asleep.

Across town, a restless Kaobi paced from one end of his office to the other. For the last hour, he had been distracted. Somewhere, something was wrong; he could feel it. The shiver down his spine was incessant. He jumped at every phone ring, at every knock on every door, even when he heard his Personal Assistant sneeze he ran out to ask the bewildered lady if she was alright.

'Do you want a drink?' she had asked him then. He shook his head.

'You look awfully pale and you are making me nervous pacing about like that,' she had said worriedly.

He apologised for his weird behaviour and went back into the office. The sound of silence and inactivity was deafening him slowly. He sat still and waited!

'What should I do now?' Olga asked, tears finally streaming down her face as she stared at her friend in total disbelief. Leila scribbled a number on a piece of paper that lay on the untidy floor.

'Call him,' she whispered. It was Kaobi's mobile phone number.

Olga was nauseated by the difficulty Leila had in holding the pen. Her palms were badly injured; but she got on with it.

Half a ring later, a desperately nervous Kaobi answered.

'Kaobi? It's Olga'

'Olga hi…'

'Come now,' she said blubbering over her house address, which she was reciting down the phone to him in half words.

'Bayswater?' he asked, grabbing his car keys as he literally flew out of his chair, still scribbling.

'Bayswater. Yes,' she responded.

'I'll be there as soon as I can.'

'Don't you want to know why?' Olga questioned.

'It's Leila…' he said and then hesitated for a bit, blinked rapidly a couple of times to clear his head; he cleared his throat and added a bit more calmly, 'It's Leila, isn't it?'

'Yes… yes it is,' Olga replied hurriedly. He put the phone down without another word.

A good few ignored traffic lights and swearing pedestrians later, Kaobi arrived at Olga's home. He could not possibly have been any quicker.

'What, did you fly here, Kaobi?' Olga asked concerned.

'I was...er… sort of in…in…in the area already,' he lied, hastily making his way across the room to where Leila lay helplessly.

'Well, mentally, I was,' he added.

'What?' Olga looked up, puzzled. Kaobi shook his head dismissively.

'Should I give her a bath?' Olga asked.

'Let me take a look at her first,' he replied reaching over to Leila and kissing her gently right in the middle of her forehead.

'Oh, sweetheart,' he muttered empathetically just under his breath.

'Is that glass in her hair?' he asked Olga, obviously alarmed at the level of violence involved.

Olga nodded. 'I'm afraid so, Kaobi,' she confirmed. Kaobi shut his eyes for a couple of seconds, obviously hurt by it all.

'Leila, I think you need to go to the hospital,' Kaobi whispered.

'I mean it, KK, I mean it!' She shook her head in blatant stubborn refusal. 'You are here. Take care of me. I will be fine. Olga will help you,' she managed to whisper back. Just one look at her ripped clothes and the give-away bruises on her thighs and he knew what had happened.

'Did he...' Olga attempted to ask Kaobi, referring to the bruises on Leila's thighs, but her words trailed off as Kaobi kissed his teeth repeatedly in anxiety and anger. He looked at Olga for a few seconds but said nothing.

He asked Leila, 'Sweetheart did he...?' but he couldn't even bring himself to complete the question either. He just stared at Leila. Leila shook her head, still lying, too ashamed to reveal all. It was something she told herself no one was ever to know. Be it ignorance, shame, or fear, she would never tell a soul what had happened. It just seemed irrelevant. She was free of the man and that was all that mattered. Still, it was not rocket science. Olga had figured it out already and was cringing at the thought, and Leila must have forgotten then that Kaobi who was examining her was a cardiologist; a cardiologist was a doctor nevertheless. The signs glared at him bare faced, winding him up so badly because he felt helpless about being unable to protect her. Kaobi's eyes burnt, blood shot red. It was a similar shade of red to that of Akash's earlier that night. Nevertheless, Kaobi remained calm, if only for Leila's sake. In his mind, he cursed Akash Yoganathan. How could anyone do this to a woman?

'Wherever you are, I hope you get what you deserve for this. I hope your pain is triple this,' he muttered resentfully under his breath. Leila probably had her fair share of blame in the marriage breakdown, but nothing she could possibly have done was any justification for what he had done to her.

'How will you live with yourself, you idiot? What kind of comeback will be enough?' he pondered. 'Dear Lord, be it not for me to judge, but

I am furious!' he added. 'I hope you die!' he thought, and was instantly alarmed by his anger. 'I did not mean that. I am sorry. It is not for me to judge. I am not without sin myself, but my goodness gracious!' he concluded shaking his head as he tended to Leila. Kaobi was special. His words were powerful, his instincts, foresights were spot on, his dreams were usually premonitions. Even Leila had figured this out already and it was often the subject of many a debate in her head. Perhaps regardless of his utterances that night, the following event may have come to pass. Who knows? Only fate and destiny can decide that in entirety.

And so it was on a deserted road in the middle of nowhere in particular that a small crowd had gathered around someone. An ambulance distress signal could be heard screaming in the distance, heralding other road users to make way. There was someone on the ground bleeding profusely. The source of blood was not identifiable. He looked like he had been soaked in a lake of blood! The ambulance had hardly halted when the paramedics leapt out and ran across to the body imploring the crowd to disperse or at least make some room.

'He just jumped into the road,' a confused man persistently explained, tripping over his tongue and shivering as he did so. Everyone, including the police officer he was talking to, ignored him and concentrated instead on the motionless body on the ground. There was a life to save!

'Are you left handed or right handed, sir?' they asked following their routine checks.

He could hardly move and definitely couldn't speak so he wriggled the forefinger of his left hand.

'Can you feel this?' they asked poking him here and there and doing the things paramedics were trained to do.

There were no answers from the injured man so in about 20 minutes, they checked his pulse and bandaged his wounds. Carefully they lifted him on to the stretcher. They got him into the ambulance safely.

'Drive, drive, drive, go!' one of the paramedics screamed across to the driver. 'If we don't get him to hospital in the next few minutes, we might lose him. His blood pressure is dropping and I am not getting a clear sinus rhythm.' He was critical and unstable, still breathing unaided, but not for much longer they reckoned. He was very weak with multiple wounds, which were exacerbated by the collision with the car. When asked by the duty nurse what they thought had happened, the paramedics' verdict upon their examination was possibly a poor attempt at suicide, with wounds further goaded by an accident involving a 4x4. He was whisked straight into theatre, but not before his wallet was retrieved from the back pocket of his trousers.

'Akash Yoganathan.' The doctor read his name from the fading national insurance card.

'Someone please give... his wife? Yup. Probably his wife. He also has her driver's licence for some reason. Someone find her number and give her a call. Match the number on his phone,' the doctor added, handing over Leila's ID card, driver's licence and Akash's phone over to a nurse. The nurse took the card and dashed across the hallway to a phone. She did not bother to cross check with his phone. She had a feeling the card was all she needed. She picked up the receiver and stood for a few seconds squinting, trying to make out the phone numbers because the numbers were faint. She had to do a little bit of *eenie meenie miney mo* with the digits, but she got there in the end. The first number was the landline. Obviously, no one was home. The nurse was relieved when she rang the mobile phone and a voice answered and confirmed that it was Leila Yoganathan's phone.

'What a week you've had, sweetheart...' Kaobi said as he stroked her hair. In her mind, she thought the same thing. For now, on this cursed blessed day, Leila walked away from her old life and in her heart, consciously embraced the new one before her. Her mobile phone rang interrupting her thoughts and bringing her back to reality. As she couldn't answer it, Olga did. Olga had only picked it up from the house by chance when she was snatching a few of Leila's clothes to take along with her. As soon as it rang, Kaobi felt that familiar cold shiver down his spine. Olga answered it hoping it was Akash so she would tell him what a bastard she thought he was and how she would make sure Leila went to the police and they locked him up for a long time, until he had many grey hairs. But it wasn't!

'Yes, this is Leila Yoganathan's phone. Hospital? What? When?' Olga shook her head in disbelief. How much more dramatic could the day possibly get?

Leila listened with her eyes shut.

'They say he is dying, Kaobi,' Olga whispered.

Kaobi said nothing.

'I mean, he is a bastard for doing this, but is it not better that he rots in jail than die? Would that not be too easy?' she asked.

Kaobi said nothing.

'I think I should go!' she stated.

Kaobi nodded.

'What if this is the last we hear from him? Don't we need answers? He is an only child. His parents are in India!'

'What do you want me to say?' Kaobi asked.

'I want you to tell me whether you think I should go. I have to see him. Leila would want me to see him.'

Kaobi nodded.

'I know what you are thinking. I abandon my injured best friend to visit her husband in hospital who is also my friend, but who is responsible for beating the shit out of my best friend and maybe worse un-confessed atrocities even, but who by some bizarre stroke of ill fate (or fucking karma, or whatever) is injured and in hospital in – according to the nurse – a critical, unstable condition.' Olga sighed. Even the thought of it all sounded like some sort of TV Drama series or something out of a Danielle Steele novel and even Danielle Steele, the reputable love drama queen was never quite that dramatic.

Kaobi nodded his reassurance.

'He is human, Olga and he ha…ha…has problems, big problems. Someone should sort him out really. Everyone deserves that much.'

'His parents are in India and he is an only child,' Olga repeated, justifying her reasons for wanting to go.

'I think Leila might want you to go,' he said.

'Might?'

'Olga!' he exclaimed. 'Just go!' he urged and when she still stood there, he pushed her gently and added once again, 'Go!' He pushed her towards the door. Olga went.

In Leila's half consciousness, she thanked God when she heard Olga's car engine kick off. Kaobi was right. Everyone needed someone. Akash was Olga's best friend's husband, but he was also her very good friend from even before he had met Leila. He was a human being with frailties (or in his case a mental illness as Kaobi had rightfully pointed out), who needed attention quite quickly. Despite her anger, Leila did not want to see him dead. She wanted him mended. Besides, who needed police? She had thrown his damned diamond ring into the Thames, metaphorically speaking. She understood that it would be punishment for Akash. Even if he did not know now, he would find out. As it happens, he did know.

Olga spoke to the doctors who informed her that Akash had stabbed himself, but the multiple wounds were not deep enough and fortunately had not hit any arteries or major veins, so he had proceeded to try and get himself knocked down by a car. Olga was horrified.

'Can I see him?' she asked the doctor.

'Yeah, sure you can. He will be fine. He was very lucky, not too much damage was done internally and he was treated in time as well. We nipped any potential damage in the bud.'

'So he is alright then?' Olga shocked herself because a part of her obviously was disappointed that he was OK. This was a thought that horrified her. She shook her head. She could do with a drink.

'Before you go in…' The doctor stopped Olga in her tracks and pulled her to the side, whispering suspiciously. 'There is a scratch on his face, it's quite deep, and we suspect that a fight might have triggered all this off, but when we asked him, he would not confirm,' the doctor finished.

'If there is another party involved and there was some sort of violence, then it is our duty to report this to the police,' she added.

Olga nodded, but said nothing.

'See what you can find out,' she urged.

Olga went in and stared at him. He was sitting up. He had a prominent fingernail scratch right down his cheek, all the way down to his neck. Olga recognised this as probably Leila's. 'Wow! She must have developed tigress claws. She must have been fighting desperately.' Olga sighed and looked to the heavens above for strength.

'How is she?' Akash asked.

'Stupid question! How do you think, Akash?' she asked annoyed.

'How have you managed to reduce yourself to this? Extreme measures to get attention, you fucking spoilt brat. What the hell is wrong with you? What now?' she asked in disgust, unable to restrain the tears that followed. He looked so frail; she had conflicting impulses ranging from extreme anger to deep sympathy. His mental imbalance was apparent.

'That woman lived to love you, Kash – how could you?' she asked perplexed by the whole situation.

'Olga, I am so sorry. Just let her know that I love her. If I could turn back the hands of time, I would and I wouldn't dare. Things would be very different. Things got out of hand. I don't know what I have done! And I did not die. How sad. I can never look her in the eye ever again!'

'Damn right! You cannot go near her or I will call the police myself! You cheated on her, Kash – several times – and to be honest, that was not even the main problem. Both of you could have worked through that, but when it comes to emotional inconsideration, your list of atrocities is several A4 sheets-joined-together long! You made her go, because hand on heart, you cannot say that Mulatto did not try! You have treated her like dirt in the last few months and I warned you so many times, Kash. I warned you. I warned you that she would walk away!' she reminded him angrily. 'She was not blameless, I know that, Kash but jeez, look what you went and did...' her voice tailed off for a few seconds, but she found the calmness to continue.

'You had no right, Kash. All she ever did was love you. She had her own weaknesses, but how dare you?'

'Olga, she is my life. I know that now. I was stupid. I was afraid to admit that the rest of my life had begun. I love her. I realise this now,' he explained as he wept bitterly, and clutched the stab wound which obviously hurt. He lamented: 'What have I done?' repeatedly half under his breath.

'Tell her I am sorry. I cannot bear to live any longer.'

'Suicide? Really? How pathetic. Next time you decide to kill yourself, please give me a call. I will be right there with a big bag of salted popcorn to watch, you coward!' She sighed deeply.

'Has she reported it yet? Will she?' he asked.

'Are you scared?' Olga asked and then continued when she got no response '… because if you are, I must point out that this will be nothing you don't deserve. You will go to prison, definitely!' she said sternly.

'I am ready to take full responsibility for my actions,' he said in a muffled whisper.

'The scratch on your face?' Olga asked.

'Leila,' he whispered, nodding.

He said nothing more, but wept uncontrollably until the nurses asked her to leave.

'He needs to sleep.'

'He needs to be sectioned!' Olga muttered under her breath.

'I'm sorry, what was that?' one of the nurses asked. Olga felt it was not her place to say anything. She shook her head.

'Did you say he needs to be sectioned?' the nurse asked. 'Why would you say that?'

'Sweetheart, you must have slipped a couple of pills in your coffee. I said I need a cigarette.'

'Cigarette, coffee…' the nurse compared holding out both hands, raising one after another, and then raised an eyebrow at Olga. 'Damn, these guys are curious,' Olga thought. She rolled her eyes.

Olga watched him for a few minutes. She stared down at a normally verbose Akash Yoganathan, reduced to this emotional wreck. His normal impressive eloquence condensed to strange mutters of incoherent gadzookery and in many instances that night, downright gibberish. She only heard the bits that concerned Leila. She also heard him refer to his nickname, 'Cash Kash!' followed by some rant in Hindi – *Mani jeetai jagjeet – He who conquers the mind, conquers the world.* She tried, but she could not make out the rest of his words. On her way out, the doctor pulled her over.

'And the scratch on his face?' she enquired beckoning Olga to a quiet spot in the corner. Olga hesitated for a second; the thought of revealing all crossed her mind. She did think it was justified. But she then decided that she was in no position to play judge. She would not decide what was 'in the best interest of Leila or Akash'. Leila should have reported the battery straight away but as she did not, Olga decided to respect her wishes. She had to remind herself that her decision to withhold this information was nothing to do with the pity she felt for Akash. She decided that in this instance, her loyalty was to Leila and Leila did not want to report it. She looked at the doctor and shook her head.

'Nope. Nothing!'

'Thank you anyway,' the doctor said, obviously disappointed. Olga nodded and left.

Upon arrival, Leila was fast asleep with Kaobi stroking her hair. It was now glass-free. She noticed Leila had been washed, but said nothing. One day, Leila would reveal all, until then, it was irrelevant. She smiled sadly.

'How did it go?' he asked. Olga shook her head and sighed. 'Well, he ain't dying!' she said, and paused for a second, choosing her words carefully. She was still battling with her feelings because there was disappointment in her tone.

'But?' because Kaobi could sense the hesitation.

'He is in a very bad way, Kaobi.' Olga continued. 'I think he needs professional help.'

'I don't think we should tell Leila just yet. I don't know that she has enough space in her heart to deal with this as well,' Olga said.

'You think not? You underes…es…estimate the magnitude of her… her…her heart,' Kaobi said. He understood that it probably was right to wait, but not to withhold this information. They did not ponder too long.

'Pray for him,' Leila whispered and closed her eyes. She had heard everything. Olga and Kaobi glanced at each other. Olga reached over, kissed Leila's forehead, and then kissed underneath her left eye to distract the tear that was crookedly making its way down her beautiful bruised cheek. Kaobi just stared. He had tears in his eyes. He forgot his anger for Akash. All that mattered was Leila. At that moment (if it were possible), Kaobi fell even more deeply in love with her (…or something).

It was a simple moment with simple words, simple thoughts, yet the most complicated, most relentlessly emotional moment.

Kaobi began to pray out loud. He reached his hand over to Olga who had one hand on Leila's head, stroking gently. She was yet to experience anything of the sort, but thought it best to go with the flow. Kaobi prayed for Akash, for Leila, for Olga and himself, their families; they committed the moment to God and accepted that He knew best. It would all make sense in the end, they believed. Kaobi found religion in Olga that night. Leila listened carefully and was amazed. Olga had been raised Christian, but it was the first time she had heard her acknowledge it in any form. They chorused their 'amen', and the rowdy multiple voices indicated that they were not alone. They opened their eyes and looked up. Leila's two sisters had walked in.

'Sorry Olga, you left the door open.'

'How long have you been standing there?' Olga asked.

'Long enough,' they said, making their way across the room.

At the sight of their sister, they both had tears trickling down from their eyes.

'Yesterday's sorrows, today's incomprehension, tomorrow's blessing,' Kaobi assured them, heartbroken that they had to see her in this state. They nodded in agreement.

'And I promise you that, Leila,' Kaobi said softly, the words replaying in the minds of everyone present as they all looked around at each other thoughtfully. Olga and Kaobi gave them some privacy and took a break to convalesce from their nursing duties. The sisters hugged and then shared light-hearted stories about what they hoped the future would bring their way. Olga and Kaobi emerged 20 minutes later with drinks for everyone. Leila was at peace with herself. Olga and Kaobi were fussing over her. Leila's sisters had driven three unbearable hours due to road works to be with her that night. Olga had asked them to turn around and go home, but they had insisted that there was no mountain high enough to keep them away. That night she experienced the inculcation of love. A smile whispered on her lips. Though it was brief, it was a demonstration of happiness hampered by the soreness of her bruises – physical and emotional. Still it was obviously soul-deep. The assembled group sat drinking brandy, rosé, coffee or water and chatting about the latest shenanigans with the National Lottery and the British reaction to it, but at that precise moment when she smiled, they all sensed a peaceful presence, possibly supernatural. They shared an unplanned moment of silence as the room (almost literally) lit up with Leila's smile. 'Bruises don't last forever,' Leila thought to herself. A new era would begin then! Chapter closed…for now!

'The moment a thousand voices unite in praise, then
comes silence; then in that silence God is born'
- Ngozi Opara

Chapter Eighteen

Two Red Lines

She stood by the post box, letter in hand, looking quite like a statue. Her eccentric, yet softly beautiful smile lingered only for a moment. Lost in a trance, her mind wandered, traversing backwards down memory lane. The past was recaptured in detail as moment-by-moment flashbacks caused her eyes to sparkle, widen and/or squint erratically. She remembered the night in the hotel room.

They had had their moments, but that night was unusual. The intensity of the two hours they had spent tangled in an untidy heap, looking like something out of the game Twister always left her with a longing she felt right in the pit of her stomach. The one thing she learnt that night was this: sex does not mean love. It was possible to have the most amazing, intense sex without the accompanying emotions that love brings. On the other hand, maybe it was intense for her, but not for him? This was a confusing thought because the look in his eyes bore into her soul. Whenever they looked at each other, she felt their souls communicate; besides eyes don't lie, right?

Or maybe it was the fact that the news she brought him threw a spanner in the works. 'That's not possible. Two red lines? Positive?' he asked. She nodded like he could see her. 'What about my family?' he asked. 'What about our baby?' she asked in return. His response – 'What do you mean our?'

She put the phone down and sobbed. A million teardrops, one broken heart, a severely dented ego, and an open, yet un-drunk bottle of brandy later, she did a diary entry. This diary entry would be the letter she would stand by the post box holding in frantically trembling hands.

'A friend of mine always says to me that soul mates do not exist. She says that all that fairy tale rubbish is fiction and belongs in Disney cartoons. I always say to her that once two souls connect, nothing can stop them from being together; that there are shades of grey, which only the two people in love can understand. Today, I find it is black and white. I find that you are either in or out and it's as simple as that. I find that "it's complicated" is either just an excuse to be a coward or your way of telling me that you just do not love me. I realise that when you love me in that bed, you are able to go home and love her, probably in the exact same way. I am hurting because every time you look me in the eyes, I am deceived into believing that you are the victim, because you are not able to tell the world about your love for me owing to your personal circumstances. Today I realise that I am the victim. I am the one who has put my life on hold in the hope that one day – one day you will do the right thing and realise that if we are together, nothing else matters. I now know that no matter how complicated the situation is, it is actually always quite easy. Either you love me, or you do not. So today, I will forget what your eyes say to me. I will forget what happens to my body when you pull me around my waist and into your arms. I will forget how short of breath I get when I suspect that you are going to kiss me. I will, in fact, forget the way you hold me after we have united our bodies. I am sitting here remembering our last night together. I believe it was in the course of the third go that night – when you told me you loved me – that was when our baby was conceived. I also realise that this was a fairy tale, which could only have existed in that moment. I will now stop replaying every second of those few seconds when you said those words to me – words I had ached to hear. Today I walk away from you and I take our unborn child with me. This is my closure. Right here – me, these two red lines, and my non-existent shades of grey!'

That indeed was her closure. She did post that letter.

Three days later, she awoke from the misery that had become her life. It seems unborn baby had decided to give her a break and she had been vomit free for six hours. This was worthy of celebration. She decided she would head out and pick up soft mints, a kit-kat chunky and some vitamins. She even sang along to the radio after she realised that she could brush her teeth without the familiar nausea. Therefore, she sashayed across the room to the door, until she froze in her tracks. The postman had been and there was a letter waiting. It was his handwriting. She sank onto her bed as her clumsy fingers repeatedly tugged at the envelope. On her fourth attempt, she opened it. It read:

'Everything my eyes said was true. Every fairy tale we created was reality. When your heart sensed a response, it did not imagine it. It was the fifth time round that night – the time you wept as you gently called out my name – that was when we conceived this baby. All I wish is that circumstances were different. There are shades of grey, babe. In our case – indecipherable shades of grey because if you think you are confused, you need to take a step back and walk in my shoes. Life is hell without you, but life with you does seem like a fairy tale. I do not understand. So now you have walked away, all I have is memories of your two red lines, this indecipherable shade of grey and a one coloured rainbow because as of now, I stare out my window reminiscing about the other night and realise that without you, my life has no colour!'

Her traitor heart rejoiced for a few minutes until she put her logical hat back on. What was he saying? He said nothing. Nothing! There was nothing indecipherable about the shade of grey. In fact, the situation had never been any clearer. She shook her head and ripped the letter into pieces.

The end? (Is it ever?)

P.S.

This is one of the many scenarios we encounter in life when we spot those two red lines. There are simple Cinderella stories as well – boy meets girl, they fall in love and get married and have babies! It is not always that simple though. Whatever your story is, let's hope finding the two red lines brings you joy.

Cheers!

Leila x

Chapter Twenty

It was a little under six and a half months later, Valentines Day of 1996. She wondered it if it was a leap year for a second.

'Nope. That's next year,' she realised. She had only just finished a blog-type back-and-forth conversation with Toks and Joy on email. Leila was at her desk at work holding a conference call with both of them. It was actually partly business for a change. Joy was managing and consulting on a new marketing strategy that Leila had put together. In terms of assets and investments, she was growing every day.

'How is your new house then?' Toks asked.

'It's taking shape. I need to go out and buy some curtains on Wednesday.'

'I thought you were done decorating.' she exclaimed.

'I don't like the ones I bought for the spare room.'

'I can't believe that it's over between you and Kash.'

'Don't call him that,' she said dismissively and was almost shocked at her response. She had a 20 second flashback about a couple of instances where Akash had begged her to call him Kash instead of Akash. When she called him Kash, it meant everything was OK. She did not mind when Olga referred to him as Kash, but it irritated her when anyone else did, including his mother. Why was she thinking about Akash?

'Leila? Are you there?'

Leila was reluctantly dragged back to reality.

'It is. I received a copy of the Decree Nisi from the Court today,' she said.

'I just can't believe it,' Joy persisted.

'It is over,' Leila simply replied. Sometimes she could do without the lengthy discussions and goodwill messages partly because she was still a bit taken aback by the dramatic turn her life had taken. She would never ever have guessed that somewhere along her path in life she would be a divorcee. But then, she supposed no one ever went into marriage expecting to call it quits after four years. It was just one of those unknowns and she just wanted to get on with life. The last thing she needed was a constant reminder of how awfully wrong it had gone so far.

'Any way, I will see you Thursday, did you say?' Leila asked finalising the conversation.

'Are you trying to get rid of us?' Joy questioned.

'No… it's just you should see the pile on my desk. I haven't been feeling up to much these last two weeks, so I haven't done that much work at all and it's piling up.'

'Why? What's wrong?'

'I can't quite place my finger on it… it might be the weather. It's suddenly gone colder.'

'You need to look after yourself, Leila.'

'I will,' Leila said, trailing off because she suddenly felt a twinge of nausea and dizziness.

'Ugh… please don't fuss,' Leila half snapped, holding her head in agony. These days, her tolerance level was low. She despised sympathy or over-concern; she just wanted to get on with life by herself!

'We are only trying to be supportive, Leila,' Joy said rather angrily. 'You are so bad at taking advice,' she added.

'I don't need advice. I don't need reminders of how wrong it has gone. I don't need anyone fussing. I simply don't need a mother in every friend I have.'

'But…' Leila did not let either of them speak.

'I am sorry, girls; I just want to get on with it! I don't want to talk about it constantly. OK? My life is not a fucking soap opera.' Leila hoped they would take the initiative and let sleeping dogs lie.

'Don't swear, Leila, all I was trying to say is that what if...' Joy began.

'Joy, forget what ifs and maybes. I am sick of those words.' Leila truly snapped this time and she even slammed a file on the table. It was loud enough. They heard it through the phone.

'We'll leave you to it then,' Joy said abruptly, obviously hurt.

'I'll speak to you guys soon.'

'Will you?' Joy asked. Leila sighed.

'Yeah, I'll call you later both. Toks, it's going to be a good episode of EastEnders on tonight,' Leila said conclusively and with polite goodbyes said, she put the phone down hastily to take three deep breaths and a glass of water – this seemed to be her cure for just about any ailment. She was just on time as well. A second later and she would have been vomiting furiously. For months she had been feeling nauseous and dizzy at sporadic intervals during the day. She was also unable to wake up in the mornings and when she did, she felt like she was hung-over, except alcohol tasted weird as well. She told herself that it was her psyche adjusting to her new life, that her diet was not clean enough, that she needed to re-commit herself to kickboxing and pole dancing lessons and the pity party had to stop! She had grown a size bigger but that did not stop her ordering her favourite Chinese take out, which she would have delivered all the way from the City. This happened especially on nights when Kaobi did not come over. She felt fat and unattractive, but simply could not be bothered to do a damned thing about it! (She cried when her super skinny D & G Trousers – the one with the gloss – did not fit, but other than that, she replaced broccoli and sweet corn with duck and crispy seaweed convincing herself that it was protein and green leaves which were good for her muscles!

Following weeks of nagging from Kaobi, she had booked and cancelled several doctors' appointment, but was determined to make the one next Thursday. 'There! Its booked KK. Now can I have two croissants and boiled eggs?' she had asked rolling her eyes. The last time she felt this way, she actually had a stomach infection that was literally nipped in the bud so this time she was not taking any chances with her overly sensitive body. Leila had grown up realising that she was highly prone to infections and diseases.

Her thoughts drifted back to the conversation with her friends. All she wanted to do was forget it all and move on but their words haunted her, specifically Joy's two favourite mini phrases… 'What ifs and maybes'…

Tomorrow is too distant a dream
Could be rainbows or dust or rain
Who knows?
Moments of gold and gain or cold moments of pain
I stare at my lost expectations
In awe of unexpected realities
Perhaps my dreams are but shadows
Fear to dare and what ifs and maybes

If I?
Should I?
What if and Why?
Visions too vague for even a heteroclite mind's eye
So let it be for me to see one moment at any time
To appreciate, be content, hope to recognise a sign
Of fruition that is nigh

For basic foresight of mere mortals will only go thus far beyond
To learn from my past
Hope for my future but of today, be fond
Forget what ifs and maybes but accept the surprise of my legend
Be the best I can be
Today is a gift, the here and now, the present!

Leila smiled. She would make the most of today and let tomorrow worry about itself. It was also in the Bible, she reminded herself; Matthew 6:34 – '*So don't worry about tomorrow, for tomorrow will bring its own worries. Today's trouble is enough for today*'. Satisfied that even God was on her side and therefore content with her life as it was, she got on with work.

'Bianca!' Leila called out. 'Where is the Cross-Somerset part two file?'

'I'll get it in a minute... it's on the top shelf in the 'R' corner,' Bianca-Maria called out.

'Why is it there? It should be with the 'C' files, you know that Bianca.'

'Yeah but I put it according to the names for that section, as you said, Leila. It belongs to Mr Routt. Just give me a second, Leila and I will fish it out for you.'

'Did I say that? I want this category placed according to the projects. They are much easier to find that way.' Leila grumbled bitterly under her breath about dissatisfaction and inefficiency. She knew she was being unnecessarily irritable, but she could not help herself. Bianca-Maria was the epitome of efficiency if she was honest. However, at the moment, all Leila wanted was lunch and she had to get that file sorted before then – if not, it would break the chain of her already planned schedule.

'It's not her fault that I am a routine freak,' Leila mumbled to herself admitting that Bianca-Maria was doing an excellent job.

'I'll be two seconds,' Bianca-Maria called out once again to Leila.

But of course, Leila was impatient. She kissed her teeth, sighed and twiddled her thumbs for all of ten seconds, before she took it upon herself to reach for the file herself, whilst still mumbling untrue, silly, silly words under her breath about the best PA in the world. She could not reach so she climbed onto her swivelling, three-legged, unstable chair. The predictable fall from the swivelling, three-legged, unstable chair was quick and agonising. The second she hit the floor, Leila fell unconscious.

'I've never known anyone to faint quite so often, sweetheart.' She recognised the familiar voice instantly.

'KK, what happened?' she asked, annoyed because she already knew the answer. She remembered climbing onto the chair.

'Apparently, you f... f... fell off your chair. Bianca-Maria had you rushed h... here.'

'Am I badly hurt?' she asked.

'You'll live,' he replied sarcastically, smiling.

'The doctor will be here to see you in a minute,' the nurse informed her and politely left them to get on with it.

'Leila, you need to rest. You are probably really stressed out and tired.'

'I'm not!' she protested.

'Well, it ought to take more than a li...li...little fall to knock the Lei...Lei...Leila I know unconscious.' Leila nodded detachedly and rolled her eyes.

'You are not my father you know,' she reminded him. She loved him dearly, but fortunately (for lack of further complication in her twisted life) not quite romantically, or at least those feelings had suddenly turned dormant, or were frozen somewhere in the archives of her heart and Cupid had halted the archery. She cared deeply for him and vice versa, and they had become best friends in the true sense of the word. Even Olga was jealous.

'But you have Chris and a fabulous lion's mane for hair!' she had commented on the day Olga had complained bitterly about being overthrown.

'I'm not jealous. My hair is unmanageable. Chris is my husband. There is nothing exciting about that!' she had said. They had both giggled. Since that night of passion, Kaobi had implied no sexual innuendos nor had she. She could strip her soul before him without a second thought and they even spoke about potential lovers for Leila and shared a jealous-free joke or two every time a man showed any interest in her. Leila was appreciative of this. Still, she did not date! She claimed to be too busy for a love life! Hhhhmmm ☺

'Is there someone you... you...you would like me to call?' he asked

'Well KK, who do you suggest needs to know right now?' she asked sarcastically.

'Well...' he responded, smiling.

'Really, it's no big deal... I'll be home soon and I can tell whomever I wish about my great big fall.'

'Olga?' Kaobi asked.

'Olga will have a good laugh with Super C.' Leila could just see their faces. Leila smiled at the thought of how content she was with her life at that moment. Initially she had found it difficult to be alone. At her lowest moments, she would even ostracise Kaobi from her world, resentful of the fact that he had a partner, even though she did not quite want him for herself. She did not get those kinds of thoughts any more. Rather than wallow in self-pity recounting what she could have had, she concentrated on counting blessings. Topping the list, head and shoulders above most, was of course her ever-loyal Kaobi. His priority was his wife and twin boys but she never felt like she was second best in his life although that part of his life, he preferred to keep separate from Leila. There was never any contact with his wife and she called him strictly only on his mobile phone. She questioned him about this once and when she got some sort of waffle for a response, she never asked again. Sometimes she wanted to meet Ada, but as she knew it was more to do with curiosity than anything else. What exactly would she say? I shagged your husband? Whom would she be introduced as? She was just grateful for his presence in her life.

'Who the potatoes is Super C?' Kaobi asked distracting her drifting thoughts. Leila smiled. His aversion to profanity was extreme.

'That's her husband,' Leila replied, smiling.

'Chris?' Kaobi asked, amused.

'Yeah, she calls him Super C.'

'I wonder why…' Kaobi muttered mischievously. They both chuckled and shared further rude enough jokes until the doctor came in.

'It's good to see you smiling; you did give us quite a scare…' he began.

Leila stiffened. Doctors made her nervous. They usually never had anything good to say.

'… But that is a tough baby you've got in there; probably just like its mum, I dare say. I have not seen any of your notes though. It is a rough guess, a safe one; I hope that all is well with you two,' he said smiling.

'Who two? I don't understand,' Leila stammered.

'It was a nasty fall and apparently you hit the floor face down. Although you bruised the tip of your cervix, the baby's heartbeat was a bit irregular, but it's doing just fine. We need you to come back in a couple of days to run some tests and for another ultrasound scan because we don't want to take any chances.' The doctor rattled on blissfully unaware of the effect of his words on his patient, and, in fact, Kaobi whose mouth was ajar in total astonishment.

'Baby?' Kaobi asked, shocked.

'What ba… baby?' Leila asked.

'Forgive my indiscretion,' the doctor began. 'I thought that as the foetus is nearly twenty-four weeks old, you most likely would be aware that you had conceived? By now you should have seen the midwife.' The doctor was genuinely shocked. It was not her regular hospital, so obviously her medical records would take at least a couple of hours to track down, but what a blunder!!!

'Foetus? Midwife?' Leila asked. 'What a load of bullocks,' she thought to herself. She could not be pregnant. How?

'You are pregnant,' the doctor spelt out to her plainly.

'Pregnant?' Leila whispered, her eyes pacing the room frantically.

'I don't want it…' she began. In her mind's eye, the scene that flashed before her was the look in her husband's eyes as he thrust himself harder and harder into her angrily; the confusion in his eyes, the hatred, the venom he spat, the filth! For the next couple of minutes, this scene played repeatedly in slow motion and she shook her head from side to side frantically.

'It's too late for that; you are too far-gone.

'Too far-gone? It's not 24 weeks yet, is it? I understand the law states that…'

He cut her off.

'I just told you, Madam, with all due respect, that you are indeed very close to 24 weeks pregnant. I am not even going to contemplate this procedure with you, Mrs Yoganathan. It will not be in your best interest. We did our best to save this baby and any attempt to terminate this pregnancy might result in infertility or the loss of your own life, and no law in this country would permit it quite frankly.'

'What's the loss of a foetus compared to bringing forth into a world a child who was conceived under such malevolent conditions?' She could not love this child. Leila had always thought that the greatest gift God could ever bring her way was a child, but never in her wildest dreams did she imagine that it would be this way.

'There must be something you can do surely?' Leila asked. 'You don't understand… this baby was not intended… I cannot…' Her voice trailed off.

'I understand that, but for reasons to do with your own personal health, I do not recommend this. The termination of this child is also illegal, I'm afraid. In my professional opinion, I think you need to consider other options,' the doctor said.

'Still, it's my decision, right?' Leila asked.

'It is not your decision in this country.'

'Good. I'll go elsewhere,' she snapped rebelliously. 'I am not having that bastard's child.'

'Still, in my opinion, Leila, I think you should consider other options.'

'Like what?' Leila spat aggressively.

'Hey… don't shoot the messenger…' Kaobi whispered sympathetically but sternly.

'But Kaobi, you know I cannot have a baby…' She turned to Kaobi. These days she only deviated from calling him Prince or KK when she was upset, shocked or felt some sort of strong emotion.

'Why not?' he asked, reaching for her hand. 'I'll be here,' he offered.

'I'll be back later on. I need to know the results of some tests I ran earlier and then I'll get back to you,' the doctor said in the most professional voice he could muster. He was obviously taken aback, but walked out with his head held high.

'Thank you,' they both said in stoic unison.

'He is gay!' Leila said.

'What?'

'Did you see his cat walk?'

Kaobi shook his head. 'Lord have mercy woman; you are so random'. He said, giving her a confused look.

'Kaobi, there is something I didn't say before now,' she began.

'You don't have to say, Leila, I know…' he said still holding on to her hand.

'Leila, I know what he did. I am a doctor, you know. I specialise in hearts, but it doesn't make me any l… l…less able to detect gyne stuff.' Kaobi had started therapy and practice with Leila to correct his now mild speech defect and Leila noted that even though it had only been a few months, his speech had improved drastically already.

'What should I do? This cannot be happening to me… I don't know what to do.' Leila burst into tears still shaking her head from side to side totally confused.

'Shh… it will be fine… shh… Everything will be right as rain…' he whispered still holding onto her hand.

'Remember your own words the other night, Leila,' he began. 'Yesterday's sorrow, today's incomprehension, tomorrow's blessing… It looks really bad right now, but in the end you will be very happy. I promise, Leila.'

Leila just shook her head in total disbelief.

'No...' she whispered over and over again.

The journey back to hers was in total silence. Kaobi had offered her a lift home. Even he seemed somewhat lost for words. He was distant and the look in his eyes came across to Leila as cold and unapproachable.

'What's wrong?' Leila eventually asked breaking the silence.

'It's nothing… it's been an awfully long day, that's all.' Leila nodded.

'Come in for a coffee please,' Leila requested upon arrival at her flat.

'I have to come in to put you to b… b… bed anyway. You heard the doctor. You need to rest.'

'I don't need looking after… I don't need any rest and I am not having this baby, Kaobi… I am not. This baby is the product of an incident that I had already managed to forget, it's in my past, and all I want to do is to move on,' she snapped.

Kaobi ignored her, took her things into the house, and made her a hot chocolate.

'Leila, God had given you a gift,' he explained in a half-snap. 'Many women pray for this all their lives and still are denied the joys of motherhood. You have been given this chance, and you want to throw it away? I will s… s… support you; I will do whatever you want; whatever you need I… I… will give you, Leila, just please, don't harm this baby,' he pleaded.

'You don't understand, you can never understand. You are not its father, so what's your problem?' Leila spat, engulfed by dolour and the impulse to hurt him. 'I'm so sorry…' she said.

'You've made your point, Leila, goodbye.' And with that, he stormed out of the house and drove off in a fit of anger.

Leila sat at the entrance of the front door. She had found a quarter packet of cigarettes in the corner – probably Olga's. Leila sparked it up; a quarter way down the stick she was choking because firstly, she did not know how to smoke and secondly, her pregnant body despised the smell of tobacco. Leila spat viciously and threw it as far as she could, went back into the house and slammed the door hard behind her. She opened it and slammed it shut again. She took of one of her four and half inch Nero Vernice Calf Pumps off her foot, and threw it at the door and paced the room with one shoe on. All the while she was panting heavily, determined to blink away the tears.

'No tears!' she screamed, tugging at her hair.

Leila went to the corner of her room that she dreaded. Out of a carrier bag, she brought out the items, which for a long time she had been unable to look at without cringing and feeling sick to the pit of her stomach. She brought out her torn clothes from the fateful night her husband raped her. She had kept it all, down to the underwear she had on that cursed Tuesday. The items were all blood stained. She held the clothes up in despair and once again recaptured the events of that moment. She could hear her desperate screams and his angry voice echoing in her head. She held the clothes against her face and wept into the bloodstained fabric. Fed up of crying, she clutched her stomach in total disbelief. She put them back in the bag, put the bag in her wardrobe, sat in the corner of her room, and stared into space incessantly.

Two hours later, a remorseful Leila rang Kaobi's phone repeatedly. For the first time ever, he (probably) consciously did not take her calls. She was worried by his behaviour, but she was also annoyed and irritated. He was not the one carrying the child, so why was he being such a 'drama queen' about it? Perhaps it was the principle of the whole thing for, despite his shortcomings, he was of quite high moral standards. What exactly was upsetting Kaobi so much, Leila was not sure.

Meanwhile, sat in front of the beach, Kaobi wept. He felt the need to protect an innocent, unborn child. Leila was his best friend; he felt her pain but did not feel it was justification enough to end its life. Why did she think he was the enemy? He only wanted her to do the right thing. Could she not tell that he felt her pain? 'Leila could be so blind sometimes,' he thought to himself.

A puzzled Leila sat in bed staring at her phone. She was confused. She did not want this baby, but the gratification of holding a child close to her bosom brought tears of joy to her eyes. At that point, she reminded herself time and time again that she had dutifully, happily made passionate love to her husband on countless occasions. That did not discount her resentment. This child would have been conceived on that night. Before that, it had been endless weeks since she and Akash had indulged. Since that incident, she had been with no one else. She frantically did the maths, hoping that she was wrong, hoping that there was a slim chance that it would have been one of the last few episodes of numb sex. Days before that, she had completed a normal monthly cycle. She looked up at the ceiling. God could not possibly want to punish her for leaving Akash. Leila was worried because the Bible did speak very strongly about issues of divorce. Still, her decision to leave him was inevitable. Being married to Akash had felt like punishment, and besides, she had begged for God's forgiveness and she was sure He had heard her persistent cries. Remaining in that loveless marriage would certainly have sent her to an early grave and she knew God understood this. The conclusion was, she wanted this child more than anything in this world, but then again, she did not want it. So badly did she not want the child that she looked out of the window and thought that perhaps it would be a good idea to 'accidentally' fall out of it dropping two floors. Then she realised how stupid and selfish that was and so she sobbed instead, then she called the greatest polyhistor she knew. This woman she turned to had a halo over her head, invisible to the world perhaps, but clear to Leila. She was prim and proper and strict; a perfect lady, but never judgmental or naïve and in Leila's opinion she had all the answers. 'She would know what to do,' she thought to herself.

'Hi grandma.'

'Hello my little one, how are you?' Leila felt safe. 'Oh Grandma…' and Leila told her grandmother everything obscuring nothing, coating nothing, baring all as she knew it to be in all honesty. Her grandmother in her invaluable wisdom explained that it was not in her place to tell Leila what to do. 'Ultimately, it's your decision, love,' she had said, having spent the better part of two hours outlining the pros and cons with her granddaughter, although reluctantly admitting that logically, there were more cons than pros.

'But I will leave you with a thought,' she began, paused and thought for a few seconds, and then she continued, 'let go and let God.'

'How do I know when he takes over, grandma?' she asked.

'Well, whether you turn to the left or to the right, your ears will hear a voice behind you saying "this is the way: walk in it" and then Leila, then, you will know. Trust the whispers of your soul!' she said.

Still Leila was confused and scared and 'where the fuck is Kaobi at a time like this?' she thought out loud to herself apologising to her stomach for the unnecessary profanity ('children shouldn't hear people swear,' she thought), and helplessly she dug out her diary, writing frantically.

Dear Diary,
I turn left and then right
But however hard I fight
There's no relief from by borne load
Because it's down the same old road
I'm walking right round a square
Another strange path should I dare?
For a moment, I thought I'd won
But it's right round this same square I'd gone
I scream for help, I hear a faint noise
Oh, it's just the echo of my voice
It's the same old patch of the sky
No matter what I do, how I try
Head back the same way I came?
Why bother it's all the same
Different methods of the same game
What do I do, I'm going insane.

Leila put down her diary and lay down in bed staring at the ceiling. She was reviewing the dramatic events of her life so far.

'Oh Lord, all this is a bit too much for me to handle on my own. I need to know if you have a plan. Please tell me, show me a sign,' she said over and over again, rocking back and forth on her bed, pillow held tightly to her stomach.

'Hello crossroads!' she said yawning. Sleep was, however, not forthcoming!

At that same moment, Kaobi's mind was willing God's wisdom to Leila's heart. Repeatedly he was asking God to minister to her, to heal her from the pain of her past and to protect this innocent child.

Leila lay in bed, eyes intently on the ceiling counting the squares, trying hard to ignore the voice of the screaming baby in her imagination. Her gaze wandered from square to square on the ceiling, second by second. Occasionally she would sigh, occasionally she would cry.

'Speak to me, Lord,' she cried.

Kaobi also lay in bed unable to sleep. His eyes were fixated on the ceiling for some strange reason. As he counted the squares, he mumbled incoherently under his breath. It was hours since he had been by the beach; he pleaded still, praying on Leila's behalf. Occasionally he would shut his eyes; occasionally he would look out of the window up high to the skies as he whimpered.

'Speak to her, Lord,' he whispered.

Many miles across town, a gentle, elderly lady lay on her bed unable to sleep. Thoughts of her granddaughter's words were echoing relentlessly in her mind. She had read all the relevant scriptures she knew, she had said all the required prayers from her little green prayer book, but somehow she could not sleep. More so because it brought back bad memories of a time she had forgotten. It was forty-five years ago. It had been the wrong decision. Could she impose her memories on her granddaughter? What was it her lawyer husband used to say? Each case is judged on its own merits. That was it. Moaning with restless discomfort, she lay down in bed furiously counting the squares on the ceiling.

'To have said to her that I know it all would have been to lie, but in my own way, you saw, Lord, I tried. I beseech thy mercy, Lord up high, hear my cry and speak to her,' she sighed.

Leila held on to her book of psalms, which comforted her, praised with her, or guided her depending on the circumstance. It was a present from Grandma – one of the many random gifts she received in the post. The portion that caught her eye for that moment was one that had been very familiar to her in recent times – *'Psalm 61 - O God, listen to my cry! Hear my prayer! From the ends of the earth, I will cry to you for help, for my heart is overwhelmed. Lead me to the towering rock of safety, for you are my safe refuge, a fortress where my enemies cannot reach me. Let me live forever in your sanctuary, safe beneath the shelter of your wings!'* Leila read this very passage repeatedly until slumber snuck up and engulfed her.

It was fifteen minutes later. This was a world so far away from Kaobi's or Grandma's, but implausibly close because their three hearts were united in common prayer. Leila was soundly asleep; both her hands crossed over her stomach, protective maternal instinct was slowly kicking in. It had just been all too much for Leila to take in, but unconsciously, her heart had welcomed the baby. The decision came in her slumber, as she dreamt dreams of smelly nappies and first teeth. She had not made this decision alone. Her grandmother and Kaobi both had jointly contributed to her acceptance of this child. This was possibly as a result of the popular biblical belief that 'where two or three are gathered, He (God) is there in their midst'. She thought that if the Bible were ever edited, that they needed to consider including: 'physically or otherwise' to the popular prayer. When she awoke everything felt different. Her perception of the baby had changed dramatically but rather than wait for explanations and answers to previously unanswered questions, Leila embraced the gift of life that she was privileged to give for what it was. She stood staring at herself in the mirror. As she slipped her t-shirt off slowly, she stared at the words above her mirror. They read:

'Even though I walk through the valley of the shadow of death, I will fear no evil, for you are with me; your rod and your staff, they comfort me' – Psalm 23:4.

Leila read these words over twice and then simply said under her breath, 'Thank you Lord' and with that, she was ready. She smiled as she admired her nudity in the mirror. Her stomach was still pretty flat for a pregnant woman, considering the fact that the doctor had pronounced her nearly twenty four weeks into her forty; little wonder she would never have guessed. She did think a couple of weeks before that her waistline felt a little pudgier, but she would never have guessed she was pregnant. She wasn't sure she agreed with the stretch marks lurking round the crevices of her body, behind her knees – really? She kissed her teeth. She was astounded because she had a normal monthly cycle, although she did miss two if she remembered correctly. It was irregular most of the time anyway so she never paid attention, and besides she had been on long-term contraception plan that had only just started to wear off. The doctor had told her that she would have irregular periods or none at all and even though she was now officially off it, it would take a while – about six months, he had said – for the body to adjust; in some cases, a little over a year. Akash and Leila had not wanted children straight away, so she had remained on the contraceptive until such a time when she thought that it was best to get off it if she were to consider conceiving in a year or so as the doctor had advised.

'Mummy loves you, my beautiful baby girl….' she whispered to her stomach in the mirror. Upon closer examination, she did notice that her belly was slightly rounded, but it was perfect. It was beautiful. It had to be a girl she thought smiling to herself. She smiled even more when she peered in her mobile phone and saw a text message from her grandmother saying that she would support her regardless of her decision. There was also a missed call from Kaobi with no voice mail. Leila breathed a sigh of relief. Life could not be better. She scribbled a note to her grandmother to put in the post later. She sealed the envelope with a kiss and then her thoughts swiftly swung back to Kaobi, her backbone. He had not abandoned her for good then, she thought joyfully. Leila called him.

'I'm so sorry about last night,' she said to him. 'I was panic stricken and self-absorbed and I do know that I won't go through this alone (?)' – it was a statement, but more in the form of a question because her tone indicated that she needed some reassurance. She paused for a few seconds and when he said nothing, she continued… 'And even if you won't be there, this baby will be the most important thing in my life regardless and I can understand why you would be so upset with me.'

A relieved Kaobi sighed gratefully and smiled. Even Leila could see the big smile from the other end of the phone.

'You know I w…w…won't abandon you…' he said, 'and I am sorry for storming off like that. Perhaps I should have been more considerate of what you were feeling. I should have tried to be more empathetic to what must have been going on in your mind at the time and broken down my thoughts to you more subtly.'

'Will you come round for a bit then?' she asked.

'Sure,' he said, adding, 'do you w…w….want anything from the shops?'

'Mmhhmmm, croissants and eggs,' she replied. Kaobi laughed out loud because recently this was all Leila ever ate and it had only just occurred to him that the cravings a pregnant woman had kicked in and he had never suspected.

'And let me guess… crispy sea weed as part of your five a day?'

She nodded.

'Are you nodding sheepishly, sweetheart? I can't see you, can I?' he said teasing.

'Then how do you know I am nodding?'

'See you shortly,' he said giggling. Smiling, she snuck back into bed dreaming of croissants and boiled eggs. She embraced the cravings and smiled; thoughts of bigger breasts were appealing to Leila who looked down at her normally A-cup sized breasts. At that point, she felt a flutter in her tummy. She had felt it before but had put it down to wind. It was not something she had ever experienced before, so how was she to know? When she put her hands over her lower abdomen and felt the vicious flutter again, her suspicions were confirmed. It was her baby kicking away. She went into the garden, sat in her bright red rocking chair, picked up her phone and made an appointment with the midwife. Yet another era would be born!

A grand adventure is about to begin
Winnie the Pooh

Chapter Twenty-Two

Leila was going through her mail one morning at the office, thirty-three weeks in – May 3rd, 1996. The letter, which was of particular interest to her, was the one she had dreaded opening for a couple of weeks now. She was afraid because she recognised the envelope. It was her 'decree absolute'. Her divorce was final! The grounds for divorce – the marriage had broken down irretrievably and that Akash had behaved in such an unreasonable manner that she found it intolerable to live with him. He did not contest.

'Why would he?' Leila had asked Kaobi when he had asked her if he had.

'After what he did to me? He would not dare. I could tell the police! His career, his life, he would lose everything. He would probably go to jail as well,' Leila had commented. All Leila needed now was Akash's signature on some other documents and they could officially go their separate ways for good. When she had announced to him that she wanted a divorce, he sounded calm and withdrawn. Down the phone, she had heard something that she suspected was an escaped sob, but she could not have been sure. Somehow, despite the animosity she was entitled to feel towards him, they had managed to be civil to each other. She was not angry with him. On the contrary, Leila felt some sort of pity towards the man she once shared her life with. She had heard through the grapevine (meaning of course Olga and two or three others) that Akash was but a mere shadow of himself. He was rarely seen in his usual hang out spots, and when he was, he was alone and seemed to have lost his gambol. No habitual loud jokes, no confident gait, even the slick in his hair lacked lustre. According to Olga, for weeks he looked terribly unkempt and desperately unhappy. Occasionally Leila actually missed him. She would smile when she remembered a moment they had shared or laugh at the thought of his silly jokes and many times she was tempted to call him when something dramatic was happening in their favourite TV soap operas. She chuckled at the memory but was always just as quick to wipe the smile off her face when she remembered all she had been through. He was not her first love, heck, he was not even her first true love, but he had waltzed in from nowhere at the perfect time. Perhaps this had something to do with why Leila was yet to go out on a date, or end up in another man's bed. (That, and the little matter of her pregnancy! And there was Kaobi. No there isn't. Yes, there is. ***sigh *).** She had also become distrusting of men! Besides, she had nothing really to give. The first cut as is often said is the deepest (Leila always sang the song by Cat Stevens, at this point), and Leila knew that it would take a miracle for her to love another man. It was all too complex, never straightforward. Kaobi had once suggested that she might end up back with Akash eventually; she had taken offence and given him a good scolding. At that point, he had waved the white flag and cocooned her in a hug until she shut up. Akash had never really apologised to her, but she knew he was sorry. Leila was a wounded but arrogant tigress. Deep down in the secret corners of her heart she hoped he had sought help and was happy, because in a weird kind of way, she was content with her life as it was. She had the baby to look forward to. Leila had learnt to enjoy her own company and go out with friends when she needed to. So no, she did not want him or anyone. She was independent and more successful now than she ever was in all those years. Now, she was her own boss in every aspect of her life although she could not explain why she kept on scribbling her 'Yoganathan signature' repeatedly on the envelope that contained her freedom. It was such a pretty signature, she thought. 'No regrets,' she said preceding a sigh. She picked up the phone and called him.

'Hi Kash…Akash…Kash…OH MY GOD! Whatever you call yourself these days…it's me… Leila. The divorce papers just came through and all that is left is your signature on all the other documents to do with our joint finances. Yeah, you can pass through if you want and pick your copies. Ok. See you then.'

As soon as Leila put the phone down, she had alarm bells ringing in her head. Akash was not aware that she was pregnant. He had not seen her for months and somehow, every time she had decided it was time to tell him, she found a 'good reason' to never get round to it; she was scared of his reaction. The baby was hers, not his. 'Nothing to do with him,' she had concluded, and for Leila, it was as simple as that. Non-negotiable!

'Leila, Akash is here to see you…' Bianca-Maria called out, interrupting her thoughts.

'That was quick.' But her thoughts had actually been drifting here and there for the better part of an hour.

'Send him in,' Leila responded after taking a quick deep breath.

She did not get up. She sat frozen and concealed in her chair.

'Leila,' he muttered humbly, weakly. She just flashed him an unsure smile, waving her Chopard-clad wrists nervously, and then using the hand to conceal the space between the table and her stomach.

'Kash,' she said, nodding her head noncommittally.

They chatted in monosyllables for about ten minutes on the weather and miscellanies as he stared blankly at the papers. He took his time to sign them. He was emotional about it all and for the first time, he apologised to Leila. He put his pen to the dotted line and paused.

'You deserve a lot better; someone who will love you for who you are. I am sorry for everything I put you through. Leila, it's my loss. I am nothing without you. Until you actually left me, I had no idea how much I loved you. Funny how you always told me this would be the case. But you did give me a long rope to hang myself, Leila; I know that now. I was a fool. But I just want you to know that I love you and I will love you for the rest of my life.' As Akash rendered this little speech, a tear trickled down his cheek and almost followed the same rough path of the scar she had left him with. She was amazed that it had turned out permanent. It trailed its way from half way down his cheek and then cut off and continued along his neck. It had faded, but was still eye-catching against his pale skin, a constant reminder for him of that night, she thought to herself.

Akash continued this speech with the occasional stutter, choke, and hesitation in-between. Leila never said a word nor interrupted him. There was nothing to say.

'I bid you adieu,' he said rising. 'At least I got my air time,' he said slicking his hair and licking his lips, but without the imperiousness that usually accompanied the habit. 'I bid you adieu? Who says that?' Leila raised an eyebrow but said nothing.

'Akash, believe me, it was the worst thing you could have done, but guess what? I made my peace with it. I forgave you the instant it happened and although I probably should, I don't hate you. I would just like to think there were a few screws loose in your head and that you have sorted yourself out now. It's all in my past now, so let's just let it go. I know I have. But, I have a question for you.' He stood akimbo as usual, hands in pocket, with his back to her and waited.

'Did you marry me for British Citizenship?' she asked. 'I need to know,' she added in a lowered tone.

As Akash turned slowly around, obviously thrown off and about to begin another speech, Leila knew this was the moment. She braced herself. She stood up. Akash stared at her with his eyes wide.

'You are... you are... is it? It is... our....it's our baby' and he dashed across the room over to Leila and leaned over to her stomach. He held the stomach, kissed it, and wept.

'Is it my baby?' he asked and then he concluded, 'It is, it is... I know it is. It is our baby,' he said excitedly.

'It's my baby,' she replied calmly, coldly. She had anticipated all sorts of reactions, but she had not expected this one. She just stared down at him, knelt down before her, face to face with her stomach.

'I knew you looked different. You look radiant. You are glowing. You have put on a bit of weight but you are absolutely beautiful,' he said happily, ignoring the look on her face.

'Leila, we can make it work, we can...' Leila shook her head indicating the hopelessness of the situation as his voice trailed off in disappointment.

'Kash, I forgave you. Let us leave it at that. This baby is mine,' she repeated sternly.

'You can't be serious...' he said with the old cold Akash eyes coming back in his fit of annoyance.

'I have never been more serious,' she replied calmly.

'But it's my baby too...' He started to raise his voice.

'The doctors said an abortion would kill me, but I was prepared to take the chance. Death would have been a small price to pay. Yes, that's how messed up in the head I was about it.' For a minute, he looked confused but Leila went on, 'Do you not remember the sexual intercourse-less few months before our marriage crumbled? When do you think this child was conceived? This child is mine!'

'Leila we were man and wife, it's your duty – my right,' he said.

'You are an intelligent man – selfish and inconsiderate, an imperious, myopic bastard, yes, but intelligent nonetheless! Penetration without consent is rape, Akash.'

'Don't call me Akash!' he whispered.

'Did I look like I was enjoying the privileges of a wife that Tuesday?' Leila was agitated because his expression was blank. He did not seem to be assimilating anything she said. 'You beat me up, you raped me,' she argued.

'I am sorry I beat you up, Leila; I know I did. I am sorry,' he sobbed.

'You raped me!' she reiterated.

'I...I....' he began.

'Oh forget it,' she said dismissively. Akash remained kneeling in the exact spot. Leila had long since wandered off and was staring out of the window. She turned round and noticed how the sunlight was seeping through the glass window from the south. The rays engulfed Akash, and as she watched his face glow in the sunlight, she realised she was unafraid of him. He was neither the dangerous hyena nor dangerous lion. Akash resembled a little white canary with a broken wing and claw. Hands over face, he cupped endless drops of tears and drenched his hair when he slicked it, licking his lips along with tears and catarrh. He needed a haircut, a shave, some sleep, heck – he needed a doctor! Leila sighed and spoke quietly. 'You need help! I heard you had lost the plot but now I can confirm that for a fact!' Olga had told her that he was suffering mentally but even the memory of that Tuesday night was not enough preparation for the reality. Now she knew what Olga had meant.

'No! I will never let that happen…' He began to throw a tantrum. It was not his usual bombastic, daunting attack. He resembled a spoilt child throwing toys out of the pram.

'You think she will call you daddy? Congratulate you for bringing her into the world with such a spectacular performance?' she questioned.

'Did you say '*she*'? It's a girl?' he asked, tears forming in his eyes, not paying attention to Leila's questions.

'It has nothing to do with you!' she spat angrily, frustrated. It started out as a whisper but ended up more like a 'bark' of some sort. The kind of uncouth outburst only Akash could bring out in her.

'You can't do this, Leila,' and by this time, his voice was unreservedly loud. She was aware of Bianca-Maria's nervous, concerned footsteps lurking just outside the doorway. Bianca-Maria was under strict instructions from Kaobi and her brother to watch her like a hawk.

Leila felt cramps that felt like really bad contractions, the worst she had had so far (and she had had quite a few in the last week) and although she put it down to Braxton's Hicks, she realised that this situation was not aiding her condition. She resisted the urge to massage her lower abdomen. She shut her eyes tightly for seconds.

'Bianca?' she called out. She could hear her footsteps rushing towards her in a flash.

'Please bring in security,' she requested.

'You never answered my question, Akash,' she said as he was led out. He looked back. 'Did you marry me for British Citizenship? I need to know.' He did not respond.

Leila seethed for endless moments before she picked up her phone.

'KK, hi... yeah I am fine. Can you meet me for lunch please?'

'You are at work?' he asked, concerned.

'Yeah Prince, I am!' she admitted, dreading the lecture to come.

'You are not supposed to be at work, Leila. Haven't you heard of maternity leave? Your blood pressure was high last week,' the familiar voice on the other end of the phone scolded subtly.

'You nearly no longer have a stutter' she said, smiling and crossing her fingers, hoping he could distract him. Nope!

'Leila!'

'I know, I know... I just had a few things to go through that's all... Fifteen minutes? Okay, I'll meet you at the café. Bye.' In the few minutes before she walked across to the café, Leila sobbed. There he was insinuating that he had done nothing wrong. Olga had said that Akash had been suffering some sort of mental confusion. Now, she understood the gravity. Apparently, he was seeking help. This stopped neither Leila's flashbacks nor her hurt.

Over at the café, Kaobi found a cushion and suspended Leila's swollen feet so that her body carried no weight. He busily set about taking her shoes off, inspecting her ankles as she ranted on about what Akash had said.

'Your oedema is pretty bad today,' he said calmly, running his fingers over her tattoo. He then beckoned one of the attendants to bring over a hot chocolate.

'What's oedema? I don't want a hot chocolate. I'm burning hot. I want a coke!' she demanded, and then added, 'Are you listening to me? Did you hear what I said about Kash?'

'No coke. Fresh orange juice or water. Your choice. Don't worry about that. Akash can never take this baby away fr...fr...from you,' he replied, still rubbing her ankles.

'Mango juice. What if he decides to take me to court and sues for joint custody or something ridiculous like that?'

'Cranberry juice? Ice?' and then he shook his head. 'Leila, trust me. It will be fine. Sweetheart, let me check your temperature.'

'Cranberry's fine. Ice. Ouch!' Leila exclaimed grasping her tummy. Kaobi looked up instantly.

She paused for a few more seconds and then said, 'Braxton Hicks! Bloody hell, that hurt!'

'No bad language in front of the baby!' Kaobi teased.

'She's not even born yet...psycho Godfather!' she responded, glaring lovingly at him. He smiled.

'Are you in pain? Should we expect contractions?' Kaobi asked.

'Hopefully not yet, KK. Baby is not due till second week of June. Back to Kash and the baby...' Leila continued.

'Forget Akash and concentrate on you. Akash is irrelevant!' Kaobi snapped. Leila did as she was told.

'Should I take you home?' he asked.

'Aren't you supposed to be working?'

'I am done for the day. I could give you a lift.'

'Ok then. Just let me finish my drink,' she said, and added, 'Your stutter is fading.'

'It is,' he agreed.

'When was your last therapy session?' she asked concerned.

'Two days ago,' he replied, smiling nervously. He was watching her glass.

He reached over to help her up. She held onto him with one hand, with the other hand on her waist.

As she stood up, she felt a very sharp pain and held her stomach, curling as she did so. She instinctively held onto Kaobi for support. The contraction came from nowhere.

'Are you ok?' he asked panic-stricken but putting on a very good act.

'This isn't Braxton Hicks, is it?' he asked, aware that the expression on her face meant that she was in more pain than normal.

Leila shook her head.

'I think the baby is coming, she might be coming, and it's too early,' she shrieked.

'Ok, take deep breaths, Leila, don't panic, I am here,' he reassured.

Leila's waters broke. As it trickled down, Leila was thinking how grateful she was for the subtle episode, when '*whoosh*!' – oh the embarrassment! Although she had hoped for a less theatrical water-breaking episode, the pain was too excruciating for her to care. She watched helplessly as the 'stuff' drowned her Ostrich Birkin bag, which she had temporarily placed between her legs.

'She's too early,' Leila panicked, holding her legs apart. She was unable to close them from that moment on. She clutched just below her stomach as if to prevent the baby from falling out. Kaobi rushed her as quickly as he could across the road to the hospital, all the while beckoning her to remain calm. Leila was hysterical.

'I am here, Leila,' he said repeatedly.

'What if I lose the baby? It's too early'

'Think positive, sweetheart. You know this baby is not going anywhere. The baby is here to stay. Say it,' he instructed firmly.

'This baby is here to stay,' she repeated dutifully, feeling the urge to push.

'Don't push yet, sweetheart. It's not yet the right time for that.' He held onto her.

'This baby is here to stay,' she muttered in-between her well-practised breathing.

'You will be fine.' He reached over and held her hand constantly assuring her that she would be ok.

Upon arrival at the hospital, Leila was taken into a room and seen by a doctor straight away and tests were run (There were some advantages to being friends with the hospital staff). Leila was informed that following her fall a few months before, the scar underneath her cervix had reopened causing the infected cervix to open (dilate) without contractions.

'In a normal pregnancy,' the doctor began, 'the cervix dilates in response to uterine contractions.' He explained to Kaobi (because Leila could hardly pay attention) that as Leila's cervix was weak anyway without the trauma of the infection, it probably would have opened just from the pressure being put on her uterus as the baby advanced. The baby was slightly distressed, but fingers crossed, everything would be fine as this was not uncommon. Thirty-three weeks was not terribly risky for the baby to be born. She was not fully dilated yet, but if things did not progress fast enough naturally, they would be looking at having an emergency caesarean section so that the baby wouldn't have to struggle for too long. As a scar could leave the skin more sensitive than normal skin, the baby being a good size, considering it wasn't full term was probably pressing against it causing it to reopen.

'Too many eggs and croissants then!' she thought to herself at that point.

'Will the baby be OK?' she asked, concerned.

'The baby is a fighter like its mum. You just remain calm,' the doctor replied encouragingly and confident in his words.

'The week of the double odd number! It could all go wrong!'

'Don't be silly. Everything will be fine.' He said, taking her hand in his, and then added: 'do you want me to wait outside?' He was unsure of what role Leila wanted him to play.

'I need you here,' she said to him, hot tears streaming down her cheeks.

'This is bound to be the most un-dignifying moment of my life' she giggled nervously, 'but I do need you KK,' she repeated.

He nodded trying to retain some sort of composure. He had never been in a labour ward with a woman before. His wife had given birth in the States. He had intended to fly out to meet her but the twins arrived two weeks earlier than planned.

What good would it do if he too panicked now? he asked himself.

While she was being prepped, Kaobi popped out to call her sisters to inform them that the child was on its way, and to get a hot drink. He had established a good rapport with them since the night they had spent nursing Leila.

'She is asking for you to come in now,' a nurse ran out to inform him. Squeamish Kaobi took a deep breath, braced himself and confidently walked into the room.

'Push…' the nurse was urging already.

'I can't do this,' she lamented.

'Leila, you are fully dilated; the baby is ready to come out. Can you give me a big push?' she asked gently.

'I can't!' Leila yelled.

'Hold her hand, encourage her.' The nurse turned to Kaobi. Kaobi held her hand gently. It was alright to watch when it was a patient but it was actually very difficult for him to watch her in that much pain. Leila screamed, Leila cried, she cursed, she pushed with every fibre of strength she had in her being, but at that time, she still was not pushing hard enough.

'Leila, your cervix has opened sufficiently and the baby is beginning to move down the birth canal. I need you to do what we have practised already. Your abdominal muscles need to push this baby out, Leila,' Kaobi said to her gently.

'The baby is in distress,' the midwife was saying as Kaobi stood squeezing her hand, urging her on. He did the breathing with her, stroking her hair, because he knew that in less complex situations, that was the key to relaxing her. The idea was to get her as calm as possible.

'Push Leila.'

It was possible that Leila's voice rang through the entire ward and possibly beyond, as she begged God for strength from somewhere to push this baby out. She eventually got there in the end. It was a very complicated labour due to the fatigued baby. The whole process lasted all of four hours and a bit. The final push brought into the world a good sized (just under five pounds), but adorable little girl. She insisted on seeing her before they cleaned her up for a brief mother/daughter bonding session, skin to skin. Leila held her in her arms and wept tears of joy thanking God for this little bundle of joy. It was nothing like anything Leila had ever felt before. It was not even similar to anything she thought it would feel like. The moment she held her baby in her arms was the best moment of her life; no moment came remotely close. The baby did not cry. She stared slightly squinted at Leila as though she understood instantly who she was. Her little eyes shone with what seemed like love and adoration. Leila stared back with just as much love. This was the one moment that Leila would cherish for the rest of her life. When she had tried to describe it to her sisters later, she simply could not. All of the pain of the labour, the breathing, and contractions and all the agony meant nothing after she was born. She could remember absolutely nothing but her beautiful daughter.

'It's something you have to feel for yourselves,' she had said.

Kaobi admired from a safe distance, unsure and scared to share in the moment until Leila invited him with her eyes.

'KK, look…' she showed her off, proud of her latest achievement.

Kaobi smiled as he stroked the baby's little hand. He opened her little left palm and stared at it for a few seconds smiling thoughtfully, but said absolutely nothing.

'Dahlia…' he whispered and peered in Leila's face searching for approval. She nodded and smiled.

'Dahlia…' she whispered leaning over and kissing her forehead; and then added, 'Mummy loves you, precious flower.' She did have this angel-like innocence and the natural beauty of perhaps a delicate white flower - a dahlia ☺. Remembering that night of torture, fear and indecision when she had not wanted this child, Leila looked at the ceiling and said a silent prayer of thanks to God for the spirit that had ministered to her and then looked over to Kaobi and whispered 'thank you' across to him. She could not control her tears.

'Yesterday's sorrow, today's incomprehension, tomorrow's blessing; remember you said that night?' Kaobi asked.

'Yes?' Leila said nodding and trying so hard to shake away the tears, 'and you promised it would come to pass.' She sobbed, remembering those words spoken that fateful night she was raped.

'This is the blessing I promised,' he said, smiling. Leila smiled nodding.

'How does it feel?' he asked in a whisper.

'It feels… it feels…' But Leila choked on her tears. She was speechless and so she just shook her head in disbelief, hoping Kaobi would understand what she was trying to say.

'I know,' he said to her, smiling; the twinkle in his eye could easily have been a teardrop, but Leila was too emotionally charged to wonder about that just then.

Kaobi laid his hand gently on her forehead and whispered, 'Thank you, Lord, for this day that you have made and thank you, Lord, because we know that this baby will move mountains to your glory!'

'Amen,' he and Leila said in unison, short and simple but a highly potent prayer nevertheless.

The baby was taken away for a little while by the doctor who explained to her that the human foetus is forced through the birth canal under extreme pressure and is intermittently deprived of oxygen. During this time, the baby secretes the hormones catecholamine, at levels that are higher than they are likely to be at any other time during his or her life. It should help open the lungs, dry out the bronchi, etc and thus achieve the switch from a liquid to an air environment. She wasn't producing too much of it and needed assistance, but shouldn't take too long. Leila switched off when she heard all the medical gibberish. The doctor sounded like a boring textbook in her opinion so she allowed Kaobi to take total control. She was confident that he knew better and would protect the child no matter what. So as there seemed to be no reason to panic, she remained calm, the smile on her face never ceasing. She tried her best to sleep in the interim when the doctors took her away, but the excitement was too intense so she found time to dig her diary out. She had to capture this feeling in words. It was totally indescribable – the world had stopped, it seemed!

If there was ever such a perfect moment,
A blessed moment, my best moment
And in that favoured moment
When…
Eyes will cry
Hurt will die
Lips will smile
With tears down faces' aisles
Hearts will melt
And chains will link as these hearts unite
Whilst behold – the perfect sight

It's the beautiful moment an innocent soul is born
Be it dusk, be it dawn
Not many an emotion could be stronger
nor intensity last longer

T'was a heavenly moment granted emotional eternity
when Dahlia's doctor
Placed Dahlia in my arms
Worth every second of strain, of pain,
Paid in full was nine months' fee
As her beautifully sincere eyes
Stared down at me with adoration and glee

If there were ever such a perfect moment
It was
When…
The world paused as my baby girl breathed life
It was…
A blessed moment, my best moment

A few hours later, a washed, beautifully bright-eyed Dahlia was brought back healthy all round staring at her new world, still looking intently into her mother's eyes through severely squinted eyes as newborn babies do with nothing but peace, affection and an obvious sense of belonging.

Shortly after, the crew trooped in. Leila's parents, Leila's grandparents, Leila's sisters and brother were all present.

'Meet the new addition to our family,' she said, gently pushing Dahlia into her mother's arms.

'Mum, meet Dahlia, Dahlia, meet Nana,' she said.

'Come here, darling,' her mother whispered gently as she cuddled her first granddaughter, happiness absolutely festooned on her face. Leila's mum had bought her a little hat with the pink inscription, 'Nana loves me' on it, so Leila wasted no time in swapping the plain white one Dahlia had on at the moment for her brand new hat.

'She's beautiful,' her mother said and everyone agreed, offering opinions about her varying features. She was darker skinned than Leila but then Akash had a drop of African blood so that was understandable. Dahlia's hair was dead straight, although that was usually the case for most babies, regardless of biological make-up, and a subtle blonde.

'This little one will turn heads in her youth,' Leila's sister commented. Everyone giggled and the commentary on Dahlia's physical features ran for hours. By this time, Kaobi had slipped out, but not unnoticed. Leila caught his eyes and they held their gaze for a few seconds.

'Thank you,' she whispered across to him. He smiled and left the family to it and when the nurse brought in an enormous colourful array of dahlias in a pretty bouquet, she did not need to ask where they came from. No matter what, Kaobi was never too far away from her. He would watch her closely, be there for, her rain or shine, she just knew. She was grateful. She had multiple reasons to feel blessed, she thought, as she looked round a room surrounded by family; a room surrounded by love in its most original form.

'They both need to sleep now, they have both had a very gruelling day,' the nurse said politely requesting their departure. When she was settled, Leila gave her best shot at breast-feeding; silently cursing the fact that no one had told her that even this task required some getting used to. That done, the cot could not have been any closer to the bed and so, left hand outstretched protectively, Leila fell into a light snooze still smiling. It took a while for sleep to set in because she kept on waking up to stare at Dahlia. She had reached some kind of excitement peak, but every time she fell asleep, she missed her so much that she woke up to check everything was OK. Leila thought back to the last couple of weeks of pregnancy when she had had about enough. She had grown a dress size and a half bigger (if that was humanly possible! Her Anna Osmushkina jeans certainly did not fit - she cried when she made that discovery). Her body had been taken over by horrible dark stretch marks in the most unforgivable places (she was not even aware they could exist in 'those' places). Her face had red patches and randomly spread blotches of rashes all over. Not even her most expensive concealer would cover; and she perpetually looked like she had been punched in both eyes. At those moments, it was a wee bit difficult to comprehend that there would be a blessing at some point; she could see no light at the end of the tunnel. Now, she admitted, she would do it all over again. It was simply amazing!

'So far so good,' she thought at about 2.15 am, then added, 'I give up'. She stopped fighting sleep, and shut her eyes.

In the left corner of the room, the wrinkly old fortune-teller with the scrawny fingers stood bent over a crooked wooden stick. In the history of Leila's relationship with her, this was the first time she had smiled. Her smile looked like it originated from her heart. Leila did not glare at her, not this time.

It was about 3.30 am that her slumber was stirred by footsteps in the dark hospital room. She heard two very familiar voices but did not open her eyes. She was a bit confused. These two voices were never heard in the same place, never at the same time. 'KK and Kash? Now that's odd!' she thought, thinking that post-traumatic stress did weird things to the imagination.

'I really appreciate this kind gesture, doctor. I realise you should not be doing this, but I am desperate. She is my daughter and Leila would not have let me otherwise. Dr...?' Akash enquired as to the name of the kind man who had let him in to catch a glimpse of his daughter.

'Dr Chetachi-Uba,' Kaobi replied in his well-known husky whisper. They both stood over the cot and looked down at Dahlia in what must have been admiration and awe. For a few seconds, Leila was annoyed with Kaobi for bringing Akash in, but she mustered up enough emotional energy to release some unselfishness. She willed herself to see it all from Akash's point of view. She also knew Kaobi was being sympathetic. It was not his place though, a rebellious part of her thought. But then, she knew he would never deliberately do anything to hurt her, so she did not relax, but she did not launch an instant attack. She observed. That was until Akash attempted to bring Dahlia out of the cot, and she was a second away from screaming the hospital down – well her mind was; her physical body was on standby!

'Err… I don't think that's a good idea. Do you?' Kaobi asked restraining him gently by putting his hand in the way. Akash said nothing at first.

'I really want to take her away. She is my daughter!' he said scratching his head.

'You won't get very far – security will be on to you in a flash. Don't bother. There are other ways of going about this,' Kaobi whispered, possibly wondering what he had gotten himself into. He hoped Akash would not throw his help in his face by stirring Leila and causing a scene. He knew all hell would break loose if she woke up. Leila would be furious and probably accuse him of playing God. It was not in his place to decide that Akash could see Dahlia if Leila did not think he deserved to. His own personal opinions should not count.

'Don't make me regret this, Akash. If I do, you will too' he whispered to sternly to him.

Akash wept silently.

'Shhh…' He signalled to him with his forefinger against his lips.

'I cannot explain why I have let you in here, I don't want Leila to wake up. She will be pissed off. But trust me, the spirit in me that will kick your arse if you try anything stupid is stronger than the spirit in me that asked me to do this.' Then Kaobi softened again after a deep breath.

'I'll leave now,' Akash said in-between not-so-silent sobs. There was no response but Leila was aware that Kaobi stayed behind. She opened her eyes partly but not so much that it would be obvious that she was awake. She watched closely as he stood staring at the baby. He whispered something to Dahlia, and with one look of respect and admiration at a seemingly sleeping Leila, he left the room. A tear trickled down Leila's cheek. The tear was of joy and intense emotion and nothing at all negative (not even towards Akash who had just contemplated kidnapping Dahlia).

And outside, in the hospital car park, Akash was beside himself with grief. His hands trembled incessantly so that a worried Kaobi feared to leave him by himself. He clung to Kaobi and wept bitterly.

'I never meant to hurt her, doctor. I love her. I want my daughter. I love my daughter. I cannot go on like this. I need help. I love her!' These were the only words Kaobi could make out. His sentences were more-or-less an endless waffle. Kaobi felt sympathy for this man and wished there was something he could do to help him.

'Mujhay mera parivara chaheye – I want my family,' he cried over and over again.

'There are procedures for this sort of thing, Akash. You need to take this up with Leila later. This is no…no…no time to stir up trouble. No one would even let you out of the hospital with the baby,' Kaobi tried to explain to him. Akash was clearly mentally unhinged in his medical opinion. The signs were glaring.

'I am going to give you a colleague's business card. You need to speak to this woman. She will make you feel better. She can talk you through all this and advise you on the best way to proceed.' Kaobi reached into his wallet. The card was for a renowned psychologist.

'In the meantime, I want to take a look at you, Akash, so could you step back into the hospital for a few minutes?' Akash nodded and just did as he was told, obviously physically and mentally worn out.

About an hour later, Kaobi came back out with some medication.

'Mani jeetai jagjeet – He who conquers the mind, conquers the world,' Akash was chanting.

Kaobi handed him sedatives and a referral to see this psychologist the following week. Akash got into his car with a bottle of water. With head rested on the steering wheel, he stuffed the tablets in his mouth and banged his head continuously against the wheel crying like a baby until, extraordinarily, he fell asleep right there with his head resting on the steering wheel.

Kaobi watched from the window. When the banging against the wheel stopped, he was relieved, but was unsure of what to do. He rang Olga and informed her firstly about the news of Dahlia's birth; and after the general jubilation and recount of events, he returned to matters at hand.

'Someone needs to take him home.' Olga agreed. It was not until Olga arrived and drove Akash away that Kaobi shut his blinds. They exchanged knowing glances and Olga signalled to him that she would call him to let him know what happened thereafter. Two hours later Kaobi was still sitting in his chair staring at the drawn blinds. His thoughts were of fear and uncertainty, of pity and of many other such sentiments. When his phone rang and it was Olga, he was relieved. Apparently, Akash was in bed and calm for the moment but she had left him a note begging him to see someone as soon as possible. He had to take control of his life.

'And does Leila have to know about this?' Olga asked. Kaobi hesitated a few minutes and then replied, 'I am not sure!'

When he put the phone down, he looked down at the open bible before him. God had told Abraham to sacrifice his only son to him. Abraham did not question God. He did it. There are many reasons why this situation is different from the story in the bible, but the compulsion to let Akash see Dahlia was so strong, Kaobi had battled with it for a while, but gave in. He would lay his life down for that little girl in a heartbeat, but there were times when certain actions he took seemed to be directed by something greater than himself. At those times, he trusted and plunged on regardless of the fact that he questioned his own sanity. This was one of those moments; maybe it would become apparent in future, maybe not.

'Dahlia' he mouthed her name. He smiled.

And after the little drama with Kaobi and Akash coming into the room, a puzzled Leila was still in high spirits, albeit slightly unsettled. Should she ask Kaobi some questions? She shook her head. She was petrified of what his response would be, so she archived the moment. She picked Dahlia up and stared at her. She memorised every strand of hair, every contour, every expression. Unable to put her back into the cot, she held her against her breasts. Dahlia made some barely audible sounds of contentment that pleased Leila. She smiled as she likened the sounds to that of a purring, content cat. The purring and rhythm created by both their hearts beating in unison caused a peaceful vibration within Leila and she was lost in a world of unflawed love. This was, by far, the best gift God had ever given her; she needed companionship, God sent her a best friend, one whose soul harmonised with hers naturally; no questions asked.

Ifeyin(ro)nwa – There is nothing, absolutely
nothing that compares to a child
Ibo name for a female child ☺

Chapter Twenty-Four

POST-NATAL BLUES – Forget the Medical Jargon – what it means to you and I!

The moment a baby takes its first breath is one of those moments that tower head and shoulders above all else. The first cry, confirmation of its gender, skin to skin contact with mum, loving and doting look from dad; it's as close to perfect as it gets! The love created by this moment conveys one through the next stage because short of this love to keep one afloat, let's just say the suicide rate owing to post-natal depression would be a lot higher! Why? We hear about this illness and all the medical jargon accompaniments, but in our everyday world, what does it mean? Let's break it down Leila-style!

OK, just a little bit of medical jargon – Professionals of the Royal College of Psychiatrists refer to depression as falling within the group of illnesses, 'puerperal psychoses'. 'Puerperal' means the six weeks after having a baby and 'psychosis' a serious mental illness. So, post-natal depression is a serious mental illness, developing in a woman shortly after she gives birth. This is thought to be as a result of shock as there is no other reason why she should feel so deflated. The pregnancy was neither unplanned nor unwanted or less than perfect. It affects 1 in 500 mothers and has been around for a while. While this seems rare enough, the truth is that dealing with a baby when you do not even claim to have this condition is hard enough – the feeling is overwhelming in its entirety so look out for the signs of post-natal depression and get help before it's too late.

Below are some feelings expressed by new mothers… and me! You can see why anyone would get depressed dealing with scenarios below as 'everyday life'!

OK so you've had your perfect little bundle of joy and it's now time to leave the hospital. Believe it or not, unpleasant as the hospital is – intense feelings of vulnerability, horrible meals, practicality prevailing over comfort and prison-like conditions, when you get home, the daunting prospect of reality sinks in. All that attention you got from the midwife, health visitor and doctor are over. You might get one or two visits at home, but after that, you are on your own, mate. There are the series of first times doing things yourself, bathing the baby, changing baby's nappy and cooking dinner at the same time, and if you have other kids, listening to them scream 'mummy I'm hungry' while the baby cries (no, shrieks!) simultaneously. But for me, by far the scariest moment is trying on your 'normal' clothes after the comfort of wearing strictly pyjamas in hospital. The reassurance of pregnancy is that you are able to successfully convince yourself that you only look like that because you are carrying a baby inside you. It's only temporary. Now faced with the reality of trying on that sexy black top, it's the moment of truth; the truth is that the rows of flaccid and loose skin hanging out in front of you is your tummy AND there is no baby in it; the flabby wings, humongous butt, unsightly stretch marks and of course let's not forget the gigantic breasts, is your new look! The injustice is unforgivable and so if you can get as far as the fridge without the baby screaming for a cuddle (or a change or a feed or a burp), you celebrate by consuming the whole tub of Haagen-Dazs ice cream with drops of your tears in it as well. When your partner asks you why you are shedding buckets of tears over the J'Adore advert (you know the one where the model cat walks towards the camera whilst taking off her clothes bit by bit?), you shrug your shoulders and tell him to leave you alone! He insists on knowing what the problem is. 'I can't have a cigarette!' you reply and immediately realise how dumb this sounds. 'But honey, you don't smoke. You can't smoke. You are breastfeeding,' he says with a confused look on his face. 'Yeah but I would like the option!' you retort and cover your face with the throw pillow, concealing your sobs!

What calms you down? Your partner knows the cue. He gives you a cuddle and tells you how he loves you, stretch marks and all (of course you don't believe that crap for a second but it's all the soothe you need just then) and you decide to spend 20 minutes in the bath by yourself day-dreaming about the new Billy Blanks DVD (because of course going to the gym is out of the question. What the hell are you going to do with the baby?) and how it's going to transform your body to a super sexy size 0 model. Eight minutes into your bath, your day-dream is rudely interrupted by the baby shrieking (maybe the other kid screaming, 'mummy can I have a biscuit please?') and your ever understanding partner who advised you to go take the relaxing bath in the first place screaming, 'love, I think the baby is hungry!' and you can hear his footsteps lurking around nervously outside the bathroom door. Thank goodness you locked yourself in. Oh well, at least you got eight minutes. You rush out, feed the baby, tuck the other kid in bed and only then do you manage to settle down and have 'breakfast' over EastEnders at 8pm; and then your partner declares that he's popping out to the shops and wants to know if you need anything. You glare at him because you are the one stuck on the couch breastfeeding the baby all day (and night because both are merged and any previous distinction is blurred), that of course means you can't, of your own accord, decide to get up and go to the shops to buy random stuff! Of course the problem is not that you want to go to the shops yourself, the problem is that you begrudge the fact that he is not 'imprisoned' like you are. It's not his fault that he has no tits but it's very annoying that he gets to be called 'daddy' and in your books he hasn't quite done much to be worthy of that title. You are the one shaped like Winnie the Pooh as a result of nine gruelling months of waddling around pregnant; now you are the one who is suffering a custodial sentence like the pregnancy was not punishment enough. What would you have him do? You don't know but somehow it all seems a bit unfair.

Let's take it one step further. So visitors troop in and out telling you how beautiful the baby is and bringing in the same size sleep suits that s/he outgrew the week before. Oxfam would be grateful! What happened to practical gifts – packs of nappies? Or breast pads (because you know you only have three pairs left)? Anyway Nazerinne and Jania come in the middle of the afternoon. They were meant to be there at 10 am but they arrive at 2 pm because they slept in. Why? They go into details of their encounters with sex, drugs and rock and roll. They were binge drinking all night and Nazerinne has a cough that makes her sound like a 60-year-old smoker. OK so you are not envious of the lifestyle (Ha! Liar!), you just would like a little bit of time by yourself or with your friends but you cannot exactly take a baby to Stringfellows now, can you? What's more – Jania has been on holiday and so to celebrate her tan, she's wearing this top that reveals the whole of her toned back. The bitch!

AND all your family have decided to chip in and help you but someone does your shopping at 6.15 instead of 6 pm, another dries your clothes in the washing machine for 20 minutes longer than you would and amongst your red cutlery which match the vase and (wilting) roses in the middle of the dinning table, another 'helpful' family member has laid out a yellow spoon in its full glory! Strewth! All hell breaks loose and you throw the mother of all tantrums. Tears, snort, you name it... all emissions present and everyone is staring at you open mouthed as you storm off to your room and SLAM the door!

Now this is the reality of life post-childbirth. While these scenarios are even a tad bit humorous, they can easily escalate into the more serious post-natal depression. Many articles, films, books and Chinese whispers depict a new mother as the epitome of efficiency with her perfect ponytail, unblemished white apron and a house that is permanently tidy with the smell of baking in the kitchen. Women often try to portray themselves this way but if you wonder what's going on in her head, it is the tremendous change in her life. She is probably on maternity leave and has to be a mother for a few months leaving her with Barney, the Tweenies and the singing kettle as her only companions for hours during the day (all her friends are at work). A lot of her relationships will never be the same again and indeed her life has taken on a new meaning. If you ask this woman whether she wants to give the baby back, the answer is a resounding NO, of course not! The baby is the best thing that ever happened to her and she is not lying either. There is the remarkable ability to go from extreme joy to intense sorrow in the space of one minute. When it gets to more serious conditions like those mentioned in paragraph 1 above, speed is of the essence to ensure that the relationship between mother and baby is disturbed for as little time as possible. The effects of psychological treatments are not usually evident for weeks, or more often months, whereas drug and physical treatments work within days or weeks.

If this article speaks to you, do not despair, for you are not alone and depending on the level of unease you feel, there are people you can speak to – midwife, doctor or health visitor are there to guide you, so you are not alone. What's my remedy? Well my best friend gave me vouchers for a massage because she sensed my aggressive joints (I bit her head off in every second sentence I made), but I personally have been dreaming of the perfect pedicure. In other words, think about what works for calming your nerves and do it. And one more thing – condoms, diaphragms, 'the pill', depo-provera injection... these are my best friends, at least for now!

Leila x

Chapter Twenty-Six

'It's just you and I, chick!' she whispered to a purring Dahlia and she let her fall asleep, spread out across her bosom. It was only then that Leila fell asleep properly. That first cuddle lasted the whole night, except on three occasions when she breastfed her. That in itself was fraught with some difficulties of its own (sore, cracked, bleeding nipples, latching on problems, lack of flow – you name it). However, Dahlia's first night was magical for both mother and daughter.

And a few days later there was of course the tricky issue of registering Dahlia's birth. Leila hesitated many times before she named her Dahlia Cranston-Jasper. It was her maiden name, which she had reverted to. She embraced her new life with mixed feelings albeit thankful for her daughter, the most important person in her life at that moment and forever on.

The months to come were not without their fair share of complications. Leila had serious adjustment problems. It was not unusual for her to pick up the phone and ring Ifi, Toks or Joy about one baby problem or the other. When the Dahlia was not colicky, she had teething problems, or trouble sleeping or cradle cap or…the list was endless.

'For goodness sake, this is non-stop!' she thought to herself. Her life did not belong to her any more. She could not as much as sneeze without having to think twice about how it would affect Dahlia. She loved her baby girl with all her heart, but sometimes she felt like a prisoner in her own life. She often felt guilty when she had these thoughts, but she could not help them. She found herself resentful of Olga when she would call from Petrus, where she would be having lunch with a mutual friend. She almost did not want to know. It was worse when long lost friends trooped in at very short notice to say hello and welcome Dahlia. She hated seeing them in fancy pants that looked like they were tailored for Barbie! She missed that she could not just grab her keys and dash out of the house to grab some chocolate or toothpaste or chicken, whatever!

On that day, she sat on her bed, clothed in her bathrobe and nothing else, with no desire to change this situation. If it ain't broke, don't fix it, eh? She lacked the motivation to get dressed or undressed, brush her hair and teeth, much less cook. Her diet consisted of whatever she could lay her hands on, except days where Kaobi was around to take care of her. He would cook or order take-out. He would vacuum, he would iron, take out the bin, do the recycling, sort out the electrical problems, defrost expressed breast milk and serve it to her while she lay on the couch (and he got it to the perfect temperature every time. She longed for him to get it wrong so she could use it as an excuse to be grumpy). He would even re-arrange her wardrobe if he had to. He filled huge voids. Leila was grateful, but...*sighs*. That in itself presented its own issues. She was aware that his bond with the baby was not biological and she was sometimes furious about it. She was also enraged by the fact that he was not her husband. She wanted him to be so that she could understand why he looked after her and Dahlia so effortlessly. By the same insane token, she did not want him. She did not want anybody! She took her anger out on him at the slightest opportunity, and attacked him from time to time. Bless him, but for his good nature, she was sure he would have run miles, but he stuck it out and took her unprovoked verbal attacks.

'Why the fuck are you asking me if I want anything from the shops? Why are you rubbing it in my face that I cannot up and go just like you, that wherever I go I have this *thing* attached to my breasts? And look at the state of them?' This was typical and once, at that point, she snapped open the buttons of her blouse. Kaobi hurriedly walked (no, ran) away shaking his head and sighing.

'Don't use that kind of language in front of the baby,' he would say gently. And Leila would both melt and burst into tears, lean in for a hug, which was always on offer, or explode and scream at him for sitting so far up his moral high horse that he was no longer visible. Kaobi never knew which version of her to expect. He knew the pressures of hormones and understood that with the right care, she would be a lot better. This was normal; there was no reason for him to be medically concerned just yet. All he did was all he could do – he persevered with patience and love.

A journey of a thousand miles begins with a single step.
Lao-tzu

Chapter Twenty-Eight

Violently craving substitutes…

Haagen-Dazs. Haagen-Dazs will melt between my lips and cause me to 'mmmm'. Haagen-Dazs will not part my lips slowly, or fiercely. He won't taste of stale tobacco or Listerine or just man. He won't put his arms around my waist and pull me close until I feel feminine or dainty or sexy. Haagen-Dazs may flirt on my lips, but won't intentionally tease my senses or stare at me, inveigle me into predicting the pleasure to come.

I can stick my tear-stained face out of the window on a typical winter's night. The wind will dry my tears. The wind will whisper, whisper so soothingly, so alluringly, but it will be incoherent to my ears – to my temporary deafness. Dear Wind, do you not know that an aching heart can cause the ears to stand oblivious to the beauty of nature? The wind will be great and reassuring, albeit automatically; the wind will not kiss them away, neither will it employ whispers of sweet nothings to ensure a genuine smile.

If I listen hard into the night, I might catch a love song in the air. It might be the combination of emotional overdrive plus beautiful wind. The dancing trees might even inspire me. And as the trees dance in accordance with the rhythm of the wind, I may sway side to side and convince myself that I feel incomplete because it is not summer and there are therefore no green leaves to dance with me. Failing that, I might imagine that the void in the moment is simply because there are no chirping birds to inspire some vocals.

If I shut the window and head to my bed in dire need of some slumber, my Judas tears will start again. And if I long for some comfort and lay forth on my pillow, duck feather-filled pillow will accept my head into its bosom, but will not dry my tears either. My pillow will soak in my tears, but will not kiss them away – not naturally anyway.

My huge teddy bear will not wrap its legs around mine. It will not force me to entangle with it. It will not take out my trapped hair strand from my earring or kiss me down my spine. It will not send a familiar breath into my face, stare at me when I sleep or say 'I love you', or smile before I drift into slumber. Not even a last call of the night should I expect.

So Mr Pretend Phallus will perform his duty, but he is poor at multi-tasking. He cannot take instructions regarding anything other than to do with south of my anatomy. In addition, even that requires the assistance of my fingers and imagination. And where finger takes over, finger needs tongue. Sigh!

And when I dream, I dream happy because that's the only substitute that works…somewhat. However, the fantasy within my dream always takes flight before I awake. See…that's the problem.

The dream doesn't last so I do not get to wonder if there's a single rose on the empty pillow beside me to make me smile, or better still, that familiar breath saying 'good morning, gorgeous', or the smell of breakfast coming my way in bed, or even an invigorating first call of the day.

And if I get through work and pretend that it's OK because none of these things should exist while I make a living, but do drinks with the crew after work, I can sit with the crowd and be normal. I can laugh and joke, I can wine and dine, but cannot ignore that all twelve of them are simply amazing, and I can happily drink straight out of the same brandy bottle as the lot of them. My goodness – the germs! However, when it comes to the germs of the passion I offer, not one of them is entitled to accept.

So I get home way too early, I even catch EastEnders, and it's a brilliant episode. But my half-full or empty wine bottle can't understand my superficial giggle. My half-full or empty wine bottle can't share the stories about the sordid twelve and how much they crack me up. It can't even hear about my day at work or empathise. Sympathise? Ha! Now, that's a luxury!

And the half-full or empty wine bottle won't dim the lights either. No, I have to get my pathetic tipsy arse up and do that myself.

So tonight in my pity party for one, I know that it will be Haagen-Dazs and wind and pillow and teddy bear and no call or kiss and the option of Mr Pretend Phallus. I will wake up tomorrow and it will be work, smiles, and the crew of twelve with a bottle of brandy and later, the wine bottle over EastEnders. Therefore, as I reach to dim the lights I look forward to my slumber. There I will dim the lights and reach out and there will be you. You will pull me in your arms and we will slow dance to Kenny G before you kiss me. I shall have no need for Haagen-Dazs or wind or pillow or telephone or teddy bear. You will singularly do all that for me, and the bonus will be that you will be real. I will cry out in sheer delight. I will be complete in my mind and body.

Obviously, I am violently craving substitutes of you. I am going out of my mind, with the basic needs of every woman that only you can fulfil. I long for you. I am hungry for your existence within my inner circle. I want to de-ostracise you from emotions and hunger and inherent desire I want to share… with you.

There is only one tragic spin to this story – even if you accept my proposal, you can't really – you don't exist!

Good luck! ☺

Leila x

Chapter Thirty

She missed having a spontaneous life, an adult life, with adult conversation (she had taken a year out on maternity leave). She knew she wouldn't swap her new life for the world, but truth be told, even for a couple, she could imagine it would be hard – to be a single mother, Leila learnt patience, determination, strength from deep within, continuous prayer and to give up on her love for seven hours' sleep every night. One night, lying in bed, it hit her. It had been dinosaur years since a man had touched her. She was horny. Her dildo was overused, the showerhead offered no surprises, but strangely, she lacked the motivation to do anything about it. She knew she violently craved substitutes – ice cream, chocolate, massages, but she knew at that moment, all she wanted was a man, a life-size man. She lay in bed wondering if this was all life was going to offer. She felt guilty about that as well, but could not help herself.

'Kaobi...' She had picked up the phone.

'You called me Kaobi. This is serious!' he joked. She ignored the joke.

'I'll arrange for Olga to watch Dahlia tomorrow night. Do you fancy going out to the cinema or something?'

It was all arranged! It was platonic and honest, but she could not help wondering why she had asked him. Should she not be in search of a date?

'It's all arranged then: 18th September at 6 pm!'

The next evening Leila looked gorgeous in her simple James Perse's olive sheer jersey scoop neck tank, Vivienne Westwood jeans and Alexander Wang olive open-toed boots. She had a young pretty face; she was 34, but could easily pass for 28, Kaobi had said. Her hair was done up in a loose bun, her make-up nearly non-existent, but perfect. But for her Chopard necklace and Nixon gold-tone stainless steel watch, she wore no jewellery (obviously her wedding ring was long gone). Leila felt like she was missing out on life and decided she would travel by public transport.

'I'll meet you at Aldgate East,' she said to Kaobi.

'Right!' Kaobi responded, a bit shocked. Leila drove EVERYWHERE. Kaobi humoured himself, musing that motherhood and the winds of change were obviously doing funny things to her.

Leila took her time when she walked to the station, taking in the fresh air and noticing the world as it was. She was conscious of the strangers in the street, wondering what their stories were. At the station, she bought her ticket and flirted with the ticket inspector. He looked a bit like Akash and, for a minute, she wondered how he was. But it was only for that minute. Somewhere on the district line, a few stops before Aldgate East station, there was a beautiful man with his Italian girlfriend. His hair was tidy and his blue jeans and light brown shoes blended perfectly, which Leila loved. He wore a dark blue French Connection polo shirt. He must have been about six feet and two inches tall. Strapped around his right shoulder and left lower waist was a guitar. He played the guitar effortlessly and beautifully. It was an unrecognisable tune, but it appealed to Leila's senses. She got lost in his music. He seemed lost in thought himself, although he was looking at his girlfriend. Leila guessed that he might have been looking at her, but thinking other thoughts, which she knew nothing about. She wondered if that would have been the thoughts of passers-by when she sat in the park with Akash and he sang to her. Leila felt the impulse to reach out to him, to hold him in her arms. As he played his confused, hopeful, but beautiful melody, Leila lusted after him. She wished he would stare at her, sing to her, hold her, and play her as he did that lucky, lucky guitar. Each stroke on the guitar strings was deliberate and sensual in her mind. She was jealous of this stranger and the Italian beauty that called him 'my man'. She eventually called him Jeff, and she thought how the name suited him. She wondered what his story was. This scene was irrelevant in the grand scheme of things. They were strangers; he would never be anything other than her random fantasy from the underground. She would probably replay this scene with many endings during her daily showerhead episode. Maybe she would imagine sitting opposite him and telling him how much she wanted to sit astride him and have them make some music of their own. All this was inconsequential, however; Leila was knocked for six by her sudden realisation – she was lonely… and horny and wanted to do something about it!

'You look breath-taking!' Kaobi said as she walked up the stairs at the station. Leila had hesitated after her sudden realisation; she had been tempted to go back home and call the 'date' off, but – too late – Kaobi had caught her eye. She did not want to get caught up in an awkward situation. She loved Kaobi platonically sometimes, sometimes romantically and sexually, but deeply. She loved his soul. Regardless of that fact, he was always firstly her best friend, her rock and the one person she could not live without. They often listened to the 'I'm lost without you' song by Bebe and Cece Winans together. The song was one of the most beautiful gospel songs she had ever heard, but she knew it was also their song. She was lost without him, but could bet her last penny on the fact that he would not swap her for the world. She made a note to ponder later. For now, she would concentrate on the wide-grinned Kaobi who was smiling adoringly at her.

'Thanks,' she said, smiling shyly.

'Are you OK?' he asked. She nodded.

'Actually,' she began. 'Should we just have a drink instead? I quite fancy a more social activity.'

'Whatever you want, sweetheart,' he said. As they walked down Brick Street – The Lane Bar – Leila tugged at him to go in there. He smiled. It was dimly lit, but there was no live band. The huge wide screen TVs were tuned in to MTV Base and Tony Bennett's *The way you look tonight* was playing in the background but the TV had other ideas. It was an unidentifiable movie. Kaobi and Leila talked about this and that, but at the point when a stunning brunette stood, hands up and pressed against a wall with a man nibbling on her neck, Leila felt that twinge of jealousy once more; she also felt a twinge of something else just at the entrance of her woman bits.

'I'm jealous of a fictional video?' she thought to herself, alarmed by her own thoughts. Therefore, it was back to Kaobi and his words. Kaobi and his sexy birthmark in-between his eyes and his nose, Kaobi's beautiful light brown eyes – she still was in awe of their luring shade of brown. Kaobi had supple, soft lips. As she examined the top of his head, his broad shoulders, his sometimes-husky voice, his stutter, his aura, she wanted him. She remembered how nicely shaped his bum was as well, and she bit her lip whilst she stroked her tattoo. Kaobi was aware of her preying eyes. He seemed to take her in with deep breaths. She knew he wanted her as much as she wanted him. She remembered the first day they had spoken in the dingy café. She remembered the construction workers and the fact that he had to speak into her ear. She remembered his breath on her neck. She wanted him more! Today!

Kaobi had the willpower of a bulldog. The electricity was exhilarating; Kaobi would not hold her gaze! Nothing happened!

When he kissed her goodnight, she breathed deeply hoping that he would take it a step further. He looked at her and cupped her face in his hands. Leila's heartbeat throbbed loud and irregular.

'Leila, you are beautiful. You are breathtakingly beautiful. There are ifs and buts, otherwise, right here, right now, I would run my fingers through your hair and make an untidy mess of it. I would dishevel you until you lose all composure. I could make you scream uncontrollably, you know I can. You know sometimes I look at you and I cannot believe that a woman as amazing as you would ever want to be in my arms?' He shook his head. Leila smiled and nodded. She knew, she believed, she accepted. She sighed!

She lay in bed later on that night, dressed in her Christian Dior peach lingerie set and stared at the ceiling. This lingerie business was totally pointless and served no purpose but the 'feel-good factor' it offered. Tonight, it was not working. She wanted an old rumpled t-shirt. With her desire for Kaobi choking her, she was unable to concentrate on anything else. She loved him so much. She sat up for a minute and sat before the mirror, analysing the situation.

'If I am honest, I simply cannot deal with the fact that he has a relationship with anyone other than me. I don't really care what she calls herself as long as he is mine. Mine! It's selfish, I know. Still, my head and heart want two different things. My head understands that the void he fills in the practical sense really works for me. My head also knows that I do not always need him. There are times when I am content to have him because I know he will go home and I will have my space. When I am in this mode, I am unperturbed by his circumstances – in fact, I don't care – I even share jokes with him about it. The main problem is my heart. My heart adores him and looks to him as my alpha male. He makes me feel like Cinderella. I feel sheltered and spoilt by him – a feeling that no man (including Akash whom I adored) has been able to induce. I feel like succumbing to him and being 'submissive' because I trust him infinitely. I am independent; I had to otherwise I would not have survived Akash. Kaobi has broken down my walls and reminded me to be vulnerable again. It was great to start with – the flattery, attention, the liberation, the wisdom – it was all good fun. But then he put his heart in mine. He says 'bless you' half a second before I sneeze and naturally, I do the same. Under different circumstances, it would be different, and we both sense this! Meanwhile, in losing myself and becoming vulnerable again (human), I forgot to keep a little bit of myself to myself…' The analysis shocked her. She concluded: *'but his friendship is the best thing that happened to me this year – this decade! This lifetime!'*

She fell asleep. In her dreams, she was reunited with Kaobi in the Lane Bar and the same thing had happened. Only this time, they walked to the station, arms intertwined. On their way there, there was a dark alley. It smelt of all things unpleasant, but their senses were aware only of each other. He loved the perfume she wore and she could not get enough of his male scent. She was so aware of his masculinity. She wanted to bite his biceps and tear his shirt apart with her teeth. He swooped her in his arms and stared into her eyes. He kissed her lightly. That kiss sent electricity all the way down her throat, to the pit of her stomach and ended up contracting the muscles of her hungry bits. He took one deep breath and his hands were unleashed all over her body. Her breasts, her back, her bum. Damn – he even unclasped her bra with two fingers, it was that intense. Moments later, he pushed her against the wall and pressed his hardness against her, Leila gasped, and it was the end. She woke up sweaty and 'moist'. Leila was cursing under her breath, referring to Kaobi as Mr *'Custos Morum'* when she reached for her dildo and put it to good use. Breathing heavily, she lamented about the many tortures endured by a single mother. There would be moments of insanity, stemmed from sexual frustration and/or lack of companionship. She groaned deeply and subsequently fell asleep after realising that her phone book was empty. There was nobody who wanted to take her to the cinema or to dinner or to cuddle her, or even a midnight 'booty call'. There was Kaobi of course, but then again, no, there wasn't! *sigh*

Kaobi lay in bed unable to shake his uneasy feeling – emotional and physical. He had to conceal the physiological reaction to Leila from his wife because he wanted Leila and no one else would do at that moment – not even for the release (relief!). Leila had pushed buttons that evening and awoken his sexual urges. His imagination was running wild with thoughts of what he would have taken absolute pleasure in doing to and with her. It hurt him that she was lonely. He sensed her longing. He wondered if his being drawn to her was born out of the resemblance to his late twin, or if he had actually waited till nearly forty to fall hopelessly in love. His heart had declared her his soul mate. Everything she did made him smile. If she made him angry, it was short-lived and never tampered with what he felt. He wanted to know even the tiniest detail. He was interested in her every sneeze, and then of course, there was Dahlia. He smiled.

By morning, the phase was over. She was no longer horny, but more bizarrely, Kaobi was her good old BFF once more. When he called, it was not unusual and the electrifying moment in The Lane Bar was irrelevant. It was business as usual!

'Until the next episode…' Leila thought to herself. She sighed!

#NoCleverQuotes

Chapter Thirty-Two

Dear Ex

Remember when I was a little seedling, young and full of promise, vulnerable and in need of nurturing and tender care? Remember how you rotated between showering lightly and pouring down aggressively with raindrops that felt like heavy bricks against a little me. Remember how you felt when it seemed to intimidate me. Did you relish the power?

Remember how my eardrums hurt when I heard loud noises? Remember how I held my two hands over my ears? Remember how you threw at me the loudest thunder you could muster, thunderous roars that equated to grenades set off – the type that sent people running helter skelter for cover. The type of grenades that killed people. When I recovered and opened my eyes, remember how you blinded me with lightning.

Remember when I was a thirsty little skinny stem in need of support? Remember how you took me away from the window that was my support and made me stand in my skinny glory, ever so wobbly and dangled a drink two inches from my reach?

Remember when I said I liked the flowerpot I was in because it was red? Remember how you teased me with the machete before you cut me out of it? You left me naked. I had no hands to protect the wicked eyes of the world from my nudity.

*Still, remember when I eventually became that tree. Remember my buds became flowers, my leaves were several inches bigger than expected. Remember my stem became a huge bark, bearing other stems off it, all big and strong. Remember when you approached with an axe. The biggest axe I had ever seen. Remember I was unbreakable. *smile**

I did not go deaf from your roaring thunder. My eardrums are just more powerful than the average. Grenades do not move me either. Raindrops bounce off my leaves and where they do not boomerang, they split into ten to twelve droplets and tickle little leaf clusters. I hear my leaves giggle. I stand un-naked too. I am covered in the brightest, most beautiful colours and these do not sting my eyes. I am beautiful.

Beside tree-me lives my huge ivory tower that shields me from the world and you. I can say that if you hurt me I will hurt you back. I could suck you in and throw you from stem to stem, have the leaves swaddle you and listen to them chuckle subtly while you choke.

OR

I will stand behind my shield and watch you try. Bring your roar and your machete or axe, and stand before me like a huge, ugly monster. Before my eyes you were big and ugly, and I cowered before you for your untold strength over me. Now you are a laughable teddy bear (except you are not cute) and you don't bother me.

Dear Ex, I am untouchable. I am no longer hurtable!
**pouts **
Leila x
(One weird moment, one weird day)

Chapter Thirty-Four

'I got you some sweeties,' Kaobi said smiling down at a beautiful thirteen-month-old Dahlia, who sat contentedly in Leila's lap. She was in good spirits, smiling back at him.

'You are spoiling her, Prince,' Leila said allowing him to plant a kiss on her left cheek. It was a beautiful sunny afternoon in June 1997 – 30th to be precise, so they sat out in the garden. Leila had attempted some hectic DIY gardening, which had partially failed leaving her totally exhausted. Instead of brooding over it, she sat in her new garden shed, sipping on a cocktail she had invented that afternoon, and was trying to tempt Dahlia into repeating familiar words after her. So far, Dahlia had picked up 'mama' for 'mummy', but that was about all she could say with confidence. Other times, she just stared at her mother through glittering eyes of adoration and fascination as she said this one word over and over again.

'She walked four steps unaided yesterday,' Leila said excitedly to Kaobi.

'Really?' he asked, sharing in the joy.

'Will you walk for Prince?' she asked, whispering to her daughter who bore a striking resemblance to Leila as a child, but with a darker complexion, and her light brown hair was more curly than straight now. She had light brown eyes and some facial expressions that reminded her of Akash. Dahlia smiled. Leila put her down on the floor and urged her to walk. She was shy. She had that look Leila normally had on her face when she was embarrassed about something. Kaobi walked to the other end of the garden and held the goodies he had bought her, dangling them to tempt her in to walking towards him.

'Come flower…' he lured. 'Come and get your sweeties,' he called out. Dahlia stared at her mother and then at Kaobi and the sweets that she desperately wanted. Seeing the look of encouragement and approval in her mother's eyes, she took one step forward, and then made her way across the garden.

'Good girl!' Leila called out to her daughter in excitement. She did make it right into Kaobi's arms and gratefully grabbed her reward. Leila skipped happily across, to where the pair of them stood underneath an un-shaded part of the garden. Only a few hours ago, it had rained heavily after a severely long dry spell. The typical British weather could not decide between spring and summer. Leila and Dahlia had sat enjoying the petrichor, ceasing the moment to indulge in the not-so-successful-but-absolute-fun DIY.

'That's the rainbow,' Kaobi was saying to an ecstatic Dahlia, pointing up to the skies. It was colourful as per normal and the brightness reflected much of the happiness Leila felt. She smiled and wandered off to check her plants.

'When is a good season for daffodils?' she was making a note to ask her mum. No matter how many times Mum told her the correct seasons, she would still ring to ask.

She could hear Kaobi whispering to Dahlia about the significance of the rainbow, and how it symbolised God's promise never to hurt the world again by flood.

'Do you want to know what my promise to you is?' and he whispered in her ear. Leila would have given anything to know what the promise he had made her was, but she stayed out of it.

'You've done a brilliant job, sweetheart,' Kaobi whispered not so quietly to Leila. 'You are a really good mum,' he added, smiling at her proudly. 'Adjusting to life as a working single mother is tough!' he added.

'I have you, KK. You help. A lot!' she said appreciatively. Thankfully, Leila's job was flexible. Failed baby-sitting arrangements, sudden illness or general logistical problems associated with childcare did not throw her off entirely. She would sit and let out a long sigh every now and again, but she never wallowed.

'You do most of it yourself. I am just your back office. You are a bri…bri…brilliant mum,' he said, smiling.

'Mam,' Dahlia called out repeating after Kaobi; and when she got praises from Leila and Kaobi for that one word, she said it over again as she wriggled herself free from Kaobi's protective grip onto the floor, walking and crawling on the grass with her toys.

'Maam,' she called out to her mother from across the garden. Leila looked over to her.

'Yes, petal?' she answered delightedly.

'Un,' she said pointing up at the sun as she had seen on *'Teletubbies'* on TV.

'What's she saying?' Kaobi asked.

'Sun,' Leila whispered thoughtfully.

'Very good, Dahlia. Can you see the rainbow?' Kaobi called out to Dahlia, but Leila was lost for a few seconds. She had flashbacks of the twelve-second moment on the beach with Kaobi. A shiver ran down Leila's spine. It was the precise scene she had seen when they planted those seeds. Had she seen her future back then in Kaobi's eyes? She had always known there was something unusual about him, but had never quite been able to place it. She knew that whenever she was upset, Kaobi felt her pain in a way that no one else could. She also knew that he sensed things. Whenever he predicted something, it came to pass. She had never probed further for fear of what she might discover in her quest to uncover the mystery behind him. There was one thing for sure though: he was not like any other person she knew. Still if she said this to anyone, they would dismiss it as ridiculous so she had always convinced herself that these were just figments of her overactive imagination. She thought to herself that she loved him so much, that she had created a mini-god out of him!

Kaobi watched her intently, but said nothing. She regained her composure, went over to her daughter, and planted a gentle kiss on her forehead.

'Who's mummy's little girl?' she asked, smiling sweetly.

Dahlia grinned from ear to ear. Her favourite moments were when she got her mum's smile of approval and encouragement.

Leila walked over to the table and opened her diary. Over a year had gone by and rather than dispose of the previous year's diary, Leila simply stapled the new one over the old one. She had done this for four consecutive years running. She slowly turned to the page in question and read what she had written about the 'twelve seconds'. She stared at the page, and then at Kaobi, and then at Dahlia. Still she said nothing.

'What are you reading?' Kaobi questioned.

'Oh it's just something I wrote a long time ago, Prince.'

'Can I read it?' he asked.

'Errrr, yeah, go ahead,' she replied, hesitating initially, but turning the diary slightly so that he could read the words. He absorbed the words and then asked her:

'Wh…wh…when did you write this and what is…is…is it about? I know the words in…in….in your diary are always a true reflection of the way you…you…you feel at any particular time, and you sometimes transfer those thoughts to your weekly blog for *Silent Symphonies*…' he questioned, curiously peering in her face.

'It's just something I wrote, that's all,' she said dismissively.

'Are you psychic?' she whispered. He turned round slowly and looked directly into her eyes. He spoke so eloquently, Leila wanted to marry him on the spot!

'There is this silent difference between being psychic and prophetic. Some people say it is impossible to be psychic and Christian, Leila. I think the word you are looking for is prophetic! I am more comfortable with that, shallow as it sounds, because I do fit the bill for a psychic, I guess, but a prophet particularly gets his spirit from God. But I don't know. I don't know what I am. Am I? Leila?'

She held his gaze for as long as she could but in terms of the conversation, that was as far as she could handle. It was never discussed again. She said no more, he probed no further so the conversation drifted on other things, mostly centred around Dahlia and her day-to-day needs. She would be starting nursery soon. She had not heard from Akash regarding the child support he had written to offer. Leila was thankful. She did not want his money raising her child. She was not angry with him, she had forgiven him, but she did not want him in her life any more, and the biggest part of her life was Dahlia. Since Dahlia's birth, Akash had phoned her once begging only to hear the sound of Dahlia's voice.

'She's sleeping'

'Please Leila'

'Akash, leave me alone,' she had barked.

'Don't call me Akash,' he had said softly.

Leila had then put the phone down. That had been the last call. Kaobi had suggested to her that despite her hurt, which was understandable, she still had to face Akash some time and thought it wise to consider how much of Dahlia she would allow Akash access to. 'None' was not an option that would work.

'He is her father after all, isn't he?' Kaobi had asked her, inviting her into his arms. Leila had bitten his head off at that point.

'How can you even suggest that, Kaobi? Do you not understand what I went through? He RAPED me,' she reiterated angrily.

'Leila, I know. You did not call the police. You refused for him to be punished. You asked Olga to go and see him in hospital. Why?'

'I don't know what you are talking about, Kaobi.' She had gone ballistic, throwing things about in a blind fit of rage. Only Akash could reduce her to this; it made sense – she picked up the damned bad habit from him anyway.

Kaobi had grabbed her at that point and held her in his arms. She sobbed burning hot tears.

'He shouldn't have done that, KK, he shouldn't have,' she mumbled in-between her sobs.

Then there was the issue of the wrinkly old woman with the scrawny fingers turning up to give her two pence worth on the issue. Leila saw her constantly in daydreams and she made it impossible for Leila to ignore. Apparently, regardless of whether Leila turned left or right, she was always right there – in the left corner…watching! Leila shooed her away, along with thoughts of Akash. For a little added complication, at such times, the only comfort she truly desired was in Kaobi's arms. This was her haven.

'Do I fly or fall?' she asked.

***sigh ***

Leila, Kaobi and Dahlia sat in the kitchen. Leila was cooking and cleaning simultaneously. The phone rang.

'Hello,' and as soon as she heard the voice on the other end, Leila put the phone and sighed.

'Hello, hello, hello,' Gucci the parrot repeated. Naturally, Dahlia joined in from her high chair where she had been otherwise engaged in making a mess of her chocolate mousse. Leila flashed a loving smile and signalled Gucci to be quiet, although she had bought him for Dahlia for mutually inspired speech.

'Who was that?' Kaobi asked.

'Wrong number,' Leila said frantically cleaning the table.

'Leila?' Kaobi called out, raising an eyebrow.

'Prince, it was Kash,' she replied throwing her napkin across the kitchen sink. 'No lectures please,' she snapped sternly.

'No tantrums,' he responded. Leila stared blankly at him.

'Leila, let it go!' he said. Leila made a mocking face at him. He looked at her and shook his head.

'It's not that easy, Prince. I have forgiven him,' she said, frustrated.

'You haven't forgotten. It's a package, Leila and you know it. You need to forgive AND forget,' he stressed.

'It's not that easy, Prince,' she said again, this time, in a muffled, hurt whisper.

'I know, but you have to try and rise above it. You ha…ha…have Dahlia now. What more do you want?' he asked.

'Let's not talk about it, Kaobi.' This was one of Leila's biggest faults. She swept things under the carpet. She would confront an emotion with such determination and when she got stuck, she would shy away from it, completely abandon it. This had invariably contributed to the problems she encountered during her marriage to Akash. They were both really good at it.

'Prepare yourself for it, Leila. He will come knocking. He may not get custody, but the courts will hear him out. With regards to the rape, no one was present. It is your word against his. To complicate things further, English Law has only just in the last few years come to terms with the fact that a man can indeed rape his wife.

'No is no!' Leila said.

'No is no, but yours is a special case. It's your word against his. He will not admit it in court and you never reported it. Leila, Akash won't get access, but it will have nothing to do with the rape!'

'What do you mean? What other reason?' Leila had turned on the tap. She abandoned it, put her cleaning cloth down and turned to him; but Kaobi had disappeared. Her ears pricked up as they drew her gaze to the faint sounds of laughter. She looked through the sliding glass doors. Kaobi had settled Dahlia into his lap, telling her tales about a beautiful princess called Dahlia and singing her hopefully meaningful Nigerian songs. She momentarily forgot about her problems with Akash and her inability to forget what he had done to her so that she could let him share in his daughter's life. She smiled as she listened to his song. Dahlia's absolute favourite Nigerian song was about a rat and a cockroach in a car, with the rat as the designated driver. Even Leila was familiar with the lyrics of that song, often chanting away with Kaobi and turning it into a song-and-dance routine, clapping hands, with Dahlia giggling and performing her best dance. This normally involved a rhythmic 'squat-stand, squat-stand' wiggle. It was hilarious to watch, but the sweetest sight ever to behold. When Kaobi had given her a literal interpretation of the song in English, Leila had laughed endlessly for long minutes. Dahlia was giggling as she repeated easy words after Kaobi and seemed excited at the prospect of being a princess. When the story ended, she clapped her hands exuberantly and threw her arms around a pleased Kaobi, planting him a big saliva-filled kiss as she tried to bite his nose. He tickled her tummy and his eyes softened as he enjoyed her screaming, kicking and fighting in wild excitement. She was a bit of a tomboy. Leila marvelled at just how much Dahlia loved Kaobi. As Kaobi unleashed the child in himself, indulging Dahlia, Leila stood smiling at both of them. They played on, oblivious to her loving eyes, Leila had forgotten about the kitchen tap. The noise of the water had long since been drowned out in the midst of Dahlia and Kaobi's laughter. There was also the rustling winds and the leaves, the rainbow, the butterfly that flew past, mesmerising Dahlia for the second when it danced just on the tip of her nose. Leila heard music, her best song.

'Out of Zion, the perfection of beauty, God has shined'
Psalm 50:2

Chapter Thirty-Six

'Did Nana send you this lovely 'Postman Pat' book?' Leila was whispering to an excited Dahlia who was still ripping the wraps from her presents.

'Book,' she repeated after her mother.

'Yes darling, book… because it's your birthday today. My little girl is two today. It's the 3rd of May.' Leila was saying to her. Dahlia was more interested in persuading Leila to read it to her straight away.

'No darling, this is for bedtime.' Dahlias impending tantrum was halted by the sound of the doorbell – anything to keep the little busy-body active, besides it was often one of mummy's friends with sweets and presents regardless of whether it was her birthday or not.

'Should we have a look and see who's at the door?'

'Door,' Dahlia repeated after her, running towards the door and pointing excitedly.

'Prince, Prince,' Dahlia said excitedly.

'Yes darling, it could be Prince.' Her nappy made her look like a little bow legged soldier ant, Leila noticed, smiling.

Leila chased after her. It was Kaobi with a huge parcel for Dahlia. She jumped on him and gave him a big hug. Kaobi carried her into the house singing 'happy birthday dear princess' to a grinning Dahlia; he held her in one hand and her lit-up birthday cake in the other. Gucci joined in as well. Leila followed closely behind with the presents he had bought. As Dahlia blew out her two candles, there was another knock at the door.

Leila signed for her delivery and came in with a puzzled expression on her face. She tore the envelope open, half smiling as she listened to Kaobi and Dahlia. Seconds later though, the smile was wiped off her face.

'What's wrong?' Kaobi asked, immediately aware of her tense disposition.

She handed him the letter and stared, smiling at Dahlia trying to disguise her lack of equanimity. Kaobi read the content of the letter but said nothing. Dahlias antennas were always the first to pick up her mothers ambience.

'I need a few minutes, Prince, can you watch her for a bit?' she asked.

Kaobi nodded. 'Can I help?' he asked.

'I will let you know. I just need to make a phone call.'

He nodded.

Away from the inspecting gaze of her daughter and the watchful eyes of Kaobi, Leila collapsed into her red rocking chair outside in the garden, shutting her eyes. The chair was always her comfort. It had soothed her when she was heavily pregnant, rocked her and Dahlia to sleep whilst breastfeeding, and she often sat in it when she needed a moment to reflect. She was so engrossed in her thoughts that she did not hear the doorbell ring.

Akash had served her notice of his contact order application. The hearing was in two and a half weeks. There was a further letter inviting her to a conciliation appointment to discuss the possibility of reaching amicable terms ahead of the trial. Leila sighed and picked up her phone.

'Hello Patricia, it's Leila. How are you? I need to discuss something with you. Is this a good time?' And Leila gave Patricia a summary.

'That's a bit ambiguous. Contact means the arrangement for the non-resident parent to write, telephone, visit or stay with the child. What is he asking for?'

'I think he wants visitation rights, Trish,' Leila said scanning through the document quickly with shaky hands.

'Can I come and see you tomorrow? Lunch? 1pm it is. Thanks hun. See ya!'

'Who is Patricia?'

Leila jumped. 'KK, I didn't hear you approach. Where is Dahlia?'

'Bianca-Maria just dropped by with a few more pressies and Dahlia has enticed her into reading her Postman Pat book.' Leila shook her head smiling.

'Persistent like her mother!' Kaobi said and then asked - 'Who is Patricia?'

'I didn't even hear the doorbell,' Leila said and when she realised Kaobi was hell bent on having the conversation, Leila caved in. Sometimes it amazed Leila just how patient Kaobi was with her. To think that he owed her nothing and yet still was so good with her – and Dahlia could not go a week without a dose of Kaobi either.

'She is my Godmother's daughter and the best lawyer money can buy. I can trust her as well.'

'Is there a conciliation meeting?'

Leila nodded.

'Do you want to talk about it?' Leila looked over at Kaobi for a second and then back down at the documents in her hand.

'KK I don't know what to think, I don't know how to react. I don't want him near my little girl, I just don't. I don't know if these are selfish thoughts and actions but I can't bring myself to think in any other way. I am really trying, but I hate him for what he did to me,' she said very quietly.

'Hate is a very strong word, Leila,'.

'How could I not? Who wouldn't?' and then meekly, quietly, humbly, she opened her Bible and read out to Kaobi:

'*The Lord is my light and my salvation – so why should I be afraid? The Lord protects me from danger – so why should I tremble? When evil people come to destroy me, when my enemies and foes attack me, they will stumble and fall. Though a mighty army surrounds me, my heart will know no fear. Even if they attack me, I remain confident.* Psalm 27,' she said as she looked up at Kaobi and handed the Bible over to him. 'Still I derive no comfort from this, Kaobi and I am in a bitter feud with God at the moment and I think he hates me. Why wouldn't He? I look at these words and comforting as they are, I am unable to find enough strength to let go and trust God.'

'He is not angry with you, Leila,' Kaobi said smiling softly then he in turn opened it up and read:

'*... and forgive us our trespasses, as we forgive those who trespass against us*...Matthew 6:4,' Kaobi whispered back to her and waited for any response. When he got none, he added, 'God knows you are human, sweetheart.'

Leila shook her head saying, 'What is the right thing?' Kaobi held her hand. 'The right thing is whatever your heart truly believes to be in the best interest of Dahlia. Dahlia – not you.'

'And what is that?' she asked.

Kaobi replied by reading:

'*Dear friends, never avenge yourselves. Leave that to God. For it is written, "I will take vengeance; I will repay those who deserve it," says the Lord.* Romans 12:19.' He looked in Leila's eyes pleading these words to traverse straight to her heart.

'He has hurt me, Prince...' she sighed and he scrambled through the pages quickly.

'*If your brother sins, rebuke him and if he repents, forgive him.* Luke 17:3. Leila, he...he...he...he is s...s...sorry,' Kaobi whispered to her.

'Why are you crying, my Queen?' he asked softly

'I am crying because...because Princess Diana died in a ghastly car accident in Paris. Every time I have to meet clients for Silent Symphonies in Paris, I go through that tunnel! How horrible! I hate Charles!' she commented.

'I bet you are!' he said laughing. He pulled her in for a hug.

Leila laughed sombrely.

'You haven't stuttered in ages, Prince, only now and again,' Leila remarked, happy for the excuse to break away from the intense conversation. When she got no response to her compliment, Leila sighed once more. There was no escaping this conversation. 'But he is not sorry, Prince. He is still fighting me. He won't leave me alone.'

'Only God is perfect. Fight him if you must, but make sure you are clear in your mind that denying him visitation rights is the best thing for Dahlia.'

After this little sermon, Leila burst into tears in the corner of the garden, well hidden from Dahlia's thoroughly probing eyes. She pulled away from Kaobi and sat rocking in her chair. Kaobi joined her in the chair. He held her, rocked her, and he listened as every sob broke his heart. Unable to stop himself, he joined his lips to hers softly; he wanted to French kiss her pain away.

'I will be inside with Dahlia,' he said tousling her hair fondly. 'I will always be there for you Leila; I just want you to know that it is not the end of the world, sweetheart.' And with that, he left her alone.

As he walked away, he sighed. Nothing would give him greater satisfaction that to take charge of this situation. He wanted her future sorted out. He wanted to know she was safe and happy.

'What a kiss…. WHAT A BEAUTIFUL KISS!' he said in a faint mumble. It felt so good, so natural. Something in him told him this relationship was not to be; not in the way he would want it. He had pledged his life to another, but by the same insane token, he would give up his life in a heartbeat to ensure that her future was paved with naught but love and eternal happiness. He loved every bit of her, and there was, of course, Dahlia. He smiled!

It was a good few minutes before Leila went back into the house to Dahlia, Bianca-Maria and Kaobi, and when she did, she swooped Dahlia into her arms, planting a big kiss on her forehead.

'And who's mummy's bestest little girl?' she asked. Dahlia grinned choking her mum as she overwhelmed her in the biggest cuddle possible. Dahlia was such a happy child; the last thing Leila wanted was to introduce her to some random stranger as 'daddy'. So far, they were doing just fine without him. Inwardly, Leila shivered with fear. Her future was insecure and she hated the lack of control. Even if she forgave him, which she could swear she had done, she did not want him seeing Dahlia. Dahlia was hers! Sensing her thoughts Kaobi looked over to her and offered her a reassuring smile. Leila smiled back; the return smile though was beset with doubt. She thought about his kiss, how good he tasted. She could not believe she still felt exactly as she did at the beach. She would think about it later. For now, Leila had a birthday party to organise.

And it was the night before the conciliation meeting. Akash was sitting in the kitchen staring out of the window with the cordless phone in his hand. He was a cleaned up version of what he had been in the last few months. There were no empty brandy bottles or half-finished cigarette packs anywhere in sight. His speech was coherent once more. He was still seeing the psychologist that Kaobi had introduced him to.

'Olga, I am not trying to make her life miserable,' he said, slowly standing up. He stood astride with his right hand in his pocket. He was quiet for a few seconds while Olga ranted down the phone. He licked his lips. He slicked his hair. He kept trying to speak but she cut him short every time. 'Listen, I don't want that. What can I do? All I want is a share of my daughter's life. I don't even know what she looks like! Do you know what that feels like? I see other parents with their children and I am surmounted with jealousy. I know I hurt her in the past and I have let her move on. She has moved on but I just want to share Dahlia's life,' he was saying.

'And you realise she might have to relive the fact that you have physically abused her in the past, Kash. The past is going to raise its ugly head once more. Are you sure you can deal with that? What happens if the court decides in Leila's favour? Then what?' Olga questioned.

'It's a risk I have to take, Olga. I can't see a way forward. I need to see my daughter,' he replied.

'Well Kash, in that case, I only hope that it all turns out for the best. Leila is not happy about this at all and she will fight you with everything she has got.'

Akash sighed and nodded.

'I don't expect that it's going to be easy but I cant give up,' he said.

'Alright then…Take care then.'

'Bye!'

If only he was as confident as he sounded. He was clean-shaven, he had not had a drink in a while (not excessively anyway), he held his hands out before him and watched them tremble incessantly. Since Leila had turned him into a mad man, he could not stop shivering. He thought himself a coward or a fool, or both.

'Meray ander mardaangi khatam nai hui mein abhi mard hoon! – I still have manhood in me. I am still a man!' He willed his hands to stop

trembling and when they did, he slipped them into his pockets. He stood by the kitchen window and stared at the clouds. All he could see was Leila in her stringy thongs, hanging off the pole in their bedroom. Upside down. Her eyes beheld him with love. He approached the pole. She remained hanging off it and she reached out and cupped his face in her palms. She kissed him lightly on the lips and smiled. Her smile reached her eyes and made them twinkle. She squinted. He carried her off the pole, and on to the bed.

'I need you. You know me. You are the only one that can take care of me. My condition is seasonal, you can take care of me, and I can love you the way you need to be loved. I still love you, Leila,' he said. 'I want to know Dahlia. What a beautiful name. If she has your smile, does she have my hair?'

In the days to come, Leila was overcome by guilt. She did not want to deprive Dahlia of knowing her biological father, but she could not come to terms with the fact that Akash would cuddle her, play with her, love her after all they had been through; all he had done! It just did not seem right. On the other hand, the circumstance surrounding her conception was not Dahlia's fault. Overall, it had not turned out bad, had it? Dahlia was her pride and joy. So what did Leila do? She took indiscriminate days off from work, days off that she sometimes could not afford because the work just piled on her desk and she was behind on her blog. But she took Dahlia to the park. She took her to toddler groups, she took her to shopping centres, play centres, baking classes, pottery making classes, and as many kiddies' parties she could find. Leila was juggling a full time job and trying to overcompensate as a mum. Mother and child suffered.

'Is this really necessary?' Kaobi asked her one evening after a day out to the toyshop, the park and then a two-hour long toddler group.

Dahlia did love the playgroups, interacting with other children and playing. But she had too many toys, met too many people and played so hard during the day that sometimes eating supper was too much activity at the end of a long day and she passed out mid-meal.

'You are a good mum, Leila. You don't need to burn yourself out to prove that!'

'But she loves the playgroups,' Leila said.

'You have taken her to two playgroups in one day! She must be drained! You do not even talk to any of the other mums, so what do you gain from these groups?'

'I want the best for her. The other mums are snotty and they wear sunglasses all the time, so I can't see their eyes!'

'I understand that, sweetheart, but you do enough. Just cut down a little bit,' Kaobi said gently. They both sighed.

Before Leila went to bed that night, she thought long and hard as she stared at a crashed-out Dahlia. Work was suffering, her mental state was suffering and she was physically exhausted. Two groups a week, no new toys for at least three months, trips to the park would be no longer than twenty minutes, and she would trust a nanny! She stroked Dahlia's hair. This motherhood thing was new, with no manual to tell you what was right or wrong; it was all down to her intuition. Her intuition was sometimes a lonely place and was tainted by the guilt she felt. Kaobi was right. She was overcompensating. She would slow down…just a little bit.

'Hello? Olga, hi! How are you?'

'Do you want to speak to Olga?' she asked, lifting Dahlia up on to her lap. Dahlia seemed pleased at the thought and babbled on. It was not the most coherent conversation, but Olga went ahead with it. With the pleasantries out of the way, they talked about the impending case. Olga had initially tried, and failed miserably to act as a conciliator, so all she could be was Leila's best friend.

'I just don't want him in my life Olga. I have forgiven him but he won't let me forget it, will he? Let the courts decide. He says his intention isn't to hurt me but what do you want me to think?' Leila was getting worked up and Dahlia was stealing intermittent glances at her.

Leila looked down at her and kissed her, smack on the lips. That kept her happy for a few minutes while she rounded up with Olga.

'Well at the moment, Olga, I have more pressing issues to attend to. Dahlia needs a bath with Mr Quacky,' and of course Dahlia looked up as her antennas picked up her favourite words. It was time for fun with

Mum, she knew. 'Don't you darling?' she asked, turning to Dahlia who was nodding excitedly.

'Who?' Olga asked irritated because thus far, she had zero maternal instincts. Leila knew that would change eventually.

'Her yellow rubber ducky,' Leila replied, still smiling at Dahlia.

'I wonder if I'll ever be ready for all this,' Olga mused and then continued, 'well have fun with err… Mr errr… whatever, just give Dahl a kiss for me, will ya? And take care, honey, I will see you soon.'

'Akash.'

'Leila.'

And they both stared at each other uneasily, both unsure. Neither of them wanted to fight but while Leila was angry, Akash was desperate.

Not nearly soon enough, it was 8.30 pm. The day had been punishing and they were in their respective homes.

'How did it go? I didn't want to ask while I was driving down,' Kaobi asked Leila as he walked into the house swooping Dahlia into his arms.

'Terrible!' Leila remarked, putting the kettle on for a cup of chamomile tea.

'What happened?' he asked.

'Nothing was agreed so it is going to full hearing. The first hearing is in a couple of weeks. Trish thinks that they are going to try dispute resolution one last time at the first hearing and after that, it could take weeks or months before it will go to a final hearing. I still don't know how to react to Kash. I am battling with that and battling with the rationale behind dragging this out for so long, but Kash is not willing to compromise and neither am I, I guess. I just don't know what to do really,' was Leila's long frustrated response.

This was always an uncomfortable conversation to have with Kaobi. He seemed to distance himself unconsciously from this issue. Leila was right. Kaobi was careful. Leila was unaware of what happened between Akash and Kaobi after they left the hospital room the night Dahlia was born. He knew there was a chance Leila knew they were both in the room, but had said nothing about it. He understood the trauma Leila was left with, but in his professional opinion, he knew Akash was mentally unstable when he raped Leila, still, his loyalty tilted towards Leila's feelings naturally and if his instinct told him she was safe, then she must be. Then there was the protective fatherly bond he felt towards Dahlia. She mattered most. Everything else was secondary, including the tinge of jealousy he felt at the thought of Akash being a dad to Dahlia. The rational, unselfish part of him that loved Dahlia and Leila unwaveringly told him he could live with it.

'Prince?' Leila called out loudly, waking him up from his drifting thoughts. 'Did you hear what I just said?' she asked.

Kaobi nodded and then sighed.

'I'm sure you know what you are doing, sweetheart'.

'What the fuck does that mean? You want me to let him see her as he pleases? How could you?'

'Leila don't do that. Please.'

'Do what?'

'Don't swear. Don't put words in my mouth. Don't!'

She gave him an uninterruptible expression and they had dinner in silence. The only sound in the distance was Dahlia having a full-blown 'adult' conversation with Gucci the parrot as they both danced away to Stevie Wonder's 'Signed Sealed Delivered'. When Gucci said 'my name is Gucci' and Dahlia clapped with elation, Kaobi and Leila broke into a smile but never looked up at each other. Dinner continued in intoxicating silence.

'He can't do that, can he?' Leila asked infuriated.

'Ask for interim custody? Yes he can, Leila.' Patricia then began explaining to Kaobi because Leila was hysterical and impossible to communicate with at that moment.

'The grim reality of the court process is that it can be extremely slow. This is normally what most people in Akash's position would seek pending a full court hearing.' Kaobi nodded nervously, staring at Leila quietly. He walked over to her and wrapped his arms around her.

'You'll be just fine, sweetheart, you...you…you just need to calm down.' Patricia noted the intimacy between them but never asked.

'I'm sorry, Trish. I am calm,' Leila said to Patricia.

'Leila, you can't fly off the handle like this. You need to remain calm and lets strategise. There is a possibility that Akash will have an interim order in place in the next two weeks because the hearing could take weeks or even months. Lets plan our response to the request.'

'What about the fact that he raped me? What about that? It would be too damaging emotionally for me to watch them establish a relationship,' Leila said quietly to Patricia.

'We are going forward with this, Leila. However, in these kinds of circumstances, we have to be prepared for the courts to ask us all sorts of questions. Why wasn't it reported? Where is the evidence? We have to sit down and talk this through properly and I need to explain to you what we will have to do if we are going to bring this forward. So far all we have said to the courts is that they need to take into consideration your broken down relationship and the fact that to date, there has been no sort of relationship between Akash and Dahlia. Leila, are you prepared to relive the rape? Are you ready for all the questions? Rape is a very serious crime. Akash could go to prison if he is found guilty. Can you handle this? What if he opposes, calls you a liar? What happens if he tells the court that you are a vindictive so and so? You heard Olga. Akash is desperate. He is not out to get you, but is hell-bent on being a part of Dahlia's life. What do we do then if he succeeds? Can you live with that? All I am saying is that we need to approach this with extreme caution, as we cannot afford to get it wrong. Leila, are you ready for all this?' Patricia was gentle but brutally honest. There was total silence in the room.

'Leila, come to my office in the morning and we shall go through it all in detail. For now, I think you need to have a nice warm bath and get some sleep. All I ask in the morning is that mentally, you are prepared.' Leila nodded.

'Thank you, Trish. I really appreciate your honesty and patience.' Leila said, reaching out for a hug.

'See you in the morning? 10am?' Leila asked.

Patricia nodded and with one last quick hug, rooted out her umbrella and headed for her car through the rain.

'Kaobi… Kaobi, I want you to tell me what you think about all this,' Leila said, sitting down and inviting Kaobi to sit with her.

'I guess it cannot be easy for you to stand back and watch him take over like this and I wouldn't be human if I said to you to feel nothing, sweetheart. I just want you to be careful and that would have meant being a bit flexible… you know… a bit sens…sens…sensitive to Kash's rights, but you clearly don't want him anywhere near Dahlia. Personally, I think you should try to work towards some sort of out-of-court settlement with him, but if it isn't what you want then I will back you up all the way.'

Leila sighed. 'You don't express too much of an opinion when it comes to this issue, do you, Kaobi?' she asked almost annoyed but trying her best to disguise it.

'But I just gave you a long speech!' he protested.

'You didn't stutter!' she said excitedly.

'I did. Only a little bit though.' He indicated with his thumb and forefinger.

They both smiled, and then just as quickly, it was back to the matter at hand.

'Don't blame me, sweetheart. This is a very delicate situation. It is one time – I do realise that. I ca...ca...can't tell you what to do, but I can support your decision and be there for you regardless. I am human, Leila; it would be impossible to be totally confident in what I say all the time,' he said softly. Leila thought it was odd for Kaobi to say that. Kaobi was ALWAYS confident in what he said so much so that whenever he said something, Leila took it as the gospel truth without question.

'There is something else, Leila.' Leila looked up.

'Sounds serious…' she commented uneasily.

'It is!' He nodded. 'In a week and a half I have to go to Nigeria with Ada and the kids.'

'Nigeria?'

Kaobi nodded again.

'But I need you to be with me for the trial,' she protested.

'My mother is dying, sweetheart. She has cancer,' he said softly.

'I'm so sorry, Kaobi. I noticed you hadn't been yourself in the last week and I didn't even ask. I am so sorry.' Leila reached out to Kaobi, apologising.

'That's OK, sweetheart; you weren't to know. I will try and be back before the first day of the full hearing. I should not be too long. I just want to assess the situation for myself and if it isn't too late, I might bring her back with me for surgery over here instead.' Leila nodded her understanding.

'And Adrian and Armani are going with you as well?'

'Yeah, it will be a good opportunity for them to learn more about their roots.

'They are only young…' Leila said smiling at the thought of the two little boys being told all the Nigerian tales that she had grown to love. 'I bet they love those stories as well, Prince, don't they?' she asked.

'Oh they do! Just like Dahlia, they get excited. In fact, under different circumstances, I quite hoped you and Dahlia would have liked to have flown out for a break as well, but not this time – it isn't appropriate and you have this case going on as well.'

'Have you bought your ticket yet?' she asked, her tone becoming sombre to match her sudden change of mood. 'I wish you were going under more pleasurable circumstances,' she added.

He nodded and smiled, appreciative.

'The travel agent will ring me with a quote in the morning and I will let you know when exactly.'

'Do you want to talk about your mum?' she asked softly.

'I'm scared to talk about it Leila. Every time I think about my trip to Nigeria or Mum's condition, I get a very weird feeling in…in…inside me. I am not sure what it means. I'm scared, Leila. I am scared of not being here for you and Dahlia, I am scared of losing Mum, I feel guilty because I am worried that I haven't spent enough time with her since my sister died.'

'Hey!' she said, reaching out to his arm. 'Where is all this coming from? You don't owe me anything, Kaobi. Having you by my side is a privilege. You go and be with your mum. I am sure she will be fine and I am sure she knows that you would spend more time with her if you could. You have just built a life in a foreign country. That's not your fault!' Slowly, Leila closed in on the two feet or thereabouts between them and engaged him in a long, long comforting hug. It wasn't one sided. Both Leila and Kaobi derived mutual reassurance from that hug. He went over to where Dahlia lay in the corner in her make shift bed by the aquarium. Many nights when her mum had guests, Dahlia would talk to Gucci endlessly and when they both knocked themselves out with senseless conversation, she would lie there and watch the fish until she fell asleep. This had been one of those nights. Kaobi planted a kiss on her forehead and smiled at her lovingly.

'Leila, I'll come by the house a couple of times before I leave, yeah?' he whispered softly so as not to wake Dahlia up. Leila nodded and they both tiptoed to the door. With a quick peck on either cheek, he ran to the car. Leila stared on after him, watching the rain pour down aggressively. When his car was a little dot in the distance, she shut the door and then gently carried Dahlia upstairs into her bed. When she eventually lay down to sleep, she realised how much she and Dahlia loved and needed Kaobi and she took for granted that he would always be there for her. She knew he would, but ultimately, he had his life to live as well and the nature of their 'lover-homie-friend/secret-lover/soul mate' relationship was such that there would be times when something else would come before her. She understood that, but it also hit her that second how dependent she was on him. She felt that stab in her heart again. She wanted, but could not have him. She sighed. She had to be mature about it. She sent him a text message saying that all would go well and he needed to think positive like he had always preached to her. Somehow, she could not help but lay awake thinking of Akash and the situation at hand, although her thoughts occasionally drifted to Kaobi, her prince, her rock! At that point, the vibration of her phone interrupted her itinerant thoughts. It was a text message from Kaobi, which read:

'Sweetheart, it gets only worse to get even better, trust in the Lord and his words will come to pass. Just believe... I know I do...and I love you!'

'Lord, please heal Kaobi's mum and bless her with long life...and please sort me out!' she said to the ceiling. She yawned. She saw the wrinkly old fortune-teller with the scrawny fingers. She was dressed in black and the look on her face was vacant. Leila ignored her completely.

Albeit the dark clouds that surrounded her skies, Leila slept peacefully. In her dreams she slept in Kaobi's arms. Bliss!

The majority of her morning was of course, spent with Patricia, working out the details of the case before them. In between her busy day, she pondered on how Kaobi seemed distant, she wanted to make sure it was just his mothers health that was worrying him – nothing more. She rang him later to confirm, but Kaobi was giving nothing away. He did in fact, sound quite irritated by her questions. He accused her of having an over active imagination, then apologised. For the sake of peace, they talked about the weather!

It was Tuesday night, 5th of May when Kaobi passed through quickly to tell Leila that he had eventually booked his flight for the next day!

'Wow! That is soon!' Leila remarked uneasily.

'Yeah there was a can…can...cancellation and I…I…I need to get on that plane because Mum is not getting any better unfortunately. Ada and the boys will have to join me later on in the week,' he said as he gulped down a glass of water.

'Thirsty?' she asked.

'Parched,' he responded.

Leila wished there was something she could do to calm his nerves. She knew he was worried. She could tell just by looking at him. She knew how much he loved and respected his mum and thought that perhaps this was his way of dealing with things.

'I shouldn't be gone too long though, sweetheart. I am sure the trial will be fine. Whatever the outcome, it will be for the best and I…I…I will always be here right behind you, you know that, d…d…don't you?' Leila nodded.

'When is the hearing for…for…for interim contact?' he asked.

'Next Tuesday!'

'A week today?' Leila nodded.

'Well I shall be ringing you for the update, and to find out how you are bearing up.'

'You have to go now, don't you?' she commented, noticing how fidgety he was.

'I d..d..do!' he replied, smiling at Dahlia who was in his arms.

'Is there anything I can do to help, Kaobi?' Leila asked.

'You've done everything you need to, sweetheart. Thanks,' and then added as an afterthought, 'well you could both walk me to the door though.'

'We would walk you all the way to the car, Prince, but it's pouring down with rain AGAIN!' Leila remarked as she took a protesting Dahlia out of Kaobi's arms. She was half-asleep and irritable and had been very comfortable in Kaobi's nice warm arms.

'It hasn't stopped raining since I left here three nights ago, has it?'

'It doesn't feel like it has,' she agreed, noticing that they were both just making polite conversation. Kaobi would be back in a couple of weeks at the latest. She was being unnecessarily clingy.

'You will take care of yourself and come back to me and Dahl in one piece, won't you?' Leila asked. Kaobi smiled.

'Of course I will. I should only be a couple of weeks at the most.' Then he turned to Dahlia

'Princess, will you take care of mummy?' he asked Dahlia who was by this time fully wide-awake.

Dahlia smiled at Kaobi, but was blissfully unaware of what was going on. She was conscious of the fact that she had to say goodbye to Kaobi and it was a special goodbye because he was going away to Nigeria for two weeks and her mum had explained to her that Nigeria was far, far away.

'Bye bye, flower,' he said planting a little kiss on Dahlia's lips. Dahlia stretched her little hands out waving bye.

'Sweetheart, take care of you,' he said and he kissed her lightly, softly on the lips. Although slightly taken aback by that, Leila was too emotionally distraught that she was on her own for a couple of weeks to ponder upon the slow, light, deliberate brush against her lips. It was not their customary parting gesture (well at least it had not happened since the night they had made crazy love. Hang on, oh yes it had – in the garden, in her rocking chair. That was comfort, this was…this was different. She would ponder later). Maybe she would have been more reactive, seized the moment to get a decent snug, if she had felt something sexual in the kiss, but as far as she was aware, it was honest, heralding a message Leila was unable to decipher.

'Prince, your mother will be fine, OK?' she reassured him once more. He smiled.

'Please, please, please keep in touch, OK?' she reiterated and then added, 'She will be OK; your mum…she will be OK.'

'Will she?' he asked for reassurance.

'Of course she will.'

'Go!' she whispered to him, giving him a mini push.

And without a second's delay he ran straight into his car, started the engine and with a final kiss blown to Dahlia and Leila, he drove off in a hurry. Like the night before, she stood by the door, although this time, she had Dahlia in her arms. They both stood staring after Kaobi. She was trying to distract Dahlia by talking to her all about the rain, and how it's God's way of watering the plants. He watered all the plants that were outside, especially those that had no homes. Dahlia was intrigued. All the while, she told the stories perfunctorily. Her mind was with Kaobi. She wondered if there was something he was not telling her. What was that she sensed in his aura? She couldn't believe he would be out of the country either. Kaobi was normally the first person she called if she had any news, if she was in any crisis, if Dahlia learnt a new word, anything! At that moment, Dahlia started to cry.

'Prince, Prince,' she was saying over and over again as the tears streamed down her beautiful face.

Leila cuddled her soothingly saying, 'Shh! He'll be back soon, darling!' and so that night she kept an upset Dahlia in bed with her. Once again, who was the comforter and who, the comfortee? Leila was not sure, but she sure held on tightly and cried…for no apparent reason.

Through the rear view mirror, Kaobi could see that Leila stood staring on after him with Dahlia in her arms. He knew she sensed his weirdness. He had intended to tell her that his journey might take a little longer than scheduled, that she needed to prepare because he might be away for a while depending on his mother's situation but somehow the words never came out right. Besides she would have asked him loads of questions, loads of questions that he would have been unable to answer and then she would have accused him of keeping things from her. The truth was that every time he thought about his trip to Nigeria he got that customary chill down his spine. If his mother was going to die, he was not prepared. Somehow, he didn't think that was it though, but he knew that whatever it was would be something so devastating that he would struggle!

'I'll try and be back soon!' he said to the mirror, as their images faded into the distance until they were a tiny speck. If only he could get himself to believe those words. He would work towards keeping his promise but that was the absolute best he could do. Whatever it was, he would have to face up to it somehow. His mother could die; everyone had to die at some point. What could be worse than that? That was the worst that could happen, right? Was it?

The elements were furious! It was raining cats, dogs and lions. Kaobi was grateful when he turned into a less busy road. He stopped outside a not-so-familiar house. It was a beautiful little mansion, but he could sense the loneliness from afar. It was certainly no home. He braced himself, and then pushed the button. Ding Dong! He still was not convinced of his sanity at that moment. He took a deep breath.

Akash answered the door and stared with no expression on his face, until he raised one eyebrow slightly. Kaobi did the same.

'You're the doctor, right? Chetachi-Ubah?'

'Indeed,' Kaobi replied in the most confident voice he could conjure up. He repeated his last name, pronouncing it correctly. Akash nodded non-committedly.

'Can I help?'

'I have a message for you.'

'From Leila?'

'No. From me.'

SILENCE.

'Listen carefully. She has been through a lot. Something will happen that will change your lives forever. If you get the chance to be with her again, do me a favour and get it right. I understand your diagnosis. You have been depressed and borderline bipolar. I get that. But practise some honesty and you should be OK. Love her right!'

SILENCE

'And this is a message from you?'

'Yes.'

'In your capacity as?'

'That's not important. If you hurt her again, I will hurt you…my… my…myself!' 'The damn stutter!' he thought.

'OK, agony aunt. I thought I was the crazy one! You can't string a sentence together and you think you can hurt me.' Akash stood akimbo marking his territory. They matched each other in size, but were of different dispositions. Akash was bold, loud and confident. Kaobi's confidence was silent but intoxicating. He stared back at Akash, not intimidated by his stance, or the fact that they stood so close to each other that it was a definite invasion of personal space. Kaobi smiled from the corner of his mouth. 'A tiger does not proclaim his own tigritude… he pounces!' he said quietly through squinted eyes (no stutter! Kaobi rejoiced inwardly!), and he jerked forward slightly.

'You what? Tigri who?'

'Goodnight.' And he made his way back to the car doubting his sanity!

He had not planned that, nor did he know what to expect. He accepted the encounter for what it was, believed in the fecundity of the words. He could not question it even though, of course, it made him even more nervous about the not-too-distant future.

For most of the night, he packed his suitcase like an automated service. Ada assured him all would be well repeatedly, but it seemed to have little or no impact on her husband. She reached out and rubbed his back. He normally would get the hint. She was asking to help calm his nerves, give him a release, comfort him and be one with her. He shrugged his shoulders and when he eventually turned to look at her, his eyes stared back void. The phase Kaobi was going through was difficult for him to understand mentally because for the first time in the history of his abnormal prescience, he was unable to predict the future.

When Ada went into the kitchen, she scratched her head in frustration. She picked up the phone and dialled Kaobi's mother.

'Is Mama Kaobi there?' she whispered, making sure the kitchen door was shut.

'Mama, Kaobi is acting really weird. He seems to be grieving your loss because the doctor exaggerated it.'

'My daughter, it has been over thirteen years since my son returned home. My daughter died in the white man's land. Will I see him before he suffers the same fate? Who will inherit his father's title? Who will learn the herbs for the village women? Will he not take on an *Ozo* title? If we need to lie to him to bring him home, then so be it. He will forgive me when he gets here!'

'As you wish. But I do not support it.'

'I married you to him. It is not in your place to support or not; you will do as I say!'

Ada hesitated. 'I go along with it to see if you can give him something to save our marriage. His heart never belonged to me, Mama, but his loyalty and faithfulness did – but now these waver. He is distracted. When he touches me, it is obvious he does not want to.'

'It is well, my daughter. There is nothing that cannot be fixed. Goodnight.'

Ada put the phone down and ran upstairs. She watched her husband weep for a few minutes. He was putting an envelope into his suitcase.

'What's that?' she asked.

'Nothing.'

What's the matter?' she asked.

'I don't know.'

'Why won't you let me comfort you? I know there is someone else. All I have ever wanted is your love.'

Kaobi turned to her and smiled sadly. 'We never dated. There was neither an electrifying first kiss nor moments where fireworks went off.'

'I learnt to love you,' she said desperately.

'I didn't.'

SILENCE

'We could not produce these boys naturally, Ada, but you stood by me for years and supported me. For that reason, I gave you myself and dedicated all that I had to you and the boys.'

'Kaobimdi! You have not had sex with me in months!'

'I have not had sex with anybody in months! That is the truth.'

'You are lying.'

'I am not. But I admit that for the first time in my life, I found an emotional connection. Please find it in your heart to understand that it was not for lack of dedication to you. If I was not dedicated, I would have left you.'

'Why do you tell me these things? Can you not see how bad it hurts?'

'Because I am uncertain of the future. I look at you and I do not know what I see in your eyes. All I ask is that you are careful. Do not do anything you will regret and harbour no hatred in your heart for me or anyone else that you feel might be to blame. You are my wife till death us do part, I still promise.' He cupped her face in his hands for a minute and added, 'You are the beautiful mother of my two sons and you carry my name because it is rightfully yours.'

'That's not enough!' she said with bitter resentment.

'I know,' he responded.

Akash's sleep was disturbed. Kaobi's words were on his mind. He needed Leila because no other person could understand him. If he told her of his condition – his being prone to depression, his bipolar symptoms, she would stand by him. Most people would run. Leila was loyal. He needed her. As for the crazy doctor, Akash shook his head. 'The man fucking threatened me! Tigritude?' Akash rebuffed. 'Is that even a word?' and then he thought, 'but he pretty much encouraged me to get her back. What the fuck!'

We human beings are strange creatures and still
reserve the right to think for ourselves.
Marilyn Monroe

Chapter Forty-Four

Thursday, the 7th of May, 1998

'Right KK, you arrived safely then?' Leila was excited for Kaobi. Despite the grim nature of his visit, she hoped he appreciated the fact that it was sunny Nigeria. He was home! Kaobi told her all about the buskers at the airport, the people who had sniffed the foreign air around him and tried to make away with his pounds. He had arrived in Lagos and would be making his way to Onitsha to meet his mother. He was traveling by road and was dreading it. Apparently, there were more potholes than before he left and even then, it had been quite bad. The country was in economic and political disarray with strange happenings. The president of the country, Abacha had died and was succeeded by Abubakar. Abiola had died in custody a month later. He died in detention of a heart disease before he could be released in a general amnesty for political prisoners. That week, rioting in Lagos had led to over sixty deaths, so it was chaotic. Kaobi explained that he had to travel by road through Benin, which had a bad reputation, but was worse than he remembered. The rate of armed robbery had risen because poor people simply had no food and no opportunities were provided for them to take on gainful employment. Still, the artwork from Benin was amazing!

'Yes Prince, I remember the bronze sculptures. The Oba and his wife, right?' she asked. Kaobi obviously agreed on the other end of the line. Leila smiled. She loved Nigeria because she saw it all through his eyes and heart. On a brighter note, he had said, he had just had a delicious meal of assorted meat suya garnished with onions, tomatoes and pepper. He explained once again what it was and Leila salivated. She had acquired a taste for spicy food because of Kaobi and pregnancy. He explained that he would travel to Onitsha. He would probably lose reception, but he would call before he set off. He did! Leila was glad and she thought he sounded a little less distant and more positive. He was probably glad to be there finally, where he had more control. He spoke to Dahlia and told her how much he loved her!

'So we are set for tomorrow then?' Leila asked

'Yeah we are. Go and get some sleep Leila. We have a nerve-racking morning ahead of us.' Patricia urged.

'Thanks Trish. See you in the morning, 7.30?'

'Sure. I am half way through my day by then.'

Leila put the receiver down and brought out a couple of suits. Should she wear a dull suit to reflect her current mood or something bright to disguise her gloom? She picked up her Helmut Lang dress. It was a sleeveless dress in black. It had a scoop neck collar and a button-loop closure at the back and at each side seam. She matched it with a blue blazer. She turned to sort Dahlia out for the night and just as she put her to bed, the phone rang yet again. She was getting tired of this. Exasperated by the pranks (at least she thought they were pranks), she picked up the phone and naturally gave a very irritable 'Hello!' After a few seconds of Leila pleading with the person on the other end of the phone to speak, it went dead. The voice on the other end just hesitated and put the phone down. This was the third time in the last hour. She tried to trace the call by redialling, but it was a withheld number. Sometimes of course, this meant that it was an international call. For a second she thought it might be Kaobi trying to reach her, but when she spoke to him, he was on his way to Onitsha to drop off his stuff and head the little village to meet his mum who was with relatives. He had mentioned that he would have very dodgy signal, as the area was still quite remote and underdeveloped. She realised at this point that she did not have his telephone number. Although this left her a tad uncomfortable, she knew there was no reason to worry.

'Could it be Akash?' she wondered. She discarded the thought. Other than the stupid quest to win access to Dahlia, Akash seemed to have matured somewhat. The phone did not ring again so Leila fell asleep. She dreamt of Kaobi. He was moving his lips frantically but there was no sound. She knew he was talking to her but lip reading his frenzied speech was impossible. The protruding veins in his neck indicated that he was screaming.

'I can't hear you' she screamed back, reaching her hand out to him. Every time she reached out, he held out his hands to accept, but he changed position without moving his feet. Sometimes this happened in slow motion and at other times, she dreamt the scene in fast forward. This frightened Leila back into consciousness with a jerk. Leila's pillow was soaked in sweat and her breathing was heavy. She peered in her clock. It was 3am. She made her way to the bathroom and threw some cold water over her face, checked to see that Dahlia was ok and then settled back to sleep. But for the wrinkly old woman making an appearance to remind her that destiny would be fulfilled, her slumber was dreamless and unperturbed… for a while.

The phone did ring again and Leila put on the bedside lamp and noted it was 5.15am. Cursing incoherently under her breath, Leila reached for the phone.

'Hello' she answered sounding groggy.

'Leila?'

'Yes?' She didn't recognise the voice but… hang on… where had she heard that accent before?

'This is Mrs Chetachi-Uba…Senior'

Leila jumped, and sat upright in her bed.

'Who?'

'Kaobimdi's mother!' She threw her duvet off

'OK something is wrong. What's wrong?' she asked. The line was unclear.

'Take down this number!' Leila obeyed without question. It was a number in Nigeria. Leila recognised the pattern of the digits from various occasions when Kaobi had scribbled a number for one long lost friend or the other.

'Whose phone number is this? Kaobi's?' Leila asked impatiently. She was so sure at this point that her heartbeat was definitely louder than both their voices.

'That is the number to the Benin Teaching Hospital, Benin City, Nigeria'

Where? Benin? Kaobi had spoken of Lagos, Onitsha, and a village on the outskirts of Onitsha but had never mentioned Benin. Hang on – yes, he had. It was the half way town between Lagos and Onitsha, the town with the ritual killings and bad roads, but beautiful art. Leila gulped.

'Our Prince was in a ghastly car accident yesterday on his way to Onitsha'. She said hurriedly.

'Accident?' she asked alarmed. She definitely was not expecting to hear this.

'Both his legs are amputated from above his knee. He seems to have an infection. We do not know what will happen.' She said.

'What?' Leila asked in a horrified whisper.

'He is in intensive care and awaits a third blood transfusion. There are moments when he is conscious and clear. He wants to speak to you.' This was followed by an undertone murmur that sounded like an incongruous grumble/protest of the most grotesque nature.

'Amputation? Third blood transfusion?'

'Just call, they know who you are and they will put you straight through to speak to him'.

'OK. I will call now' She had so many questions. 'Is he going to be alright?'

'I don't know,' and without another word, Mrs Chetachi-Ubah Senior hung up, leaving Leila to decide if she was still in her nightmare.

'Strewth! What the flipping heck is going on in Nigeria?' she asked out loud.

With shaky fingers, Leila picked up the receiver. A million and one horrible images were flashing through her mind; horrible images of HER PRINCE with amputated legs.

'...from above his fucking knees?!' she cursed out loud.

She shook her head repeatedly to block out the images. She could not dial the number because her trembling fingers would not let her. She paused for a moment to compose herself, and then she called out the digits as she punched them in.

'Hello, this is Leila Cranston-Jasper. I got a message to….'

'Hold on please' said the voice on the other end of the phone. She heard shuffling noises and running feet in the background.

'Leila!' it was distressed, weak, but not unrecognisable.

'Prince? What happened? Are you OK? Is there anything I can do? KK, please talk to me. Do you want me to come and see you? Anything you want, just tell me… because I will… you know I will…'

'Sweetheart, I sensed this. I am sorry. I am so sorry. You need to know that Dahlia is….' His speech was muffled, and devastatingly slow. She imagined he was in a lot of pain. It did not help either that the telephone line was crackly in parts, breaking up his already broken sentences.

'It's such a bad line Prince. What did you say? Dahlia is what?' she asked him but when he attempted to speak again she still could not make out what he was trying to say and so with all the noise in the background she attempted to make up his words for him to the best of her ability.

'Dahlia is fine Prince. She misses you too'.

'Tell her I love her Leila. Leila, I love you. Leila, I am sorry. Leila, sweetheart, it will be ok, trust me. Leila I am so sorry!'

'Why are you sorry Prince? Of course it will be ok Prince. You are going to get better. They are taking very good care of you there'. Leila did not realise that by this point, she was screaming and there were hot tears streaming down her cheeks.

'I'll take the first flight out to you. You just hang in there. I will. You know I will', she said. And she meant it. Who cared about the court case? Kaobi needed her right now. She would be crazy not to fly out there. She would leave for Nigeria that minute if she had to.

'Leila, Dahlia… Leila, I…' and the line went dead. The whole conversation had lasted a meagre three minutes or thereabout. She had to speak to him.

'Hello? Hello? Hello?' No… no… no… no…. Prince? Kaobi… Hello?' Frantically, Leila re-dialled a gazillion times. It was the same: *'The-number-you-are-calling-cannot-accept-this-call-at-the-moment-Please-try-again-later'* message. She sat there redialling for the better part of two hours. She had to get through. She had to speak to Kaobi.

'Both his legs amputated from above the knee? How could that happen?' she wondered. The dismay! It sounded like a horror movie – one that her prince had no business being in. She had to speak to him. She had questions. Eventually, she put the receiver down very slowly.

'You tried to reach me in my dreams Prince, didn't you?' she whispered clutching her pillow to her chest and saying many prayers for his life. 'I'm sorry Prince. I didn't understand. I'm sorry!' she said. 'Lord, come on, plllееееееееааааssssеее…he is your son. He is your son Lord. Lord have mercy; protect your son. Take anything else. I don't care about the court case. Please don't take him from me.' She had her bible open before her, but she wept unto its pages. She felt incompetent to conjure up the relevant verses. She hoped God understood. He knew her heart, he could see it. She was taught to believe that it did not matter how incoherent the prayer was, God could make it out, and so she hung on to that promise and kept interceding on his behalf.

'I'm so sorry Kaobi. I am not there, I am so so so so so sorry!' Out in the garden she went, in nothing but her underwear. It was May, but it was still cold, especially as it was only the wee hours of the morning. Back and forth she rocked. Her rocking chair offered no comfort. Her prayers and tears never ceased.

Mrs Chetachi-Ubah stood trembling by his bedside.

'I would have made it, amputation and all.'

She nodded.

'It's the stomach infection. It was the allergic reaction to the mixed herbs.'

'The drink that would make you love your wife. If you did not love her still, you would never have forgotten your responsibilities at least. You fell inlove with that woman like they do in the white mans land. We lost Kamsi to the white mans land. Do you know men here have multiple wives? They apportion love equally, even though they may keep a favourite. I have never understood you, my son. I was scared I would lose you like I did Kamsi.

'So you…you…you pretended you were ill and even when I…I…I came back, that was not enough control for you. You have given me herbs that my body does not agree with. I lost control at the wheel because of the pain.'

She sobbed.

'I got this wrong. How will God ever forgive me?'

'I forgive you, but on one condition. You must do as I say.'

'If I don't?'

'Mama, you will never sleep again and my blood will be on your hands.'

'Ah. All this for a foreigner? You choose her over your own mother?'

'You say you are my mother. Look at what you have done to me. That car crash would never have happened if the pain did not take over my body.'

SILENCE

'And if I do as you say?'

'You will be ok.'

'You love her'

'I do'

Leila sat still rocking and staring at the phone. She was back in her room as the change of scenery had been of no use, except the bad cold she would catch. It had gone very quiet indeed. When it came back to life again, it was 8am. Leila had not even realised it was way past daybreak already. The hours seemed to have gone by in minutes, seconds even.

'Hello!' Leila picked up probably half a second into the first ring.

'Kaobi?'

'Leila?' the voice on the other end sounded surprised and confused.

'No Leila, it's me, Patricia. I thought we were meeting for 7.30?'

'It's still early isn't it?' Leila asked stuttering through her sentence. Straight away Patricia could tell there was something wrong.

'Leila, are you ok?'

'Patricia, it's horrible; it has been such a nightmare. How can I get a flight out to...'

The phone started beeping, indicative of an incoming call.

'I have an incoming call Trish. I will call you back' and she swapped the calls instantly.

'Hello!' she took the other call in a flash.

'This is Kaobimdi's mother'

'The line went dead and I... I....' Leila swallowed hard and continued, 'and and and I tried to call back and and and.... It just wasn't going through. How is he? What's going on?' Leila swallowed even harder again as she waited. It was a few seconds.

'Go on...' Leila urged painfully. She sensed what she was about to hear.

'It is no good news, I'm afraid'. There was yet another loud silence.

'Why? Does he need another blood transfusion? Are you flying him back to England?' Leila began to pray frantically within the agonising seconds of silence. Kaobi's mother sighed slowly and breathed deeply before she spoke again.

'He passed away at 5.30am shortly after he spoke to you. I have a few things to talk to you about but I need a couple of hours.'

SILENCE

'I am...' she took a deep breath after she nearly choked. 'I am so sorry' Leila summoned up the courage to say, and once again, with no warning, the woman terminated the call.

The news did not actually sink in for a good few minutes and so Leila stared at the phone sniffing. She had a bit of a runny nose. Sitting in the garden in underwear at that time of the morning had done her no good. When it did sink in, Leila was not sure how to react. She felt like she was hyperventilating and could not breathe, then she felt choked with too much air, then she felt an unnatural calm. So far, she had never lost anyone close enough to her. There had been of course Yardua who died a couple of years before and that had really really hurt and she could now really imagine how Toks had felt back then and exactly what Yardua's family would have gone through. This was her Kaobi. This was Prince. Her rock! The pain was impossible. Where would she find the strength? She would never have imagined it in a million years. Is that why he was acting so weird? Was that what the dream was about? She dug out his passport-sized photo. It was the one she had accompanied him to take when he had his drivers licence renewed. The one she had teased him about. 'Looks like a mug shot!' she had said that afternoon. He laughed loudly and tickled her. He had six. She took one and slipped it into the back pocket of her jeans. Later that night, she slipped it into her wallet. She heard Kaobi's hearty laughter from that night as she stared at his photo.

'I have questions!' she said as the tears began to build up. 'I have questions and if you don't answer them, I will go insane.' She paused for a moment before she continued:

'Don't think for one second that I didn't know you were psychic. I know you were.

Then she heard his voice in the form of a conversation from the past: *'There is this silent difference between being psychic and prophetic. Some people say it is impossible to be psychic and Christian, Leila. I think the word you are looking for is prophetic! I am more comfortable with that, shallow as it sounds, because I do fit the bill for a psychic, I guess, but a prophet particularly gets his spirit from God'*, he had said that day. Leila had thought about it and said nothing further..

'Prophetic/Psychic…whatever Kaobi! You knew this would happen, didn't you? Didn't you Kaobi? You knew. You always know these things before hand. You knew this would happen, Kaobi. That is why you were acting so weird before you left. A bloody indecipherable kiss on the lips Prince… is that all I get as a goodbye? Is that all I am worth? How the hell is that supposed to suffice? How was I supposed to read that as a sign that you were never coming back? Then it was getting too late for you to get the message across to me, to…to…to tell me and then I had that dream? Was that you doing that? That's just not fucking good enough Kaobi!' she yelled at the photo amidst heavy choking sobs of unquantifiable devastation.

The doorbell went and it sounded so loud that Leila screamed. Then she thought of ignoring it for a few seconds. Then she thought it might be Kaobi. Then she shook her head because she knew it wasn't and never would be, not ever again, and she knew that this was one hurdle she was not expecting and instead of running straight over, she stopped in her tracks and stared at it until the doorbell went off again. Leila tore towards the door and flung it open.

'Kaobi!' She said and she fell into a heap on the floor and cried heart-breaking tears that startled Patricia. Patricia joined her on the floor.

'I can never get over this one' she said over and over again staining Patricia's expensive suit with many tears and other rude emissions.

'What's happened?' Patricia asked gently.

'Kaobi died this morning Trish. He died. Kaobi.' Patricia held on to her for a good few minutes as Leila sobbed hysterically.

'Alright, I will have to rush back to court and try and get an adjournment. You obviously can't attend in this state and I will definitely need for you to be there…' and then as an after thought she added carefully,

'Leila, I know that you and Kaobi shared a special bond but I never really asked specific questions because I always felt it was none of my business. Just for the record, was he…were you guys… what I mean is…'

Leila shook her head knowing what Patricia was trying to ask. Leila did not blame her for being confused about the nature of their relationship. She was not so sure herself, but….'he was my best friend!' she said with a weird half smile on her face. 'He was my soul mate!' she added.

'I know it sounds like some...some…some old cliché but its complicated. Patricia nodded her understanding. She picked up her phone and rang Leila's sister asking her to come over and lend a hand with Dahlia as Leila was totally beside herself with grief, with good reason it seemed because as soon as Leila's sister heard the news, she too sobbed loudly.

'Leila, let me go and sort out a new hearing date for the interim contact. I will be back in two hours, alright?' Leila nodded

'Do you think it will be a problem?' Leila asked

'Well, let's just say it might be time to cash in on a few favours. I will do my best. It is not impossible to get it adjourned'.

She left Leila to her thoughts. Leila grabbed Dahlia and held unto her tightly praying for strength, praying for direction.

'KK, you are all I know. Where do I go from here?' and Leila was petrified because Kaobi never responded.

At court, Akash was pacing.

'Adjourned? What do they mean postponed?' he was asking his lawyer.

'It seems there has been a bereavement in your ex-wife's family you see'

'There has been a bereavement in the family? Who died?'

'I haven't been told more than that, but as Miss Cranston-Jasper is in no fit emotional state to attend… the court has to be reasonable you know. It has only been adjourned by a week Akash'

'Leila is in no fit emotional state to attend?' Akash asked.

'A week is not that long?

'No, what I want to know is…' and then he spotted Patricia and ran after her.

'Trish! Trish'! He called out breathlessly tearing down the corridor in her direction.

Patricia was furious at herself for being discovered. She had managed to hide away up until that point. She had spotted Akash earlier on but had done well to stay well clear from him. She knew he would be asking questions and she was unsure as to whether it was in her place to answer the questions or not. Somehow, she had hoped she would escape from the premises without having to reveal anything. In the split second before she turned around to speak to Akash she had to make a quick judgement within herself. Should she be discussing Kaobi's death with Akash or shouldn't she? She decided it would do no harm to give his name, after all, that would be barest minimum detail. She did not want to be in Leila's bad books but she did not want to deprive Akash of the information if Kaobi was a friend of his as well.

'Trish…morning…' he said catching up with her.

'Morning Akash' she replied uneasily. Akash either did not notice or ignored her unease.

'I heard about the adjournment. Is Leila OK? What is this bereavement in the family?' he asked breathing hard from running down the corridor.

Patricia hesitated and then said, 'It is a friend of hers, Kaobi'

'The doctor? Dr Kaobi Chetachi-Uba?' Akash asked horrified.

The surname sounded familiar enough to Patricia and she knew he was a doctor so she nodded.

'What happened to him?'

'I'm not sure of the details Akash. You might have to ask Leila.'

'How is Leila?' Akash asked

'Well she is upset but we should carry on as normal in a couple of weeks' she said giving a professional nod.

'No, I don't care about the trial. I want Leila to be ok.' He said

Patricia nodded again, just the single nod, and bid him farewell.

'Tell her that I am really sorry Trish' and with that he turned around and wandered down the corridor, sitting on the steps outside. He rang Olga at once. She had not heard and sounded bitterly upset about it as well. He tried to fish for some information about their relationship; Olga was not forthcoming so Akash gave up. The man was dead. He put the phone down and stared into space. His mind naturally travelled back in time. Kaobi had visited with that strange message for him, all that gibberish that Akash had been unable to get out of his head.

'I don't know what the fuck is going on here. I don't know who to ask,' he thought out loud. 'The man died… how bloody bizarre!' He sat there for an hour engrossed in curious, confused thoughts.

An hour and a half later Patricia returned. Leila's siblings were in the house. Nobody spoke. Not a word.

'The hearing has been adjourned Leila' Patricia whispered.

'When is the new date?'

'Its next Thursday, 15th of May, same time'

'Thank you' she replied. There was a beep from her mobile phone and she retrieved it from her pocket. It was a text message from Olga, which read:

'I heard from Kash… I am here if you need me…'

'She heard from Kash?' She did not have the emotional energy to contemplate the connection. She tucked the phone back into her pocket.

'Should I call Olga? Will that help?' Patricia asked. Leila shook her head.

Dahlia was awake and had been washed and fed. She sat in the corner talking to Gucci as usual. It was hard for Leila to conceal her grief from Dahlia but somehow she managed. She knew that at some point she would have to find some words to explain to Dahlia what was going on but she would need a bit of time to think about what it was that one said to a two year old about death. The phone rang and there was absolute silence in the room because they knew that Leila was awaiting a return phone from Kaobi's widow.

'I need to take this. Could you guys watch Dahl for me?' Leila asked grabbing the cordless phone and making her way to the garden. It turned out to be some sales representative trying to sell her some sort of insurance. She did not want insurance, not unless he sold insurance for the heart of course. She tried hard not to get too angry but she couldn't help herself at that time. She cried buckets after she was overly rude to the unlucky cold caller. Oh well…

She sat in the bright red rocking chair and stared at the skies before her.

'Insurance for the heart…' she thought out loud to herself chuckling as her mind journeyed back in time to the afternoon when she had spoken to Kaobi for the first time. When she asked him what he did for a living, he had cheekily responded that he mended broken hearts. Well he wasn't bloody here to mend this one he had just broken now was he? In a weird sort of way, he had in fact actually mended her broken heart back then and restored her faith in herself and in love but he obviously had offered no insurance for a time such as this when it all went horribly devastatingly wrong. Leila was angry with Kaobi for leaving her in the lurch like this. She did not know what to do. He was the one that she would normally call to comfort her. How was she supposed to react to this? How was she ever supposed to get over this? She remembered the dream, but that had come too late anyway. It was not even clear enough. She thought back to the kiss that he had planted softly on her lips before his departure that night. That had been too subtle. There was nothing suggestive about it. It was not platonic and although unusual to a certain extent, it was not something she would have fussed over. Somehow, she just was not satisfied; it just was not good enough. What was worse was she could not contact anyone to ask what had happened, get a better insight. She had to wait for a call from his mother!

The phone rang again and her heart skipped many beats. When it did beat again, it hammered so loudly against her chest that she could see the vibrations from underneath her blouse.

'Hello'

'Leila, its Kaobi's mother'

SILENCE

'How are you?'

'Ironically I will be just fine.'

Leila shook her head. There was more silence.

'I have a message for you from Kaobimdi!'

'Go on, I am listening' Leila said choking on her words.

'He said you should attend his funeral. It is in two weeks time'

'In Nigeria?' Leila was taken by surprise

'No. In Timbuktu. Listen, don't irritate me! Of course in Nigeria!' she said sarcastically.

'Yeah I know but…' The rudeness did not interest Leila. She was talking to Kaobi's mother about attending Kaobi's funeral…in Nigeria. Nothing made sense!

'It is important that you do. He died with your name on his breath.' The phone went dead.

'Leila…' Patricia called out. Patricia was soft spoken, so always sounded like she was whispering. Leila had decided that it was because she was vegetarian. She needed a little meat to kick in some 'roar' in her. At that moment, Leila could not decide if she wanted to wrestle her to the ground and punch her or hug her. She glared at her for no apparent reason.

'I saw Akash in court. He was worried about you. He wants you to know that he sends his condolences.' Leila forgot her irritation for a second. 'They didn't know each other'

'Well, he sounded like they did'

'I'll ponder about that at a later stage' Leila said wiping her eyes and shrugging her shoulders.

Patricia knelt down in front of Leila and took her hands in hers.

'Where is Dahlia?' Leila asked

'With your sis…'Patricia said pointing towards the house. Leila nodded.

'My darling, tell me about Kaobi, tell me all about your Prince… that's what I used to hear you call him right?' Leila nodded slowly.

Leila told the greatest love story. 'I was inlove with him. I think he was inlove with me too.' She told the 'Kaobi story' Kaobi played a major role in her life and she was aware that people often mistook them for an item but she never set anyone straight neither did she ever concur. She told Patricia about the café, and their endless talks. She spoke about their debates, his stuttering, his dreams, his wife, and their twin boys. She hesitated slightly. Then, she spoke of their kiss and their one off sexual affair. She spoke of their inimitable friendship, the fact that he was always the one there, for example at Dahlia's birth (he had even named her) and finally how she loved him in a way that had been new to her.

'He named Dahlia' Leila said sobbing.

'And what did he say when you spoke to him before he died?' Patricia asked

'He said he was sorry and he said something about Dahlia but I'm not sure. I think he was just trying to acknowledge her or something. There might have been a message for her.' Leila responded retrieving more tissues from the nearly empty box. Patricia looked around thoughtfully, still nodding.

'What was it like when you made out that night?' Patricia was very reserved and under normal circumstances, would not be so intrusive, but her thoughts were leading somewhere and she did not want to frighten Leila outright.

'It was beautiful. The world stopped!' Leila said smiling mischievously and then added, 'but it was wrong Trish' she added hastily, stammering.

She continued, 'we both realised that almost straight away. I don't know, sometimes these feelings can get so tangled up, cant they?' it was not a question, but Patricia nodded her agreement nevertheless.

'No-one is judging you love, we all make mistakes.' Patricia said

'After that, it never happened again. I wanted him. Don't get me wrong, I wanted him so badly, but he was married. I could not have him so I got on with my life, but he was in my life.'

'Did anything more happen?' Leila shook her head.

'We never made love again, if that's what you mean. But…the way he looked at me Trish, the way he held me, his love for me, his love for Dahlia. We kissed once or is it twice? I don't know', Leila responded. 'But it wasn't anything worth losing sleep over. We just had moments', Leila said.

Patricia nodded waiting for the right moment to get her point across. She was not overly interested in the rationale behind their passion.

'Then you never went home again? You went to a hotel.' Leila nodded.

'I just needed to clear my head Trish.'

'I know, I know' she said still stroking Leila's fingers softly.

'You went home.' Patricia urged her on.

'To get my stuff and that's when the other horrible stuff I told you about happened. That's when Kash… you know….'

'I know. You don't have to say it love, I know'. Patricia smiled.

'Leila…' Patricia began pulling herself even closer to Leila. By this time, they were both sitting on the ground in the garden holding hands and talking. Leila looked up.

'There is something you haven't ever considered love, and quite frankly, I don't really understand why that is'

'What's that? And don't tell me I was in love with Kaobi and all that bullshit'

'Oh no, no nothing like that. Well, we can always argue about that another day…'

'Then what?'

'I hate to frighten you Leila. You know Kaobi was trying to tell you something during your conversation with him before the line went dead?'

'Yeah' Leila said urging her on

'You know you said he was psychic?' Patricia plodded on.

'He did not like that word. He preferred prophetic', Leila said rolling her eyes at the sky. Patricia smiled hastily and nodded.

Leila nodded and wept on. 'There are many reasons why anyone would. There are many other examples I could give you as well. It is true.'

'I am sure there are darling.' Patricia said and then carried on, obviously treading carefully. She cleared her throat subtly.

'You know you made love with him before you went to see Akash a few days later?'

'Yeah'

'Well…' Patricia said hesitating and edging in even closer, bridging the gap between them.

'Well, the thing is you never even considered it but it is such a strong possibility and I would be surprised if I am wrong but darling, Kaobi could be and probably is… Dahlia's father!' and they both fell silent and stared at each other for a couple of minutes with Leila looking expressionless. This made Patricia hold her breath nervously as she waited for what seemed like eternity for Leila to speak.

'Patricia, Kaobi couldn't father children naturally. It took him ten years to father his twin boys and that was all as a result of IVF and all that'. Leila replied although still in shock by Patricia's analysis of her 'Kaobi story'.

'I know, but…' Leila cut her short. 'He's black. Look at Dahlia. She's not black.' She sounded worried.

'Leila, are you black?'

'I don't know what I am'

'Did Kaobi look racially mixed? He had an Afro for goodness sake'

'Dahlia has curly hair!'

'I have mixed blood Trish. Kash's mum has Sierra Leonean blood. Of course her fucking hair is curly!'

They both stared at each other.

'You said so Leila, but I think you should go to Nigeria for the funeral and hear what his mother has to say. Do you agree?'

'No! I don't know' Leila replied getting up and making her way across the garden.

'Have I frightened you?' Patricia asked worried.

'No.... No… not at all. Its just I never even… the thought never even crossed my mind... I just never….' and it trailed off as she asked herself whether that statement was in fact the whole truth. At that point, she could not answer the question.

'I wouldn't even know what to do when I get to Nigeria. I don't know how big or small it is, where to go, whom to ask for, where I will stay? I just know little bits and pieces from Kaobi's stories to me' Leila continued her eyes dancing about like ping pong balls.

'If I were to embark on that kind of journey, where would I begin? Personally, I am not adventurous. Nigeria is apparently a beautiful place but according to Kaobi, just not the kind of place you get up and go to. Did you hear on the news about the situation in Lagos? They are killing innocent people!'

'Do you want my advice?' Patricia asked

'No'

Patricia ignored her and carried on. 'This is a once in a lifetime chance for you to go and say your good-bye's to Kaobi properly and to get answers to your questions. In my opinion, it is not optional. YOU HAVE TO GO! KAOBI WOULD WANT YOU THERE. How can he have a send off party without you?'

Leila shook her head.

'How else are you going to pay your last respects to him?'

'Yeah but what about all the things I just pointed out?'

'When last did you speak to Lala?'

'Lala?' Leila asked puzzled.

'Yeah. Lala. Haven't you seen her since that weekend we spent at yours renouncing our dependence on men?' Patricia asked.

'Lala, what has Lala got to do with it?' Leila asked.

'Oh you dozy mare, Lala is Nigerian, isn't she?' Leila's face brightened as the picture came together for her. Lala paid an annual visit home if Leila remembered correctly and all she had to do was find out if she was due one anytime soon, if she could speed the trip up and if she would do her the biggest favour ever.

'What about you Patricia? Will you come?' Leila asked

'Who will keep an eye on things here? After the interim hearing next week there will be a lot going on here.' Leila was impulsive and one to make things happen straight away, so she flicked anxiously through the address book on her phone and dialled the number.

'Don't you want to think about it first?' Patricia asked alarmed at her swiftness.

'What's there to think about? Shhh… it's ringing…' she said

'Lala, how are you babe? Listen, can I be cheeky and ask you what you are up to today? At work? Ok, what do you say to dinner at mine tonight? I know its short notice but something has happened (and her tone dropped pitch at this point) and I really want to see you. I need to run something by you… well you know that favour you said I could cash in on at any time? Put it this way, I have a huge favour to ask of you. 7pm? See you then'. Leila concluded and put the phone down. She shut her eyes, breathed deeply, clenched her fists, and gritted her teeth tightly trying to prevent the thunderstorm that threatened in her eyes. Patricia sensed it, and walked across to her and hugged her again.

'There is one more thing I need to clarify with you Leila' Patricia began

'If it all works out and come next weekend you set out to Nigeria, I want you to ask for a sample of Kaobi's DNA. I know it's not something you considered in the past but just to rule out the possibility with regards to the case; it's something I need you to do for me. Will you?' Patricia asked holding her breath.

'I don't know if I can. What am I supposed to say? What rights do I have? It was just the one night Patricia. His wife spent a decade trying to give him a child. It will crush her.'

'I am sure you will find a way round it Leila, but in my opinion, call it lawyer/friend/third party intuition, it is something that has to be done' Patricia concluded. Leila nodded her understanding but sighed at the heftiness of the consequences.

Death ends a life, not a relationship
– Mitch Albom, Tuesdays With Morrie

Chapter Forty

'Who could that be?' Leila turned to a delighted Dahlia. Both her sisters and Patricia had stayed the whole day, and subsequently earned themselves dinner.

'Prince, Prince,' Dahlia responded, making her way to the door as usual.

'She thinks its Kaobi.' She would have to explain to a two year old about death. *sigh*

It was Lala!

Leila hardly saw Lala, but they kept in touch by phone and email. Lala had been out of the country when Dahlia was born so naturally she came bearing two years' worth of presents, which kept Dahlia distracted and delighted. The night ended well. After a hell of a lot of hesitation, doubt, and questions hanging in the air, Lala agreed to go with Leila to Nigeria the following week.

'Fine! I agree to be your official tour guide,' she said smiling and accepting a hug from Leila. Leila made her book with her usual travel agent right there, so that it was more or less agreed that Leila, Dahlia and Lala would fly out on Tuesday, 22nd of May, to arrive at Lagos, Nigeria on the morning of the 23rd. The funeral would be the Friday, the 25th, by which time Leila would have somehow sorted out things with Kaobi's family. Leila paid for all three tickets. Apart from checking to make sure her North London based restaurant would not collapse in her absence (she was chef and partner/manager), Lala was fine with the arrangement. She was curious about the relationship with Kaobi but knew that this was no time for silly questions.

Later that night, after Lala, Patricia, and her siblings had bid them goodnight, Leila called Kaobi's mother to let her know she would attend his funeral. After they sorted out the details of the flight, they both courteously wished each other a good night and deferred further discussion until their meeting in Lagos. All Leila knew was that Kaobi had been travelling from Lagos to Onitsha to meet his ill mother. The fatal accident occurred half way through in a town called Benin, he had been rushed to the hospital in Benin where he died and now, his body had been flown back to Lagos (although it would end up in his hometown – Onitsha), which was where Lala's family lived and where the main international airport was as well. According to Lala, Lagos in Nigeria was the London in the UK, but Leila knew that already. She knew many things about Nigeria; she just never thought she would have to piece all the information together without Kaobi.

She sat with Dahlia and Mr Quacky in the bath, and was involved in their playtime activities but her thoughts were drifting. She was examining her daughter closely, as Patricia's words played repeatedly in her mind. She was thinking about Kaobi's relationship with Dahlia. Her flashbacks did not come to her in chronological order. They were random pop up memories, which caused her heart to skip several beats. She remembered Dahlia's birth: Kaobi had named her. He had peered in her little left palm and smiled. Leila paused and took a deep breath. At that time, she had been too high on gas and air to wonder what he was smiling about, but coming to think about it… (and she peered in Dahlia's little left palm)…what was he looking at? What she saw in the little palm sent Leila's mind into further flashbacks of the moment at the beach and the weird twelve-second mini-vision. Following the kiss, she reopened her eyes, took Kaobi's hands in hers and she kissed them both and had noticed that he had a birthmark right in the middle of the middle line of his left palm. Adrenalin-filled, she had thought it strange and sexy, she remembered. In Dahlia's little left palm was the very same spot in the exact location as it was in her father's left palm… (Hang on:

did she just refer to him her father? Leila's spirit nearly jumped out of her body) ... in Kaobi's left palm (Kaobi is not Dahlia's father; she scolded herself). How she never noticed that spot on Dahlia's palm was beyond her. Ordinarily and naturally so, she knew every inch of her daughter's body, but somehow she had missed that one. At the birth, Kaobi had whispered something to Dahlia. She would give anything to know what he said. Dahlia did not have suspiciously strong African features, but one could tell that she was of mixed ethnic origin. Dahlia seemed to have Leila's skin complexion, but her eyes? Where were they from? She examined her nose, her mouth – 'Oh this is impossible,' Leila decided, letting it all go. What she also decided then was that she would find out, if only for her sanity, otherwise she knew it would haunt her for the rest of her life. There would always be the 'what if' question and she hated 'what ifs'.

'If this is the case and this is what you are going to make me handle on my own, you have a lot of explaining to do, mister,' she whispered under her breath. Finally, she convinced Dahlia to get out of the tub and into her pyjamas.

As soon as she got Dahlia settled in bed, the phone rang. She had been nervous at every ring so she did not answer. She waited to hear who it was on the answer machine and then, she thought, she would pick it up if she wanted to speak to the person. Just as she suspected, it was Akash. He said he was just checking to see if she was alright. Leila was specifically avoiding his call. She did not know what to say to him, especially now that she had had this discussion with Patricia, and she was going on this weird mission to Nigeria. She just did not want to speak to him. Perhaps it was guilt for what may be to come, but she just was not ready to deal with other emotions just yet. She would have to see him at the interim trial coming up the following Tuesday. He would ask questions. She would avoid as many questions as possible until she knew for sure what exactly was going on.

'One step at a time, one day at a time,' she said to herself and Gucci echoed that after her repeatedly until Leila was sure she was minutes away from strangling the witty bird.

Still...'do I fly or fall?'

Leila sat staring into space. Gucci had finally shut up so she could think once again. Unable to help it, her mind drifted back to Akash and the message he had left on her answer phone. She decided she would deal with him upon her return from Nigeria. She would say her goodbye to Kaobi, get the results of the DNA test, and then she would speak to Akash. Fair or not, this was to be the order of events. There was no manual for this sort of thing; she was therefore making it all up, as she went along.

'What is the appropriate reaction, Kaobi?' She recounted every second of every minute of every hour she had spent with Kaobi right from the day at the café. She giggled, she frowned, she wept, she sniggered, and she sighed. They had been through it all together. The sun was rising when she settled into bed. When she did eventually sleep, she dreamt Akash was holding her, comforting her and she found succour in his arms. For some strange reason she seemed to be at peace then. She obviously was in a state of mental mystification, she concluded upon reflection later. Then there was the wrinkly old fortune-teller with the scrawny fingers. She seemed to appear in every dream. Even when she did not speak, she stood bent over in the corner, her eyes looked sad but she wore a smile of some sort. 'What the potatoes do you want?' How bloody bizarre!

Tuesday came quicker than Leila was prepared for. She was finding it hard to concentrate on the trial now more than ever. Her eyes were forward looking to her trip to Nigeria where she would find peace once again.

'Leila, how are you?' It was Akash.

'I'm alright, thank you.'

'I heard that you were a bit upset about this doctor's death. I called you a couple of times and left you messages. I just wanted to make sure you were alright.'

'I am fine...'

'He was such a nice guy, wasn't he?'

'He was. You didn't know him, did you?'

'To an extent,' was all Akash said. Leila wondered about this because apart from the night Dahlia was born when Kaobi had let Akash in to see her, she was not aware that they had ever been in contact with each other. Leila asked no further questions. She had enough to deal with. Her sanity had been at stake since Kaobi's death.

'Was he your boyfriend?' Akash shocked Leila with that. Thankfully, Patricia arrived just in the nick of time.

'Leila, there you are.' Patricia pulled her to a corner. Leila was glad.

'Are you ready for this?' she asked.

'I have no choice, Trish. I want this over and done with. Do you think they will give a decision today?'

'It depends on several factors, love, I couldn't tell you. They may well ask us to come back in a week or two for their decision depending on their interpretation of what we say and what Akash's lawyer presents.'

Patricia squeezed Leila's hand, reassuring her that all would be well.

Leila's mind drifted constantly throughout the hearing. In fact, she only picked out bits of the arguments. Patricia was called up to speak for Leila.

'We would like the courts to consider the status quo. This child is well adjusted to her routine. It will not be in her best interests to introduce a life she is not accustomed to. Maintaining stability should be paramount in our minds,' Patricia was saying.

Akash's lawyer argued that Dahlia was still young and if visits to her father were introduced, chances are that before long she would not remember that life existed when she did not have a father. How could denying Akash contact be in the best interests of his child, if the courts were of the view that contact with both parents was important for the emotional development of the child. That was a good argument perhaps, because in Leila's opinion Akash gave her an 'I-told-you-so' look. She paid no attention.

Then the big moment came when Patricia brought up the issue of the physical abuse by Akash. The whole story was dug up once again in more detail than Leila cared to recount. As this was a family court, she was not going to be cross-examined about the intricate details though. For this, Leila was thankful.

Unfortunately, the judge had so many factors to consider, and Akash's barrister tore Patricia's argument to pieces. She did not look too perturbed though, so Leila remained calm (outwardly at least). Why was it never reported? How sure was Leila that she had conceived then? They were after all husband and wife. Even if eventually proven, this did not mean Akash was automatically unfit as a father. He had been diagnosed with a mental imbalance. They had proof – consultation visits, prescription drugs, and expert witnesses to testify. The most important thing here was that, ultimately, Akash denied the rape charge. He admitted to physical violence on the one occasion but claimed it was an isolated episode and there was no rape.

In summing up on this point, the judge pointed out that the courts would always take into consideration physical abuse especially if the mother's emotional state is affected by the granting of contact. The tenors of the times, judges are allowed to bend over backwards to allow either parent to win contact with their children. Where allegations of physical, or most especially sexual abuse are being made, there had better be rock solid evidence against the offending spouse. When proper evidence is not established, there is sometimes the presumption that the accusing party is trying to use the courts to punish their spouse; the reality is that it does happen. However, as suspected and even convicted physical abusers had increasingly been awarded custody of their children, the courts would tread carefully. They were therefore adjourning their decision for two weeks to consider the positions carefully, to give the parties time to amend the flaws in their arguments and consider their legal positions properly. If Leila wished to proceed with the allegation of rape, she was going to have to report it to the police and allow criminal proceedings to go ahead as the family courts had no jurisdiction to hear the matter. Still, they had to deliberate on the other issues identified so far and in two weeks' time, whether a criminal investigation was underway or not, they would have an interim contact decision for the parties and this would of course be subject to change at the main hearing or in light of any new evidence before then.

Outside the courtroom, Patricia and Leila discussed the outcome. Leila was not sure about the legal jargon.

'How do you think we did?' she asked nervously.

'Well, it could have been worse. This gives you literally enough time to go to Nigeria, get the sample and send it to me for testing. By the time you come back on the following Tuesday, we will be going straight to court.' Patricia said.

Leila nodded.

'Leila… hi!' Akash came up behind her hesitantly.

'Kash!'

'This is nothing personal you know. I just want a share of my little girl's life. I swear that's all it is.'

'You still don't remember the rape?'

He did not respond.

'Is this the truth, Kash?' she asked just a little bit louder.

He said absolutely nothing.

'You see, Kash, the only problem I have with you is this: that you have refused to accept what you did to me. You damaged my spirit. For the sake of closure you need to take responsibility for your actions. I know you went through hell and I was not there for you, but I had no clue that you had any issues. You have picked yourself up. Good for you, but you cannot erase that Tuesday afternoon from your memory. That is not fair on me! I not perfect, but I am a human being with feelings.' They both stared. 'Don't do this to me, let me go!' she added in a gentle beseeching whisper. He said nothing. Licking his lips, he slowly turned around and walked away.

'Akash.'

He stopped in his tracks.

'You never answered my question. Was it for British Citizenship? I need to know.'

He walked on.

It was all still hanging in the air and there was the decision to deal with as well but Leila was proud that she had attended the hearing. She knew what she had to do now and could only look forward to the future. The only thing she was not sure about was whether she would take this to the police. That seemed to be too extreme a length to go to just to prevent him from seeing Dahlia. Nevertheless she was confused about his state of mind. Was he playing a game? He seemed normal enough to her. Did he actually have a problem? He was not that good an actor. If he thought in his mind that he had done nothing wrong, then he definitely had a problem. He needed to speak to someone and she would advise him about that upon her return from Nigeria. If the DNA test proved that Akash was indeed Dahlia's father, would she send him to jail to prevent him from seeing Dahlia? Leila needed to decide exactly how angry she was with Akash and what she was willing to do about it. How much did she want to punish him? Lying on that kitchen floor on that Tuesday afternoon, Leila had forgiven him and she was sincere in those thoughts, so why dig it all up again? She dug out her diary to begin an article. Her mind was blank. Since Kaobi died, she had not written a word.

'Oh this is impossible!' She flung the diary to the left of the bed. It landed at the feet of the wrinkly old fortune-teller with the scrawny fingers. Leila stared at her toes for a couple of seconds before she found the strength to raise her head. The woman was dressed in white. She was holding a crystal ball and but a quick glance at Leila's journal, her eyes were fixated on the ball. Leila closed her eyes and kept them that way.

Akash sat at home by the windowsill in the kitchen. That seemed to be his favourite spot in the huge, empty house. Kaobi's words were playing over in his mind and then, intermittently, Leila's words at court that morning would jump in and take over. He had gone back in time to even before he married Leila to face his demons. He had come to terms with everything that had happened between them. He knew where he went wrong and knew what he had to change if he ever got her back (unlikely as that seemed, considering the circumstances). But she was accusing him of rape. 'Rape? Could a man rape his wife?' He wished he could take her back to India and throw her in some remote area in Punjab where they would knock some sense into her head. These modern women sure did take the piss! He turned around and stared at the dining table. Leila usually had a colourful array of flowers in the middle of the glass table. When she did not have time to put flowers there, she had a sparkling silver fruit bowl. There was nothing on the table. He cared nothing for flowers, fruit or beautiful arrangements. Leila loved that table. It had cost him triple what the average table would cost. Several times they had had arguments at breakfast before she went to work or over dinner and he had always slammed his fists on the table. 'It is a fucking glass table,' she had said one day. What a rude bitch she could be sometimes, and Akash's breathing quickened. God! She got to him. But he wanted her!

He licked his lips and slicked his hair, but then he sobbed. He regained his composure quickly.

'Mani jeetai jagjeet – He who conquers the mind, conquers the world!' Akash jumped off the chair and kicked the dining table with rage that came from somewhere deep down inside. The table came crashing down. As soon as it happened, he regretted it.

'Oh this is impossible!'

Sometimes getting completely lost is
the best way to find yourself.
A Beer Ad

Chapter Forty-Two

She had a lot to organise before the trip. She had to get Dahlia some summer clothes. She had to sort out travel insurance and jabs as well. She intentionally went nowhere near Kaobi's hospital, and of course, that included work. That would have spooked her out. The week dragged on. It felt like forever waiting for Tuesday night to arrive. Lala arrived in the afternoon ready for their trip. All they had to do was turn up at the airport. Leila must have asked Lala a million and one questions on the way. This trip filled her with so much excitement, good and bad. She would come face to face with the reality of Kaobi's death and be able to say her goodbyes; she would also be visiting a country she had heard so much about, a country that Kaobi had spoken about with so much love and passion. She knew he would be proud of her right now. He always told her that he knew without a doubt that one day she would visit Nigeria. The circumstances could not be any more painful though. Dahlia seemed excited as well. She knew that Dahlia had a vague idea in a sort of 'toddler' way where they were going and what they were up to.

'Everything will be fine, Leila. Just ring me as soon as you have the information I need and of course to tell me how you are getting on.'

'I cannot believe I am doing this, girls,' Leila said to both Lala and Patricia.

'Boarding time!' Lala announced, standing up.

They hugged and the three travellers made their way to their appropriate boarding gate while Patricia made her way home. Leila remembered to explain everything to a stunned Dahlia. She was not sure what was going on. It was her first time on a plane. So far, she seemed excited. Lala made a quick call to make sure her parents sent the chauffeur to pick them up at the airport and that was the last phone call made. They got on the plane. It took a while for Dahlia to settle down. She cried incessant tears of unsettlement, but when she did settle, she fell asleep and was peaceful thereafter. They all sat in the same three-sitter row in the same aisle so Lala and Leila were able to catch up on their lives. Leila revealed most of what was going on. She was glad to be able to talk about Kaobi. Lala was empathetic. She cried with Leila and told her how brave she was. Many people would be happy to pretend the situation with Kaobi and Dahlia's paternity did not exist. She was not sure she would be strong enough to do the same. For that reason, she was very proud of her friend and promised to be with her every step of the way. Leila was grateful for the loyalty. It turned out to be a mind-settling, pleasant flight. The only problem was Leila picked up her diary, but she could not write. She had absolutely diddlysquat to say!

It was roughly seven hours later when the pilot announced that they had landed safely. Leila was delighted but the butterflies in her tummy just would not stop somersaulting. She wondered what Dahlia felt. Upon exit from the aircraft, it was exactly as Kaobi had described – the heat! It was different from the London summer. There was a dryness about this heat. It was almost penetrative. They managed to get through customs and although it was a struggle, they retrieved their luggage amid total chaos. Leila was glad when it was time for them to leave the airport, clinging tightly to Dahlia who looked dazed to say the least. They got into the car safely and were soon sitting in Lala's family mansion in Lagos, Nigeria. Yes, mansion!

'Wow!' Leila was in awe.

Most houses in this area were detached. They were huge, with massive gardens. They had a concierge of some sort on guard. An elitist neighbourhood perhaps, she concluded. The houses topped anything she had seen in most of London in terms of size and beauty. She did not think the government would let people get away with owning this much land in England. Saying that though, she remembered the many stories of corruption Kaobi had told her about. The rich got richer and the poor got poorer. Leila wondered if Lala's parents earned an honest living or had been sucked in by the norm. It turned out Lala's father was an oil merchant. Oil was the main source of Nigeria's revenue. That obviously explained the life of luxury. Leila was grateful for the warmth with which Lala's family received her; she had been unsure of what to expect. She bathed Dahlia and had some private time to reassure her and make sure she was OK and then tucked into some Nigerian food. She had tasted some of these before as Kaobi had taken her to a Nigerian restaurant in London from time to time. She had some fresh fish pepper soup and 'suya' (dry roasted peppered meat) on the side. Dahlia settled for dodo – fried plantains with a less peppered beef stew, and some spring greens, which came directly from the back garden. With each event, Leila was tormented with flashbacks of Kaobi. She was living all the stories he had told her.

The next day, they went sightseeing in the morning. First port of call was the most amazing resort Leila had seen in a long time called 'the whispering palms'. The drive-through was long and narrow, lined with palm trees. As the sea was close by, the soft breeze caused the trees to waver and literally whisper. Leila could hear the melody in her head and took deep breaths…she wanted to share this tranquillity with Kaobi. The cubicles were like little caves. Leila picked up beads and shells to take back as souvenirs. As there was so much to see, they did not spend as much time there as Leila would have liked. On the roads, the environment was dusty and dry; the air was electrifyingly boisterous as the overpopulated city went about their daily business; they were so excitable, but it seemed normal to everyone. One of the biggest puzzlements to Leila was the random 'stop and search' attitude adopted by the police. Still, one could get away with murder if they had a couple of hundred naira to give to the hungry looking policemen who all referred to her as 'ebo', 'oyinbo' or 'onye ocha' which all apparently meant 'Caucasian'. She thought she could actually remember Kaobi referring to her by the last of the three. She did not approve of the children hawking in the streets either. Were their parents aware? The laws were in dire need of reform. Back in England their parents would be in jail for child abuse. Different strokes for different folk, it seemed. No one seemed to be complaining.

'How about lunch by the beach?' Lala asked, interrupting Leila's thoughts.

'Well, you are our tour guide, Lala, whatever you decide is best.'

'Whilst we have lunch you could call Kaobi's mum to announce your arrival as well.'

Leila nodded obediently. There was no time to panic. It was now Wednesday, the funeral was on Friday, and she had to be back in London by the following Tuesday morning. There was a lot to achieve in such a short space of time. They settled to another Nigerian delicacy of jollof rice (cooked with tomatoes, onions, and spices apparently), moimoi (bean cake) and the most organic looking leaves Leila had ever seen.

'Wow, we could get used to this, couldn't we, sweetheart?' Leila asked Dahlia.

Lala smiled. Dahlia tucked into her food obviously enjoying every minute of it.

'I hope you liked the meal. I'll treat you to as much variety as possible. Let's create some memories.'

'Thank you, Lala, for everything.'

'Ah it's nothing. I am just glad to be able to do something for you for a change, Leila. In any case I promised my parents a bi-annual visit this year, so it worked out well.' They both smiled.

Leila wandered a few inches away to ring Kaobi's mum and inform her of her arrival.

'Hello Mrs C, it's Leila. I am in Lagos now.'

'Welcome to Lagos,' she said unattached.

'When would you like to meet? I gather Prince's funeral is on Friday still?' Leila had seen the obituary announcement in the local newspapers. He really was royalty apparently.

'It is. Where are you?' she asked.

'We are staying with a friend in an area called Lekki, but now, we are at the bar beach having lunch. Obviously I don't know my bearing here but if you wanted to meet up I could perhaps wait here for you or meet you somewhere or…' Leila suggested.

'It's 1.30 pm now; I will meet you at 3.' She sounded dismissive.

'That will be fine,' Leila said politely.

Leila nervously sauntered back to where Lala and Dahlia were busy watching the marines and mini parties on the beach.

Mrs Chetachi-Uba stood a safe distance from Leila and stared. She was filled with a long list of emotions, hatred topping the list. This emotion was groundless; and in her subconscious, she knew. Could it be envy? That too would be unfounded. Her son loved her. No proof required. She caressed the package in her hand. She closed her eyes for a moment and recalled the conversation.

'Give this package to her.'

'What's this?'

'It is none of your business.'

'You are talking to your mother!'

'Mama, you lost the right to say that the minute you decided to lace my drink of water with a cocktail of poison.'

'My son, I was trying to protect you. It is not poison. If you had not reacted to it, your life would have been better.'

'It is not? We know that I have survived this car accident, but my body cannot handle the last drink I had. You gave it to me. You know what you put in it. Is it not bad enough that you brought me back to Nigeria under false pretences?'

At that point, Kaobi had started to vomit blood again. The doctors had tried to prepare her for the worst. 'It is only a matter of time. We have tried to flush it out of his system. He has had a lethal dose.'

'He was only meant to take one glass. He was thirsty. He drank the whole bottle.' But of course, these were thoughts she could not speak out loud. She had not known how to react. She was not even sure if she confessed to him because she was truly repentant and ashamed of herself, or because she knew that once her prophetic son looked in her eyes, he would know the truth. The gift had come from his father. All she wanted was for him to be normal. She wanted him to embrace his talent, his heritage. She wanted him to learn the herb mixes from his father and the elders, to carry on the family business and even become the Eze (king). Kaobi was having none of it. She had been petrified since the day she lost Kamsi. She had begged Kamsi not to go to the UK, but that fell on deaf ears. Then Kamsi had died – in a foreign land. She had to get Kaobi home. Her husband had told her to desist from worry. He had said that Kaobi would bear seed of both genders. She laughed at him. She called him an old man who was losing his touch. When she asked him to swear on his integrity (more because the thought excited her and she wanted him to validate it), he had confirmed this to be the truth. As time went on, Kaobi could not even father one gender, let alone both. When he eventually had twin boys, she had assumed that his prophesy had been wrong – multiple children, not of both genders. She had laughed at him at every available opportunity.

'Papa Kaobi, please retire so that someone else can give accurate predictions. You are old. *I nwago – you have tried!*'

'You are a selfish woman. You never see beyond your own needs. You are only happy when things go your way. You have lost one child; you will lose the other and it will be your undoing.'

'*Tufia! God forbid it!*' She spat too for good measure.

When Ada had informed her about his 'distraction', she was scared. It was bad enough that the said woman was not Ibo – she was not even Nigerian. Her fear was that the white man would kill her daughter and take over her son's mind. He already sounded like them. When he spoke, she could barely understand – his interaction with them meant that his accent changed, rapidly. His views were always eccentric but to declare that he had nothing left in Nigeria? That had made her cold all over. This was probably what his father had tried to predict. She would fight to keep her son. Saving his marriage would keep Ada happy. She convinced herself that she would do something about it. It was her duty as a mother!

When she saw a woman's figure in an all-black kaftan, Leila guessed it was Kaobi's mother. But for her wedding band, she wore no jewellery. Her hair was tied in a scarf which she wore bandanna style. She also wore black flip-flops. The woman stood staring at Leila from a distance. Leila was nervous, but did nothing.

'Tell me everything, Mama.'

'I cannot!'

'I foresaw trouble in my wife's eyes. Tell me what you did.'

So Kaobi's mother explained that in trying to do what she thought was in his best interest, she had taken mixed herbs from a renowned doctor to make him love his wife to the exclusion of any others.

'Papa said you would lose us both. His prophecies will come to pass.'

'Your father is old. He was wrong. He said you would bear fruit of both genders. I got scared that it would be from this woman. She is not of our origin. Your sister died in their land.'

'Papa prophesied correctly. Mama, you are a fool, but I forgive you.' Before she could substitute stern words about Nigerian culture, respect and appropriate words with which one could address one's mother, the sharp pain came again. The cough sounded different. The pause in-between the last two was only a few seconds, but the rhythm was different. She looked up and instantly tossed the package he had given her to one side. 'Kaobimdi!!!' she was screaming. As his eyes rolled back, he opened his mouth to speak. 'Leila.' That was his last word.

Leila did her best to ignore the woman staring at her from a distance. Instead she watched the activities on the beach. Still…'I will always, always be there for you…' She heard Kaobi's voice. This journeyed its way down, somewhere deep in her soul where incommunicable emotions lived. Lala and Dahlia turned to Leila suddenly and stood they were rooted to the spot because without Leila collapsed into a heap…and wept!

She watched on as her recollections continued.

'Kaobimdi!!!!! Please o. Please. Please o. God help me. Please, my son. I am sorry o. Lord; take me in his place, biko – please. Biko.' She lost her mind in that moment as she rolled hysterically on the floor screaming and undressing herself.

'Take anything. Take me. Don't take my only son. I want to die today.' She meant every word of it. Her eyes opened. She had destroyed her own family of her own accord. People consoled her. If only they knew the depth of her lamentation. She looked around. No machete.

No cutlass. No gun (not that she knew how to use one). Nobody but Ada would understand why her she deserved to die in Kaobi's place. Mrs Chetachi-Uba suddenly stopped crying. She re-clasped her bra from underneath her top and adjusted the sleeves of her top. She re-tied her headscarf and got up. She walked to the window, looking out into the streets with burning red eyes of intense hatred. She knew exactly what she had to do. Someone was to blame. She would die. Someone had to pay. But then Kaobi's voice came to her in a flash: 'Papa prophesied correctly. Mama, you are a fool, but I forgive you.'

'Kaobimdi nwelu nwa nwanyi – Kaobi has a female child!' She spent two hours thereafter staring outside the window; her wrinkles seemed to have quadrupled.

'You have done enough, Mama. If you want me to rest in peace, carry out my wishes. Let her be!'

She did not respond. No. Well, not straight away. Then people rushed to her because the racket that followed was unexpected. When she screamed the hospital down that day, it was for many reasons – reasons that her lips would never speak of, reasons that would follow her to her grave. She collapsed into a heap – and she wept!

'I kwa akwa Alili' – To weep tears of lamentation
Someone, somewhere in Onitsha, Ibo land, Nigeria

-

Chapter Forty-Four

The last thing she remembered before the deafening bang was haggling with the four men!

'How can you be charging me ten thousand naira? It is just a woman and a little girl.'

'Madam, do you want us to get rid of them or not?'

The collision came from nowhere. It was minutes later that she regained consciousness. She looked around her and saw the wreckage. There were people running towards them but, more importantly, she remembered there was petrol in the boot. She struggled free and broke her way through the window. But for scratches from the glass, she was unharmed. She had walked a few feet away before the explosion. The four men were dead.

She left the scene dazed. She walked for a while in shock. She could easily have been in that car.

'Kaobi nwa'm – my child. I have to do what is right!'

'This woman has done you no wrong. If you hurt her, the rest of your life will be difficult – that is if I ever allow you the opportunity to. I will protect her until the end of time. We shall see who serves the stronger God!' She looked left, right, behind her, in front and to the sky. She hailed a motorcycle to take her to the beach. Leila would be expecting her.

She stood staring at Leila from a distance. She thought her elegant and pretty but was clouded by hatred and jealousy. More flashbacks haunted her.

'Mama, remember when Kamsi and I used to tell you we could sense each other's thoughts? Remember when Kamsi broke her hand in school and even before any of us knew, my hand was swollen at home?' His mother did not respond, she just stared. 'Well, that is the kind of connection I have with her. Our minds communicate. Before I speak, she knows. If I never speak the words, she knows anyway.' She had glared at him at that point.

She slapped a mosquito off the side of her neck, still lost in thought. Why did this woman seem so familiar to her?

'Chukwu Nna'm – My God! They do not even share the same ethnic origin and yet, in this woman, she saw her late daughter. How could this be possible?' And irrationally, the hatred grew.

'You say she is untouchable? You better appear to me and explain why because I do not accept. She has caused all this!'

Face to face, the woman stared piercingly at Leila. Leila had intended a handshake – it never happened.

The woman gasped!

'Is there a problem?' Leila asked uneasily.

'No,' she said coldly after regaining her composure.

'Before we carry on, I need to know if you are attending the funeral in Onitsha.'

'I thought the funeral was in Lagos?' Leila asked.

'It was initially but as Prince is royalty, it was disputed so we will take the body home to rest.'

Leila nodded her understanding. Kaobi had always told her about his royal heritage, hence, the soubriquet Prince, but Leila never actually attached too much importance to that.

'Well as I am in Nigeria, I will go anywhere for the funeral.' That was the last of conversation for a few minutes. They watched a crowd of people gather around a body. Apparently a mermaid (mami water) had lost her way somehow and ended up on the shore. Leila shook her head. This country was unbelievable – just like Kaobi had said! It was a welcome distraction though. Both women were at a loss as to what exactly to say.

'Do you want to talk about it now?'

'I think I want to talk about that Tuesday afternoon today,' he said to the doctor.

'There is no rush, Akash,' the doctor assured him.

'I know, but…' and he trailed off, staring out of the window. He looked childlike. 'I think I have to, if for my own sanity. I'm going crazy, doc,' he replied quietly and then added, 'This has gone on for way too long for me. She accused me of selective memory. It's true. It's doing too much damage. I cannot cope with it. I don't know what's going on.'

'She?' the doctor asked.

'My ex-wife,' Akash responded and sighed.

'There is no rush, Akash. Just take your time. Do you want some water? You have made so much progress; I don't want this to set you back. So…would you like a drink of water?'

Akash shook his head slowly and sadly.

'OK, what happened on that Tuesday afternoon?'

'She came in to take some of her things and I stopped her in her tracks. I think I tried to reason with her but she was having none of it. She said our marriage was over. I was pissed out of my head. I had been drinking. I could not understand or process the words she was speaking. I knew that I had hurt her emotionally and I really wanted to make amends for it. I wanted to hold her so badly, and tell her how sorry I was for everything. I wanted to cuddle her and tell her that I had now realised that she was the love of my life and that I would never let her go. I wanted her to listen to me so that I could tell her exactly what had been going on in my head these past few months and why I had been behaving like a fool.' Akash paused and sipped from his water, which the doctor had put before him anyway. His eyes were dancing about; he was reliving the day. He had the look of horror in his eyes.

'Are you OK to carry on, Akash?'

'This has to end. I cannot carry on like this. I have to face it. I have to face her.'

'OK then, in your own time.'

'I didn't want her to go. All I wanted to do was explain to her. She did not want to listen. She did not even have her wedding ring on. I was so mad.'

'What happened next?'

'She was going to walk out of the door and I pulled her back. I pulled her back and I hit her. I hit her hard because she was hurting me. She said I was hurting her, I told her she was hurting me. I did not mean for it to happen that way. I thought that…'

'You are doing really well, Akash.'

'I thought that if I showed her how much I loved her that she would change her mind and stay. I thought I could prove it to her by...'

'How did you intend to prove it to her?'

'I wanted to make love to her. Not have sex, not hurt her, not rape her; I wanted to make love to her.'

'Did you make love to her?'

'I… I… I…'

'Did you make love to her?'

Akash shut his eyes. He shook his head.

'What did you do?'

He shook his head more fiercely.

'Can you tell me what you did to her?'

He fell to his knees and wept. Of course, he remembered. He just could not bring himself to terms with it. In his subconscious, he knew but he could not admit it to a soul. All the while he had been apologising, he had been apologising for the hurt – emotional and physical; physical in terms of the violent attack. He did not think he had it in him to do 'that' to her. He loved her.

He looked up at the doctor.

'You were ill, Akash. You were not in control of your senses. I am aware of your present contact battle with your estranged wife over your daughter. Your lawyer can call me as an expert witness. We can prove that you were unwell, but Akash, for your own personal sanity and peace, I suggest you speak to her about it and when you do, everything will be different.'

'I raped her!' he said and threw his face into his doctor's lap, crying like a baby.

Dr Aisha Alli had seen it all in her career and was never moved emotionally. But this brought tears to her eyes. This supposedly brutal animal, with all his superciliousness and rudeness was nothing but a scared little boy. She could see it. The referral had come from Kaobi, one of her best friends. To date, Akash was unaware that Kaobi received and settled all the invoices for his sessions. Akash could afford it – easily. But Kaobi could not risk Akash refusing treatment. As far as Akash was concerned, it was all on the NHS. If they thought he had a problem, he would let them sort it out. He would not pay a penny towards this.

'Just sort him out please,' Kaobi had said. He would call every week, normally on a Friday afternoon, to find out how it was going with Akash. Aisha was yet to come to terms with the fact that Kaobi was no more. Could her tears be as a result of the emotions of the past week? It was the last favour Kaobi had asked of her. When she had asked Kaobi what the personal interest was, he had replied that future events relied on Akash getting better, but he had offered no further explanations.

'How bloody bizarre.' She wiped away the single teardrop that escaped.

'Do you want to talk about it?' Leila asked.

Mrs C looked rattled.

'Are you OK?' Leila asked. She never answered. She rolled her eyes and slapped (imaginary) mosquitoes off her neck and shoulders.

'I suppose we don't have all the time in the world, do we?' she replied eventually.

Leila shook her head.

'How is your health?' Leila asked. She did not respond.

'When Kamsi died, everyone was so worried about Kaobi. He would not speak to anyone about the way he felt. Everyone knew the loss was too much for him to bear. Kaobi and Kamsi were best friends. They did everything together. There was this connection between them. It was like they read each other's minds. Before this, Kaobi just had never brought anyone home to see his family, you know… never had a serious relationship. He was not that way inclined. Instead, he concentrated on his career. He was a really good cardiologist and having studied abroad he was granted the opportunity to work over there in London and he seized the opportunity, eager for a new life. You know… that highly skilled visa they offer…'

Leila nodded.

'He accepted the wife I got for him. Ada. He came home briefly, we had the ceremony, and they went back to England as husband and wife. He sorted out all the paperwork for Ada's residency.'

She beckoned on some hawkers who carried what looked like animal horns of some sort. When she asked, she was told that it was wine – palm wine. It was an off-white, nearly cream shade of white, and did not have the affluent colour of wine that Leila recognised. It also had a potent smell, which grew on her. It was delicious. It is tapped from the sap of the palm trees. Leila had never quite tasted anything like it. It was sweet, yet sharp to the taste buds and left the most unusual aftertaste, but it was rich and beautiful. The immodest amount of alcohol they consumed played a part in settling their nerves. ☺

'Kaobi could not have a child with Ada. He would have been well within his rights to take on another wife.'

'That's bigamy. I told…' but then Leila stopped. She was about to say that she knew all this already. She wanted to move on to messages from Kaobi. She did not want a history lesson, which she could score an A+ in already.

'What do you know, eh? What do you know about the ways of our people?' Mrs C kissed her teeth.

That was the point Leila nearly reached her limit. She wanted to engage this woman in a headlock and practise her boxing skills. Her coach would have been proud considering what was going on in Leila's mind at that moment. But she could not. Leila shook her head slowly. She could not be rude, not to Kaobi's mother.

'He brought to my attention that there is a possibility that he has a daughter!' Leila's heart leapt as she looked across to Dahlia. She was building sandcastles with Lala, totally oblivious to how her history was being retold! Kaobi's mother followed her gaze.

'His sperm count was low. I was right there in the room when Ada broke down. They said the possibilities were next to nothing. They said there was nothing wrong with Ada. So how could he make love to a woman one night and father a child?'

Leila gulped.

'Was it one night?'

Leila nodded. Kaobi's mother nodded slowly.

'After he spoke to you, the line cut off and it was an impossible connection to make a second time but he insisted that the hospital crew keep trying. Your name was the last thing he spoke. He said I should give this to you.' She handed over an envelope without looking at Leila.

Leila accepted the envelope without expression. She had no clue what to feel.

She braced herself. It was no impeccable timing; she knew she had to ask! Time was of the essence. She grabbed the bull by the horns.

'Now you have said all you have to say, I have a request,' Leila said, stuttering through the sentence. She steadied herself.

'I need something that you have the permission to give me.'

'Ogini? What is that?'

'Ogini?' How many times had Kaobi used that word?! Leila would have smiled if the pain had not penetrated through and paralysed her all her facial muscles.

'I need a sample of Kaobi's DNA,' she blurted out. She was not sure if this was an insensitive request, but she had to send it to Patricia as soon as possible to get it tested before she got back to London on Tuesday morning for the trial.

'Gini? What?'

Leila sighed.

'What?' she said clapping hysterically.

Leila looked around, aware of the eyes of passers-by.

'Next you will be telling me that you want to speak as his wife at the funeral?' She was loud. She was rude and Leila was embarrassed.

'No, no. I will pay my respects and go. I am not alleging anything.'

'What do you want to use my son to do? Are you a witch?'

Leila sighed. What the fuck! No wonder Kaobi did not want to go home. But she never spoke those words. She wanted to show this deranged woman how witch-like she could be.

'I know I don't have a right to make demands, but to be honest, I need to know for many reasons and topping the list is my sanity. I need to be sure.'

'You are not sure? *Eziokwu – true?*'

'I don't claim to be perfect, I really don't. It's such a long story.' Leila simply did not want to explain that it was something she had not thought about because she knew Kaobi could not father kids naturally. She wanted to say that it had never crossed her mind until Patricia mentioned it. Instead, she did not explain at all. It was easier that way. She knew the implication. Mrs C thought her son had hooked up with a slut, but right now, Mrs C's thoughts about her were irrelevant in the grand scheme of things. The sample! Mrs C could think whatever she wanted and she would not blame her. In fact, at that moment, Leila even wondered about herself. A supposedly good woman of the Christian faith was unsure of the identity of her daughter's father! Worse still, Leila wondered where she had found the guts to declare her husband a cheat! She shook the thought away and made a mental note to get depressed about it later – for now, she needed that DNA sample, whatever the cost.

'So you are an *ashawo,* a hooker, a good-for-nothing slut?'

'If it makes you feel better or eases your pain in any way to think so, that's fine!' Except Leila did not speak those words. She said nothing.

They stared at each other with more confusion than hostility. It was an emotional battle between them and Leila held her gaze. She would not back down. Kaobi's mother sighed.

'What do you need? What is the procedure?' She rolled her eyes and shook her head. She slapped her shoulders and neck again. This made Leila very uncomfortable. Every time she did that, Leila had mini spasms, she got goose bumps and jumped. Was that some sort of reaction to stress? Bloody hell! She wished she would stop doing that.

'Well actually I have done my research and there are two ways of going about this. The first is to obtain a post-mortem sample of his DNA. The second is to reconstruct his genotype based on surviving family members. Samples may be obtained from the medical examiner, coroner or other pathologist who may have performed an autopsy, an associated toxicology in the funeral home before or after embalming or even following burials for years to come, but I need it quite urgently.' Leila said quite matter-of-factly. At this point, she was fed up of walking on eggshells and thought she would just get it finished as soon as possible.

'You want a post-mortem sample?'

'I do.'

'Well, he has gone now. I can't ask him, can I?'

'What do you think he would have wanted?' Leila threw it out there.

SILENCE

'Tomorrow. I will ask tomorrow. He hasn't been embalmed; his people want to see him – he will be lying in state.'

'What does that mean?'

'His body will be exposed so that people can see him when they pay their last respects to him.' Leila shivered at the thought.

'But his legs…!' The visual image made her physically sick to her stomach.

'There are ways of getting round that,' she replied.

'So I can have the sample tomorrow?'

Mrs C nodded.

They both stared at each other and unable to resist, they looked away in two opposite directions, and wept. There was no sobbing, no sound. Still, the few, silent teardrops were salient and emotionally deafening. Each was left to their own thoughts, conscience and grief. The palm wine probably contributed! *sigh*

Thursday came quicker than anyone was prepared for. Kaobi's mother visited. Apparently their Lagos family home was in Victoria Garden City, which was just under a half hour drive from Lala's home so it was not bad, albeit the traffic was heavy. It had been a struggle. She had bribed her way out of that building with a post-mortem sample of Kaobi's DNA. Leila was grateful, but fed up of making a fuss.

'For the funeral, there is the uniform traditionally worn by family – it's called the *asoebi*. I had the tailor sew you one, and one for your little girl.'

'Oh I don't know…' Leila began.

'Well, it's up to you really. I am not forcing you and I sure as hell am not going to beg. But like you asked earlier, what do you think he would have wanted?'

'Point taken,' Leila said non-commitally.

'Also, I assume you will be flying to Enugu tomorrow?'

'Yeah, Lala, come over here for a second please.'

'The actual ceremony is at 5 pm.'

'Yes I know Enugu fairly well and we can make our way to Onitsha from there.'

'Did you live in the East?'

'No… no… my father is actually from Asaba Town originally but we have cousins in Enugu.'

'Damilola is a Yoruba name.'

'I am Damilola Dumebi Chukwuedo. My mother is Yoruba, from Lagos, but my father is Ibo, although I am from Asaba, which is before the Niger Bridge.'

'The language is slightly different but still that will come in handy. You can translate all that is being said at the funeral to Leila in that case.'

'Asaba Ibo is slightly different from Onitsha Ibo but it should be easy-peasy regardless,' Lala pointed out.

Lala and Leila sent the sample back to England by courier. When she spoke to Patricia, she was pleased that all was going according to plan and she noted that all in all Leila sounded quite happy. Leila paid an arm and a leg to make sure it arrived at Patricia's doorstep first thing in the morning on Friday. By Monday, the result would be known. Leila sighed heavily.

On Thursday night, Leila lay in bed with her eyes closed. She had Dahlia wrapped snugly in her arms because she had woken up startled. It was a nightmare about a monster apparently. That night, Leila did not see Kaobi. She saw the wrinkly old fortune-teller with the scrawny fingers. 'Now what the fuck do you want?' She shook and opened her eyes. Dahlia's eyes were piercing into hers. They were expressionless for a few seconds until Dahlia broke into an infectious smile and reached towards her mother's face. Following a kiss on the lips, she tucked her head as far into her mother's body as she could manage. Leila was grateful for the comfort and safety she felt. 'Who comforts whom?' She did not speak the words out loud but should she have had company, they could easily have lip-read them. Leila added, 'Do I fly or fall?'

'...the words I cannot speak are the holes I
punch in the walls of my psyche...'
John Geddes

Chapter Forty-Six

When Friday came finally, Leila felt like it was the first day of her trip. It was the first time she would actually come face to face with Kaobi's death. So far, she had not had to really think about it. Even talking to his mother on the beach had been a better emotional experience than she had envisaged – not that she had known what to expect, but still. She suspected that it all had to do with being in a strange land, and the fact that she did not have much thinking time either. Lala was always whisking them off to see some sight or eat some delicacy. So far, she had eaten every dish Kaobi had told her about and more. They tasted slightly more intense than the versions Kaobi had taken her to eat at Mama Calabar – the Nigerian restaurant in London.

Soon enough it was time for them to catch their flight to Enugu. Everything went smoothly and when Leila emerged wearing the outfit Mrs C had ordered, Lala smiled. It was rich lace, a royal shade of purple. It was cotton, sequined beautifully all through. The top was a deep round neck, cut quite low and nearly off the shoulder, but not quite. It was fairly fitted with loose sleeves. The bottom was a one-piece cloth, which Leila simply wrapped around herself as though she was wearing a skirt. Dahlia was in a little A-Line dress made of the same fabric. Leila tied a little pink belt, which formed a big bow in front. She wore her sparkly pink sandals and she was pleased with herself. As Leila had come unprepared, she had to do some improvising. She wore a red spaghetti string top inside the see-through lace top and dug out her red Charlotte Olympia Gummi Bear Perspex sandals. The purple shade suited both Leila and Dahlia. She was tense at first but when Lala gave her a reassuring smile, she relaxed. When Patricia called to say that she had received the sample and was taking it to get it tested straight away, Leila was relieved. So far, everything seemed to be going according to plan. Now, there was the task of getting through the day and releasing herself from the prison sentence her mind had been serving since the moment she heard about Kaobi's death.

Leila found the air-borne journey from Lagos to Enugu disturbingly rocky, but they arrived in one piece. She learnt that the people in Lagos were Yoruba and the people in Enugu (as with most of eastern Nigeria) were Ibo. Enugu, she found, was less boisterous than Lagos but it seemed the Ibo language was more commonly used in this part of the country than the Yoruba language in Lagos. Good thing she had Lala with her. They hired a car to drive them the extra hour to Onitsha, stopping once to get a dehydrated, excitable Dahlia a cold drink. Leila found herself asking an irritated Dahlia seconds after she finished her Ribena if she wanted another drink and was quick to admit to herself that her nerves had taken over completely. She was trying to prolong their arrival by even minutes if she could; her heart beat even louder the closer they got to their final destination.

'We are entering Onitsha now, Leila,' Lala announced, unable to disguise her excitement. It had been a couple of years since she had been to this part of the country. Her father seldom went home and she, upon moving to England had always ended her journey to Nigeria in Lagos. Leila, on the other hand, was nervous and swallowed hard many times. Dahlia was sound asleep.

'It'll be fine!' Lala reassured Leila, holding her trembling hand.

'What do you think of Onitsha so far?' Lala asked, trying to lighten the mood.

'Well, it's much rowdier than Enugu, and louder than Lagos,' Leila commented, indulging her friend in conversation to distract her wandering thoughts. For a while, they managed this. Fortunately, the driver knew exactly where they were going. He even knew about the funeral, as Kaobi was the Obi's (king's) son and as such, the talk of the town apparently. Leila made a quick phone call home to her parents, sisters, brother and one or two friends. She said to them that she was in Onitsha now, it was a lovely town, she was near the funeral venue, she was sure it would go well, she would be back soon, and she loved them.

Jay questioned the soppiness. 'What's this about, sis?'

'I just want you to know in case I wake up and there is no tomorrow,' she replied.

'Right!' he said rather sarcastically. He loved her really, but he was no good with emotions. Still, he had taken a liking to Kaobi, even though his unexplained relationship with his sister got him a little tense sometimes. Back in London, he was marking the day as well. Kaobi's funeral was international!

Still she felt uneasy and scared. No one was exempt from death. Not even her Kaobi. Dahlia was asleep. She was grateful for that. Lala could sense her grief. The phone calls home were potently emotional. Leila pulled a sleeping Dahlia close and kissed her forehead.

Kaobi was never coming back. No more Kaobi. She hoped this would be closure, although she knew another chapter awaited her back in the UK.

'I will always...always be there for you.' She heard his voice and wished he would stop doing that. Every time he did that, she got those spasms again. The same ones she felt whenever his mother did that weird thing where she slapped her neck and shoulders!

'Leila, in a few minutes we will be approaching the street. It will be blocked off obviously, but I have told the driver to get us as close to the venue as possible.' Lala's tone was sombre.

'I thought we were going to the church for the service,' Leila protested.

'It's on the same street. The church is the Christian version of things. After that, it's Nigerian tradition.'

'What does that mean?' Leila asked.

'You will see a lot of the culture play a big part. There are rites to be performed to send his spirit on. He was the Obi's son. There will be a huge fuss!'

Leila nodded. She still did not understand.

They turned into a street and Leila noticed the whole street was blocked off after a point. All she could see was a row of brightly coloured canopies and thousands (it seemed) of people in black, and a few in the same sort of attire she and Dahlia had on. Many others had on the same style, but in blue.

'This is as far as I can go I'm afraid,' the driver said in vernacular, interpreted by Lala.

When they got out of the car, Leila held tightly on to Dahlia with one hand and on to Lala with the other. They made their way through the crowd as quickly as they could. Upon arrival at the church, Leila chose a seat, as discreet as possible. It was in a little corner, right at the back. Almost as soon as they sat down, they were ushered to the front. Maybe the purple outfit instantly identified her as family. On the other hand, was she being expected? She wondered. Either way, she was treated like royalty, just as Kaobi said she would. Leila was not sure she wanted the attention, but decided that it would have been rude to turn the usher down. They seemed to have attracted a lot of attention. This could have been because they were foreigners or could people have heard 'stories' already? Leila wondered. Just before that one hymn that tortured Leila to her core, she jammed a set of eyes. A woman who sat with two boys of the same age, right in front, stared at her. No introduction was necessary. Ada!

'Amazing grace how sweet the sound...' it was the most solemn instrumental version, but Leila could hear the words. Four men dressed in black and white carried the coffin by its four corners. They were all cousins, Leila was told later. Strangely enough, she could guess exactly who two out of the four were. She could guess simply from all the many stories Kaobi had told her about his hometown. Leila missed Kaobi and could not believe that the body being carried in was his.

'Oh it had to be a glass encased coffin,' Leila muttered to herself, panicking as they made their way down the aisle. She could not face it.

It was interesting listening to all these people talk about Kaobi. Some of the stories she knew already and some she was hearing for the first time. Everyone had good testimonials about him so far. Ada spoke of what a kind, loving man he was. He was a true friend, loyal and the best husband and father anyone could have wished for. She said that Kaobi had asked that his life be celebrated as opposed to mourning his death. She was positive that he was in heaven.

'Would anyone like to say anything about Kaobi?'

Leila stood up. Cameras flashed. People whispered.

Walking down the aisle felt like walking down a hundred-metre track. It also felt like someone had pressed the 'mute' button on the congregation. Leila counted her steps; she could not help it, not when her heels hit the floor so precisely and noisily. Fortunately they sounded un-wobbly, un-akin to the jelly her legs had become.

The moment came. She came face to face with Kaobi's corpse. Oh the grief! In her mind, she was in an empty room tearing down thin red lace curtains, tearing them off the rails and ripping them one by one, first in half and then in a violent rage, into shreds. This happened in total silence. She could not explain it but that was how her torment was represented in her head. She stared…at Kaobi.

'Fire. Fire is proud. Fire does not die easily. Fire does not follow orders, it does not stop. Fire even after death, produces smoke, still fights, as if in defiance. Fire is proud. The wind. The wind is invisible and unseen, but its presence is ever felt. It can be gentle or ferocious but never unnoticed. The wind is undeniable. The heart. The heart will endeavour to do the right thing. The heart knows where home is. The heart need not speak but even in its silence is deafeningly audible; immutable. The heart is the core of the being. A good heart never dies!'

Leila paused as she beheld the lifeless body of the love of her life. She could not divulge the extent of her grief in order to pay respect to his personal circumstances, but she would be damned if anyone would deny her the moment to give him a eulogy.

'Does anyone recognise this quote by Wole Soyinka? I ask because it was a favourite of his – a tiger does not proclaim its own tigritude, it pounces –' She smiled as she put her hand on his coffin.

'Kaobi will be remembered because there is no other Kaobi. Kaobi is fire, he is wind, he is the heart. His memory will never die because his 'tigritude' is proclaimed – today and evermore.'

The journey back to her seat felt like she was dodging bullets. Between Ada and his mother, she was unsure of whose bullet would hit her first. When she sat down, her head was held high.

I am always…always with you,' she heard. 'Oi, don't make this a habit,' she said with an inconspicuous smile.

'Who are you talking to?' Lala asked.

'I said that out loud? Private joke,' she responded with an unnerving calm. She tilted her head and closed her eyes as she felt Kaobi's hand wipe the disobedient tear that ran down her cheek.

'That was beautiful,' Lala commented.

'I know,' and when Leila turned to smile at her, she noticed that Lala was in floods of tears.

Lala reached across over Dahlia and put her palm on Leila's left cheek. Leila accepted the comfort. Lala read the words on Leila's lips. 'My Kaobi,' she said, holding her right hand up against her chest. Lala smiled sadly, nodding. Leila mouthed it again, 'My Kaobi!'

Of course by this time, she realised she was at war with Mrs C and Ada. Her little speech had not gone down well. Leila sat trembling, but insolently confident. She pouted. Kaobi would protect her regardless of whether he was alive or dead. He had promised. Simples!

'We walk with our hearts, but the winds push us down fiery paths that sometimes leave indelible portraits in our hearts'
C. Beluchi Egwudo

Chapter Forty-Eight

There were purple canopies about fifteen feet long and wide with about a foot in-between each. These were in rows on either side of the road, and ran the whole stretch. Some of them were labelled with family names or organisations. Musical groups loitered around the road, dancing the length of it; some had Kaobi's picture held up high. They would stop at various canopies and dance in front of them. People from the canopies would put naira notes on their foreheads. Leila could not identify with some of the beats, but some, especially when they used horns, were catchy.

They were ushered to a canopy where there were seats reserved for them. Leila was not sure what her place was but she knew she had to go with the flow. There was no point leaving until Kaobi was finally six feet under. Looking around, she noticed a pair of eyes on her. Ada was in a designated area, but she sat on a mat. She was dressed in black and her hair was cut scalp-short. Lala explained that by virtue of tradition, Ada would have had to shave her head and be isolated for days. So, no, it was not some rebellious fashion statement. It was a taboo to bury one's child, but in fact Kaobi's mother was only present because he had hit 40 and was, therefore, no longer considered a child. She noticed Mrs C walk across to the canopy where Ada sat. She observed the tension between them and wondered if it had anything to do with her, because every now and again, one of them would look across at them.

'Mama, I thought you were supposed to help me get rid of her, not invite her to join in the family.'

'You will do well to remember who you are talking to. Don't question my actions.'

'Far from it, Mama, but Kaobimdi is dead and it seems you have accepted a second wife for him.'

Mrs C spat. 'Kaobi had one wife. So it shall remain. But you better put away those silly emotions and brace yourself.'

'What does this family have in store for me?'

'There is a strong possibility that Kaobimdi has an *ada – first daughter.*'

Ada just stared in disbelief. 'You will accept her?'

'She is my son's blood.'

'So much for loyalty.'

Leila's glance was just in time to watch Mrs C slap Ada hard across the face. She was taken aback. A little crowd gathered around them quickly distorting Leila's view.

'What's all that about, Lala?' Leila asked tapping Lala's hand but not taking her eyes off the scene.

Lala shook her head. They were speaking too fast and all at the same time.

The moment finally arrived. Kaobi's body was going into the ground. Leila was not sure what role to play this time and just waited to be led. Kaobi's grave was a generous portion of land beautifully decorated with the brightest flowers, mostly shades of purple - must have been something to do with royalty. There was an ornamental roof like projection over a niche. It was befitting. They all stood around it, some weeping, and some staring. Leila was quiet. The priest read:

'Genesis chapter 3, verse 19 – By the sweat of your brow you will eat your food until you return to the ground, since from it you were taken; for dust you are and to dust you will return.'

Some men appeared with a bucket of sand and shovels.

It was an intimate congregation; most people had stayed on at the reception. Mrs C had sent someone to tell Leila to follow the little procession to the grave.

Mrs C appeared from behind the men. There were a few mutters at that point. Leila turned to Lala.

'Mrs C should not be here. Regardless of age, one should not bury one's child,' she whispered. Leila nodded.

The men gave a shovel to Ada and her boys. All three accepted. They handed one to Kaobi's mother. She shook her head and directed them with her eyes to Leila. Ada's eyes burned and she fidgeted until she could no longer contain herself, and she leapt forward. Mrs C anticipated this and leapt ahead of her. She stood in front of Leila. Leila held the shovel in her hand, unsure of what was going on.

'Give me that shovel!' Ada said.

'*Mba nu – No!* Don't do this. I already told you, I know what I am doing!'

'You are giving her rights.'

'You want another slap? Listen to me. Put your jealousy aside.'

'This is not jealousy. It is about doing the right thing, Mama. You cannot acknowledge her.'

'It was his last wish.' Ada looked at Mrs C, and then over her shoulder at Leila. She looked broken, but pulled herself together. The ceremony continued. Ada and her boys paid their last respects.

'Ashes to ashes, dust to dust,' they all chanted. One of the boys looked more like Kaobi than the other and from stories he had told her, she guessed who was who. They looked sad and she wanted to hug them, at the same time, she was trying to stop herself from staring. They were parts of him. But then again, so was Dahlia (maybe). She looked down at her and smiled sadly. Dahlia smiled back. Leila had two little white lilies. She passed one to Dahlia and they threw them in unison.

'Sweetheart, we have to say bye now.' Dahlia nodded, aware that there was something sad was happening, but unsure. She shared the shovel with her mother, threw the sand in and waved at the coffin. She was unperturbed by the fuss, although she looked a bit dazzled by the crowds. She stared at the mourners as well. Before they walked away, Leila added her own little bit but in a barely audible whisper. No one heard her. 'I love you. I will love you forever. Rest in peace!' This was it. She would never see him again. She was looking forward to seeing the message in the brown envelope. The instructions written in Kaobi's handwriting said she had to read it at the beach house. She would obey. Task done, Leila retreated to a corner and watched the rest of the obsequy in silence. She spoke only when she was spoken to and that was usually rare, with Lala interpreting some curious event or the other.

The rest of the night was in the same sombre silence. At the hotel, she bathed Dahlia and then joined her in bed. She was aware of Lala's eyes watching her from the settee across the room.

'Do you want to talk about it?' Lala finally asked. Leila shook her head as she stared into space. Lala let her be.

Leila replayed the events of the day, all the while staring at the picture on the wall. It was off two lovers clinking their champagne glasses whilst staring into each other's eyes. They looked happy and Leila smiled sadly, but at the same time, she desperately wanted to throw her red shoe at them. Nobody had the right to be happy right now!

Leila retrieved her foot from under the duvet and peered at her tattoo. She wondered how it had not put her off alcohol for life. When she had the eerie feeling of being watched, she diverted her gaze from her foot to the corner of the room. 'No. Not you again. Why won't you leave me alone?' Leila sighed as she glared at the wrinkly old woman with the scrawny fingers. She sat in the corner with a toothless smile; she strummed her words on a purple ukulele, reiterating her words fro the past in the form of a song:

'The true queen will never see the crown, not the one that did drown. A flower she did bear; Truth so bare. He carries her heart. Only in death do they part. No one changes that. Her name is his last breath. A bond till death.'

Leila shivered. She was trying hard not to read any meaning into these words, or the fact that the woman kept appearing at the most awful moments. If her words had played out, she could not make out the last part.

'On that day she will testify. From then you die!'

'Who?' Leila was asking repeatedly. She felt a gentle tap on her shoulder.

'Leila, wake up. You are talking in your sleep. You are burning up as well,' Lala said feeling her forehead. She rushed to the bathroom and soaked a towel in cold water. 'I have some nurofen. Let me pour you a glass of water.' Leila sat up in bed, barely awake. She swallowed the tablets and drank the water in a couple of gulps. She was panting.

'Are you OK?' Lala asked. Leila nodded. She lay down and turned her back to Lala, which meant she slept face to face with Dahlia. That night, she saw Kaobi in her little girl, so she held on tight. She did not hear Kaobi's voice, but when Dahlia woke up briefly, and peered in her mother's face before closing her eyes just as quickly, it was a familiar facial expression. Leila stared, Dahlia smiled. Naturally, Leila smiled back.

When they all awoke in the morning, the fever was gone.

'You were probably just exhausted. It has been eventful.' Leila nodded but said nothing. And so it was from then on. Leila's mourning began. His death was real. She had watched random men lower his body into the ground. For the next few days, she was partially mute.

Monday morning took its time, but arrived eventually. Leila, Dahlia and Lala were back in Lagos and looking forward to their night flight back home. For many reasons, it had been a fulfilling trip albeit the bits that did not make much sense, but in the grand scheme of things, those were almost irrelevant. She knew Kaobi approved. She was desperate to hear news of the paternity test. Patricia had promised to call as soon as she found out. So far, nothing! Even when she called, her secretary said she was too busy to take the call. She was in back-to-back meetings and then court, apparently. Dusk came and Leila thanked Lala's family for their hospitality, hoping to return the favour sometime.

On the plane, an exhausted Dahlia fell asleep. Leila turned to Lala.

'Thank you for everything.' She held her hand just as the pilot announced their safe take off and altitude.

'Don't be silly. I had fun too and I would not have swapped sharing this experience with you for the world.'

'It's the single most difficult thing I have ever had to do.'

'Kaobi would be proud.' Lala smiled, and then added, 'I am.'

They sat in silence for a while and made plans for their arrival.

'So, when we arrive, I will take Dahlia home. You are going straight to court to face whatever.' Leila nodded and called for the attendant's attention. She ordered a double shot of brandy.

'Patricia didn't call. She said she would,' Leila said, confused.

'So? She is busy. You will find out in the morning.'

Leila gulped her brandy, reclined her seat and shut her eyes. The 'what if' questioned had tortured her to complete exhaustion. Her slumber was unperturbed. She was motionless until the pilot announced that seat belts were required ahead of landing.

Leila freshened up in the airport. It was lovely to smell the English (cold) winds once more. Nigeria had been great, but England was home. As soon as Lala went off with Dahlia, their luggage and all the souvenirs, Leila hailed a cab. Off to court she went, wondering what this day had in store for her – the 29th of May 1998 was potentially a very big day in Leila's life.

'Trish... I have been trying to call you,' she said almost angrily.

'So sorry, Leila, I have been busy.'

'Busy?'

'I'm sorry, Leila; I didn't want to disrupt your trip.'

'Fine Trish; whatever; what's the verdict?' She was more anxious than rude.

Patricia hesitated for a few seconds. 'Kaobi IS.'

Leila's heart stopped beating for a few seconds and she gasped for air. How would she break the news to Dahlia? To Akash? 'Where's Kash?' she asked aloud. She wanted him to find out from her and not in the middle of the courtroom.

'Leila...' Akash called out.

'Kash, I need to speak to you.'

'No. Me first. You have to hear this before we go in there.' He pulled her to a corner.

'I have something you have to hear too,' she interrupted quickly trying to catch her breath to speak. She was in shock. She had known all along that this was likely to be the outcome of the DNA test, but still managed to be terribly ill prepared. She tried to concentrate on Akash but it was a particularly unsettling moment. Akash looked very excited about whatever it was he could not wait to tell her.

'Leila, my sessions with the therapist are over. I am finally willing to take responsibility. I am really, really sorry. It must have been distressing for you, but I want to speak to my lawyer. Let's not fight. Let's sort this out. I was sick, Leila. But I am willing to accept and find another way. Can we work round this? I mean we could...'

Leila interrupted him.

'Erm...wow...great. I forgave you already. I am glad you are feeling better but Akash, there is something you need to know right now. It's about...'

'Leila, come on in. The judge is calling for us to come in.' It was Patricia's turn to interrupt.

Akash's lawyer was after him as well.

'We will talk about it later, Leila, I am going to speak to my lawyer,' Akash said loudly as he hurriedly made his way across the hall to where his lawyer stood. Despite the circumstances, he looked curiously happy. Leila rolled her eyes, calling after him, 'No, it can't wait.'

'It will have to...' he said as he walked away. For some strange reason he was smiling. He added, 'everything will be alright, Leila, we will sort all this out, I promise!' and he walked off in his usual conceited gait, except this time, he had a spring in his step. *sigh*

'Patricia, he can't find out in there!' Leila said, panicking. 'Do something!' she added desperately.

'I have indicated that there is new evidence already, Leila. I cannot take that back!' Patricia said. 'For what it's worth, I am sorry.'

'Not a lot,' Leila muttered, exasperated by the situation.

Both Leila and Patricia looked at each other, and Leila shook her head. Leila was going to have to forgive Patricia for this blunder. All Patricia had wanted was for Leila to have a stress-free trip. She thought she had been acting in her best interests, but clearly she had not thought it through in its entirety. Akash was about to hear that Dahlia was not his biological child in a crowd full of people. How humiliating.

Leila's heart was beating frantically. She contemplated not attending, but realised what a cowardly thought that was. Patricia approached the bench.

'Now in the light of new evidence, the decision will have to be reviewed,' the judge was saying. Patricia nodded.

'Can we hear it?' she asked.

Patricia walked across to the judge and whispered something. She was obviously trying to rectify the situation, but as the judge was shaking her head indicative of a negative response, Leila guessed it was too late. The only and last sentence Leila made out with a clear head was... 'We have DNA evidence to suggest that Mr Akash Yoganathan is not the biological father of Dahlia Cranston-Jasper (the child in question). In light of this new evidence, it seems Mr Yoganathan has no claim.' The case instantly collapsed. Leila was unable to look Akash in the eye. She felt culpable.

Outside the courtroom, he approached Leila.

'Why did you put me through that?' he asked, both hands in his pocket, legs wide apart. He looked down at Leila through squinted eyes.

'Kash, I wanted to tell you, but I only just found out.'

'Who is her father?' Akash asked, tears of anger and who knows what other emotion welling up in his eyes.

'That's not important at the moment.'

'Who is her father? Leila, I am doing the maths here and it does not add up. You were my wife. Who is her father? You owe me that much, don't you think?' He sounded stern, but calm. Leila could not deal with it.

'Kaobi!' she replied quietly. She almost whispered.

'What? The doctor?' he asked, alarmed.

Leila nodded.

Akash walked off angrily. Leila made her way out of the building, ignoring Patricia's plea for her to stop. She walked into the streets away from everyone, feeling an overpowering need for solitude. She needed time to come to terms with what had just happened. The guilt she felt was beyond measure, overwhelming in its vast bulk.

'Kaobi!' she said aloud. It was the only name on her mind and for many moments, the only word that was perceptible; the rest was silent or gobbledygook.

She searched her bag for the brown envelope and dug it out making her way for the trains – off to the beach house she was. Many questions needed answers!

Akash sat by the stairs once again. How strange these months had been. Leila had blamed him for the breakdown in their marriage. She said she was upset about the rape and for that reason did not want him to be a part of Dahlia's life. After fighting so hard for contact, it turned out that he was not the child's biological father; and what's more, his squeaky clean wife had been committing adultery at the time for, according to Dahlia's birth certificate, they were still married at the time of her conception (even notwithstanding the fact that she was born prematurely). He had beaten himself up over his alleged infidelity. He was guilty to an extent, but he had not even had penetrative sex with most of these women. Leila preached fidelity and loyalty to him. So was she a hypocrite? A self-righteous so and so! Either she was just as much to blame for the breakdown in their marriage or... he had pushed her into the arms of another man. Yet still, this same man let him see Dahlia when she was born. He offered his support that dark, lonely night. This same man offered him counselling. The same man came to his house with some random message about honesty, and what's that word again? Yes, 'tigritude'. He died? Akash was fuming because he wanted to punch him in the nose! How could he be Dahlia's father? He was not here to explain. Then Akash replayed the scene. The man stood tall, proud, confident. 'A tiger does not proclaim his own tigritude, he pounces!' he had said and his eyes had widened as his head launched a fraction of a mini inch in Akash's direction. That line would probably haunt him for the rest of his life. Was he gloating? Akash slicked his hair in anger. There was a lot to take in. Many questions needed answers!

Patricia stood in her little space, lacking conscious awareness of the world. She thought she was doing the right thing by not telling Leila about this result on Monday. Leila was obviously very upset and she had seen the heartbreak in Akash's eyes. It was too late to mend it all now. Patricia was pleased the trial was over for Leila's sake because now she could move on. She was also very sorry. For the life of her, she did not understand how she could have handled such sensitive information quite so haphazardly. She had thwarted any hopes of Leila and Akash remaining friends. She decided she would try to make it up to Leila somehow.

Leila approached the beach house. She opened the envelope, took out the keys and with trembling fingers, inserted it in the lock. It opened after three tries. She navigated her way to the back where the beach was, momentarily forgetting Akash's forlorn look, her anger with Patricia and her confusion at the outcome of the DNA test. No, she left all that behind. Instead she remembered every second she had spent with Kaobi. She re-lived it all, moment by moment, unhurriedly. She could hear his voice whispering and laughing. Somehow, she found herself by the beach overlooking the waters as they had done the day of the beautiful revealing kiss and the weird twelve-second moment. She found the suitable spot where she and Kaobi had picnicked together and then, from her bag, she dug out the envelope, pouring its content onto the sand. This was the last meeting with Kaobi; it had to be perfect. She wanted unblemished memories of him. Leila had more flashbacks. Kaobi speaking.

'My twin sister lives in my heart forever because her memory can never die.'

Leila's eyes danced about. The sky was that epileptic shade of brown again with the energised waves overwhelming the rocky shoreline. She could hear his voice just as it was that day, the same tone, the same seriousness, the same emotion, his Nigerian accent. His voice said:

'This is rare. The sky looking like this. Whenever you see this, remember me. Remember our kiss; what we shared today.'

The tears poured down. Had he known that today would come? A day when he would be no more and she would be left to deal with the consequences of what had started then? She tore open the envelope and emptied its contents on the sand; the title deed to the beach house, another set of keys for the house (she assumed) and a letter. She picked up the letter.

Sweetheart,

I lie here tonight putting this together, a love letter. I hope that I will have no reason to give it to you. If you have received this, I am dead! Although you and I both knew about my prophetic nature, it was mostly silent communication between us. I never said anything because I was not sure, or I hoped I was wrong. You felt it in my aura. You know my connection with Kamsi was such that we could read each other's minds – I had that connection with you. Don't cry! It is the will of God. Who are we that we question this? As you always say, sweetheart, for everything in life there's a time, a place, a season, sometimes there isn't but sometimes there's a reason, remember? You said that to me. Well, this is one of those times. Take it for what it is and instead of mourning my death, celebrate my life for what it brought to yours. There are a few things I really want you to know so brace yourself.

1. I have packed my suitcase and jetting off tomorrow and guess who stands before me? Kamsi. She has been watching me for a few days. She is beautiful. She is just like you in every way. My memory served me well indeed. It was not my imagination. The moment I laid eyes on you, I saw her.

2. Leila, the gift of love is going to be yours until the day you die. When the time is right, be happy. Do not hesitate. I will not let you go alone. Do everything you can to get it right. Be happy.

3. The love I feel for you is in every way identical to the biblical sense of the word. We had a rather unconventional romance, but I am sorry that we could not explore the husband and wife thing; it was never for lack of desire. I have always tried to do the right thing. You are my soul mate. I have no doubt about it. I think this is a mutual feeling. It also created a new path in life. I was perhaps not blameless but still, I love you like a sister, like a friend, like a companion, like my other half, I love you in every sense of the word, yet in its purest form. I accepted it for what it was.

4. Speaking of new paths in life, remember we planted seeds? Pause for a moment; go to that spot. I had to go and find out for myself too.

Leila stopped reading and scurried across to where they had planted the seeds on that crazy day when she had almost certified him insane. Before her was a single stem, a beautifully blossomed flower. It was a long, elegant three-foot stem; the flower was a breath-taking lilac pink and white mix, about eight inches in diameter. It was a dahlia. Leila shut her eyes for a few seconds. There were times when no words, no tears, nothing could describe an emotion... this was one of those times. She read on.

> *And the moral of the story is: for every second, every action makes the difference between what will or will not be. We did not have to go to the beach house that day, but you and me are written in history. There had to be proof of it. I knew Dahlia would exist, but until I met you, I had no clue how; and even then, I was too scared to believe it possible. However, when I looked in your eyes, Leila, I knew and I told you. Remember? Once again, it was a vision to you; it was communication of the minds to me. A dahlia emits sentiments of dignity and elegance, just like you. It is a symbol of love that lasts forever. Ironically, it is used to celebrate love and marriage – something I could never offer you, but Leila, you are my queen.*

Leila paused for a second. She remembered the mini-trance; she remembered how she had seen Dahlia even before she was born through Kaobi's eyes. She wished she had confronted him about it, but she was too scared of his prescience. Even now, she had to prick herself to check that she was not dreaming. Kaobi was indeed prophetic. It was a fact. She continued.

> *5. She is my little princess. On her 21st birthday, tell her how much her father loved her, tell her that her father watches over her every day and tell her she is the most beautiful girl her father has ever seen. Tell her my story, Leila, as you hand over the keys to her. This beach house belongs to Dahlia. My lawyer will call you. He knows what to do. I hope it is as fulfilling to*

her as it was to me. I hope she finds answers to questions in the tranquillity of these surroundings; just like her father.

6. I have to tell you again how much I love you. I loved you from the microsecond our eyes met. You touched my soul like no one else ever has. Your smile, your scent, the way you shake your head when you are confused, the way you sneeze like a cat (lol), your perpetually pink and/or cold nose, the way you hold Dahlia, the way you cry. Leila, I love everything about you. I will always love you. Maybe in our next lifetime, Leila, maybe then our relationship will be much easier to define. You and I could have shown the world the way love works. For now baby, be happy. I love you!

Lots of love,
Your KK xxx

2 PS's (because I know you don't like odd numbers!)

'KK, you weirdo!' She paused to laugh and cry hysterically before she carried on.

Firstly, there is something I never told you. Kamsi calls me KK. Can you imagine my shock when you called me KK at the café that afternoon? ☺

Leila screamed. Good thing no one could see her. She could have created an entertained audience right there.

Secondly, I had to proofread this letter out loud, and guess what? You will be so proud. Not one stutter. I have met some beautiful souls and interesting people in my lifetime, but you stand out by far. You subscribe to my school of thought. It is the little things. Leila, for all the reasons God brought you into my life, I am humbled by you, I am in awe, and I thank you! See you in the next life – the afterlife! I'll be watching you, I'll be guiding you, I am always…always with you.

Leila held the letter tightly against her bosom whirl winding through a myriad of emotions.

'I do not sneeze like a cat!' she screamed at the skies, smiling.

In spite of the anger, Leila felt relieved.

'KK, thank you. Thank you for this letter. Thank you for explaining it all to me. Thank you for everything you represented in my life. Thank you for OUR daughter. Thank you because, finally, you have answered my questions. It was too sudden, too confusing, and too hard. Finally, you have unhurt me, unchained me, un-kindled it all – you have set me free! I love you too, KK, my Prince. Goodbye!' She yelled this at the top of her voice as if that meant that he could hear her. In her shivers, she felt Kaobi's presence. She knew he had heard her. The downpour that followed was belligerent and with further flashbacks of Kaobi taking her hand in his and running to shelter, Leila collapsed into a powerless pile by the single dahlia and wept for a long time. When she dried her last tear, she was calm. She had said her goodbyes. It was over. Maybe now she would even write again. Once again, a new era would begin!

The day, which we fear as, our last is
but the birthday of eternity.
Lucius Annaeus Seneca

Chapter Fifty

It took two weeks to realise that she needed to help. She was unable to draw her curtains and let in sunlight. How fucking dare the sun shine? Did it not know life was over? Anything normal irritated her. She hired a nanny who looked after Dahlia. Fortunately, Dahlia loved her and was comfortable with the arrangement. It might have had something to do with the fact that the nanny accorded a lot of respect to Gucci. She barely noticed her mother's unsociable behaviour as Leila still showered her with cuddles and kisses; and nearly every night, she ended up in Leila's bed. But the grief! Leila had thought that reading Kaobi's letter on the beach was the all the medicine she needed to solve her problems. How mistaken she was. Every fibre of her being ached for Kaobi's voice, his flesh, his presence. There was a huge antique red clock that was positioned in the middle of her wall. It had the tick-tick sound which either infuriated Leila to the point of gulping down irresponsible amounts of brandy or soothed her to sleep because she fell into long daydreams about the clock being life-size and her jumping on to its minute hand and turning it backwards a good few weeks. Her days went thus: wake up, make sure Dahlia goes off to nursery with everything she needs, have some chicken soup, go back to bed, wake up, have a few more sips of the chicken soup, turn off phone if it has been ringing, receive Dahlia and overcompensate with copious amounts of hugs and kisses, kiss her goodnight, drink near enough to a pint of brandy, puke in middle of night, repeat puke process in morning.

The cycle went on for two weeks, except for weekends when she had to be a bit more discreet because Dahlia was at home.

Leila booked an appointment to see the doctor. Nothing reasonable came of that so she called in on Dr Aisha Alli – Kaobi's psychologist friend. She could trust her. Aisha agreed to an emergency session. By the time she walked out that office, Leila might as well have been bipolar for she suffered an immediate personality transplant. She had refused to acknowledge her grief and the doctor had to guess her symptoms; however, suggesting the 'D' word was all the kick up the backside Leila needed to immediately send her in the opposite direction. Depression! Hell freaking no! Leila became the epitome of activity. She grocery shopped, paying particular attention to their five a day (yet all she could manage was chicken soup and brandy), attended conferences she cared nothing for. She went for a run twice a day and took Dahlia swimming. She bought new curtains. She googled Nigerian recipes and cooked them (and Chinese, and Indian, and Romanian too!), but she never ate them. She put them away in the freezer. Three days later, she went back to see Aisha. They sat in opposite chairs facing each other. Aisha's eyes were intensely piercing and intruded the privacy of Leila's soul, so she ran away mid-session. Leila spent the next few days running away from herself. Anything that gave her a moment to think was avoided. She cleaned, she paid bills in advance, and she got on the train for no reason. One night, she lay in bed staring at the clock and trying not to get worked up by the tick-tock sound. In the corner of the room, the wrinkly old fortune-teller with the scrawny fingers stood filing her nails slowly. Occasionally, she looked up at Leila. She said nothing, no toothless smile; she looked almost nonchalant every time she blew the nail chaff away. Leila took a look in the mirror and realised how much she resembled the wrinkly old fortune-teller with the scrawny fingers. Her eyes looked sunken, she looked years older. She had dropped a dress size and a half – and not in a good way.

Leila sighed and called Gaurav Verma. He was her boss's boss, but a good friend nonetheless. Pleasantries were exchanged and she asked if he was in London. He was. She wanted to meet up for a coffee.

She wanted to talk about a working holiday. As *Silent Symphonies* was based in Zurich – Switzerland – she wondered if he would give her the opportunity to work from the Zurich office. She would deal with neighbouring clientele. There was a potential little magazine based in Itzehoe that was winding up. Itzehoe was about an hour on the train from Hamburg in Germany. She knew Gaurav had delegated some of the guys in Legal – Asif Minhas and Mark Davidson – to look into the potentials of a possible take-over bid. These two colleagues she knew in a professional capacity, but somehow she felt they would back her up with her plan. Mark Davidson had a gentle persuasion about him. He talked and people listened. He often talked in Leila's favour ☺. Asif Minhas was a good Muslim man with a strong professional wit. She always felt the urge to give him a hug because in his company she felt safe and worthy. But she had never seen any hugs in the office, so she guessed they were inappropriate – she never hugged him. She did tell him though that she hoped that Dahlia would marry a man just like him. He had smiled. Anyway, there was a business case underway, and Leila thought that perhaps she could project manage that venture. Both Mark Davidson and Asif Minhas were consulted. They approved. Leila smiled as she realised that, in life, God sent guardian angels in the form of everyday people. There was no other explanation for the encouragement she received from these two men; she would be grateful to them for life. As they spoke, Gaurav thought carefully.

'Where will you live?' he asked, eyeing her up and down. 'Sorry, just a bit distracted by the size zero look,' he added.

'Surely Gaurav, that's the least of our problems. The accommodation, I mean, not the err...weight loss. That bit wasn't planned. Long story.'

He nodded. 'What does Akash think?'

'Akash?' Leila was perplexed. 'You lost me there, Gaurav. This is nothing to do with Akash.' Leila did not care about Akash's opinion at this point. She owed no one any explanation.

He nodded again.

'Ok. My penthouse in Zurich – the one quite close to the Raddisson Blu Hotel. You and Akash enjoyed your last stay there, didn't you?'

'But your family will visit in three months – I was eavesdropping on your conversation the other day,' Leila confessed.

'How long are you running away for?' he asked her through inquisitive light brown eyes and one raised eyebrow.

Leila smiled. 'A year? Maybe two? Who knows.'

'Oh.'

By the end of the night, it was verbally agreed. Leila was going to work from the Zurich office. She would resume her weekly column as usual whilst attracting potential business in Switzerland and its environs. She would not stay in the main penthouse; she would live in the guest chalet, which was a beautiful self-contained two-bedroom luxury apartment.

The next day she called up a select few nurseries for Dahlia and had them fax over their information straight away. Leila had no time to lose. A week – max. She would get out of the UK for a while. She was unsure about whether she was running from, or looking for herself. She would find out one way or another.

'Do I fly or fall?' she wondered. Leila slept soundly that night.

By the end of the week, arrangements were finalised. As the nanny would live in the appending quarters to the chalet on an all-expense paid basis, with days off included, she decided the adventure was certainly worth her while. Dahlia had been worried about leaving Gucci behind but in addition to that, she wanted a cat as an additional complication. Leila got on the phone to Edna Karungu who had sold Gucci to her. She had no cats, so Leila called a colleague – Paul Edwards. He passed on a one-eyed cat called Horatio, with promises to give regular updates on his development and return him whenever she got back. It would be a holiday for Horatio. Horatio was a gorgeous two-toned grey Mackerel Tabby - Dahlia fell in love with him instantly. Leila sorted out pet insurance and they were good to go. Dahlia was content with the arrangement. Leila was comfortable that it was the right thing to do.

In the two years that Leila remained a resident of Zurich, she isolated her old life to concentrate on herself. She kept in touch with her family, but it was not as regular as it could have been. She became sociable and did things she would not normally do. She had a couple of pointless affairs – nothing that was worthy of archive or debate, but helped her along her journey to self re-discovery. Amongst these was a French Business Analyst with whom she companied and conversed with regularly (well, daily really) at the bar in Raddison Blu. She thought him the epitome of all knowledge and nicknamed him 'Mr Google'. On the days when Mr Google was not available, she sat in the Angel Bar in the Raddisson Blu by herself watching people walk in and out. Her laptop was never too far away from her and she took notes. She chitchatted with strangers and was on first name basis with the staff. The wine bar intrigued Leila every day; it always felt like the first time her eyes had beheld its beguiling lure. It towered all the way up to the ceiling with dim lights that went on and off at intervals. The flying bar staff – or 'wine angels' – soared up and down the Wine Tower retrieving bottles of wine and champagne were led by a sequence of LED light to the correct bottles, and equipped with individual holding gear. This was cleverly executed by computers, which took them by ropes to the tower's top and then back down to the appropriate bottle. It was not unusual for them to serve guests hanging upside down. In addition, they entertained guests with acrobatic displays at regular intervals. Leila was a big fan. Deep down in the archives of her memory, it reminded her of the pole in the middle of her bedroom in the house she had shared with Akash a lifetime prior. She had loved that pole and learnt to assume impossible positions hanging off it.

One night, after her affair with Mr Google came to an end, she met two of the most random, but most interesting people. A seemingly ordinary guy – Ricky – he always looked tidy and sexy, and his best friend, Ricky – a girl, a lesbian tomboy, a dyke! She was always in some form of baggy, sagging jeans and displayed abdominal muscle that most spent lifetimes trying to attain. She was perpetually drooled at. She moulded a comfortable friendship with the pair and when they informed her that they were from Itzehoe in Germany, an instant bond was formed. They were referred to as 'Ricky Boy' and 'Ricky Girl'. For work purposes and taking over the little unfortunate magazine that went under, these two became her useful tour guides. What's more, on a not-so-drunken night, Leila had the pleasure of Ricky Girl's company in a one-on-one honest conversation. Ricky Girl told her about her life of solitude, with all her family dead or not speaking to her; Ricky Boy had rescued her from a self-destructive life of Class A drugs. Leila got adventurous and shared her own story. Completely drowned in a world of woe-is-me, Leila had her first and only lesbian encounter. It was new and intriguing and took sexual to a whole new level for Leila. It felt good to bare her soul to a stranger and dabble in a bit of excitement. It was emotionally safe, detached but helpful so Leila let it carry on for a couple of weeks, that is until Ricky Boy got a bit fed up of being the third wheel, and it ended just as quickly as it started. Nobody got hurt, nobody drew the short end of the stick. It was what it was. Leila noted a few conclusions from that experience – girls' kisses were more passionate. Only a woman knows what a woman wants because it is what a woman wants. Leila archived the whole experience and thought about it sparingly with a cheeky smile. The end.

Leila took over the little magazine in Itzehoe on behalf of *Silent Symphonies* and although Itzehoe was a tiny, geographically insignificant town in the grand scheme of things, it ended up being one of the most fruitful ventures *Silent Symphonies* had acquired. Leila could not have pleased Gaurav any more than she did. Her bonus was huge; ultimately, Dahlia lacked nothing!

On an unplanned trip to the zoo in Zurich, Leila and Dahlia met a French mother and daughter – Chimene and her daughter, Chirene. So began regular weekend trips to Paris. On one of the trips, she rekindled things with Mr Google who took her on the most romantic nights out in Paris. When she reached the top of the Eiffel Tower, she wished Kaobi were with her. She gave Mr Google her all for the purpose of the moment, but he did ask: 'what is Leila searching for?' and Leila was unable to answer. Once again, just like that, it fizzled out, but not before she got him to make love to her with his reading glasses on. She loved the way he looked in those glasses. ☺

During her Zurich tenure, she dreamt of Kaobi twice. Both times he held her tenderly. The dream was always accompanied with the words – 'I will always…always be with you.' These words were usually timely and Leila found her comfort and strength to plunge on. Her journey of self-discovery had taken a new turn and she had found renewed strength. She was almost ready to face the ghosts of the past. Throughout her stay in Zurich, the wrinkly old fortune teller with the scrawny fingers had failed to make a significant appearance. She was probably uninterested in this little interlude of Leila's life. Still, from time to time, her last sighting of the old witch resurfaced – she filed her nails in the east of whatever room Leila was in and watched with that same nonchalant look on her face, as she blew the nail chaff. Nothing new.

One Tuesday evening during a deep meditating yoga session, Leila realised two things. Firstly, she had not had a conversation with God in over two years. Secondly, she no longer had a craving for chicken soup followed by brandy. Dahlia had turned four and it was time for real school. That evening, Leila gave Radisson Blu a miss and went to church. She sat there with a hymn book. Choir practice was on but she paid them no mind; instead she heard her favourite hymns in her head as she read the words. She listened to *'All things bright and beautiful'*, *'How great thou art'*, *'This is the day that the Lord has made'* and *'You are worthy'*. When her soul failed to connect deeply enough with these hymns, Leila wept; she dried her tears and sighed. The metaphoric winds blew and Leila knew it was time to go home. She spoke to Gaurav, Asif and Mark and was convinced it was the right thing to do. Just like that, Leila, Dahlia, the nanny, Gucci and an obese Horatio packed up their belongings and returned to London. Her brother met her at the airport and indulged her in a hug that lasted a couple of minutes. The hug told so many stories that evoked a variety of emotions in Leila. In his arms, she wept refreshed tears.

'Do I fly or fall?' she asked out loud. Her brother's expression was vacant. 'Never mind, please find me a grande soya Americano.' He nodded. 'That, I recognise. I'm on it,' he replied, tangling himself free.

'What the fuck did you feed that cat, Leila? If I didn't know any better, I would think he ate Gucci!' he exclaimed as he flicked through photos of Zurich. Leila giggled. 'Ask Dahlia…and the nanny!'

'I would like to be a fly on the wall when you hand Horatio back to Paul Edwards!' When Leila smiled, she knew it was because for the first time in two years, she had picked up her laptop and written a few articles and some diary entries…straight from the heart! Maybe she would get her life back. A new era!

"A change is as good as a rest."
– Stephen King, Hearts in Atlantis

Chapter Fifty-Two

Does 'it's over!' mean 'it's over!' OR 'it's over... for now'?

From a lady's point of view, it was one hell of a rollercoaster ride getting over the ex. X number of days, months or even years have gone by since you played 'Romeo and Juliet' with him. You can never watch 'Friends Series 3' because every episode reminds you of him. For a 'Friends' fanatic such as yourself that's a pretty disastrous state of affairs, so for him to muscle up the balls to waltz back in, you think he must be high on some cheap stuff! For the gentlemen it's sometimes more about the serious battering your pride took and how your friends called you a big wuss for blubbering so unashamedly when she left you (and they probably threatened to post a mobile phone video of your unwashed 9-day-old stubble on the www). For you, it's about the cold look on her face when she walked out and never looked back. Did the devil-woman ever love you? She's back. Why? Is her biological clock ticking that loudly?

Having promised each other eternity and failed, some people say 'it's over' means 'it's over!' and I say fair play to them. But I pose this thought for you to ponder: upon your mind retracing paths down trails of many yesterdays, you cry at some junctions and laugh at others, you remember steamy nights of passion till dawn and the first day s/he used the 'L' word (no, not liar, silly, love!). These memories haunt you, tickle your psyche and your heart betrays you by smiling at your mental memoirs. Regardless of who did what which led to the end, does 'it's over' really mean 'it's over' or 'it's over for now'?

OK so you don't want to even entertain the thought of reconciliation. What crime did h/she commit? Murder? (Well, in a sense because at that time you felt like you died but for the purpose of this article I was merely being sarcastic.) Or was it that you were shown so little a befitting thought in the perfection they sought? Did h/she decide it was absolutely within the boundaries of normality to wake up one day and just not love you anymore? Did you walk in on him/her having sex with someone that was not you? Let's summarise your feelings: (a) you are hurt or (b) h/she was generally poor at dating? If (a) is the case, then read on. If (b) is what bugs you, then turn the page and let's say no more on this issue – you have no business reading this article UNLESS time did not stand still. For if time stood still then he/she is definitely the same scumbag you dated (and I agree), but if life moved on and you even went on to attain that desirable qualification h/she always urged you to pursue, then read on and I'll make it worth your while ;-)

In playing devil's advocate (and some of you are going to kiss your teeth but listen with your hearts… and 'good sense' hat on), if life continued albeit reluctantly at first, do people not change accordingly? In this time, things happened – the environment changed – maybe they started recycling or their siblings had kids or their cat died – after which life brought on maturity, new perspective, new beginnings and ends, new meanings but all in all, one thing remained constant – their love for you (if you love someone do you not always love them in a sense? Maybe?).

We learn every day in love songs, in books by renowned psychologists, in films, etc that in love there are no guarantees. So if you say 'fuck you, fuck off!' and show them the door, they may walk away forever and take their love for you with them, whose loss is it then? OK it's theirs but is it not also yours? For when they said to you 'it's over', perhaps they meant 'it's over… for now'. '… for now' may be an undefined period of time in which h/she needed to broaden their horizons, mature, understand the requisites of a serious relationship that will weather tough storms. So maybe '…for now' has now lapsed (?). Sometimes '…for now' is so indefinite that it's 50 odd years later and you are all grey and wrinkled and realise that they actually never came back (ouch!). Yes it does happen that way occasionally. But if you are still in love and you suspect your brand new ex is too, will you, for fear of a tomorrow that you will never know today, give up on a chance of happiness tomorrow, today?

I'm no expert but I present to you from relationships which are close to my heart (OK, OK you twisted my arm – JO and CO are back together and getting married. The date is set for spring next year – you heard it here first), the new thought for the day – 'it's over… for now', trust me! ;-)

Leila x

Chapter Fifty-Four

'Bloody hell, Leila… Come on, Leila! I know you are there. It's Kash. You know we need to talk. I know you are back from Zurich, Gaurav told me.' The answering machine relayed the message. Leila sighed. It was over two years since that historic day in court when the whole trial had collapsed. It was the 1st of September, 2000 - but for the occasional text messages to say she was OK, and no, she did not want to talk to or see anyone, nobody had seen or heard a peep from Leila. Everyone had heard she was back though. She must have had a million messages from Patricia, Lala, Olga, her sisters, but half of these messages were from Akash. She was still not quite ready to face the world. Be it shame or discomfiture, fear of what people would think, annoyance for letting herself down, Leila did not know. She always took pride in doing the right thing, being on the straight and narrow. Christianity was not very flexible with morals, and she liked to believe that she was a good Christian. However, not only had she had a baby out of wedlock, she had done so whilst still in a marriage, so she had in effect committed adultery, the world knew, she had subsequently run away. This was against everything she portrayed herself to be and, what's more, she had, intentionally or not, given people the impression that her failed marriage was not her fault. Akash had been guilty, but she had outdone herself by far. Now it seemed God had punished her for it and taken Kaobi away anyway. She had turned her back on Him and He had obviously turned His back on her. It was nothing she did not deserve. The world was such a crazy place. Look how hard she had struggled to be good most of her life, all she asked Him for was little pleasures of life like a happy marriage and look – her life was a mess. She had been back from Zurich for a week and yes, it had been a great hide-away, but Leila still felt let down by God. She glanced over to the side table where her Bible lay. The cleaners had done a good job keeping it from gathering dust. Leila looked away, focussing her attention on the phone. She had to do it sometime. She picked up the receiver and dialled the number.

'Kash, it's Leila,' she said in an almost timid voice. The guilt she felt was inestimable.

'How are you?' he asked calmly. He did not even sound angry.

She didn't know how to respond to this question, and quite frankly she was baffled by it. Perhaps he was just making conversation. She decided not to answer it. How pointlessly rude she could be sometimes.

'I'm sorry I...' He cut her off. 'Can I come over sometime? We need to talk...face to face.' There was a mixture of irritation, hastiness, sadness, and confusion in the tone of his voice. Perhaps this was an example of one of the reasons why they had to talk face to face. With over-the-phone conversations, it was easier to lie/disguise emotions.

'We do?'

'We don't?'

'Tonight?' she sighed.

'What time?'

'What time is good for you?'

'Is 8 pm OK?'

'Yeah, 8pm is good.'

'See you then,' and he put the phone down. Leila sat panicking on her bed until Dahlia and Gucci interrupted her thoughts. Horatio was uninterested as usual and perched himself in the corner, glancing over occasionally when the pair reached some high pitch or Dahlia shocked the bird into furiously flapping her wings. Leila drifted off into random thoughts of her ex husband once again; she found herself wondering about things that should be no concern of hers. Well these things should be no concern of hers if she were no longer interested. She wondered who was hugging him these days, who was putting trespassing hands into the two back pockets of his sexy blue jeans. She loved those sexy blue jeans, she had bought him those sexy blue jeans, and his arse looked so taut in those sexy blue jeans. She wondered which lucky woman had the privilege of staring into his squinting eyes after a night out boozing with the boys… those eyes always meant one thing: they were going to bed but there would be no sleeping. Leila smiled at her stupidity. After he raped her? 'This is a joke! Really?' This was guilt talking. Guilt and grief. Possibly loneliness. Maybe starvation – sex (love) starvation. Yes! That's what it was!

At quarter to eight, Leila thought she heard a car pull up in her driveway. When at five minutes to eight there was still no knock at the door, she took a step towards the window with the intention to peek outside, but she chickened out and walked straight back to the breakfast bar and tapped her fingers on it. On the one hand, she blamed him for her mistakes, and yet on the other hand she was sorry. The doorbell rang finally. She was expecting it, but still, she jumped. What the flipping heck was she supposed to say to Akash? Her mind was blank!

It was quarter to eight when Akash drove up Leila's drive, but as it wasn't eight yet, he sat in his car and waited. What was with the disappearing act? Leila had a child while she was still his wife, and disappeared on some adventure (or something) to Zurich. Gaurav had not given him any details. Who exactly was Leila? He did not recognise this person. It was 8 pm finally, so he got out of his car and braced himself as he walked towards her door. He slicked his hair with his right hand, and he rang the doorbell with his left. What the flipping heck was he was supposed to say to Leila? His mind was blank!

'Kash.'

'Leila.'

'Come in please,' she said ushering him into the living room.

They managed the barest minimum of pleasantries and when the weather was too obvious a diversion from the reason for his visit, they shared an uncomfortable silence. Akash was the first to speak.

'I don't understand it. Maybe if you explain to me I can understand how you let it come to this. I know I hurt you, but I pushed you this far?' and he waited a while for a response.

'Kash, I don't know. I didn't know till that day at court.'

'You could have stopped that from going ahead. You could have made sure I heard this outside, not in court,' he said, shaking his head in despair.

'I tried to, but it was too late. I wish I could answer your questions. In our marriage, I felt so alone, so frustrated and I wanted to leave you, but this was not intentional.'

'How long did the affair go on for?' he asked.

'Affair?'

'Yes. How long?'

'I did not have an affair with him…not in the manner you think.'

'Then explain to me,' he said and when he did not get an answer, he added, 'Do I not deserve that much?'

Leila took a deep breath.

'Kash, when we got married, I was the happiest girl in the world. You were everything I wanted in a man. You gave me all of you. Over time, I watched you change. I know you knew when things started to get a bit rocky. I did not know what to do. I wanted us to last forever. Yes, I met Kaobi back then. He was only a friend. I talked to him about our marriage, amongst many other things. I became quite close to him and we slept together once, Kash. It was when I found out that you were having an affair. After that, it never happened again. I prayed to God for forgiveness for that but obviously for every action taken there is a new path in life created and these are the consequences. God has turned his back on me. He died; you hate me. I am a hypocrite, a laughing stock who has begged for forgiveness and been denied. Everything I believed in has been thrown back in my face. Love, life, God! I don't really know what to believe any more. I hate myself for what life has brought my way!' Before Leila knew it she had said everything. She poured out thoughts that had been tormenting her. She hated life and was unsure as to what her beliefs were concerning the existence of God at that moment.

'God? What has God got to do with this?' Akash asked, bewildered.

'I did my best, Kash. My best is never going to be good enough,' she replied.

'Leila, I was ill when we got married. I only realised that after that horrible incident between us. I was closed when I should have been open; I turned to other destructive ventures for comfort when I should have turned to you. When I decided to put it right, it was too late. I'm sorry.'

Leila was taken aback. Was this a game? She expected a shouting match, violence even.

'Kash, you hate me. There is no need to pretend.'

'Leila, I don't hate you. Pointing fingers at each other won't help. I am sorry it didn't work out. I am sorry for what I put you through. If I could go back in time I would, I am sorry!' he concluded and he stood to make his exit.

'Kash,' she called out.

He turned around.

'I am sorry,' she said and by this time, she was weeping. His eyes were not dry either. He closed in on the distance between them, but Leila shook her head and shrugged him off. Unable to decode her reaction he made his way to the door.

'Kash.'

He stopped in his tracks. Customary pose. Hands in pocket, feet slightly apart, but this time, head bowed.

'Did you marry me for British Citizenship?' Akash slicked his hair. He took a few steps towards the door, but then he turned round and looked at her.

'Initially, I, well, what happened was…'

Yes or no?'

'Yes.'

SILENCE

'Yes, Leila, but...yes, but I…'

'It's OK. I needed to know.'

He began to speak but no words would come out. He made his way to the door and left. He never looked back.

He sat in his car for a few minutes. He was trembling. He was furious with her, but he could not deny his part in this disaster. He was relieved that he had spoken to her about everything and then there was the question of citizenship, which she had tortured him with for a while now. Well, there, he had said it. What did her tears mean? Leila renouncing God? That was bizarre! He wanted her back. He could rescue her, be her knight in shining armour again. He had to play his cards right. Kaobi popped in his head for a second but he shrugged that away quickly. He needed Leila for himself. She was the only one that knew how to be there for him; no one else would do. This had nothing to do with teenage crushes. This was grown up stuff, a symbiotic relationship. He would take, but he would give too. How would he fix this? This is not a game of chess! Oh yes it is...well, in a sense. Prince Charming got Cinderella. He would win her over and it would be in their best interests. How? He turned the key in the ignition with such annoyance that the engine shrieked. He closed his eyes for a few seconds trying to calm down, and then he screeched off.

Leila stood with her back against the door still weeping. Despite her feeling of relief, she felt guilty...and alone. He had been so composed, so calm. She heard him screech off and wondered if he was angry. But then, she replayed his words, 'initially, I...yes!' and she gnashed her teeth in frustration. Her ego was still bruised. The thoughts in her head were haphazard and confusing. Once again, Leila had the sinking feeling of hopelessness she had felt in the days before she met Kaobi, but this time for a totally new reason. She felt like she had lost God, lost Kaobi, and even managed to outdo herself by hurting Akash – the emotionally untouchable beast!

It was two weeks after her meeting with Akash and still, the only person that had laid eyes on a brooding Leila apart from Dahlia and the nanny was Akash. Leila had spent the two weeks literally staring into space. She had no idea how to get on with her life. For some reason, she almost did not hear the doorbell – the world was at a total stand still. The time in Zurich had helped, but she realised that was temporary. Life went on without Kaobi, but cruelly, her problems waited for her to come back and regardless of whether she was ready or not, they just sat there, unchanged.

Akash lay in bed thinking about his visit to Leila. It had been two weeks and yet he was able to think of nothing else. Leila lived for her beliefs and if she had given up on those then she was in trouble. He would know about depression. He had conquered it, and upon reflection of his attitude back then, he would not wish the fucking disease on his worst enemy. He stared at the Bible on what was once Leila's dressing table. He picked it up thoughtfully and caressed its pages through squinted eyes. Leila's words came back to him – 'It's the little things, Kash. The things you think don't matter,' she had said in a whisper one night.

He had an idea. He smiled.

It was the postman at the door with a package for Leila. Five roses – single elegantly long stems, de-thorned; four white and one pink. Accompanying these beautiful roses was a note. It read:

> *'Ephesians 1:6–8 says:*
>
> *…to the praise of his glorious grace, which he has freely given us in the One he loves. In him we have redemption through his blood, the forgiveness of sins, in accordance with the riches of God's grace that he lavished on us with all wisdom and understanding…*
>
> *Leila, don't give up. God has forgiven you. Forgive yourself.*
>
> *Kash'*

Leila was puzzled and read the note repeatedly. Throughout their married life, Leila had read the Bible every day, sometimes out loud so it was no surprise that Akash would know the parts of the Bible that were relevant to certain circumstances. She half smiled, but did nothing. That night she read the note 28 times before she fell asleep.

And when the postman arrived the next day, he brought with him a beautiful bouquet of white daffodils. This time the note read:

'Psalm 62:2

He alone is my rock and my salvation; he is my fortress, I will never be shaken…

Leila, God is with you. His words remain in your heart. Do not be afraid to live them again. Be strong

Kash'

And the postman came again on the third day. This time when she opened the door, he even managed to share a light-hearted joke with her. It had been the same postman three days in a row. He had for her five white lilies.

'John 11:25

Jesus said to her, "I am the resurrection and the life. He who believes in me will live, even though he dies"

Leila,

It is very hard I know but according to God's word, Kaobi lives on. I'm sorry for your loss. Be strong!

Kash'

On the fourth day, Leila received a dozen red roses. As Kash knew that this passage needed no introduction or elucidation, he skipped the reference and the personal note and signature at the end. This self-explanatory passage was Leila's favourite passage.

'…Love is patient, love is kind. It does not envy, it does not boast, it is not proud. It is not rude, it is not self-seeking, it is not easily angered, it keeps no record of wrongs. Love does not delight in evil but rejoices with the truth. It always protects, always trusts, always hopes, always perseveres…And now these three remain: faith, hope and love. But the greatest of these is love…'

And on the fifth day she received another dozen red roses with a white rose in the middle. This time the message read:

'Romans 8:18

...I consider that our present sufferings are not worth comparing with the glory that will be revealed in us...

Leila,

I believe in you...

Kash'

And finally, that cracked her. Leila smiled. She sat on her bed for a while staring at the notes, and with drawing pins she stuck all five notes on her wardrobe studying each one with scrutiny. After an hour, she knelt by her bedside and opened her Bible. She was scared at first, but soon she was in familiar territory. Leila prayed for a long while, catching up on all she had wanted to discuss with God and as she closed the prayer and the Bible, something strange happened to Leila that night. She had tears falling freely from her eyes, but she did not know if she was crying or if it was just the blast of wind that came through the window she had opened wide. She gave up trying to figure it all out and she fell asleep. When she woke up two hours later, she returned all her phone calls and made polite conversation. By the end of the night, Leila had even promised to be at Olga's lingerie launch party. Leila had not seen Olga since before Kaobi died; she had obviously missed out on over two years of success, for this lingerie brand was all work in progress the last time they spoke. It seemed her friend's dream had come true. She was sorry she had missed every phase of this wonderful development, but she had been through her own issues. Occasionally, one needed a retreat from the world; Olga understood. Not many best friends would be that forgiving. This was one reason why she loved Olga with all her heart and with no conditions.

'You bet I will be there, babe, speak to you soon. Take care, bye!' she said as she put the phone down. Leila felt ready for the war, to get her life back on track and be normal.

The lingerie launch party was even bigger than Leila had anticipated. It was set under four cream and soft turquoise marquees matching the theme of Olga's brand. On display was a huge projector churning out photos of the various ranges. One of the clips was a two-minute introductory speech by an elegant looking Olga. She was initiating all women into the wonderful world of 'Olga's' where women's practical needs were met without ignoring the sensual feel expected. She introduced her debut selection of high-waisted thongs, designed to hold a woman firmly in place, accentuating her best qualities whether her clothes were on or off. She winked at that point. There were a few women all glammed up in little cream and turquoise satin off the shoulder dresses. They were handing out sample goody bags to guests. This was all thoroughly thought through. Leila was a little sad for not being a part of the organising. Good thing she had dressed appropriately – she had not quite realised what a big show Olga was putting up. She was wearing an outfit Akash had bought for her following a business trip to Europe somewhere. It was a simple white Chloe dress, cut at the top, shirt-style. The collar and trimmings were gold with an apt gold belt. She finished the look off with gold Lanvin Degrade python shoes, which had a detachable buckle-fastening ankle strap. It was nice to wear anything other than underwear and a bathrobe. With her hair up in a loose bun, and wearing hardly any make up, Leila looked simple, but exquisite. There were many 'big shot' faces present. Leila recognised them from contracts both she and/or Akash had spearheaded. She spotted Akash. She decided to hide – too late; their eyes met!

'Leila.'

'Kash.'

'I got the flowers and the notes, thanks.'

Akash half smiled, and nodded.

'A bit of research went into that. I had to pick the right verses…you know, get it right.'

Leila wondered if she detected an attempt at nonchalance, but she nodded regardless.

'You look beautiful,' he said looking at her from her hair, down to her gold painted toenails, which were sheltered within familiar shoes. He ignored the tattoo.

'You bought this dress.'

'I remember! I didn't think you liked it. You never wore it. Except that first time when you put it on…and I took it off.'

Two red faces. SILENCE

'How are you Leila?' he asked.

'I'm much better than the last time we spoke, thanks, Kash,' she replied.

'Glad to hear it.'

'Would you...' but he was cut off.

'Leila, Kash...' It was Olga.

'Congratulations!' they both chorused.

They chatted happily about the lingerie range, which she had decided to call simply, Olga's.

'Wow Olga... your dream has come true,' Leila was saying.

And a few feet away Patricia stood. She was approaching Leila. She stopped when she saw Akash heading in the same direction. From then on she had watched them. Curiously so, she thought, if she didn't know any better she would say there was unfinished business there! She was not going to butt in (and she imagined that she would be the last person Leila would want to listen to, especially since the DNA saga), but she thought that a harmless comment would not hurt. As soon as Olga spoilt the moment (in Patricia's opinion), Patricia joined them as well. It was the first time she had seen Leila since court. They had talked on the phone, but only briefly – mostly about settling invoices. Leila was pleasant. Patricia had not been sure what to expect. Patricia was glad when Olga dragged Akash away, talking marketing.

'Leila, I never got the chance to say how sorry I am for the way I handled the DNA results. I didn't quite think it through properly.'

'Obviously!' Leila rolled her eyes, but smiled and took Patricia's hands in hers. 'It's forgotten, Trish. These things happen. I didn't take offence. I was upset at the time but I know it wasn't personal,' Leila replied.

'I would never do anything to hurt you,' Patricia reiterated.

'I know,' Leila said and then added, 'and I am sorry that I never got the chance to thank you. Had it not been for your insight, who knows how this might have played out. I would not have gone to Nigeria either and that was an amazing experience.'

'And you and Akash are on speaking terms now?' she asked.

'I think we have worked through the hard bit. We need to forgive each other,' Leila replied.

'And have you?'

'You know, I think we have made our peace with everything!' Leila said thoughtfully.

'I am not even going to ask what you mean by that but I have something to say.' Patricia then waited for an invitation to share her thoughts.

'Last time you had intuition…' they both smiled.

'When you do not know where you are going, all roads lead there. It's a Roman saying,' she said all the while staring across at Akash and Olga who were both staring at Leila, it seemed. Patricia smiled.

'And in English please?' Leila asked.

'Think!' she said, sipped on her cocktail and questioned Leila about this Olga's new exciting lingerie brand.

'So you seem to be getting on quite well with your estranged wife…' Olga said to Akash obviously fishing for information.

'I'm going to be careful,' he said.

'Do you think you might get back together?' she asked.

'Do you think there is a possibility?' he asked. Olga said nothing initially and Akash added, 'Would I be stupid if I thought there might be?'

Olga thought about it for a second.

'She loves you – love makes people do the craziest things.'

'What does that mean?' he asked.

'Think!' Olga said.

'That's good enough for me!' Akash said smiling as they both looked thoughtfully over at Leila. Leila was so deep in conversation with Patricia that she never noticed their eyes. Patricia did though. She winked!

When Patricia wandered off Leila thought about her words and all the while she had her gaze intently fixed on her ex-husband. He was making his way across to her.

'Leila, I am leaving now. I have business to take care of, but erm... before I go, I was wondering if I could ask you something.'

'Yeah?' Leila replied, her heart racing for no reason.

'I was wondering if I could take you out to dinner some time next week,' he blurted out.

Leila stood rooted to the spot.

'Think about it. Ring me...or text, or you know...whatever...'

Leila was grateful for the space to think about it first. He knew her too well.

Later that night, Leila sat by her phone thinking. She picked it up and dialled his number.

'Hello.'

'Kash, it's me. Let's do dinner. Not Petrus. And no chicken.'

'Tuesday, and not Petrus. And no chicken.' Leila nodded and then remembered that he could not see her, so she waffled on about how she wanted to eat duck instead.

'Fantastic. I will pick you up at eight then.' He sounded pleased.

'OK then. See you. Bye!'

'Leila!' he called out before she dropped the phone. She paused and listened. Her heartbeat tripled for no apparent reason.

'Nothing,' he said in a tone that she had not heard in a long time. That tone reminded her of being wrapped in his arms in moments so light, yet so heavy. A particular night came to mind. It was a night when she had come back from work after a disastrous day. She had snapped at him for no reason.

'You are tired,' he had said pulling her in for a cuddle.

'You are rather tall for an Asian bloke, you know,' she said, standing on tiptoes, whilst tilting her head up for a kiss. He had smacked her on the bum playfully which triggered off their messing around like kids. They destroyed a pillow together that night. By the end of their play fight, they had duck feathers all over the living room. They did not have sex that night, but they slept in a tangled mess. They had sex as soon as they woke up though, and then argued over who would hoover the duck feathers! Bliss.

'Are you there?' Akash asked.

'Sorry, I wandered off for a second there,' she replied, sighing deeply.

Upon further reflection, Leila decided that she had agreed to dinner because it would have been much easier to say no and she was tired of being a coward. She had no clue what she was doing, but she would do it anyway. Patricia had pointed out that no step would take her nowhere. This was no time to sit in her rocking chair. Back-forth-back-forth. How else would she arrive at a destination? Satisfied that it was the right decision, she curled herself up in bed and slept soundly.

Tuesday night came. Leila wasted no time searching through her wardrobe. She did not want to appear like she was trying to make an effort, but she did not want to look too casual. She settled for all black – a high-waisted knee length Camilla and Marc skirt with a gold tone wrap-around function zip. She wore this over a Zimmermann black sleeveless bodysuit with sporadic shimmering gold bits and cross over straps. It was simple, so she relied on her make-up and nicely straightened hair to finish it off perfectly. When Akash smiled, she smiled too. She knew him well enough to read his thoughts. He did not look bad himself. Akash had the most fabulous wardrobe and that night he scrubbed up good and smelt subtly sexy – black jeans, a brown shirt, brown suede boots and a navy blazer. It was by Thom Browne – irregular patch-effect with alternating hound's-tooth-patterning throughout. Typical Akash. He took her to a jazz club where the music was beautiful, but not too loud and they served light meals. Leila had a salad in the end. Akash wanted to speak to Leila and not have his voice drowned by the music even though he hoped some of the love songs would act as some sort of aphrodisiac, or at least soften her heart up a little bit.

That night Leila and Akash talked about their failed marriage. For the first time, they both accepted their faults and did not point fingers at each other. Leila accepted that she could be imperious sometimes. In her quest for perfection, she often paid him too little a befitting thought. A good example would be the fact that she never agreed to a Hindu wedding; after all, what is in a little ceremony to please him, a little ceremony to honour his own culture, to make his own family get their say in their celebrations and to feel a part of their union. It was more about how she was feeling, than his opinion on certain issues. She did not take time to notice when he was upset about something because she was too busy reiterating how hurt she was and was often quick to play the victim without first trying to work it out. On the flip side of the coin, Akash's list of flaws was an inexhaustive list. Where would they begin? His truancy, blatant disregard for her feelings, marriage under false pretences, violence and sexual abuse! Leila nearly threw up going over the details, but he was ill for the most part. Was that enough justification to dowse all that had happened? In the end, they both agreed that in the areas of their marriage where he was good, he scored highly. They marvelled at how easily things could be resolved if only they communicated; and while Leila accepted that Akash needed a bit more attention, Akash accepted that it was the littlest of gestures that made the difference. Overall, they both understood where they had gone wrong. When the heavy talk was over, Leila spoke to Akash about Dahlia and her development thus far. Akash's interest seemed uncomfortable initially but once that over, he was genuinely interested in the detail. Then they spoke about other inconsequential matters arising, and as the night progressed, it was filled with less awkward silences.

For Leila, it felt like she needed time to be alone and gather her thoughts. She needed to focus on Dahlia and build a new life, one without Kaobi. But that was just it. There was no Kaobi, there would never have been Kaobi. If Kaobi had lived, would she have ended up with him? She had no crystal ball, fact! In reality, and factually so, it seemed unlikely. He had dedicated his life to someone else; Kaobi did not do divorce. That much was obvious. Did she have the emotional strength to deal with someone new? With all that had happened to her thus far, probably not. Was this feeling temporary? It was so strong, it did not feel like it would fade any time soon. Maybe she would change her mind at some point? Leila did not feel like she could be bothered. Ultimately, it boiled down to this – she simply did not want to invest her time or effort in anyone. It was too hard. If there was no Kaobi, then so be it! She had somehow lost all faith in Cinderella-type romance, but did that give her the excuse to settle for whatever was first in line? Akash was not first in line. There was no line. 'Oh for goodness sake, line? Settle?' Was going out to dinner and having a cosy time with her ex-husband settling? No. It was dinner. And conversation. Did it mean she was getting back together with Akash? Not particularly. Would she rule out the possibility though? Not at this stage. That was how tiny the scared little voice in her head was to admit it. She rebuked the voice instantly and sent it to the naughty corner. She locked the door and threw the key away…for now!

Akash was in control to a certain extent. Did he want Leila? Yes. Because he was madly inlove with her? He did not know any more. With her he felt safe. If they got back together would he do things differently? Definitely. Was that for love? Akash had never been the type to throw himself into love, not in the romantic sense that rendered one silly. Did he want to go out and search? No. Not particularly. Leila ticked all his boxes. She would look after him and he would look after her. They could exist in a reciprocal relationship of give and take. Could they be happy? Sure. He had learnt what to do to make her happy, but most importantly, he was now of sound mind. Everything that happened henceforth would be by choice, by maturity. Drawing from that, he knew he could love her the right way and give her everything she wanted. Did it mean they were getting back together? Not particularly, but he was willing to give it a go.

'Would you like to come in for a drink?' Leila asked and instantly regretted asking.

'I better not; it's a long day tomorrow,' he said.

'Yeah, it was a bad idea anyway.' She had to redeem herself somehow.

'No it wasn't!' he replied.

Leila got out of the car, not waiting for Akash to drive her down the driveway.

'Well, thanks for dinner, Akash. I will call you,' she said politely and hurriedly made her way to her front door without a second glance backwards.

'Don't…call me Akash, please!' but she had slammed the door before he could finish the sentence.

Leila got in and slammed the door shut. She was annoyed with herself for asking but more irritated by her vibrating phone. She reached into her purse. Probably the nanny, asking if she would be much longer. She had said she would be back at about 10 pm and it was midnight now. Still she had paid her to stay the night. But it was not. It was Akash.

'Ak..Kash?'

'Are you still offering coffee? You know I can only have de-caff.' If she had looked, she would have seen him smile.

She paused for a couple of seconds. She could tell him that the offer had been withdrawn, that it was too late in the night anyway, and it was a bad idea. But she did not!

'I have de-caff!' she replied. Leila smiled.

'I like what you have done with this place,' he commented as they sat in the kitchen waiting forever for the kettle to boil.

'Thank you. We are actually moving soon.'

'You are? Where are you moving to?'

'There is this house just around Stroud...' and Leila took a deep breath and explained about Dahlia's inheritance and how she had decided to move there for the tranquillity of the surroundings and because she wanted to live in it to make the most of the house anyway. Her bond with Kaobi was something she decided was best to leave out but she felt compelled to inform him of important decisions. It was awkward but Leila was happy that they were open enough, civil enough, and mature enough to be honest about these issues. They soon drifted on to other topics and just like the good old days when they had only just fallen in love, they talked until the wee hours of the morning. At 5.30 am Leila saw Akash to the door. He stood outside, she, inside. The open door separated them.

'I had a good time, Leila,'

The typical aggressive winter was yet to hit Britain, but it was quite early in the morning so it was cold; yet standing face to face with a seemingly reformed Akash even with no jacket on felt warm.

He held out his hand to her. She accepted.

'How on earth could I ever have been stupid enough to let you go?' he asked quietly.

'I was stupid too,' she replied. With that, the bridge between them was no more.

'When I look at you like this, all I can see is the hurt I put you through and how badly I want to right that wrong,' he said.

'Let's not be hasty!' she said, but she knew what was coming next; every hair on her body sensed it. He was going to give her a taster of the past, the bit that had once pleased her, something to tease her mind a little, and to stir those almost forgotten memories just a little bit. It took what felt to Leila like forever before he kissed her. He teased her many times, touching her lips with his only slightly and then retreating until finally, he enclosed them totally with his. The kiss was soft and purposeful. It heralded many messages within it, which Leila read quite clearly. If she read the messages right, he said: 'I'm sorry', he said 'let's make it work'.

'Do you understand what I am trying to say to you?' he asked gently.

Leila nodded. The kiss was delicious; thinking was a bit tricky!

Akash woke up with a smile on his face. For the first time in a long time, the future looked bright. He was determined that this time he would get it right. He had learnt an invaluable lesson. It took two to make a marriage work, it took a lot of communication because it was just as important to speak one's mind, as it was to listen; and love is very important, but marriage is hard work - love with no accompaniments is simply not enough!

Leila awoke with a smile on her face. She was not a hundred percent sure of the details but she knew the kiss felt right enough and she was not going to ask too many questions either. If they got back together, she would be careful. She had learnt an invaluable lesson. It took two to make a marriage work, communication and compromise were absolutely essential, it was just as important to listen as it is to rant, and although it is very important, love is simply not enough!

Love never dies a natural death. It dies because we don't know how to replenish its source. It dies of blindness and errors and betrayals. It dies of illness and wounds; it dies of weariness, of witherings, of tarnishings.

Anaïs Nin

Chapter Fifty-Six

Letter to Santa

Dear Santa,

It's that time of the year again. Everyone has sent you their requests and I am sure you are inundated at the moment. I am sorry to bother you.

I have tried, but haven't particularly been the best I could possibly be this year. I have made a few mistakes. I hear, though, that you have a big heart so I hope you can forgive me. The last time you would have heard from me would have been when I was 8 years old or thereabout and I asked you for a dolly. Thank you for that; she was beautiful. I haven't come to you in a few years because I have been busy growing up. Shortly after that request I went into my teenage years and my eyes began to see the world differently and I lost my prelapsarian childhood/youth. Now, things are not that simple any more. Being a woman has brought with it all sorts of responsibilities and challenges that I never imagined possible as a child. Maybe if knew then what I know now, I would have asked you for something a little bit different.

In light of this, Santa, this year, I ask for something pretty intangible. Santa, this world is such a crazy maze. A lot of times I find myself going left or right and still ending up in the same spot. Santa, this world is fraught with winding roads. I know I am merely human and should expect nothing supernatural about my foresight but sometimes I wonder if a little peep ahead would have been asking too much. Santa, this world is full of disappointment and shock and twist and pain and Santa, tell me, who created death? Why can we never be prepared for the pain?

So I was telling you about my request for something ethereal this year, I won't ask you for a dolly. But, I won't ask you for courage or good vision or the power to deal with emotional trauma. This year, Santa, I ask you to reduce me to love. If I am able to love as God intended love to be, then I think I will be alright. I will be able to forgive, I will be able to forget, I will be able to accept people for who they are and despite flaws, they will be endeared to me. I will be able to rise above disappointment and I will be able to see the bigger picture when I know that I will never mortally see someone I love ever again because they have died. I will be able to look at my maze or winding road and embrace the challenge and where I would normally complain and wallow in self pity; instead, I will smile and be thankful for the two feet of straight road that is within my vision at that point in time. When a baby cries, Santa, I will forget about the panic of what baby needs at that time, but instead tickle baby's gorgeous toes and bask in the most beautiful sound of baby giggling, for God who created ten perfect little toes obviously has a sense of humour – amazing! When my friend rings me up at midnight with a problem too big for her shoulders, I will love her enough to not look at my watch every other second or yawn or bring my own problems into the conversation. When I wake up and go outside to breathe in the fresh air of the morning and the neighbour says good morning, I will not try to read between the lines, I will not wonder what she is trying to say or if she stole my bin, I will, in breathing that morning air, breathe in enough love to say good morning back and mean just that! I hope to receive the gift of love that when I behold a beautiful daffodil, I will stop to appreciate the beautiful things in life.

Santa, yesterday morning, my daughter put a striking flower in my hair and she was convinced the flower made me the most gorgeous woman in the whole wide world. 'It's yovyi, mummy,' she said. Something in her outlook to life softened my heart instantly. Therefore Santa, I reckon that if I could love, love and love with her naivety, that I will be able to see life through her eyes, the eyes of a child. If I can do this, the world will be brand new again and when I smile, it will come from somewhere deep down in my heart.

OK so maybe this is a bit premature, Santa, I forgot to ask, do you do intangible gifts? Thank you and merry Christmas!

Merry Christmas All!

Leila xxx

Chapter Fifty-Eight

It was December 1st 2000, and Leila had just about finished unpacking. Leila and Dahlia had successfully moved into the beach house and were settling in quite nicely. Akash had been instrumental to the success of the move but as they both wanted to get their relationship absolutely right, he was not moving in (or at least not yet). They, in fact, had not officially announced that they were seeing each other again. There was a lot of speculation but Leila had not confirmed it. She had not even told Olga, although she was sure that smart as Olga was in deciphering her many moods, she had probably worked it all out for herself. Leila and Akash jointly decided that if things were still going as good as they had been going for a while then they would let people know at Christmas. For now, it was best not to jinx it. Leila had also decided that in the true spirit of Christmas, she was inviting as many of her friends and family as were dear to her heart over for a sleepover into Christmas Day. There would be the loud squish squashing of wrapping paper, disorderly cheers and happy faces on Christmas morning and a beautiful buffet of sausages and eggs for breakfast; what more could she ask for? There were conditions of course. Firstly, beds were on a first come, first served basis (with the kids taking priority of course) but there were loads of spare blankets, duvets and sleeping bags. She knew most of her friends would jump at the opportunity of togetherness. That was what Christmas was all about after all. So far Dahlia and Leila were looking forward to their first Christmas in their new home with Akash, Leila's parents, sisters and brother, Olga and Chris, Toks, Gerald and their son, Joy, her husband, Jose and their baby, Lala, Jennifer and her kids, Tia, Patricia and Bianca-Maria. Every one arrived on Christmas Eve with bags of presents to put under the Christmas tree. Leila's Christmas tree was over six feet tall and she had done the majority of the decorating with Dahlia. They had organised a 'Secret Santa' game which involved all their names in a hat with each person drawing a name from the hat and buying that person a present without revealing who bought what for whom. That way, no-one was left without a gift. There was of course the obvious exchange of gifts between individual families as well. As assistant hostess, Dahlia had the majority of the presents because everyone had bought her something. They all sat round the erratically scintillating Christmas tree singing hymns and sharing jokes. The children played games in their own little corner joining in when the hymns got exciting enough. At midnight, Leila looked around and loved the joy of sharing her home. It made the season that bit more special. With thoughts of Akash and their future on her mind, Leila made her excuses and retreated for a bath and a little quiet time. She admitted to herself that she was scared. She was scared of the past, scared of the future, scared of the instincts urging her on. She wished she could be certain. Since their first date earlier on in the year, they had shared no more kisses. It was Akash's idea of taking it very slow. Something about being with Akash felt right though and she found herself longing for intimacy.

Sat in solitude, discomfort, unrest
Solo restless thoughts of your worst and your best
Says my head to my heart, 'his eyes told tales of trials and lies'
Says my heart to my head, 'bare truth thrives only truly in eyes'

I've been there, I've moved on, love's discreet, life's sweet
Lies! Conflict reflects my soul, my soul burns with lustful heat
It's his presence in physical, the awareness of him
It's my soul on fire with the burning urge to sin

But his heart may be unyielding, no, his heart could be reborn
But he can never love me, adore me. To this has he sworn?
And the past? It didn't last, all the hurt, his passiveness
Love is foolishness, love is blind, no foresight, but loves also
forgiveness

Minute per minute heart and head naively toddle, they fight,
and they struggle
Second per second body heat is at its height, feels right, hardly subtle
Ask his lips of untold truth, request your bequest
One familiar kiss says my eyes to his lips that I may begin my
quest to conquest

Leila wanted to make the right choice. She did not want to be a fool again. Still, she missed Kaobi sorely, but slowly she was learning that life simply had to go on. She said a silent prayer and wondered if Kaobi was a Christmas angel watching over her that night. If he was, she hoped that he would put in a good word on her behalf. She smiled at the thought of Kaobi (in white leotards because that's what angels wore according to her bizarre imagination) negotiating her future with God. She looked up to see Akash staring at her.

'That's a strange smile, Leila,' he said as he walked up to her. Leila nervously brushed his curiosity aside.

'On a more serious note...' Leila began but he cut her short.

'I am uncertain too…' he said, reading her thoughts. He continued, '… and it is all very strange but, Leila, you make me happy. You make me so happy. A happy life would be one spent with you. Nothing else will do. I will die alone otherwise,' and he opened his arms to her inviting her over. Leila accepted.

'I am scared though. We have been through so much,' she said timidly.

'I know but I think you and I both know that we belong together. We will make up for not getting it right the first time. We both know what to do, don't we?' he asked. Leila nodded. It was amazing how Dahlia got on with him instantly. She absolutely adored him. Leila was pleased about that. Dahlia's stability was always paramount in her thoughts.

'I'll make it right. Just leave it all to me,' he said. Leila nodded.

'Do you trust me?' he asked. Leila nodded again and strangely enough, she realised that she actually did trust him. This Akash was the Akash she had fallen in love with. He was back, and with God on her side and a lot of hard work, he was back for good.

It wasn't even 7am yet when they all gathered round the Christmas tree, each overflowing with anticipation of unwrapping presents. Leila said a short prayer and as soon as they chorused that final, anxious 'amen', they all began ripping away. Dahlia was in ecstasy. She adored presents. Barbie dolls, fairy outfits, fairy tale books, and ribbons; she got it all! Leila watched her with pure admiration. Her daughter was generally a happy child, blissful and unaware of the turmoil her mother had undergone from time to time. Leila noted though that at that moment she was actually content enough, almost happy – she was nearly there. There was just that little bit left. Leila just wasn't sure enough even to think it or hope for it just yet but she was certain she would get there at some point in the not-too-distant future. She smiled at the thought.

'Aren't you going to open your present?' Akash asked in a curious whisper.

'I got carried away watching everyone else open theirs,' she replied.

'Do you like the bracelet I got for you?' she asked.

'Absolutely love it,' he replied and showed off his wrist with his new Tiffany's Square Links bracelet on it. It had three letters of the alphabet and the sign '&' dangling off it. It had 'D', 'L' and 'A'.

'Dahlia, Leila, and Akash,' he said softly. Leila nodded.

'It's an invitation,' she said.

'An invitation?'

'An invitation to share our lives,' she said after nodding and ruffling Dahlia's hair, but staring intently at him.

'I have a normal present for you and a counter invitation.'

'Counter invitation?' Leila asked, receiving the 'normal present' first. She opened it. It was a thin golden necklace with a crucifix.

'A plus sign necklace,' he said and they both burst into laughter. 'I hope you like your crucifix,' he said. She kissed him lightly on the lips.

'Now, the counter invitation…' he said presenting her with her gift. It was wrapped – the size of a six-pack drinking glass set (which is what

Leila thought it might be for some strange reason. Akash had never been great at buying the right gift when it mattered. He was better at unseasonal gifts like the 'I'm sorry' tokens. He had once bought her a pair of marigolds washing up and oven gloves as a present!).

She undid the wrap. It was a box. Inside the box was another box and inside that box was yet another box and it went on like that for a while still.

'It is probably something tiny like earrings at the very end, right?' she happily yapped on enjoying the joke and suspense of it all. This mystery gift had of course captured everyone's attention. When she got to a jewellery-like box, she smiled.

'I knew you got earrings or something,' she said.

'… or something,' he said but she didn't quite hear that last bit. Had she looked up she would have noticed his flushed face. He was nervous. She opened the box. It was sparkling; it was dainty, and precious looking, with the most unusual, most beautifully cut, six-pronged solitaire, round diamond. It was the most breath-taking ring Leila had seen in a long time. Yes, it was a ring! She gulped and looked up at him.

'Do you trust me?' he asked in the same tone as he had asked earlier on, but this time, his voice shook..

'I am not Princess Yasmin and you are not Aladdin,' she said, because they had an audience and she was shy.

'It's no time for jokes!' he whispered softly but he smiled still.

Leila was unable to speak. He continued, '… because life may not be the party we hoped for but while we are here, I reckon we might as well dance. The last time I did not have the right dancing shoes on; this time I have. Will you dance with me?' he asked.

'Are you asking what I think you are asking?' she asked wanting to make sure. In front of most of her family and close friends, he got down on his knee once more.

'Marry me… again, Leila... Please.'

It must have been the longest minute Akash had ever waited for. Leila knelt in front of him. It was not quite déjà vu in the sense that the first time Akash had proposed, yes he had made a big show of it, spending thousands of pounds, but there was something different about this time. Putting it simply and ironically so, considering the crowd of people, it was more personal.

'I will dance with you,' she said, smiling softly, tears of mixed emotion streaming down her cheeks. She wasn't sure what she should have said or done, but she suspected she was going down the right path and judging from the prolonged applause, cheering and whistling and even a teardrop or two in the room, her friends and family thought so too. Dahlia hugged her mum. Whether she had planned this alongside Akash, Leila was not sure but she would certainly have to have a little chat with her later on. Leila also was not sure if it was appropriate to drink champagne in the morning, but what the hell…it was Christmas Day so fair enough! They all toasted to a bright future as Olga's unborn baby kicked for the first time!

'Are you not going to put it on?' Akash asked when they had a moment to themselves later on that night.

Leila smiled thoughtfully, but said nothing.

'Do you doubt my love for you, Leila? I know there was the past, but that was then, this is now. Let me show you,' he said, his eyes pleading.

'I believe you, Kash,' she said softly.

They were not sharing a room. Not yet. Akash knew her well enough to know when to let things just be. He planted a kiss on her forehead and left her alone. As soon as he shut the door, Leila sat before her dresser and stared at herself in the mirror. Yes, Kaobi had said Akash would be the one for her. She and Kaobi had been ultimately best friends with a few 'incidents' here and there. Yet, to let go of Kaobi and be with Akash was a difficult thing for Leila to do. She had lost a soul mate…she had lost the one man she loved in a way that she loved no other person in the world. There were times when, wrong as it was, she had felt married to him. This feeling was usually so overwhelming that if felt right.

She stared in the mirror.

Dear you,

Where are you?

I feel you, I ache, I long for that time, but life went on and somehow I had to leave you behind. Somewhere in my heart – where members of my inner-circle live, is this unoccupied space. Its void screams so loud because it belongs to you. Being in the presence of this somewhat empty space takes me back to a time and place where your face is as it was many phases of life ago. You will never age or wrinkle in physical. However, more beautifully I think about the fact that you retain your innocence and purity and love; the love that sparkled from your eyes. You stamp stamp stamped your way into my heart. These heartprints are so strong they overwhelm me with feelings of the kind of love that I feel for no-one else. That's why I dedicate this empty space to you. It's yours. Let time keep tick tocking, let life pause never, the image of your face remains the same and whenever I retreat to that empty space, I hide within a moment when time stands still and love is the only thing I know.

Intercept my thoughts please. I need you right now. Let me feel your presence like you are right here with me. Let me think of another and smile, for I look in the mirror and recognise the smile that belonged only to you; the smile you said lit from deep behind my eyes and somewhere beneath. The smile I said, if it were truly as beautiful as you describe, was only a reflection of the love you show me. I long for you. Hush me to calm with your lips.

And Leila subconsciously parted her lips slightly as she closed her eyes. She saw him smile.

I know we can never have a coffee together again. We can never talk again like we used to. I can never get the opportunity to explain the depth of my love for you. We said that regardless of the fact that in this lifetime we could not be together, we would love each other forever. It was a vow. I suppose you kept your side of the bargain. It now remains only a memory in time, a phase in my world, the best time of my life. I know it's too much to ask to re-live it. I know that once that tick tocks, it never goes back. I know and understand that there are certain pains that, though inconceivable at the time, and will never be erased, there are heartprints – eternal heartprints. You have stamp stamp stamped your way into my inner space forever. How then can I behold another the way I did you? she sobbed.

'What are you looking at?' he asked.

'Your photo.'

'And where do you keep that photo?'

'Underneath my pillow, closest to my heart.'

'And when you are not asleep or staring at the ceiling?'

'In my purse. I carry you with me always.' She sobbed some more.

'Well, sweetheart, I love you. I always will. What we feel for each other is frozen in time. Whatever may be will neither taint, nor alter that. It has left permanent prints in our hearts. I think in a sense you stare between my photo and the ceiling for one reason. Perhaps you want my blessing, which I wholeheartedly give. You say you will never love another the way you loved me, and though that may be true, I would hate to see you live without love. Embrace it and understand that I watch from a distance. I will guide you and hold your hand whenever you need it. I will be that little push or nudge or whatever makes you smile, I will watch for you, be there for you till it's the end of time,' he said.

'This empty space, Kaobi, this space somewhere in my heart is reserved for you. People I meet and love or even semi-strangers who leave impressions have their own space there too, but yours is different. It never grows, it never depletes, it never changes. It's constant. When I am there, time stands still and whenever I retreat there, I long to remain right there, close to you,' she said.

'You will always have me. That inner space is in you and so goes with you wherever you go. That's my heart you carry with you. I understand that life goes on and you may not visit as often as you might have...'

'Please don't say that...'

'Wait. Let me finish. You deserve to be loved and adored and reminded of how beautiful you are. You need wind beneath your wings. You need someone to put a glow in your eyes, and, babe, I give my blessing, because if you are happy, I am happy!'

'Should I marry him? I feel like I am cheating on you!'

'Even though we never dated, really?'

'It's the strangest feeling, KK.'

'Remember what you said on the day you said your goodbye to me in front of my family and friends in Onitsha? Sweetheart, I remain in that occupied space of yours. I am happy with that!'

'...but...'

'Until death did us part, we said. Even though we never pledged this in church because fate and destiny had other plans, we understood that our love was eternal. Now, life goes on...for now. Be happy, be sure. I will never lead you astray, sweetheart. Now, life goes on. Leila, I will always...always be with you.'

She nodded and smiled.

'Thank you!' she said.

And she put the photo under her pillow. It was a very big step for Leila. She took the ring out of the box and put it on.

'Life goes on,' her lips whispered as she drifted off to peaceful slumber!

'So, are we going to have the ceremony at your normal church in London, or do you want us to go to the one you have joined here?' Akash asked Leila.

'Well, actually…' she began, smiling and turning to Akash, taking his hands in hers.

'Yes?' he asked looking excitedly suspicious. He knew that tone. It always brought good news his way.

'In light of our whole new outlook to our marriage, I thought that I would show you how much I want to compromise and take your feelings into consideration…'

'Yes?' he urged her on.

'I thought we could have the Hindu wedding that we never had,' she said. That had been one of their major arguments during their wedding preparations and Leila had in fact threatened not to marry Akash if he insisted on the Hindu traditional rites, so much so that his parents disapproved of the wedding. In hindsight, she thought that perhaps there was no big deal to having a Hindu wedding, as she was sure God understood. It did not belittle her faith in any way; it just meant that she had a healthy respect for others. Her religion was personal and she would be bowing down to no other gods. Having said that, a Hindu wedding was all Akash had grown up believing in. For once, she could appease the in-laws. If it were sacrifices like these that would help her marriage, then surely God would approve. She looked at the big smile on Akash's face and knew it would definitely be worth it.

'How about…we go for a blessing in the church the day before or the day after?' he asked her smiling. She agreed with him happily: they would have a small blessing the next day at their church service and perhaps a couple of friends over for lunch or something. The wise ones who wrote books about the success or failure of marriages often said that firstly, compromise was of the essence and secondly, a woman's ability to take a step down for her husband is a skill that would yield fruitful results. Leila was reaping the benefits of imbibing these.

'Deal!' she said and they high-fived to seal it!

Akash was not moving into the beach house just yet. They were still taking it slow. They had forever together so there was no point rushing anything. As Akash had mentioned the pressures he felt the first time around, Leila was going to make sure that he knew what he was doing. No rush. There was also Dahlia to take into consideration. Yes, she loved Akash instantly and bonded with him in record time, but Dahlia was paramount in Leila's decision-making. If she were marrying Akash, it would be for life. They would take life one baby step at a time, at Dahlia's pace, so that the transition would be bearable and pleasurable for her little princess. The date was set: 25th April. They wanted to go all out – the whole shebang – mandap outside, and all. Hindu weddings usually took place outside, on the earth, under a canopy (hence the mandap). They would get little radiators in strategic places around, because even April evenings were known to bring an uncomfortable chill. They would have beautifully sequined rug pieces, which from above would give the illusion of glittering stars. Now this all sounded fabulously glamorous to Leila, but the beach house was the chosen venue! Leila was not sure. The house was Dahlia's. Leila was merely holding it in trust for her, but even apart from that and most importantly, it was once a sacred haven for Kaobi. It was his special place, which he shared with her. There were two poignant memories. They had kissed on the beach. It was, to date, the most breath-taking moment Leila had ever experienced for many reasons. Obviously, she was going through her dramas with Akash, but putting that aside, it was almost an out of body experience for Leila. The second out of body experience was his presence with her as she read his letter – the one he sent her following his passing. These precious moments would follow her to her grave. Now this was the issue – was it appropriate to use the beach house?

In bed that night, Leila tossed and turned and it took a while before sleep eventually consumed her. That night she dreamt of Kaobi.

He never said a word to her. He stood there in his beautiful, angelic glory and smiled at her. The smile went so far beyond the surface that it connected with her soul. She did try to speak to him. She asked him how he was doing; she asked him how Kamsi was. He said nothing. All he gave her was his smile. Leila awoke at 4 am, dishevelled. She had not dreamt of him for a while, not vividly anyway. Her dreams of him had almost been semi daydreams, usually when she was in that half-languid state. This one was a full-on dream. She reached for her bottle of water and had many gulps. It had been nearly three years since his untimely end, but moments brought fresh pain. There would never be another Kaobi. She knew he appeared to her once again because of her issues with the beach house. She had shared that moment with him before her mirror about the engagement ring; now there was this. From that dream, could she infer that he was alright with it? Was that his way of giving his permission? His love? Was he really watching over her? Was he her guardian angel? Before his death, he had told her clearly that she would end up with Akash. These other details in the fine print never quite came up, obviously. Leila said a prayer for his soul and thanked God once again for bringing him into her life, albeit for just a short period. She could easily have spent her life with him, but life obviously had other plans for her; other plans that she would embrace. Now she would re-marry Akash who had always been the only other man she had known intimately enough, but for the first time since she had started dating him again, she felt this tug in her heart. She was happy, she was content, and she knew that Akash loved her, but soul mate? She found that no matter how many terms of endearments she used to describe him, she could never refer to him as her soul mate. This was a revelation to Leila. 'So you approve, Kaobi, do you? I can use the beach house?' she asked the ceiling, and she drifted off to sleep. In her sleep, she smiled…back at Kaobi.

Note To Self,
Trust the whispers of your soul… That's God speaking to you
- Lynne "In his hands"

Chapter Sixty

The choice of bringing happiness…

A lot of us depend on the goings-on in life to bring us happiness. We expect to find 'it' in the most unlikely of places, external influences such as status, money, food and general accomplishments in life. More probable, it seems we expect to find happiness in the reciprocal ties we form between ourselves and other individuals, especially one-on-one partnerships.

The truth is nothing and no-one can make us happy. Why? As a starting point, searching the widest definitions of the word happiness, the following words persistently appear: contentment, pleasure, delight, bliss, glee, cheerfulness, joy, exhilaration, satisfaction, gratification and pleasure. The point is these emotions are all influenced internally. By implication therefore, there is only one person that can make me happy. That person is me!

…in a relationship (one-on-one)

Occurring often in our human minds is the expectation that what we give is what we get. The shocking reality is what an egotistical, myopic way of thinking this is. In the beginning of a romantic involvement, we see things through rose-coloured glasses because the intensity of the initial infatuation leads us to believe that life outside of this perfection we have found is void. This works well until the passage of time and the natural progression of events see to it that these glasses are taken off. Then what do you see? Do you see this person who is totally besotted by you so much so that they have given up parts of their life that were incompatible with your relationship? They didn't discuss it with you because it happened so naturally to them that you didn't notice. Or do you see someone who is so selfish and unromantic, they do not even buy you flowers or cook you candle-lit dinners and therefore have lost all appeal because they clearly do not know how to make you happy? Do you want to bring happiness into your relationship? Look at the bigger picture! Consider this quote by Khalil Gibran:

'One day you will ask me which is more important, my life or yours? I will say mine and you will walk away not knowing that you are my life.'

It is simple enough – we cannot influence other people's perception of what is right and what is wrong, what is proper and what is not! Sometimes we are searching so hard for something that we fail to see it right before our very eyes. This is usually because we expect that the unravelling of this thing, which we seek, will be revealed to us in some grandiose manifestation inclusive of fireworks and preferably labelled in a package marked specifically for our attention. Unbeknownst to most of us, the greatest miracles happen every day in our ordinary lives. Do not be upset that he/she did not buy you flowers on Valentine's Day, be grateful that on that day, the first thing you saw when you opened your eyes was him/her gently watching you sleep and you were gently stirred out of grogginess by the most heart-melting smile you had ever seen. Be grateful that on that day, he/she kissed you 12 minutes longer, 12 minutes more passionately, 12 minutes more deliberately than he/she would have done on any other day. Your friends all got a dozen red roses each and have called you to show off. Do you get jealous and resentful of him/her and of them, or smile to yourself knowing that that moment you shared with him/her when you awoke was one of the most sincere, intense, meaningful moments of your life (their flowers would last a week, tops - HA!).

Sometimes in searching for the really little things (which we confuse to be the big things by our own inhibitions), we lose sight of these big things, the essential things, the things that really matter, the things that at the end of the day make the difference, the things that, all things considered, keep us going in life, the things that bring about ultimate satisfaction, happiness!

What makes a 'happy' relationship?

a. *Speak when you need to. When words are an unnecessary evil, shut up! It is not about who wins the argument. We may have won the battle, but who won the war? Consider for example, that Ingrid Bergman said, 'a kiss is a lovely trick, designed by nature, to stop words when speech becomes superfluous'. Not taking this literally in this case, be tactical and resourceful in your approach. What is it you wish to achieve? This also involves the difficult test – compromise. Will it really kill you not to say anything this time around?*
b. *And following on from the choice of (un)necessary speech, is to accept this man/woman for who they are. Never compare him/her to an ex. They have their strengths and weaknesses. To embrace their strengths and castigate their weaknesses based on the strength of an ex is the most narrow-minded way of thinking. This other person is after all your ex for a reason. In your relationship, there are not comparables, fullstop!*
c. *To employ (a) and (b) above is to accept them for who they are. To accept them for who they are is to use their strengths to your advantage. Bury their weaknesses in the back of your mind and instead let their strengths be scribbled in the forefront of your heart in bigger, bolder font! For this reason, romance them like it is going out of fashion. Forget about routine. Be spontaneous. Be complimenting. Be sexy. Be happy! Within reason, be what he/she wants you to be when they least expect it. Elizabeth Ashley said, 'in a great romance, each person plays the part the other really likes'. Surprise him/her by keeping the sparks flying. Spend time together loving each other.*
d. *Attainment of (a), (b) and (c) means you are on the right path to respecting him/her. Hold him/her in high regard always, regardless of the situation! According to Jeremy Taylor, love is friendship set on fire! Make him/her your most cherished friendship.*
e. *And in so doing, accept that as they are human, times will come when they will hurt you. Little hurts or huge heartbreaks – if it's not worth dwelling on, then let it go. In the grand scheme of things (using this as a general example), the Bible tells us we must do – perhaps just below God's demand of 'perfection', this being impossible to attain in*

our own resources, we must forgive. Rise above it, forgive and forget. Your heart will feel so much lighter for doing so and guess what, you will experience happiness!

f. *Mozart said thus: Neither a lofty degree of intelligence nor imagination nor both together go to the making of genius. Love, love, love, that is the soul of genius. It takes a truly great mind to employ these elements but to employ them is to LOVE in the true sense of the word; our reward – happiness!*

... in non one-on-one relationships

These theories apply in principle to all forms of relationships. The fundamental key is to accept fellow human beings for whom they are, mere mortals incapable of perfection but worthy of love regardless. The supreme happiness in life is the conviction that we are loved and we all know what love is, we feel it in its absence or presence in our lives. The acceptance of people for who they are is the acceptance of life for what it is, followed by peace. Peace brings happiness.

Concluding

For many of us, finding happiness is a long process that takes time, very often only a lifelong achievement. In searching for happiness we look too hard, we then rebel, shun and belittle the happiness of others in the quest to find our own happiness. Master your mind because you own it! Exclude the world, reach into your inner self and tap into your own happiness. It is there somewhere!

My secret is in the knowledge that I am my own best friend and thus only I am responsible for my own happiness. I expect to find the emotions that create the elements of happiness in people around me (my family, my friends, my colleagues, my clients, people I meet in the streets everyday); I do not expect that the true meaning of my happiness is begotten from the acts of these people. If I laugh, I laugh, and if I cry, I cry, but I try and, ultimately, the decision to be happy is mine.

Are you happy? Yes? No? Whatsoever things are true, whatsoever things are honest, whatsoever things are just, whatsoever things are pure, whatsoever things are lovely, whatsoever things are of good report; if there be any virtue, and if there be any praise, think on these things. Happiness is not a right, it's a choice and this choice is yours to make!

Be happy!

;-) Leila

Chapter Sixty-Two

April 25th 2001 came before Leila could blink twice. It was a beautiful spring day and the atmosphere was festive. Leila woke up pleased with herself. Manicure – check, pedicure – check. Beautiful red Berhampuri sari – check! She smiled as she stroked the elegant fabric. Her mother came into the room with Dahlia.

'He will look after you,' she said. Leila smiled.

'I know, Mum,' she replied thoughtfully, but before she could have that mother/daughter chat, everyone else came in. Her siblings, Olga, and a few other friends – everyone who mattered would watch her. They had signed the papers at the registry the day before, but that was just for the legality of the proceedings. It was quiet and personal. Olga and Chris accompanied them as witnesses and they had a quiet toast after that. The Hindu wedding, and subsequently, the wedding blessing the following day would be the real occasions. When Leila re-appeared, everyone gasped and there were camera flashes going off from every angle. She looked regal. Her fabric was more a shade of maroon than red. The intricate motifs were glowing with radiance in her secular drape designed in net sari. The phenomenal drape matched the embroidered dupatta worn underneath. The sari, adorned with sequins, zari, stones, and cutdana work was glorious. Its border had rich patches with lovely embellishments. Its entire drape had intricate floral designs and traditional motifs. Her hair was simple. It had a left side pattern, and behind, sparkly maroon hairpins held it up high in a sequined bun. Hanging down her forehead was a dazzling maroon tikka. Her make-up was simple. Her eyes wore stunning black eyeliner with little maroon studs creating a pathway for her eyebrows. Her lips were a silently potent shade of red, which did not scream out on first look, but played a very important role. Her eyelashes were coated with layers of waterproof mascara. She did not wear a necklace, but she made up for that with a flamboyant vintage glamour maroon bracelet. Akash's mother had bought that. Traditionally, shoes could not be worn under mandaps so she did not bother. No one asked because no one noticed. Her sari lingered far below her feet onto the floor anyway. Everyone went outside in quick processions, but Leila remained indoors with her brother and mum. Lured to the window by the sudden energy in the music, they were in awe of the sight. The music had lacked life, but in an instant that changed. Something was happening…something different. She was stunned when she saw the mandap. It was red and stood on four pillars. Little flashing lights, banana trees, wooden pillars and an assortment of colourful spring flowers decorated it. She also noticed the central sacred fire Akash had talked about excitedly. Lit up right in the middle, it romanticised the atmosphere. Then she realised the reason for the sudden buzz. The groom was arriving. Akash appeared on a beautifully ornamented white horse with a procession of synchronised dancing relatives. She could see his smile from where she stood. The smile was infectious. Leila understood his various smiles. She knew the ones he wore as make-up, and the genuine ones. This one was genuine. He looked proud…and very handsome. She could not wait to get her hands on him. He would be her horse. She smiled mischievously. She had seen him in his outfit a few days before, but he did not look half as good then as he did at that moment. He wore his black Sherwani heavily embroidered from the neck sides to the bottom. He also wore a black turban as well, with a maroon scarf round his neck for Leila's sake. She smiled when she noticed that. His dancing relatives were chanting with drums in the background and jingling bells too:

O Ladki Ke Sahelion. Aao hum sab mehndi lagayen. Pinky ko sajayenge. Nachenge aur gayenge. Phoolon ke aangan me. Hum hasiyaan ourayenge. Dulhe ke intezaar me. Jhoola Julayenge

In accordance with their rehearsal, Leila's mum received him by putting a kumkum on his forehead, and he in turn gave her a coconut. She knew from the script that it was her cue to appear so she dashed down the stairs with her brother. When he was seated in the mandap, Leila made her appearance and felt sexy as the crowds whistled. She looked directly at Akash. He could not keep his eyes off her. Dahlia was by her side. Well, Dahlia was always by her side. Today was no exception. She made an adorable bridesmaid in the kids' version of her sari. Everything else happened too quickly. Leila was glad for video footage, and looked forward to watching it at a later stage. Overall, it had been the most alluring ceremony Leila had ever seen. The culture was rich and beautiful and she was so glad to have been a central part of it.

'Thank you,' she said at the end of night, kissing him lightly on the lips.

'I can't believe how beautiful you look,' he said, scooping her in his arms for a proper kiss.

'Don't get carried away,' she said wriggling away from him.

He grumbled.

'Don't start what you can't finish,' she added smiling mischievously.

'Oh I can finish this alright,' he said with narrowed eyes.

'I know,' she said and ran off upstairs instructing him not to dare follow. She looked down at him from the top of the stairs.

'Tomorrow,' she whispered to him. He lip-read and was satisfied with that, so he smiled and walked in the opposite direction.

She was pleased to get out of the sari. Beautiful as it was, it was heavy and stuffy. She stroked it gently, smiling as she captured flashbacks of the day. It had been amazing and she had never seen Akash's mum look so happy. She thought she would stress about the wedding blessing the next day. But she did not. She thought of Akash and his doting eyes. She knew he loved her. He loved her the best way he knew how and right now; he scored ten out of ten for effort. He would make her happy. She knew it. Her love for him had changed. She was aware of it, but she refused to worry about it. When she went to bed that night she slept peacefully. When she dreamt, she dreamt in colour. The ceremony had found its place in her heart and Leila was confident that marrying Akash had been the right decision without a shadow of a doubt.

Akash lay on his bed staring at the ceiling. He was pleased with the way the day went. Leila was officially the most beautiful woman he had ever seen. When he looked at her, he was certain like the blackberry emoticon that tickled him so much, his eyeballs were replaced with little red hearts. The depth of his love for her was unimaginable and he was grateful for a second chance. He knew he still had to make up for the past, but he was confident he would. He thought about Kaobi for a second, and his facial expression changed. 'A tiger does not declare his tigritude, he pounces!' Akash could never get that one line out of his head.

'How's this for pouncing? I am marrying her in your house!' Then he felt stupid. Dahlia was Kaobi's daughter. That was his blood for life. He also knew that a part of Leila had died with Kaobi. She was giving him her all, but it was the best she could offer. He knew he had never reclaimed Leila a hundred percent. Akash would never understand what happened between Leila and Kaobi and he was not sure he wanted to know either. Leila had married him again. Kaobi was dead! He would bring back the spark in her eyes. That night, Akash dreamt in colour. Everything in his life was falling into place once more.

The morning was less festive than the day before as the wedding blessing was a quieter affair with just close friends and family – no fuss! Leila loved the sari, but also could not wait to put her dress on. She had a shower and did her hair and make-up first. She had her hair brushed from the side, over her forehead and loosely held behind in a herringbone plait. After the glamorous look the day before, she felt the need to mellow things down a bit.

'Sometimes less is more,' she said to herself as she swapped her red lipstick for a pale shade of pink. She had not bought a wedding dress. She had been there and done that, she thought. Instead, she went for a classic Roberto Cavalli Grecian-inspired cream satin cowl-back gown. The decadent crystal-studded belt defined her beautiful figure and it was finished off with subtle sparkling gems. Her heels were simple and sophisticated Jimmy Choo silver mirrored-leather wrap-around sandals. It completed her entire look, giving it the chic effect. There was no limo, no bridesmaids (except Dahlia), no fancy cars, or elaborate wedding type affiliations. She drove in a convoy with her family to the church. She spotted Akash's car and was relieved that it would all go according to plan. She did have the traditional 'here comes the bride' song. She swapped it for Newsong's '*When God made you*'. She walked down the aisle with her dad who told her that he really did not want to have to do this again. They had laughed about it. She smiled sweetly across at Akash and fell in love with how gorgeously immaculate he looked in his cream suit. When they got to the front, her dad took her hand and put it in Akash's.

'Don't give her back this time!' he whispered, and then kissed Leila on both cheeks. He had tears in his eyes, which provoked tears in Leila's eyes.

Akash nodded his understanding and took Leila's hand proudly, but gently. The priest went through the procession. When it was time for the vows, Leila's heart beat loudly. Akash went first.

From the archives of my heart these words are true. In the memory of my past, in the core of my present and in the subconscious of my visions is the pedestal on which you stand, you stand out! As you came into my life, you brought with you your winds. These winds gently stirred my fate, caressed my destiny, fore-planned my future. When I look in the mirror it is you I see; my twin in every sense of the word except biological. Your winds whistle and the trees obey, they sway gently from side to side, dancing to the soothed beat of my heart. It is always a beautiful love song. For every moment you smile, my whole being lounges in the perfect bliss that only a lucky few ever experience. It warms my insides from heart to soul, it leashes any hole, un-whole becomes complete and whole. When you speak to me, every word is true. Every conversation is easy; our chords play the perfect harmony, naturally. Our words are music, our music is synchronised, and our synchrony is perfect.

My heart salutes you because time will pass, presidents will lay new precedents, babies will have babies and perhaps even more men will visit the moon and my love for you will blossom yet without change, ceasing or season.

With you my life is fulfilled and every dream you ever preached to me to pursue and have for myself will come true because you say so. I can have wings if I want and the star that shines the brightest, that star is mine... because you say so. Together we will move mountains because I trust you, I believe in you and with you, I feel safe enough to bare myself in entirety.

So today, I say to you, I see my future in your eyes. Time will stand still and destiny will be complete as I tell you that I love you as you love me in the uniqueness and realness of the word – the unconditionality of it. From you I have learnt love and indeed you are not without shortcomings but because of the sincerity of your heart, I love you in spite of those shortcomings. I will still love you in many tomorrows to come but for today, from the archives of my grateful heart, I pledge this undying love to you and the world will witness and share...

Today I marry you!

There were tears in Leila's eyes and she choked so much, it was hard to concentrate. There were tears in all the pews and all over the church. Heck, there were tears in Akash's eyes. It was not just the words. It was the sincerity. Leila believed every beautiful word. It was her turn.

In my prelapsarian days when my world was but fluffy clouds and teddy bears, all clowns and no fears, I dreamed of growing up. Being in love would be to find my perfect other, another that would but for biological differences, would be me – twin my soul, win my heart, never from me part.

So life came my way ushering me into a world where it was sometimes strife or strain, moments of gold and gain or cold moments of pain

But even in the ever-changing faces of my life's many phases, destiny gave me you, perfection so true.

If I were to love you, respect you, care for you, then for a brief moment I was to live life without you, my perfect gift, my soul lift.

So there came a time when I basked in every day with no you – you had no say.

I masked my confusion doing this, doing that, yet awakened with me were the once forgotten cravings of a lonely heart that bravely learnt to live without the perfection that could not be bought, perfection it so sought, perfection – its sole thought.

And the winds of fate blew you back my way.

A bewildered heart thought it late, perhaps love's gates were shut, but my eyes were suddenly open to what a subconscious me knew all along.

It is you. It has only ever been you. It only ever will be you

If ever I were scared and wouldn't have dared, in a moment that all cleared

For when I looked in your eyes and it was I that I saw,

Behold before my mind's eye, my very reflection in dreams of children who bore your eyes. In your eyes I realised – you are my future

Now when my heart succumbs to fear

I'll hold you close and pull you near

And right there with you in my arms and with the beat of your heart, my heart calms

Still looking in your eyes

I see all that I am not, but all that makes me whole

You are the missing part of me, my other half, you complete me, you complement me

Look at me; look in my eyes, for truth thrives only truly in eyes, my eyes won't lie

Feel the strength of the unspoken word and take these truths as they pour out the emotions from a heart that is bottomless with love for you

Today I rejoice in your imperfections, for they make you perfect

Today my heart sings with happiness because you are in my future's sight

My soul screams and basks in the delight that you share my dreams

And my eyes… my eyes shed tears of overwhelming emotion

Right here, right now, all I feel is love

Imperfect perfect you –

I choose you over and over again and today I prove it.

Right here, right now, let us celebrate our love as I vow my forever to you.

Before the priest could speak, Akash took her other hand as well. Now, he held both hands in his.

'Leila, I mucked it up the first time. This time we will get it right. This time it's forever! I promise.'

Leila was thrown into flashbacks of Kaobi and the mini vision she had seen in his eyes during their twelve-second gaze. 'This is what he foresaw and tried to show me!' she thought as she fought so hard to contain her emotion.

She nodded.

He cried unashamedly. She cried too. Everyone cried. The priest got through blessing their rings, blessing their union, and wishing them a lifetime of happiness. It was a beautiful service. Leila could not have asked for more. She had the fairy tale wedding the first time around; this though was effortless, but meant so much more. Cinderella had nothing on her and when she shed tears, she did so because she knew she was blessed.

The reception was equally romantic. The lights were dim; there were candles and single stemmed roses on every table. The speeches were personal and creative. Olga was hilarious. She hoped it was the second and last time she was going to have to dish dirt on both of them. The room roared with laughter. Akash and Leila both glared at her, but no offence was taken. There was so much love in the room. They fed their guests with their love when they cut their cake and exchanged pieces. The highlight of the night was Akash on the piano. He sang to her – *'Nothing's gonna change my love for you'* by George Benson. It was the first time she had heard him sing since the early days of their love. She remembered how she felt the first day that he sang to her in the park. She also moved on to flashbacks of this scene replaying in her head during their violent episode (which they both referred to as 'the incident' from time to time), and she compared it with how she felt at that very moment. It was their second wedding. The fact that she was able to do this with him just proved how evasive this shade of grey was in life's black and white story. When he finished, he swooped her in his arms to the centre of the room. He put her down, got down on his knees and kissed her feet. That was surreal. They danced. Leila had struggled with the song choice this time. The first time they danced, Akash was her everything. She loved him with every fibre of her being. Now, she loved him simply, without obsession. In travelling through life, she had discovered a different kind of love. The love she had for Kaobi had happened to her and it was something she would never be able to explain. Her love for Akash was a bit more realistic. She avoided any song that declared Akash her soul mate. She knew he was not. She had probably fallen inlove with the idea of him or maybe she did love him and when life happens to people, the dynamics of relationships change. It was a difficult change for Leila to come to terms with. It killed the Cinderella story for her. Leila learnt about soul mates and soul ties. Apparently, soul ties were people who would be intrinsically linked with your heart forever, and while they would never measure up to the natural love the soul mate could offer, a soul tie could give you a life that was equally rewarding. God loved her, she concluded. That was why she had Akash. Regardless of everything they had been through, she knew that the past was just that…the past. Akash was the best choice for her – it was crystal clear. Therefore, when they danced to *'When God made you'* by New Song and Natalie Grant, the song they had played in church as she walked down the aisle, Leila meant every lyric. As he kissed her half way through the song, Leila fell in love with her husband all over again. She would give him all of her (to the best of her ability). For the magic he created that day, he deserved it.

It was Leila, Akash and their bedroom. It had scented candles and rose petals everywhere. It could not have been any more romantic. They talked about the day and giggled a lot. The expensive champagne had a part to play of course. When they played their song again, Leila knew the time had come. Akash held her in his arms and took in the scent around her neck, and then he sat her down.

'Leila, no woman will ever come close. I have loved you from the minute I saw you. I know things were messy, but I will show you love this time, I promise!' he said.

Leila had tears in her eyes:

'The truth is Akash, I hurt you as well. You really needed me and I was not there for you. I was too busy wallowing in self-pity and discovering life without you. I never stopped loving you though. We have a second chance and this time, it is for better, for worse.'

They kissed. It was passionate and truthful, forgiving, expectant and hopeful. That kiss told stories of what they hoped the future would bring. It was not long before they were both naked. There were no clothes flying in all directions; no, it all happened naturally, intentionally. When he eventually took his position on top of her, she could not wait. Good old missionary it was, but the beauty was in the love they made that night. He did not take his eyes off her for a second and as their eyes stayed locked, so did their souls. His thrusts were commanding, yet tender. Every part of her took him in gratitude, love, and hope. She clung to him and told him how much she loved him. They had their song on repeat and threw themselves deep into the lyrics, timing their movements in rhythm with its beat. Even after their climax, he stayed inside with her.

'I want to be this close to you forever,' he said. She smiled. With their bodies still merged, he fell asleep. Leila stared at him for endless moments after. She was very happy with this soul tie. About twenty minutes later, he stirred from his slumber to find her still staring.

'What are you looking at?' he asked tenderly.

She smiled. 'I'm happy,' she said to him.

'Go boys, go…go make us a baby!' he said looking down south of them both.

At that point, Leila's spirit jumped out of her body and fled for the hills! The wrinkly old fortune-teller with the scrawny fingers made her first appearance in months. She had been standing, whistling in the corner but at that point, standing right there in the left corner of the room as usual, she cracked up, barely able to contain herself. She giggled hysterically, pointing at Leila. Her toothlessness always left Leila taken aback. Leila ignored her.

To Akash, she said absolutely nothing. Her thoughts – 'A baby? You have got to be fucking kidding me, mate!'

"We waste time looking for the perfect lover,
instead of creating the perfect love."
– Tom Robbins

Chapter Sixty-Four

It was a little over a year later, a Tuesday afternoon (because everything of significance happened to Leila on a Tuesday) in May of 2001. Leila sat in the kitchen reading her appointment letter. She was off to see the doctor the next day. According to her friends, books and articles she had read, if she had had unprotected sex for a year and failed to get pregnant, then officially, there was a bit of a problem. On the wedding night, Akash had made his intentions to have a baby with her clear. At first, she was petrified and even contemplated going on the pill behind his back, but then upon further reflection, she realised how selfish that was. Akash gave Dahlia all his love and she had started calling him daddy. Even though they never mentioned it in conversation, she knew how much it hurt Akash that she was not his. She knew he deserved a child. The last year had been everything she hoped her marriage would be. This time, it was genuine. Therefore, she ignored the selfish part of her that did not want to go through the nine-month custodial sentence, and had even started smiling at babies in the street. Still, she had spent the first five months relieved to feel that familiar bloatedness indicating the start of her monthly, but by the eighth month, she was panicking. The appointment was at noon the next day and she quickly sent Olga a BBM asking if she fancied a spot of baby-sitting the next day. It would be a great chance for her to catch up with Olga and the new addition to her world, ZsaZsa. She was a year old now. She had missed being born on Leila's wedding day by four days. Leila had an honorary invite to the christening as Godmother, but after that, the pressures of balancing family life and work had meant that she had rarely seen her in the last year.

'Sure babe, I'll keep Dahlia and ZsaZsa entertained until you get back and then maybe we can take them to the park or swimming later.' Leila was reading the message from Olga when a call came through. Her heart skipped a beat – international call…from Nigeria…and… Lala was in London at the time, they had hung out a couple of days before.

'Hello,' she answered as composed as she could.

'Hello, is that Leila? This is Mrs Uba…Chetachi-Uba…Senior.'

Leila knew who she was as soon as she heard her voice. The confirmation was irrelevant.

The gist of the conversation was thus: she was coming to town to spend time with Ada and the boys. She wondered if it would be possible to see Dahlia that weekend or possibly, first half of the next week.

Leila gulped before she told her she would see her.

She put the phone down and was unable to recall the tail end of the conversation. She stared, blinking. She had to present this information to Akash. In this case, she could not predict what his reaction would be. The drip-drop from the tap distracted her. She shut it tight, made a mental note to get the plumber in, and took Dahlia out for an impromptu swim.

'I'm afraid that isn't my only concern,' the doctor said.

Leila had been hit with the news that it was secondary infertility. There were many reasons why this could suddenly happen to her, but in her case, the most plausible would be the fact that she bled so much when she gave birth to Dahlia. Her age didn't help either. There was a chance that she would never have another baby. All she could think about was Akash and how devastated he would be by the news.

'There's more?' she stuttered.

'I'm afraid we found some irregularities which means that we have to investigate further.'

'What are you investigating?'

'The bloatedness…we need to make sure…'

'Oh no, that happens at the start of my period, it's nothing to worry about.' She cut him short.

'Has this always been the case?'

Her second bombshell came just then. Leila would be tested for ovarian cancer.

'I'm forty years old. I have a husband, a daughter! She is six years old.'

The doctor was sympathetic. 'It's not a definite diagnosis yet.'

She nodded several times. 'You are right. Of course, you are right. It's not a definite diagnosis.'

That was the last thing she said before she left his office. It was the only thing she said to herself throughout the day, throughout swimming, throughout the time she spent in the park with Dahlia, Olga and ZsaZsa; throughout dinner with Akash.

'Akash, I need to discuss something with you,' Leila said.

'When you call me "Akash" I get nervous,' he said smiling. He sat down.

She told him about the call from Kaobi's mum. She wanted to know how he felt about it.

'But she is mine now, Leila. Why are you bringing up the past? Why are you doing this? What do they want to see her for? Kaobi died. Why are you re-opening fresh wounds? Why do you want to insult me? Am I not a good enough father for her?' he asked agitated.

'The best!' Leila said turning to him. 'You are the best, Kash, but Kaobi is her father. His family have the right to see her.'

'Right? What right? Based on what?'

'Based on biology!'

'Where have they been? Why are you doing this to me, Leila?'

'Kash, I need your blessing!'

'Never!' he said and he stormed out of the living room, and in fact, out of the house. It had been a while since Leila had seen him that angry. Yes, they had their tiffs about random stuff like finances and Dahlia's education and their plans for the future, but he had never walked out since...well, not since the old marriage.

Akash drove. He beat every traffic light in sight. He broke every speed limit possible and stuck a finger up at speed cameras as he created new speed records in his Z5. He wanted a fight with someone, the police if they wanted. Eventually, he stopped at an unmarked junction. He stared at the bottle of brandy and willed himself not to drink it. It was not necessary. By the time he thought through the consequences of drinking profuse amounts of brandy, irresponsible recklessness, drink driving, slipping into old habits, allowing anger which he had learnt to manage rear its ugly head, he was already half way through the damned bottle.

'Damn you, Leila!' he screamed in exasperation. 'Fuck you! The one thing you know I want. I compromise for you; you cannot do the same!' In his lifetime, nobody had the ability to reduce him to feel like nothing like she did! Reality check – the beautiful little girl who resembled her mother in the cutest ways possible, the sweetie who called him Daddy was not his child. He had known all along, no doubt, but it rarely came up, rarely stared him in the face, and rarely slapped him hard across the face!

'What broke? Your ego or your heart?' Akash could not make up his mind. Either way it was irrelevant. He had the rest of the bottle to get through. If the police had stopped him that night, it would have been an instant ban.

Leila paced in the bedroom. One part of her told her to ignore Mrs Chetachi-Uba. The other part of her reminded her who Mrs Chetachi-Uba was. She needed to understand if she was doing this to try and re-introduce Kaobi's presence in her life – something to hold on to, or if Dahlia's biological upbringing was that important. Kaobi was no more. Life had moved on. She had her quiet moments when she thought of him, her daydreams, her flashbacks, but those would never replace him. Having said that, Dahlia was Kaobi's daughter. This was a fact! Her mind was made up. She pouted for a second as she stared out of the window. She dropped the pout. There was nothing to fight about; this was no war with Akash. It was not even a peaceful protest. It was what it was. Getting Akash wound up was and would never be the intention here. This was about Dahlia (she hoped).

Akash walked into the room and she jumped.

'You smoked?' she asked, bewildered.

'So fucking what?' and he punched the wall.

'Don't you dare, Akash! We have Dahlia now!'

'We? We have Dahlia? You have just reminded me that she is not mine and I have no say and yet you say *we*?'

'I cannot talk to you when you are in this state. You reek of alcohol!' she said walking towards the door. He got to the door before her and slammed it shut.

'Akash, don't you fucking dare!' she said looking him directly in the eyes.

'Leila, I won't touch you.' He softened, but only for a second. He looked like he was restraining himself. He was trembling.

'I FORBID CONTACT!' he said firmly.

'Get out of my way!' she said fighting past him.

'Fuck off!'

'Get the fuck out of my way!' she repeatedly coldly!

He pushed her to the bed. She was up in a flash, heading towards the door. He pushed her again. She pushed him back.

'Akash, understand this. This time, I will send you to prison!' she warned.

He stood staring at her.

'You promised!' she said to him calmly.

He walked away from the door. She walked out of the room.

'What are you doing in my bed, Mummy?' Dahlia asked through sleepy eyes.

'I just wanted a cuddle,' she replied tucking herself under Dahlia's blanket.

'Why? Did you have a bad dream?' she asked. That was one way of putting it.

'Yes darling, yes I did!'

'There are no monsters, silly. That's just pretend,' she said turning to tangle herself in Leila's embrace. Leila smiled.

'You protect me then, sweetie,' she said and they both fell asleep.

It was 2 am when Akash puked his guts out. With both hands on his head, he recollected the events of the night. He shook his head slowly as he made his way across to Dahlia's room. The door was slightly ajar and he peeked in. He watched them sleeping peacefully. Dahlia was so much like her mother. Both so beautiful and of utmost importance to him. He would be damned though, before he would be undermined as a man. Compromise – yes; direct defiance of his feelings – no way! One part of him wanted to reach out to her, beg her to come to bed. The fear of rejection was so strong, he walked away exasperated. He headed to the lonely master bedroom.

It was dark enough despite the light coming through from the corridor. Leila's eyes were wide open watching Akash. Part of her wanted to go to him and talk things through. That part of her wanted to reassure him that nobody was taking Dahlia away from him, to reassure him that she would make him a dad. But she couldn't. She sighed deeply as she watched the wounded lion make his way away. His temper was back? She read somewhere that once a man hit his wife; he would hit her repeatedly. She was worried, but dismissed the thought. Akash would never be violent towards her again. Somewhere deep inside, she understood his hurt. But then, she did have other issues to worry about. How would she get Dahlia to see her grandmother? That thought was overtaken by another thought, and so she said out loud - 'It is not a definite diagnosis yet!'

Leila stared at the ceiling and then fell asleep, that is until she awoke to a tingling feeling on her foot. She opened her eyes and Dahlia was running her fingers over her tattoo. She froze and instinctively turned to the left corner of the room. There she was in all her glory. The wrinkly old fortune teller with the scrawny fingers sat on a stool that could only have been made for a child Dahlia's age. She had that toothless smile again. *'On that day she will testify. From then you die!'* she whispered.

Leila had no clue what she was on about. She sighed and shut her eyes.

The next morning, Leila and Akash never said a word to each other. The same happened the day after that and then the next. Both were overwhelmed by pride and uncertainty, neither wanting to make the first move to reconciliation.

On Thursday morning, Leila received that dreaded phone call. Kaobi's mum wanted to know what she had decided.

'Can you text me your address? I will be there at about 4 pm!' she responded.

Leila was trembling when she put the phone down. Every fibre of her being, every motherly instinct she felt, all the love she felt for Kaobi which burned wildly at that moment whilst she looked in Dahlia's eyes told her all she needed to know. She had to pay that visit! It would hurt Akash, but she did not feel like she had a choice. Then she wondered if Akash really needed to know. 'It's the right thing to do! Dahlia is Kaobi's biological daughter. His family have a right to know her.' This was Leila's justification for what she was about to do.

She got dressed. Simple and understated – blue skinny jeans, a beige spaghetti string top, and a beige Portobello jumper by Clements Ribeiro – it had pearls all the way down both sides from the collars, with silver buttons. She dug out the pearl earrings Kaobi had bought her – one of quite a few pairs. She also wore a silver bracelet he bought her upon her request, and she slipped on her black Cavalli ankle boots. She was visiting his world so it felt right to take a piece of him with her for support. She stared at herself in the mirror, then she swapped the beige spaghetti string top for a black one. She put Dahlia in a pink dress, pink tights, and pink boots. They both wore buns in their hair. Before she had a chance to have second thoughts, she tossed Dahlia in the car.

'Where are we going, Mummy?' Dahlia asked excitedly.

'We are going to visit some relatives,' Leila responded in the calmest voice she could muster.

'Relatives?' Dahlia asked, puzzled.

Leila did not respond. She did not know what else to say.

It took ages to get to Finchley. Dahlia had managed two naps, following a huge McDonald's meal, but was sufficiently bright eyed upon their arrival. They pulled up to a beautiful detached house; the driveway was rowed with rosettes and daffodils. She also spotted three sunflowers. The building was labelled 'The Palace' in regal purple. Leila smiled. Of course Prince Kaobi had lived here.

When she hit the doorbell, Leila's heart raced wildly. She did not know what to expect.

Ada opened the door and stared.

She was bypassed by Mrs C. 'Please come in,' she said. She was neither warm nor cold – expressionless. Leila held on to Dahlia and quietly made her way in.

Nigerian clothes fascinated Leila. She stared at Ada's colourful fitted top and long skirt with slits on either side. They were ushered into the living room that had numerous family photographs. Leila spotted a family portrait. Kaobi's twin boys both bore an uncanny resemblance to him. Kaobi looked gorgeous in his two-piece Nigerian attire. He also wore a native cap, which had a feather sticking out of it. She looked around and felt emotional knowing that Kaobi had lived here, walked around this house, was the head of this home. He always described a house in the course of conversation. Everywhere she turned brought back memories of past conversations as she put pieces of various puzzles together.

'The boys are...' Ada was beginning to say, when they walked right in.

Leila did not know how to react. They greeted her pleasantly and turned their attention to Dahlia.

'Would you like an ice lolly?' one of them asked.

'Are you Adrian or Armani?' Leila asked quietly.

'Armani,' he responded with a smile. Leila had tears in her eyes for that smile was Kaobi's.

'Pleased to meet you,' she said. He nodded shyly.

Dahlia went off with them, feeling quite at home.

'They are the spitting image of their father – my husband, aren't they?' Ada asked, breaking the silence.

Leila smiled nervously, unsure of what to say.

'Does Dahlia know? She is old enough to understand,' Ada asked.

Leila shook her head. Not yet.

'When then?' Ada asked.

'Do the boys know?' Leila asked.

Ada shook her head.

'Why?' Leila asked.

'We probably have similar reasons,' Ada responded. Leila accepted this. Neither probed further.

Leila heard footsteps and held her breath.

'Nno! – Welcome.' It was Kaobi's mother. She was in a bubu made of adire – local Nigerian print. Leila thought it pretty. She wore her hair tucked inside a Nigerian head tie, which Leila knew was called an 'ichafo'. When Dahlia came back in, she stared at the head tie in fascination. Kaobi's mother stared at Dahlia. Her look was un-interpretable.

'Nwa Kaobi – Kaobi's child,' she muttered.

'How old is she now?'

'She's six.'

'Adaobi,' she said. Leila looked puzzled.

'This is the name we have brought for our daughter!' she said to Leila.

'This child is the first daughter of the royal palace – Adaobi. This is what we shall call her.'

Dahlia just stood, staring, not knowing what to make of all the senseless conversation.

Leila repeated the name after her. She corrected her accent a couple of times and gave up.

Leila and Dahlia both had some dodo (fried plantain) and gizzard. Leila had a little palm wine; Dahlia just had regular juice.

They spent about two hours, mostly staring in silence.

'How is your health now?' Leila asked. It had always confused her. Was she not the same person who was supposedly on her deathbed, causing Kaobi to rush out to Nigeria? He met his death there! But Leila did not dare question her.

'We thank God,' Was her reply. Mrs C and Ada exchanged glances, Leila noticed. She said nothing but decided it was her cue to leave. Mrs C handed her a parcel.

'It is a bubu. You will like it.' Leila was slightly taken aback, but she accepted it and thanked her.

'We say – Dalu for thank you,' Mrs C said.

'Dalu,' Leila repeated.

'Dalu,' Dahlia echoed. Everyone chuckled.

'I leave tomorrow, but I will be back again in a few months,' she said.

Mrs C said her goodbye at the door, but Ada walked her to the car.

'You stole him from me!' she accused.

'He was never mine.'

'You gave him a child.'

'You gave him two!'

'You caused all this. Kaobi's death is on your head.'

'What are you talking about?' Leila asked with a puzzled look on her face.

'If only you knew!' and she let out a disgusted look. 'He had no business going to Nigeria. It was all your fault! I would have talked him out of it.'

'His mother was ill. She needed him.'

'The old witch was never ill and will probably live to a hundred!'

Leila was confused. She wished she could explore the conversation more but Mrs C was watching carefully. Ada was obviously aware of her probing eyes as well. If Leila did not know better, she would have said Ada looked scared of Mrs C. Leila put up her best poker face. Ada slipped her a card. 'Call me! You and me – we have unfinished business. You need to explain to me why you could not leave my home alone.'

Leila took the card off her but not before sighing and saying: 'Kaobi loved you. That should be good enough for you if it is coming from me.' Her eyes were wet with tears.

'I married him because I had no choice. I could not marry the man I loved, so don't tell me about natural love because I know all about that. Whatever he felt for me I settled for; even that little, you took it away anyway.'

'Kaobi loved you, Ada. Don't break your own heart for no reason.' And with that, Leila got into her car and drove off.

'Who were those people?' Dahlia asked.

'Relatives.'

'Relatives?'

'Yes. Relatives. Weird ones.'

She drove the rest of the journey lost in thought. Thoughts that she would later archive in a corner somewhere deep down, because she knew she would be unable to find the emotional energy to deal with whatever potential bombshell Ada had to drop on her. She decided to leave her memory of Kaobi exactly as it was. Therefore, when she threw away the unfinished McDonald's, along went Ada's card with it – straight into the bin for collection by the council the next morning! She washed her hands.

Akash was sitting in the living room, watching TV (or at least staring at the TV, considering the fact that it was a replay of the previous night's EastEnders. Akash despised EastEnders. He did not look up, but Leila knew he was aware of their entrance. 'Daddy!' Dahlia called out. He looked up and smiled at her. She walked up to him, gave him a hug, kissed his nose, and positioned herself comfortably beside him.

'How was your day?' he asked.

Leila's heart did a quadruple somersault. She did not wait to hear Dahlia's response. She ran up the stairs to their bedroom, threw her handbag on the bed, and then straight into the bathroom. She shut the door. She held her breath for a second, closing her eyes. She knew it would be war. She shook her head for a second and then remembering the parcel in her hand, she smiled curiously. It was a bubu – a loose maxi gown. She had seen loads of them in Nigeria. She had seen quite a few in movies she had watched with Kaobi. She had seen a couple on Lala in the summer. She had never quite seen one like this. Its undertone was black, it had a bit of cerise splashed around it, but not conspicuously. All around the shoulders and draping down to her breasts, where it would have fitted like a cleavage-revealing top, it had the most intricately embroidered thread in a wavering pattern. Some of it looked like plaited thread. It was exquisite and regal. Usually, it would be quite loose, from what she understood. This looked like it would be neither figure fitted, nor completely loose. It was somewhere in-between. It also had two long slits on either side. It had the same gold thread hemmed all the way up the slits. She quickly slipped her clothes off and put it on. She stared at herself in the full-length mirror. She did a twirl and smiled. She imagined Kaobi before her. She knew his eyes would have lit up excitedly. She wrapped her arms around herself in a hug and looked in the mirror. Behind her, stood Kaobi holding her around her waist. His breath was on her neck and he was looking in the mirror too, so she could see his smile.

'I am always...always with you,' he whispered in her ear. She shut her eyes and the sudden sharp pain in her heart engulfed her. She opened her eyes very slowly, and the closer she got to wide-open eyes, the quicker Kaobi faded. By the time the knock – no, the bang – on the door came, Kaobi had completely disappeared. She slipped carefully out of the bubu, placed it among her clothes, and jumped into the shower. She heard her phone ring but she drowned it out with the noise from the shower. She put on some Kenny G and zoned out on Akash's rant as she had a 25-minute shower. For every minute that passed, she had a tear trickle down her cheek.

Akash searched for the ringing phone and found it in her handbag. There was no name – just a number. He answered it.

'Hello,' and when he heard the unmistakable African accent, he was furious.

'Who is this?' he demanded to know.

'Where is Leila?' she asked.

'In the shower. What do you want?'

'In the shower? She is OK?' The voice sounded confused.

'Do you have a message? Or are you going to keep chanting your gibberish?' he asked. She said nothing for a few seconds, so Akash threw the phone on the bed.

'What did you say to her?' Mrs C was asking Ada.

'Nothing. Why does it matter? I have had no say in any of this.'

'You idiot. You think I don't know what I am doing? I hate her just like you, but you don't listen. The herbalists washed that bubu carefully. By now she will be feeling the effects. It should not take more than two hours.'

'Do you have no fear, Mama? You told me everything Kaobi told you.'

'I am his mother. I am protecting my family. Kaobi knows.'

Ada shook her head. 'I will never be party to your evil ways. I should never have listened to you in the first place.' Mrs C slapped her hard across the face.

'That will be the last time you will do that to me. Get out of my house!' Ada barked at her.

'Me? Are you mad? You cannot kick me out of my son's house. Watch me!' and she began to ring 999. 'Police please,' she said.

Mrs C shot out of the house quicker than lightning.

Ada did not have Leila's number so unless Leila called her, she would never know for sure if Leila made it through the night. Having said that, she knew she would not have to wonder. Kaobi's love for Leila stood out like a bright star in the sky. She knew his spirit would protect her. Hocus pocus meant nothing to Kaobi. If anything happened to Leila, his mother would be mysteriously struck dead by lightning or something, and one way or another, she would hear about it. The thought of Kaobi and his love for Leila was so strong; it filled her with relief but equally with grief. She hated Leila but could never find it in her heart to wish death upon her. The right person died. Kaobi would never get the chance to walk away from her. Ada shook her head at the extremity of her thoughts. She made an emergency appointment with her reverend.

Mrs C wandered a couple of streets before she paused to think about where she was going. She shook her head bitterly and when she slapped imaginary mosquitoes off the base of her neck, she knew she had a problem. There were no mosquitoes in London. She stood outside a hotel wondering whether to check in or to give Ada a call to check that she had returned to her senses. The elders in the village would hear about this. Somehow she knew she had crossed some line with Ada, so swearing under her breath, she checked in to the nearest hotel she could find. Lying in her bed, she rang Leila's number. A man picked up. She expected to hear wailing, confusion, anything. Instead she got an angry man who was not particularly interested in what she had to say. He said she was in the shower. 'O na wu aru? She is having a wash?' she had asked, confused. Said man had been uninterested in what he termed 'gibberish' and had thrown the phone to a corner somewhere for all her 'hellos' went down in vain before she realised it was time to terminate the call. She knew Leila would have tried the bubu on and even in the event that she did not, it was potent enough to do its job. It would have recognised her from the hair strands she had saved and given to them. She lived? How? This had to be Kaobi's protection. As she lay down to sleep she reviewed the situation. Kamsi had died. Kaobi had followed the same fate. Her daughter in law had kicked her out of the house. She was pretty much alone in the streets of London. She would have to find a way home where Papa Kaobi would be waiting to laugh at her. His health was failing, but his mind was sound. He would tell her what a fool she was.

'If Kaobi does not avenge his death, her attempted murder (because he will never let you kill her) or the way you have treated his naïve wife who has done nothing but love him and respect you, then karma (maybe God himself personally) will!' Papa Kaobi had said.

'Tufiakwa – God forbid!' and she slapped her neck again.

Leila took another deep breath and stepped out of the shower. She had her towel wrapped around her.

'How could you?' he asked in a violent whisper.

'Where is Dahlia?'

'Answer me!' he screamed.

Leila walked away from him, towards the door.

He pulled her back by her towel, unwrapping it and swivelling Leila in the process. She tripped, but regained composure quite quickly. Still, she stood naked and petrified. He grabbed her by her right arm and Leila grimaced.

'Akash, you promised,' she said to him as he stared back at her with ire in his eyes.

'Akash, you promised. If you hurt me, you will not be able to unhurt me. This time, you will never be able to turn back the hands of time!' she said bluntly. He stared at her like he did not hear a word she said, like he had gone mad, like he wanted to crush her with his bare hands. His breathing was heavy. Leila suspected what was going to happen, but somehow she stood rooted to the spot, unable to think, unable to feel, unable to find the strength to flee either – or maybe actually she did not want to. She watched him, her eyes narrowed, but other than that, the look on her face was expressionless.

Dahlia walked in at that point.

'Mummy, put some clothes on, that's embarrassing,' she said, oblivious to the tension she had walked into. Leila nodded.

'Where is my pink watch? I can't find it.' Leila pointed. Akash stood, staring.

'Mum, where are the other crackers? You know Gucci does not like the organic crackers. It tastes yucky. How can crackers have garlic in it? That's disgusting,' she continued, sprawling herself on their bed. Leila did a fake laugh and all of a sudden, Dahlia looked up at her.

'Are you OK, Mummy?' she asked looking at her. 'Is she OK, Daddy? Is Mummy OK? Is something wrong?' she asked. Leila retrieved a t-shirt and leggings as quick as she could and put them on – no underwear. Dahlia walked over to her, peered in her eyes. Leila looked at her. She said nothing. Dahlia gave her a very light hug, a kiss on her right eye and walked away.

'This automatically makes me a bad guy, does it not? It automatically negates every good thing I have done for our marriage. This has set our relationship back years. Yet, I stand here, hurt and so confused. The one person I want to get sympathy and understanding from is the one person who is hurting me,' he said.

'There are other ways of putting your point across, Akash,' she said.

'Don't call me Akash,' Akash said in a frustrated tone.

'You bruised and battered me, raped me, Akash. I forgave you. No matter what happens between us, I promise to consider your feelings, but violence is not acceptable, Akash. I will fucking send you to prison if you lay a finger on me. Do you understand me?' she asked, looking him straight in the eye.

'Did you consider the way this would make me feel? Did you consider that it could tear me apart?' he asked.

'No. I suppose not. Biologically, she is not yours. No matter how much we try, we cannot undo the past. I am sorry about that. But Akash, do I have the right to prevent Kaobi's mother from seeing Dahlia?'

'We all have choices, Leila. That was your call to make on a balance of probabilities.'

'It was your choice, Akash, not to intimidate me and threaten me in our home. It is your responsibility to make me safe. This is the second near miss. Incidents like this are like déjà vu. I do not take your feelings into consideration when you treat me like this.'

'Do I have a say in Dahlia's life?' he asked.

'Yes,' she responded quietly.

'Why did you go behind my back?'

'Because when you intimidate me as a woman, talk down to me, bully me or attempt to turn me into a victim of domestic violence, you lose my respect. When you lose my respect, you lose a space in my heart and I forget to value your opinion. I will submit to you, but if you bring the old Akash back, I have the emotional strength to walk away. I will leave you and I will never, never look back.'

'Will you allow regular contact with them?' he asked.

'I don't know.'

'Leila, for the sake of our marriage, for the sake of my manhood, the answer has to be no,' he pleaded.

'And for Dahlia's sake?'

'Don't do that, Leila. I love that girl, and you know it!' he said forcefully.

Leila just stared.

'Leila, for some reason, I cannot handle this. Please tell me it will never happen again.'

'I am not here to make you feel better, Akash, not after that display.'

'Can't you see why I lost it?'

'No! Violence can never be justified.'

'You won't see them again…will you?'

'I don't know!'

There was a pause of about 15 seconds until Stevie Wonder's 'Signed Sealed Delivered' came blasting through and Dahlia's laughter and Gucci's imitation of it vibrated within the house.

Leila walked out of the room. Unstopped.

Three weeks went by and Leila never set foot in that bedroom. In fact, it was a good excuse to do some shopping, especially since Ferragamo and Vivienne Westwood had come up with some extraordinary designs,

Patrick Cox and Edina Ronay were her new discovered favourite designers, she could never get enough of La Senza and she had a new found jewellery interest in Swarovski. It had nothing to do with the fact that her bloating was getting worse. It had nothing to do with the fact that she was petrified of the effects of penetrative sex – it hurt. It had nothing to do with the fact that she did not feel cuddly or sexy at that moment; or that in fact, she was distressed that she might have to come to terms with death in a week, two, a year, ten, maybe longer, but due to cancer. There had been no diagnosis yet. Her appointment was in three days – on her birthday.

'Leila, how long are we going to do this for?' Akash asked. 'I said I am sorry. It will never happen again. I lost control. I was upset and scared. You two are my family. I want to be your husband and Dahlia's dad. I don't want anything to interfere with our family!'

Leila kissed her teeth (she picked that up from Lala. She had always tried to do it, but that was the first time it actually sounded like the hissing sound it was. She almost smiled).

'What is that supposed to mean?' he asked.

'Akash, just give me some space. You need to let me breathe,' she snapped.

'Let you breathe? We have not slept in the same bed for weeks. I touch you, you cringe, I sit next to you on the sofa and you stiffen; you avoid eye contact. Why are you doing this? What do you need space for?'

'Just leave me alone!'

'Fine! I don't know what else to do. I am going to stay in the city for a few days!' he said and turned to look at her. 'Not like it makes any difference; there is so much space between us at the moment, I don't need to be physically absent from the house.'

He stood there, quietly, hoping, waiting for her to say something.

'Leila?'

She said nothing. He shook his head and walked away. The look of pain in his eyes was unmistakable. Leila wanted to reach out, but there was some sort of barrier preventing her from feeling anything remotely emotional towards anyone. The only person that stopped her in her tracks was her Dahlia. She had dropped the phone on Olga following a heated discussion about weaning techniques, she had distanced herself from Lala because…well, mainly because her accent reminded her of Kaobi, but she said it was because she was too busy. She had eight missed calls from her mum and sisters collectively. She felt harassed, but alone. The last thing she needed was to help Akash feel better.

Dahlia was going to Olga's for the better part of the day on Leila's birthday. It was the summer so schools were on a break.

'Do you want to do something later?' Olga asked. 'Even though you have been a cow in the last few weeks,' she added.

Leila glared at her. Olga drove off.

She wore a low cut red Versace dress and red suede Louboutins, she brushed her hair down sideways, and carted herself off to the hospital.

'I'm afraid...' the doctor began. All the while he spoke, she was lost in a world of random thoughts. Why did all doctors have that weird look on their faces when they gave bad news? How long could she fight this? What would happen to Dahlia? Why did blue and yellow make green? She also wondered what Kaobi's father looked like.

'Mrs Yoganathan, did you hear what I said?' the doctor asked.

'Yes, my first chemo session is due next week.'

'Here is the letter confirming your appointment. Here is the number you need to call beforehand. Is there anyone I can call for you?' he asked.

Leila shook her head and made her way out of his office. She drove for miles that afternoon. If her mind went on about Kaobi way too much for her own good, it was about to get worse. She had never missed him so much. Everywhere she looked she saw him. His eyes, his smile, his nod, she could smell him. She longed for him. Her heart ached for him; for his presence in her life, for his presence before her, for his hug and his reassurance and his wisdom and the way she could handle just about anything with him beside her. Cancer would be easy peasy if she had Kaobi. She drove through a red light and that prompted her to park the car for a few seconds.

'Prince KK, will there ever be anyone else? Will I ever love anybody the way I love you? Will anyone ever hold me, kiss me, listen to me, be a best friend to me like you? Will I ever get over this? Is it so pathetically diabolical that I have a beautiful little six year old at home and yet the thought of dying just does not seem too bad, if it means I get to share my problems with you for eternity?'

Leila shivered frantically at her thoughts. She marvelled about how people looked at her and thought she was normal. These people did not understand the torture she underwent on a daily basis. She loved Akash with all her heart, and in every sense of the word, she was his wife. The truth was, Akash was her soul tie (for want of a better word) and she did not mean that in a bad way. Kaobi. Kaobi was...Kaobi was undoubtedly her soul mate! Kaobi was dead!

She got home to a huge bouquet of red roses. They were from Akash, who turned up 15 minutes later.

'Happy Birthday, Leila,' he said soberly.

She gave a weak smile.

'Are you OK?' he asked. She nodded.

'I was wondering if I could cook you dinner.'

She shook her head. 'I would rather be on my own right now.'

'Leila, I don't know what to think right now. Are you breaking up with me? I am sorry about the thing with Dahlia and the way I handled it. If it means that much to you, please let her have contact with Kaobi's family. I just thought...' And he just kind of trailed off because Leila did not seem to be paying any attention.

She burst into tears.

He approached cautiously. 'Is it OK to hold you?' he asked.

'Please just leave me alone!' she snapped and stormed upstairs.

Akash stared at their wedding photo on the fridge magnet. It was from the Hindu wedding. He had never seen anyone look so imperially exquisite in red. He stared at her lips. Even her lipstick seemed custom-made just for her. That day her eyes had shone so beautifully. He was so confident of her love for him. Today, he did not have a clue what to think, and more importantly, what to do to rectify the situation, if indeed it was rectifiable. He turned around towards the door, hesitated, and then walked out. There was only so much magic a man could work. The end of his marriage again? He cursed wildly under his breath. He jumped into his car and committed every traffic offence he possibly could and all the while, his language was filthy and obscene – had it been on TV, it would have been 'beeps' all the way. Did it make him feel better? Not really, but the alternative would be to beat the troubles out of Leila. He shook his head at the violent thoughts in his head.

'What a damn fool I can be sometimes!' he said aloud.

He drove to Olga's.

'She's probably just getting her period right after you pissed her off. Kash, you know what happened the last time. This time, she will see that you go to prison. Control that stupid temper of yours!' Olga said. Akash agreed.

'So she will snap out of it?' he asked anxiously.

'Give her a week or two,' Olga said, and patted Akash on the back.

He sighed, and then went on to entertain Dahlia and ZsaZsa for a bit. In the car, he decided to take Olga's advice. He would give her two weeks.

As Akash shut the door, Olga stared on after him, mobile phone in hand.

She dialled Leila's number. 'Do you want to tell me what's going on?' she asked Leila.

'No!' Leila said and put the phone down. Olga stared disbelievingly at the phone.

She snuck to the back where the kids would not see her and had a cigarette. As soon as she was done, she sparked up another. It was the first time she had felt the urge since ZsaZsa was born. She was worried. OK, today seemed like a good day to find an excuse to chain smoke. She smoked a third.

In the two weeks Akash gave Leila, she managed to shut everyone out. She had a drink or 12 every night, did not take any calls, was off work, and generally lost the will to live, almost literally. She struggled with Dahlia. Routine became too hectic a chore and the norm slipped more every day. When the bell went that morning, she suspected it was Akash. She did not move from the sofa. He let himself in.

'Leila, you look terrible!' he exclaimed.

'Charming…thanks…!' she responded sarcastically.

'Are you OK?' he asked.

'It's called a hangover!' she snapped, nonchalantly.

'Where is Dahlia?' he asked.

Leila pointed towards her room. A few minutes later, Akash came back down.

'She is still in her pyjamas, she has not had breakfast, she's playing video games!' He looked perplexed.

Leila got up.

'Where are you going? I am talking to you!' he called out after her.

'What are you going to do? Hit me? Rape me?' she said without turning around. She headed to the toilet. She was in there for 10 minutes when the phone began to ring. Akash did not pick it up. It went to voicemail. The call was from the hospital asking Leila to please call back concerning her missed appointment. Apparently, when you know someone well enough, it is easy enough to identify a problem. Akash raised his eyebrow at the answering machine. Hospital appointment? Instinct kicked in and James Akash Bond began his investigation straight away. He dashed to the kitchen and grabbed the heap of unopened letters. He tore at them wildly until he gathered enough information to fill the gaps. Leila came out just as the phone began to ring. She answered it.

'Yes, yes. You have to respect my wishes. Please do not ring me!' Akash had figured it out.

Leila turned round to see Akash staring at her, letters in hand.

'I'm so sorry,' he said in a whisper.

She had tears streaming down her cheeks.

'That's invasion of privacy, you bastard!' she said quietly.

'I know! But I had to know!' He held out his hands to her. She accepted. She collapsed in his arms and wept!

They stood a good few minutes in an embrace.

'Why have you missed your treatment?' Akash asked.

'I can't go through that. Who will look after Dahlia?'

'I will!'

'And me?'

'I will!'

'There is no hope, Kash. Let's forget the treatment and let nature take its course,' she sobbed.

'I have never known you to be a coward, Leila. You can fight this. I am right beside you! I will look after you!'

'I will lose my hair!'

'It will grow back, Leila. You need to do this…for Dahlia!'

'I am tired, I want to go to bed!' she said exhausted. She made her way to the couch and fell asleep straight away. She fell asleep because it had been days, maybe weeks since she had had a decent night's sleep. She felt like a heavy load had been lifted off her shoulders. She slept soundly. She dreamt of Kaobi and this time, she embraced his presence. His death did not hurt quite as much as it had in the last two weeks. He smiled at her and she smiled back. He stroked her cheeks gently.

Akash stood staring over Leila. He had fed Dahlia, given her a good scrub, cleaned the house and cooked a meal – roast potatoes and vegetables. He knew the weeks coming would be tough, but he had to be strong for Leila. He stroked her cheek as she slept peacefully. When she smiled, he was reassured that he was doing the right thing. He cuddled up beside her and smiled back. He wondered what she was smiling about. He wished it had something to do with him, but somehow he doubted it. They were husband and wife and Leila gave him no reason to doubt her faithfulness, but did he have her heart like he did years ago? He doubted it. Somehow she was her own woman, with her own thoughts, a lot of which he knew nothing about. He wondered what had happened between Leila and Kaobi. He knew he would never get answers. She loved him enough, he accepted that, but he was aware that part of her had died. There was no genuine sparkle in her eye. He wanted her one hundred percent. Now cancer? For fucksake!

Leila awoke to the smell of fabric softener. It was her favourite scent, and Akash knew it.

'I mopped the kitchen,' he said proudly.

Leila smiled.

'I poured the diluting detergent tablets into the mop bucket and then I put in some fabric softener, and then boiling water from the kettle – just the way I watch you do it. It smells really nice and feels lovely against the feet when you walk through the kitchen without flip flops or bedroom slippers on.'

'Thank you,' she said softly. 'Is this mine?' she asked, pointing to the mug of coffee beside her. Akash nodded.

'How long did I sleep?' she asked, trying to find her watch.

'It's 3 pm now,' Akash responded.

'Wow!' Leila exclaimed reaching over and taking a nice, long sip of the coffee. 'It's lovely, thanks.'

'Soya milk!' he said.

'You've gone all out, Kash. Thanks.'

'I have not seen you look so peaceful in ages, Leila. You slept really well. You were smiling in your sleep. What did you dream about?'

Leila thought for a second and then nearly choked on her coffee. Then she smiled and said nothing.

'It has been a month, babe. It has been four successful chemo sessions. Kash is obviously looking after you well, you even said so yourself! So why has Kash just left my house insinuating that the bitch in the house is back? Why are you being a cow to him?' Olga scolded down the phone.

'I need to put you on speaker babe, hang on. I need to…' and she trailed off. Olga could hear her vomiting and felt a pang of guilt for telling her off.

'Olga…' Leila muttered.

'Are you OK?' Olga asked, listening intently. Leila's voice was barely a whisper.

'I want some custard…please,' she said and then collapsed in a mound on the bathroom floor.

'Leila…Leila…Leila,' Olga screamed as she threw on a pair of shoes…the first she could find and screamed something inaudible to her nanny, who appeared with ZsaZsa and jumped into the car.

'Leila!' Olga screamed as she tore through the house looking for her. She found her in the en-suite bathroom upstairs in the master bedroom.

She rushed to her friend's side. Leila was conscious, but only just.

'Call an ambulance!' she screamed to her nanny.

'Am I dying?' Leila asked softly.

'Babe, God forbid that! You are probably having a bad reaction to the chemo or something. You will be fine.' Olga stroked her face. Then she picked up her phone.

'Kash…she's OK. The ambulance will be here soon. Can you arrange to have Dahlia picked up from school later? I'll sort that actually.'

'Take ZsaZsa home. Pick Dahlia up at 4. Give them some dinner, a bath or shower, whatever, then wait for my call,' Olga said to the nanny and then turned back to Leila.

'Are you sure I am not dying?' Leila asked when she awoke in her hospital bed.

'Don't be silly!' Olga scolded. 'You just reacted badly to chemo. You will be fine. You are strong! You can get through this.'

'Where is Kaobi?' Leila asked.

Olga was taken aback by the question, so she just stared at Leila, unsure of what to say. She said nothing.

'I know…he's dead!' Leila said, turned around and fell asleep.

Olga went out for an emergency cigarette. She was not sure what to do, what to say – IF to say anything at all.

Akash walked up to her mid-fag.

'How is she?' he asked.

'She is sleeping.'

'Will she be OK?'

Olga reached over and hugged him. 'She is a fighter. You know she is!' she said, smiling.

'Yes but, it's cancer!'

'She will be fine, Kash.'

'Isn't that what they always say? Then next thing they get better and then they die suddenly.'

'Kash! Please be positive. Don't go in there with this attitude. Have a fag and calm the fuck down!' she scolded.

'Kash!' Leila smiled weakly.

'Did you get me some custard?' she asked.

'Of course!' he said, putting on his most reassuring smile. Leila looked up at his smile, turned to Olga and then fell asleep.

'So are you going to shut everyone out for a couple of weeks and then collapse shortly after?' Akash asked when she was finally fully conscious and sitting up.

'Kash, I understand your big hero thing and wanting to stick by me and I am grateful. If you have wanted to prove your love for me, you have… completely. However, you heard the doctor. I have ovarian cancer. It is not looking good. I am probably going to die pretty soon and even if I don't, Kash – I can never give you a child!'

It hit Akash like a bullet. He knew this was probably the case all the while, but to hear Leila say the words was different. He took a long, deep breath.

'Leila, I have Dahlia. Call her Yoganathan and that is good enough for me,' he said, making his way across to hold her hand. 'Call her Yoganathan?' Leila had to think about this one. It gave her a weird feeling inside. Dahlia was Kaobi's daughter. But Kaobi was not here to fight for her to bear his name. Dahlia had remained Cranston-Jasper anyway. She had never really thought about whether it ought to be anything different.

'Kash, you have always wanted kids.'

'I have always wanted you!' he replied.

The road to recovery following that particularly bad bout was treacherous. She had hallucinations, she felt weak to the bone, it infected her spirit too. Her mother spent endless hours reading Bible passages to her and prophesying the longevity of her life. Leila was fighting but she was weak.

'Your light shall break forth like the morning, your healing shall spring forth speedily, and your righteousness shall go before you; the glory of the Lord shall be your rear guard.'

'Where is that from, Mum?' Leila asked weakly.

'Isaiah 58, verse 8,' her mum responded.

Leila smiled weakly and fell asleep. This cycle repeated itself for days on end. Her mother never left her side – three weeks, it was. Akash had been away in Japan on business for a fortnight and Leila's mum had stepped in to assist Olga. They took it in turns to run her home while Leila recuperated. The following Tuesday saw some colour return to Leila's cheeks. She sat in bed after a bowl of porridge. Olga had just left with Dahlia for school.

'Why do you keep staring at her, Mum?' Leila asked.

'I noticed the Jimmy Choos. They are pretty. I would love a pair of those.'

Leila gave her a sarcastic look.

'Not Olga. Dahlia.'

Her mum looked at Leila carefully before she spoke. 'Tell me about Kaobi,' she said.

Leila breathed long and hard.

'Why?' Leila asked.

'Because on countless occasions in the last four weeks, you have whispered his name in your sleep…and smiled!'

Leila's expression was vacant when she told the 'Kaobi story'. She stopped occasionally to sip on some water, go to the toilet or stare into space.

'And you did not think Dahlia was his?'

'No! Not for a second!'

'Leila!'

'I think I blocked it out of my thoughts,' Leila said dismissively.

'She does not look like Akash, she does not look like Kaobi, and she does not really look like me either. Her features are totally random!' Leila said, making excuses.

'She looks like you,' her mum said gently.

'No she doesn't!'

'Leila, you block things out when you don't want to remember! You have done this since childhood. Deep down inside you know the true story of her conception!'

'I do?'

Her mother nodded.

'What have I blocked out?' Leila asked.

Her mother got up from the chair and sat on the bed, where she could be close to Leila.

'Sweetie, I have loved you all your life. I loved you from even before I met you. Of course Dahlia's biological make-up did not manifest in physical features, of course she looks totally mixed-blooded. She took that from you. You are neither white, nor black, nor Asian even,' her mother said carefully.

'What am I?' Leila asked.

'I don't know, sweetie!'

'Why? How come?' Leila asked.

'You know how come!'

Leila sighed. She had not uttered the words in years…'I know. I was adopted! The only person who would have known where I came from died.'

'But I have loved you like my own from the moment I saw you,' she said in a soft whisper. Leila agreed with her because it was the truth.

She fell asleep in her mother's arms.

In the last few minutes before she slept, she replayed the night, the only night she had spent with Kaobi. The car bonnet incident had happened and they got on the flight to Paris. Kaobi arranged the middle aisle so they could sit side by side. The flight lasted an hour and fifteen minutes. In the first twenty minutes, they were buzzing from their previous episode, the champagne they drank and the general electrifying madness of what they were doing.

'Don't you need the toilet?' she asked him as he nibbled on her neck.

'I do?' he asked puzzled.

'Well I do…and I will need some help in a few minutes so you can join me,' she suggested. He looked puzzled for a few seconds and then, 'ohhhhhh', he said, nodding and smiling.

She was up in a flash. Off to the toilet, she scurried. She shut the door behind her and climbed into the sink. Her underwear had been long gone since the car bonnet incident anyway. She heard a tap on the door. 'KK?' she asked. He responded. She let him in. He kissed her straight away while he undid his zipper. The episode lasted only four minutes, but it was extremely gratifying. Her body was thanking her. She left him there and went back to her seat. He was beaming from ear to ear when he came back.

'You are totally insane,' he said to her. She smiled, offered him more champagne and rested her head on his chest while he put his arms around her. When they got to the hotel room, Leila remembered that she jumped into the shower. Minutes later, Kaobi joined her. There was music in the background. Leila could not remember what was playing. They held each other, scrubbed each other, kissed each other several times everywhere in the shower. They got out soaking wet and Kaobi dimmed the lights. He held her in his arms and they swayed from side to side. This time he kissed her gently and asked her to listen to the lyrics. Bryan Adams' *'Have you ever really loved a woman?'* took on a new meaning for Leila that night. In between his subtle kisses, he whispered the words, 'I love you, I adore you, you are my baby, my princess, you are my woman!' in random order into her parted lips. When he did not speak them in words, he spoke them with his eyes. His gaze was intent, focussed, genuine. He laid her wet body on the bed and went to work on her breasts. He drew circles around her nipples, and then he sucked on them gently. Leila tingled to her toes. He smiled, he leaned over and caressed her flittering toes, and then he came back up and bit ever so lightly on her areola. She gasped and released tiny yelps of deep, conspicuous pleasure. He reached out for the bottle of Baileys and tipped some into the valley that her navel created. He stuck his tongue into it and scooped drops in powerful upward movements; he sipped out of it like it was a soupspoon. Leila's heart raced. He went further down. He licked the tip gently, then hard, then gently, then hard. He licked the sides with the tip of his tongue and French kissed her clitoris. He came back up and lay beside her. She did exactly the same to him. He was mute, but she could see fire in his eyes. When he was back on top of her Leila was on tenterhooks. His initial thrust was gentle. He paused.

'Are you OK?' he asked. Leila choked on her speech. It was the same as the car bonnet, but this time he had space and comfort to manoeuvre every corner. He visited new places within. Leila was no screamer, but that night she screamed in pleasure that was so cavernous, so beguiling, so breath-taking, it was almost painful. This happened every time he hit what she later learnt was her g-spot. When he rubbed against it, his thrusts felt like a grind and Leila's prolonged groans were audible, but at those points, she did not scream, she created a melody of some sort. Leila felt his presence in little paths along her vagina wall that she never knew existed. She lost control, her inhibitions were non-existent. Even her language lost composure. She told him she loved him, she told him nobody had ever done these things to her body, not this way. Nobody had ever loved her like this. She begged him to give her more, she begged him to take her, to fuck her, and when she had exhausted her limited vocabulary, all she could say was 'please'. 'Please what?' he asked. She mumbled. 'Please stop?' he asked. She shook her head quickly. He turned her around to lie on her stomach.

'Should I stop?' He asked.

'Please don't stop!' she said and he didn't. Well not until she climaxed, really went into unbelievable multiple orgasmic spasms and concurrently, he felt fireworks of his own. They both collapsed in a heap.

'I love you,' Leila said.

'I love you too, but….' Leila turned away.

'I think we have a problem!' he announced a few minutes later. 'The condom is lost!' he said.

'What do you mean?' she asked. Kaobi made a couple of embarrassing Internet site visits to discover it was a common problem. Hard, deep thrusts could throw it far into the walls of the cervix! Kaobi used two fingers to retrieve it.

'That has never happened to me before!' she said.

'Many things that happen to me with you, Leila, have never happened to me before!' he said.

Leila lay in her mother's arms thinking of the six major things that happened to her that night. Firstly, at 33, she had had her first real sexual experience. She discovered she had a g-spot… and it worked. For the first time in her life, she climaxed. Previously, she had just lied and pretended mostly to save her partner's ego (yes, including Akash). She experienced a vaginal orgasm and a clitoral orgasm because Kaobi had been on top of her from behind with his fingers working magic against her clitoris. Both orgasms were a few seconds apart, if that. Secondly, she had a man insert two fingers into her to retrieve a lost condom. Kaobi was her 'homie-lover-friend!' This was evidence. Thirdly, she fell head over heels in love with him. The love she felt was unlike any feeling she had ever had, it was unmistakable. It was the real thing. The way he looked, the way he spoke, what he did for a living, none of these things mattered. Leila could almost physically see into his heart and soul. She had not known him that long, but it felt like she had known him even beyond a lifetime. That night, Leila and Kaobi created a love bond. Fourthly, she thoroughly enjoyed giving him a blowjob. Every attempt prior to Kaobi had left her gagging. Fifthly, Leila joined the mile high club! It had been on her to-do list since her twenties. It was on her current to-do list and she knew she would have to give it a retrospective 'tick' for the sake of completeness. Lastly (and Leila's eyes opened wide at this point)…she heard his voice in a flashback: 'something happened last night, Leila. It was the few seconds with the g-spot!' they chuckled because that bit was said in unison.

'You read my mind with ease,' he said.

'You read mine!' she responded.

'Something that will follow us for the rest of our lives,' he had said. Dahlia was conceived that night…and she had known…that night!

Leila looked at her mother. 'I know the precise moment when Dahlia was conceived!' she said quietly, her face devoid of expression.

'I bet you do!' her mother said. The expression on her mother's face was not decipherable either. Leila untangled herself from her embrace and fell asleep. She slept for ten hours. Her slumber was dreamless.

She awoke to her mother's smile.

'Hungry?' she asked.

Leila shook her head.

'Do you want me to brush your hair?' her mother asked. Leila shook her head again. She diverted her gaze from the hairbrush, which held more of her hair in its bristles than it should under normal circumstances. She ignored the urge to cry.

'Lala is coming over later. Let me go and get Dahlia settled. Olga deserves a break. Will you be OK?' she asked taking Leila's left hand in hers. As she did she and Leila both smiled at Leila's wedding ring. The smile asked a multitude of questions that Leila was not prepared to answer.

'Go, Mum,' she said. 'I have a few decisions to make,' she added.

'Are you strong enough?'

Leila smiled and nodded slowly.

'God be with you sweetie. He knows your heart.' She kissed Leila's forehead.

Two hours staring at the ceiling, Leila battled with questions. Would she survive this disease? Who would look after Dahlia? Where was Kaobi? (She knew the answer to that one, but she asked anyway). Akash! What exactly did he represent in her life? Was she being fair to him? Where was he anyway? Japan! What the fuck was he doing in Japan when she was busy dying of cancer? Running away? Did she have the right to judge anyone? She sighed…again!

'How many times do I have to ask for closure, KK? I will always love you. I will always carry your photo in my wallet. You are never far from me. I will see you when it's time because it will take more than life and death to separate us. It is not time yet. For now, I need to live.' She sighed. She needed one last gentle push in the right direction.

She was nearly mentally comfortable. She fell asleep.

She awoke to Olga's gaze.

'How long have you been staring at me, psycho?' she asked lazily.

'Long enough. OK, sleeping beauty, I have got some soup for you.'

Leila pushed the bowl away.

'So are we going to get unpredictable Leila from now on? One minute you eat, the next you starve until you pass out?' she asked, slightly irritated.

'Do you fancy swapping places then? Let's watch you deal with this better,' Leila spat.

'Oi! There is no need for attitude. If you do that, I will never be inspired to tell you what Christian Dior has done with animal print and red recently!' Leila kissed her teeth.

'And where did you pick up that rude habit from, young lady?' Olga scolded.

Leila turned her head towards the wall and brushed off more loose strands of hair that had given up the fight to stay rooted to her scalp. She was in no mood for stupid jokes. Olga visibly softened.

'Leila, we both know you are not going anywhere. You can fight this. You will live. I have no other punching bag and I know you want to see what comes of the lingerie business. I know you want to see Dahlia's kids.'

'I can't understand how I got here,' Leila whispered. 'I'm petrified and I don't have Kaobi. He's gone.'

Olga got up from her seat beside the window and sat on the edge of Leila's bed. She took Leila's hand in hers.

'You are an irritant, Leila. But you are a beautiful irritant and I would not swap you for the world. You drive me up the wall with your attitude...'

Leila cut her off.

'Errr...pot, kettle,' she said pointing to herself and then Olga. Olga smiled.

'You are my best friend in the whole world.' Silence.

'Kaobi. Kaobi died, Leila. OK, listen. I want to tell you a story,' Olga said.

'Once upon a time, there lived two mice that were inseparable. They did everything together. Literally. You know, the whole Cinderella shebang – love, etc. Mr and Mrs Mouse, they were.' She had caught Leila's attention; Leila held her gaze and listened.

'They lived in a house with a fairly aged lady who was scared of mice.'

'Why?' Leila asked.

'Why what?'

'Why was she scared of mice?'

'I don't know. Who likes mice? I don't like mice. Do you?'

'Dahlia does. I don't mind them either.'

'OK remind me to put some in your kitchen. I'll get some nasty brown ones with fat bellies.'

'No way! Yuk!' Leila exclaimed. They giggled for a bit.

'Anyway, honey, one day, the woman bought a mousetrap. She could only afford one. She put the trap in the kitchen and waited patiently. She got Mr Mouse. The snap was so gruesomely executed, the mouse felt no pain. It died instantly without a sound. His companion just stood there and watched. The old lady peered in and was pleased, but she was unable to take it outside to give it a befitting burial in the garden because the other one would not leave its side. She waited hours and the mouse just stared on at its dead companion. Anyway, when she saw that this mouse was not budging and was probably going to stay there forever, she fetched a knife and decided she would be brave, as she could not afford another trap. The mouse was so engrossed in waiting for the miraculous resurrection of her partner that she noticed neither the old lady nor her knife. One strike and she met her totally avoidable demise.'

'That's really sad!' Leila said.

'Yes it is, Leila. In standing there, brooding over her loss, she lost her own life. It probably hurt really badly, but subconsciously, Mrs Mouse did not accept that her Mr was no more. She knew she was in danger, but she took the chance and stood there trying to turn back the hands of time and then look what happened!' Leila blinked several times.

'Day in, day out, I have stood and watched this love triangle starring you, Akash and…and a ghost!'

'Sweetie, you have to let go. Kaobi is dead. Akash Yoganathan can be a prick sometimes, but you married him again because you realise there is something there. You know this! Dahlia needs you. Heck, I need you. I am useless without you. I understand you loved him, but truth be told, when he was alive, you could not even be together. What's the point of dying of a broken heart just to be with him? He would want you to live, Leila. You have a good chance. Please live!'

'I really miss him,' Leila whispered. 'I loved him,' she added.

'Yes, yes, our cross-eyed stutterer! What's not to love?'

'He's not cross-eyed. His stutter is sexy!'

'His bum was sexy, his cross-eyes weren't. His stutter was debatable.'

'He was not cross-eyed.' Leila said laughing. Olga smiled.

'Today, you let go,' Olga said and inched in on what space was left between them.

'Let's kick cancer's big arse!' She held Olga in her arms and they both had an impromptu cry.

Leila dug out her to-do list.

5. ~~Join the mile high club!~~ ✓ ☺

'If you do not change direction, you may
end up where you are heading'
Lao Tzu

Chapter Sixty-Six

Crossroads

We stand at the junction of the crossroads. Although we stand on the pavement that leads one way, it is not a final decision. We could cross over and go the other way instead. Basically, all we hope to achieve is a) the 'right' path, and b) a place that will make us happy. If we could achieve a and b above concurrently, then the fact that we stand at the crossroads would hardly make topic for interesting conversation, would it?

Today we stand examining our predicament with our hearts and head and we can see black and white in all its glory. It is emblazoned almost in physical so that there is no running away from it. What we see also is the culprit who makes it a blurred sight, even in its apparentness – shades of grey!

Both of us stand hand in hand at the crossroads. We are veering to the left, but there is a tug to the right. I pull you to the right, you nudge me left and the only place we stand that puts a smile on both our faces is right in the middle of the road. This cannot work. It is the only way we can be together and be happy, but it involves a lot of other – how should I put this? – unfortunate incidents that could result as a direct consequence of this (you stand in the middle of the road, you stand in danger of getting run over #fact!). Neither of us wants this. Neither of us can fully accept the terms and conditions that come with shades of grey. What a dilemma!

I therefore cross to the right and watch you cross over to the left. We have agreed that there will be one final hesitation. I will bear no grudge and you will live with it too.

*I know enough about shades of grey. She has got to be female. I understand the way she operates. She's honest, no doubt – she's also alluring and tempting and if accepted, makes even the most complicated situations seem simple. She is also known sometimes as fantasy because in reality she can be an excuse not to go with black or white. In some cases, she is obvious enough and is just a steady grey hue. When she is a bit more knotty is when she stands before you, blurring your vision with her evasive, indecipherable shade – sometimes light, sometimes dark! *sigh**

*It is black and white now; shades of grey disappeared, melted away into oblivion. And as I walk to on my path to the right, I am conscious that if I look back I will run back to the middle of the road. I am almost positive that you will meet me there. We both know that we will revive shades of grey. When she comes back with a vengeance, she comes armed with a discombobulating bang that throws you off course. You would never have encountered these new strange shades – shades that will take indecipherable to the next level. *sigh**

Dear Reader, are you familiar with the story of the man and woman who could not be together for one reason or the other – even when the 'love' (note – this word is used reluctantly because it has been bastardised – every Thomason, Dicky and Olivia is 'in love') was apparent? Yes? The black and white in the story is that nothing can stop love. The shade of grey here is that this is no Disney cartoon. Yes, it can be stopped. The truth – it is what it is. But let's take this one step further and make a tearjerker of it. What if in this story, they could have conquered all the odds somehow. What if she had to go on her own path not because she could not meet him on the other side, or he was not happy to go with her down the right path? What if she is walking down this path alone because neither of them had a choice…literally? What if black and white was not black and white, but was life or death? What if he died? Then what?

PS

There she goes, walking down the road to the right, alone. She is conscious that even if she looked back all she would see is his shadow. She is also conscious of the fact that if she looks back hard enough, she too will be a shadow. It does cross her mind for a second. 'At least we will be reunited!' Then the after thought: 'it's not time yet, neither is it the right decision'. She keeps walking. Fullstop!

Chapter Sixty-Eight

That night, Leila made a to-do list.

1. Beat Cancer
    a. Cut my hair. It WILL grow back with a vengeance – unbelievable volume with the help of every product Mizani, TRESemme, Phytospecific and Vitamin E have to offer (☺ I cant wait!)
    b. Wallow not in self-pity during chemo. It is what it is

2. Change Dahlia's name by deed poll. It will now read Dahlia Adaobi Adaobi Cranston-Jasper Yoganathan. (This one took considerable thought, but this is my final decision. It is the right thing to do for all involved.)
3. Change my telephone number. Cut off the Chetachi-Uba's. There will be no surprise phone calls. This is in Dahlia's best interest…for now.
4. Let Kaobi go. His memory is an indelible print in my heart, so getting on with life does not mean forgetting him.
5. Join the mile high club!

Chapter Seventy

Lala, Patricia, Olga and Leila's sisters. They all stood in Leila's kitchen talking about French Connection skinny jeans and the fact that stamp duty ought to be scrapped for first time homebuyers in the UK. Basically, the conversation ranged from sheer silliness to issues of serious global importance. Leila stared blankly from one to the other, thinking how every woman she knew had such a strong voice, strong identity and stood for her own individuality. She smiled as she watched her sister and Lala cook jollof rice – Lala's Nigerian delicacy that had everyone licking their fingers and wanting more.

'Now, which one of you do I trust enough to do me the honours?' Leila asked smiling, speaking quietly and pointing from Olga to Patricia, then Lala and her sisters with the pair of scissors.

Everyone was instantly silenced, all gazes directly on Leila. She sighed subtly.

'Who is going to do the honours?' she asked again. She paused. 'You know, Patricia has me drinking this concoction.' She rambled on nervously. 'At first it tastes kind of weird, but it's an acquired taste. It's not half bad,' she said sipping from a double pint sized calabash and feigning nonchalance with the added 'mmmmm' for effect. Nobody believed her. Heck, she did not believe herself!

'This *calabash* brings its own aura and even influences the taste a little bit – gives it character, somewhat. Besides it's a nice shade of clay, don't you think?' Everyone was quiet as Leila replenished the bowl and made her way to the living room. Everyone else followed suit.

Leila fetched a little bright red, heart shaped pillow and sat in the middle of the sofa. She sat on the smaller of the two, east of the front room, the one that faced the window. She sat directly in the springtime sunrays that seeped through the lace curtains. The rays bore the semblance of the much-celebrated spotlight and she was well aware of all eyes on the calabash, a pair of scissors, the bright red, heart shaped pillow and her.

They all sat in the living room in a semi circle. Never had silence sounded so thunderously deafening. Tears had never pricked so hard through several pairs of eyes, all beholding this woman with patches of hair that once was a voluminous head of hair, and had successfully concealed what was in fact quite a small head.

Leila's sister took the pair of scissors bravely. She sat on the sofa. Leila sat on the floor between her legs. Nothing happened for a few minutes. They all listened as Lala lectured them sombrely on the contents of Leila's calabash. Leila sipped slowly. It was a mixture of ugwu (African pumpkin leaf) and Onugbu (African bitter leaf) blended in brine.

'It does not taste bad when you get used to it,' Leila said, trying hard to persuade the others. She shut her eyes.

'Dear Lord, it's me again. I have authority to do this because you have said so. Tonight I feel your love. I see your angels all around me. You know like when we are in church and we all drink from the same cup and it symbolises your blood? Pour your healing into my calabash. Let me taste your replenishment; let me feel your restoration. Let us drink with one love, in one accord. Thank you, Lord.'

She passed it to her sister, who took a sip and passed it on. And so it went round the room in persistent silence. Banter was unnecessary, possibly inappropriate because in that room hearts spoke volumes. In the spirit of togetherness, they sipped and prayed. It was a common prayer. 'Dear Lord, please take control,' the words on Leila's lips. If their lips were read, the same prayer would be heard.

Twenty-five minutes this moment lasted. Leila's top-of –the-range front room with its Van Gogh painting in the corner, Leila's huge cinema screen TV North-Central of the sofas and the beautiful pair of kissing teddy bears made of bespoke crystal which complemented the Swarovski flower glass on the window sill, glittering as they stood interrupting and trapping stray traces of sun rays as it shone through in bright and beautiful glory. The setting was beautiful enough to be captured as a painting. But these would be inappropriate to describe, as it would detract from the illustration of what happened in this room that afternoon. The apposite description consisted thus: Olga, Lala, Patricia, Leila's sisters sitting in a semi-circle with their gazes fixed directly on Leila. Nothing else was important. Nothing else could be seen or heard. Although they formed a perfect semi-circle, each on the far end connected to Leila by gaze and unbreakable bond, therefore they formed a circle – a chain. This chain was connected by one spirit, one heart, one mind, a single thought, in perfect, synchronous accord. The energy was potent like a fertilizer within soil, which gave their prayer verve.

Therefore, as Leila's beautiful hair, once easily 8 inches, now varying lengths ranging randomly in patches on her little scalp between 0 and 5-6 inches fell around her shoulders to the floor, she said, 'Thank you, Lord, for family, for friends. Thank you, Lord for loving me. Thank you for the gift of life. Thank you for interesting contraptions like pairs of scissors.' (She smiled.)

She took out her notebook. 'Item 1a, tick' and she ticked. 'Item 1b…' she paused.

'Finally, I am thanking you because, Lord…' she choked, but only slightly, 'thanking you. I know, I feel it, today Lord, I have beat cancer already. 1b – tick!'

'When two or three are gathered in my
name, in their midst …I am there'
The Bible – Matthew 18:20

Chapter Seventy-Two

Three weeks passed and Leila would not wear a wig. She worked her baldhead as was and batted not an eyelid when she got puzzled or sympathetic glances in the streets or hospital respectively. The damned disease was on its way out anyway and the hair would grow back. She strongly believed this.

She waited till Tuesday because she knew at about 2 pm the front gates would part open and Akash would be home. His deal in Japan had taken a while, but they had Skyped, Facebooked and BBMd all the way through. Conversation had been few and far between but there had been a lot of communication, sometimes a bit too much for a recovering Leila. She did not want him to feel guilty for being away for so many weeks; it was something they had to do. They had opted for private health care because Akash wanted to be sure she got the best. He footed that unplanned forty five thousand pound bill without touching a credit card or taking a loan. The money had to come from somewhere but she knew it had hardly any impact especially with this new deal he had successfully undertaken in Japan.

It took every bit of energy she had left, but she did make her way successfully to the registry office. It took a few minutes of 'ums', 'ahs', 'just give me a second', 'can I have a glass of water please', heart palpitations and telling herself that it felt right, it was a good thing to do; but then it was done. She looked at the new version of Dahlia's birth certificate. It read: Dahlia Adaobi Yoganathan.

'Item 2 – tick' and she ticked.

That afternoon, chemo just would not give her a break! She had puked her bodyweight in fluids, or so it seemed, but the feeling would not relent. 'I have nothing left to give to the toilet bowl,' she remarked, kissing her teeth. She grabbed a cup of brine. Ugwu and bitter leaf would have to let her be today and she sat by the windowsill in the front room. Summer of 2002 was lovely. Her daffodils were sprouting nicely. There was some movement with the roses as well, but not one had bloomed just yet. The flowers danced happily in the wind. They formed a row all the way from the gate, down the driveway and round the little roundabout, which sat central before her front door. Her eyes followed each flower round the circle. The daffodils were yellow and every fourth or fifth flower was a shade between orange and red. They were not daffodils. She wondered if they were tulips. She had no clue. She smiled. Her mother would know. Mum had re-designed the front of the house just before they moved in. Leila was useless with flowers. She just knew they were either pretty or not. Her eyes continued to roam through the row of dancing flowers on either side of the driveway. She spotted a sunflower. She thought they only sprouted at the start of summer. She made a mental note to ask Mum about those too. She continued to tour with her eyes. Her eyes got to the gate. It was a bronzy red. It was the same shade of her calabash. She turned round and glanced at the centre table in the front room where the calabash sat, its contents still intact. She confirmed they were similar, not quite the exact shade though. Then she spotted the Mercedes Benz outside the gate. Akash was home! Her tummy did a little flutter and she realised that vomiting that afternoon was not just chemo – it was nerves as well. She was not sure whether to leap happily to the front door or wait for him to come in. She did not have to contemplate for long. The car just stood there, parked, neither driving off nor in. Twenty minutes she sat there, no longer interested in the flowers, but now concentrating instead on the car just outside the gate. She sat there and stared; she felt like an army of tipsy butterflies were playing catch in her head and tummy concurrently.

'I know Olga. I know! Thank you. I will see you when you bring Dahlia home later,' Akash said putting the phone down and taking a deep breath.

The business with the Japanese was brilliant – he was back on his feet now and his fortune had pretty much tripled. He had paid the hospital with a cheque and had not even flinched. He was proud to have been able to take care of his wife, but it had kept him away from her for weeks. He knew Leila dodged conversation, and, more recently, Skype because of the way she looked. He had missed the worst part of the chemo, but now, it appeared she was coping a lot better. He heard from Leila's mum and Olga that she had been a brave little combatant. On the flip side, Olga had warned him that her physical appearance would shock him. He needed to brace himself and when he did see her, he was not allowed to show shock or emotion by reason of her appearance. He was petrified. When he was in Japan, he had jumped every time the phone rang – he spent the whole time expecting 'that' phone call bearing details of her unfortunate demise. Even though it never came and Olga assured him she was over the worst, he could not believe. That was what they had said about his cousin. She recovered, but she then she died a year later. That she was on the mend was no consolation to him. It should not have happened in the first place. Japan was a compulsory trip – a welcome excuse not to watch the deterioration? Possibly. He sat there and stared, he felt like a multitude of soldier ants marched in his brain, intent on building a colony – some had made their way to his tummy!

Leila had watched him drive in, but when he turned the key in the lock, she still jumped. He walked in and spotted her straight away. Unsure of how to react, she waited a few seconds to take the cue from him. He obviously felt the same, so they ended up staring at each other for a few seconds. Then he smiled. His smile was pregnant, but she was grateful nonetheless. She had not known what to expect. She stood up weakly as he invited her into his arms. He walked a lot quicker than she did to bridge the gap between them. He kissed her on her forehead and held her tight.

'I'm sorry,' he said.

'What for?'

He did not respond. He just held her in comforting arms.

'I'm here now,' he said quietly. He sat her down on the sofa and smiled sweetly. He reached into his pocket and retrieved a gold pen.

'With love from Japan,' he said.

'For my scribbles?' she asked.

'For your scribbles,' he confirmed and they both laughed lightly. Her voice sounded like a garbled whisper. Her hair – well, no hair really. No eyebrows or eyelashes either. She had lost nearly a quarter of her body weight. Olga had placed her somewhere between size UK four and six. He reckoned she was a two – if that. It was not just the weight loss. It was the accompanying frailness that was emblazoned viciously all over. She looked like she was being eaten up. It had even caught the atmosphere in the house. He had not heard a peep from Gucci. Gucci and Dahlia usually played the 'first-to-speak-is-the-loser' game. Gucci lost every time. There was no shutting her up…usually. He made his way into the toilet. Unable to control himself, he wept.

Leila wished she could not hear the sniffles he tried so hard to contain. There was a life-size mirror in the little hallway that separated the living room from the dining area. It had a little table in front of it. She stared at her sunken eyes, her overly pronounced cheekbones, her weak shoulders (literally and metaphorically), but she knew all these would pass. She looked significantly better than she did a month ago. She was getting better. What more did he want?

Exhausted by the emotion, she sprawled herself on the sofa and waited patiently. She had the adoption papers in her hands and used it to fan herself.

'What's new?' he asked.

She handed him the paper work from the deed poll..

Leila watched as his eyes lit up excitedly. 'It has all gone through?' She nodded.

'She is mine?'

'The adoption was successful.' She replied smiling.'

'Thank you, thank you, thank you,' he said, kissing her several times on the forehead, on the bridge of her nose, on her lips.

'I am here now, Leila. I am not going anywhere. Let's eradicate this fucking disease!' They held hands.

'It's gone, Kash. I feel it,' and she said it with confidence. Akash did not say a word.

'Oi! Mulatto! Should you not be in bed? What are you doing hovering around in the kitchen like a bored vulture?'

'Olga'! Leila said. 'You mean eagle, silly woman!' she said twirling. 'I did not expect you so soon.'

'Kash has only been back two days and you look much better already. Good on you!' Olga said beaming. Leila ignored the statement.

'Actually…' Leila began, 'I need you to make this call for me. I have been on hold for ten minutes and I don't really feel like a long conversation with well-mannered customer services.'

'Oh,' Olga remarked, although it was more like a question. 'Pray tell?'

'My to-do list. Item 3,' Leila said quietly.

'Ohhhhh,' Olga said with more expression. She knew exactly what to do. Leila wandered off into the living room with her calabash. Olga took over the conversation, whilst making a cup of tea. Leila could hear bits of her conversation. Olga could clone Leila any day. Leila smiled at the thought.

'Name – Leila Yoganathan, yes, I am nee Cranston-Jasper. I changed that last year. Check your system. Address, date of birth, password Dahlia,' etc, until she got down to the nitty gritty. 'I would like to change my telephone number please, effective today…'

Leila ticked off item 3 with the golden pen from Japan. 'Tick!' she muttered with her customary sigh.

The mind is everything. What you think you become.
– Buddha

Chapter Seventy-Four

It was the morning of her final check up. It had been five months and Leila's hair resembled a shorter version of Demi Moore's in *Ghost*. It suited her thoroughly, especially with the new fiery red shade she had adopted for a bit of rebellion and character. She chose her wardrobe carefully during a conversation with God.

Her pussy-bow top from one of the Portobello Market sales – it was gold with animal print in the background. For her, the gold represented strength in royalty. It represented importance and greatness and wealth. The animal was representative of the fight her spirit had put up. It had been war!

She threw on green Dolce and Gabbana skinny jeans. The colour, green, represented growth, potency, and wealth in health.

She finished it off with her bug green Louboutins; they were a different shade of green from her jeans – in her mind, she thought the variety would give more power to the wealth she was claiming. They also had gold heels. She brushed her hair and wore no make-up. She was in tune with nature.

Grandma had sent her a pocket-sized Bible, which came in a gold case. She took that instead of her handbag and jumped into the front seat with Akash. Olga sat behind with Dahlia and ZsaZsa.

In the waiting room, Leila was calm. Olga had taken the kids to the little play area to keep them distracted. Leila held her Bible firmly;

she displayed any emotion akin to apprehension. Akash, on the other hand, was bathed in pools of sweat and paced erratically. She wanted to tell him that he was standing in the way of her positive light. She thought him a fool for not believing that all was well with her. She felt slightly sorry for him because she could imagine the turmoil his mind underwent, albeit it being futile. But then she thought to comfort him would be most inappropriate. Anyone would think he were the victim of cancer. As he gulped down a cup of water, whilst undoing his tie, she rolled her eyes. 'Selfish git!' she muttered under her breath, but decided to block him out of her thoughts. She wanted all things positive – strictly positive.

Akash observed Leila through the corner of his eye. He was almost worried at how calm she looked. He wanted to give her a hug, tell her that whatever the results, he would be there for her. He did not want to pronounce her dead before the verdict though. But he was also worried that in being overly optimistic (in his opinion), she had lost touch with reality.

'Bloody ants!' he said, before realising he had said that out loud.

'Ants?' Leila asked.

How was he to explain the pounding in his head, the grinding in his stomach, the lump in his throat? He just shook his head.

'Are you ok?' he asked her.

'Of course!' She said and she even looked quite irritated by the question.

Akash finally sat down quietly.

It was not long before it was Leila's turn. The doctor seemed pleased to see her, which was always a good sign. She smiled back.

'Mrs Yoganathan...' It was a long speech but she loved the summary version of it. Leila had beaten cancer! She sat in the waiting room to catch her breath. Finally, it was all over. It was something she had known all along, but hearing the confirmation of it was prodigious. Akash stood rooted to the spot for a good few seconds.

'Baby!' he said as he lifted her in his arms. Leila smiled

Olga came back in with the kids. She looked straight at Leila with questioning eyes. Leila smiled. Olga did her happy dance, right there in the waiting room. It consisted of the running man and twerks. The kids were amused and joined in. Leila 'face-palmed' and shook her head, so Olga cleared her throat and composed herself. She listened to the gist of it. 'Bottom line – the cancer has been eradicated. They want bi-quarterly check-ups initially, but fingers crossed, that's it!'

'Mulato!!! That's fantastic! I take it we are having champagne when the kids go to bed!'

'I don't see why not!' she responded, beaming from ear to ear. 'First, I need to have a word with Akash!' Akash's heart skipped a beat at the sound of his name. Whenever his wife called him *that* it was never a good sign.

'Now?' Olga asked. Leila nodded.

Olga wandered off with the kids in search of fruit shoot and chocolate, no questions asked.

'Did you think I was going to die?' she asked. 'It's almost like you wanted that to happen. Do you want me to die?'

'How can you get it so wrong, Leila? You are my life. I was petrified. You are much better at all this positive thinking stuff than I am. I am so sorry. I have not handled it well in the last couple of months, but Leila, I am relieved. I don't know what I would have done if it wasn't good news!' He had tears pricking in his eyes.

'You would have left me, you bastard!'

'No! How can you say that?'

'I don't know how to react to you. You love me, right?' she asked. He nodded.

'You swore you would be my backbone. Where have you been? I don't mean physically, Kash. I understand the Japan thing. Well actually, that was really convenient for you, but I worry about how quick you are to run away when things go wrong. In sickness and in health, Akash, that's what you promised. You pronounced me dead, pretty much. You left me to fight alone.'

'Leila, how could you say that? It tore me to pieces. Ok, this is my frailty. I am a selfish bastard and probably sometimes unable to show the right emotions, but I swear to you that if you had died, I would have died too.' he looked at Leila with pleading eyes.

'You are a selfish bastard, that bit is true.'

'A selfish bastard who cannot bear life without you.' It made sense to Leila and was genuine in a sense so she softened.

'Well, I ain't going nowhere, am I, Kash?' she said gently.

'And thank God for that, Leila. I will spend the rest of my life looking after you, I promise.'

She allowed a hug, but it was nearly reluctant on her part. She was sure he loved her. She was also sure that she needed him to have been a bit stronger. If she had believed him, she would have been sucked into believing in her own death.

Later on that night, Leila admitted the truth to herself. Akash only brought her own innermost fears to the surface. She believed she would live, but that was because this was her only option. If she had died, Dahlia would have been an orphan, which is a true, but bizarre thought considering she had just allowed Akash adopt her as his child. She was ashamed of her thoughts, especially considering her own origin. She had never been loved any less. It was also about her fear of the tattoo! For now, she had won. When she saw the wrinkly old fortune-teller with the scrawny fingers perched in the left corner of the room, she was chewing gum (this confused Leila because as far as she knew, she had no teeth); Leila stuck her tongue out at her!

What the mind can conceive and believe,
and the heart desire, you can achieve
– Norman Vincent Peale

Chapter Seventy-Six

My colour themed heart

My heart is big and colourful. It feels at random things most times. When I imagine my heart, I don't think of it as a huge vessel pumping away. Yes, it is red like most emoticons out there, but it also has colour injected in it. I often describe life in terms of colour. When I am happy, I see the rainbow; when I am not, I find it hard to even see shades of grey, which I heavily subscribe to…i.e. life, especially in terms of love, is never ever black and white.

But most of all, sometimes I think of my heart as a big house with many colour-themed rooms. I won't get bogged down with the details of the symbolism each colour theme represents, suffice to say my talented heart is capable of drifting from red to grey, to black to multicolours, all within seconds. Apparently, it's the cancerian in me. Does your heart do that as well?

In my journey through life, my heart engages with people. Many rooms are the colour they bear because of the impact these people have had on me. This message is particularly to the members of my inner circle.

If I open the main door to my heart and invite you in, I do so because I trust you intrinsically. It is rare that I will limit access to just one room. If therefore I grant you unlimited access, I don't expect you to take your shoes off at the door for fear of soiling my rug. I expect you to confidently hold a glass of red wine over my white carpets because I expect that when you spill it, you would have done so totally by accident. I have invited you in because I trust you to be careful. Upon going into my colour themed rooms, I don't mind if you lie down and rumple the sheets a little bit – I don't mind if you feel totally at home. Why? Because I have invited you in because I believe that in all your humanness and possible flaws, that you will not do anything that will jeopardise my position, not intentionally anyway. In the event that you do so, I hope that you will feel comfortable enough with me to attempt some damage control – honestly.

When you walk out of any of my colour themed rooms, and even when you think you might walk out for good, shut the door gently behind you. Don't slam my door. You never know, you might be more attached to the colours, you see, you just might want to come back. If I have to spend sorrow, tears and blood fixing the broken lock or re-cementing the cracks you leave, regardless of how much of a good host I am or how beautiful a guest you were, I might struggle to let you in again. Why? Because it is not in my nature to make you take off your shoes at my door before you step in or to restrict access to any of my rooms, so don't break my door on your way out.

If therefore you walk around with confidence, but gentleness, and every time you walk out of any room, you take in the colour I offer at that time, close your eyes, relish in what it offers and leave peacefully for the next room, or perhaps out of my colour themed house that is my heart, I can make you this promise. I promise that whenever I visit your colour themed house, I will not take off my shoes, I will be careful with the glass of red wine, but whether you expect me to or not, I will bring with me my vase and decorate each colour themed room with beautiful flowers.

...my randomest thoughts,

Leila x

Chapter Seventy-Eight

The years rolled by. In what seemed like the blink of an eye Dahlia turned 18 and Leila at 52 sat wondering where all the time had gone. She sat in her front room on the morning of Dahlia's birthday recounting how times were changing rapidly. There was of course the increasing pain in her bloated tummy, which she had ignored for weeks, hoping it would go away when it was done torturing her. *sigh *

The following significant events occurred in this time:

Immigration laws became significantly tighter. Even though Akash had spent years as a bona fide British Citizen, he still followed the Immigration News almost as closely as he followed Formula One. He was obsessed with these two things. But for a couple of Dahlia's school friends, Leila knew nobody who had suffered as a direct consequence of the new stringent measures introduced by the British Government. With regards to Formula One, Dahlia was totally smitten by the British driver, Lewis Hamilton, who was a welcome addition to the world famous drivers. Akash screamed, urging the cars on; Dahlia bought endless posters and souvenirs and inveigled Akash into taking her to France to watch the Grand Prix for two successive years just so she could get a glimpse of this dashing young driver. Leila often remarked that if she was going to sit with her father and watch cars go round a track eighty nine times (how exciting!), then there ought to be a few perks – e.g. something for viewing pleasure.

Leila learnt more about happenings in Nigeria than England. Kaobi was never far from her thoughts on a daily basis and Nigerian news – her only link to him – somewhat kept the fire burning in her soul. The only other way she would have kept tabs on his life would have been through his mother, Ada and his boys. She wondered often enough how his twins were doing, if Ada had found love, if his mother was OK. Occasionally, her mind replayed the last conversation with Ada, but she always concluded that ignorance is bliss. Still, had the twins grown up to be like their dad? Could they be nice, little English gentlemen, or had they taken up their roles as princes in their dad's honour? She wondered if they would ever find her again. She always mused that if they searched hard enough, it was possible. Every day she waited for that knock on the door, that email, phone call, anything. She consoled herself that if it never happened, then perhaps it was God's will. What would be would be. Every afternoon, she logged on to the website that had the Vanguard newspaper. She had kept tabs as Nigeria went through presidents Abacha, Obasanjo and now it was some dodgy fellow who constantly wore a black bowler hat called Goodluck Jonathan. She was more amazed by his fashion sense and his rather interesting first name than in the substance of his speeches (and his wife's too!) and merits of his appointment, which only came by default following the unfortunate demise of his predecessor. Abuja was replaced by Lagos as the capital of Nigeria and crime evolved from the times of Anini (some deranged armed robber/serial killer) to more modern robbery techniques, including kidnapping. As though there was not enough cruelty, Nigeria also saw the rise and rise of the Boko Haram – some religious fanatics who committed the most hideous of crimes to humanity in the name of religious justice. The country was going bonkers. Travelling by car was a hazard, travelling locally by air was not much better. Just a few days before she had heard that the country had a broken heart due to an aircraft accident that killed all on board. So many families were torn apart by this crash. It made the news in England as well. Akash had rambled on about it, while Leila stared on. Everything to do with Nigeria took on a different meaning to her; a meaning which Akash would never understand, nor be a part of. Every time Lala went on holiday, Leila was nervous. Lala always asked her to visit again, but Leila never took her up on the offer for many reasons, and foremost in her thoughts was the still bitter reminder of Kaobi's sudden death. Leila had never recovered from watching his body go into the ground. She still remembered the pain like it had happened only minutes before.

Dahlia had gone from despising the name 'Adaobi' to absolutely loving it and including it in all her schoolbooks and even her Facebook Profile Page. On her sixteenth birthday, she had scrapped the nametag on her bedroom door from simply 'Dahlia' to 'Princess Dahlia-Adaobi'. When Leila saw this, she quickly summed that it was five years left till Dahlia would learn the truth about the blood that flowed through her veins. Every time she remembered the clock ticking away, Leila felt a bit light-headed. Still she marvelled at how apt the title 'Princess' was, considering Dahlia did not have a clue about her imperial background. She wondered if Kaobi's spirit had been communicating with her. She would not put it past him really. She smiled at the thought.

After 14 years of a long distance marriage, Leila's father finally gave up his contract overseas and came back to England to age gracefully with his wife, Leila's mum. She had never seen her mother so happy. He had not featured too much in Leila's adult life, but Leila was ecstatic to have a physically present father once more. His thoughts were never too far off though and their relationship remained rock solid all through his stay in Dubai. Dahlia adored him and the feeling was mutual. He was wrapped around her pinkie easily. 'Granddad' and fluttering eyelashes was all she needed, he was at her beck and call.

Leila kept in touch with her High School crew. Ifi, Jennifer, Toks, Joy and Tia. They did not hang out every day like they had done in High School. In fact, they rarely spoke. Leila guessed that it was always going to be difficult for six women with fiercely strong individualities to maintain such a close relationship. There was bound to be conflict and many a time she deleted one or the other from her thoughts, but she was quick to realise that they always found their way back into her heart somehow. They would always be bound by High School memories – first boyfriends and kisses, puberty palavers, by virtue of their parents being friends and of course tragic events like Onyechi's fatal car crash. However, they had grown up and taken different paths in life and sometimes they only featured in each other's lives sparingly. There were one or two others from High School who featured more than these five, but life moved on and friendship happened in seasons. Leila had no hang-ups about this whatsoever. It was what it was and the key was in trying to respect individuality, preferences and lifestyle behavioural traits. Live and let live was the mantra she adopted. Her affection veered more towards Ifi and Tia. Yvonne too. Tia and Yvonne had spent the week with her a couple of weeks in her home. Patricia and Lala, she loved to the moon and back forever. As far as fondness was concerned, it did not get any closer. She had her 'constants' – people who did not shout off 'I am Leila's best friend' from the rooftop really, but who featured in her 'back office' so to speak. They helped her keep things running and they had secured their place firmly in Leila's heart. Olga had quit smoking finally ☺. She retained the title of best friend for no other reason than the naturalness of their friendship. Whenever Leila thought about Bette Midler's, '*wind beneath my wings*', these were the category of people who were in her thoughts. She thanked God for them as often as she prayed!

Leila and her family remained rock solid! Despite the circumstances surrounding her origin, the foundation of love was unshakable. It was undoubtedly, unquestionably, unconditional. She prayed often: *'Thank you, Dear Lord, for these people who love me even when I find no reason to love myself. Thank you, Lord, for the anchor to that girl who is neither a mother nor a wife, not anyone, other than simple Leila!'*

Leila's sister got married. It was the most beautiful ceremony Leila had ever attended. 20th of August 2006, Dahlia was ten years old at the time and made the perfect little flower girl. She paved the way for her aunt throwing rose petals with glittery bits down the aisle of the church. She was the faultless little princess and played her role with so much enthusiasm. Leila performed lyrical poetry, Akash was on the piano, and backed her up with subtle background echoes of her literary piece. It was the most personal present Leila could think to offer. It lasted eight minutes and the atmosphere was electrifying. The room was particularly dimly lit and so the ambience encouraged love, especially romantic engagements where applicable. The grey wall had 'Mr and Mrs Moon' sparkling on and off in exhilarating glitter throughout the rendition. They had the smoky effect as well. Her parents cried buckets and did a lot of cuddling and staring reminiscently in each other's eyes.

'Look how happy our daughter looks,' her father commented. Leila's mother could not stop smiling. Interestingly, Leila's sister married Leila's childhood friend - Charlie Moon. In the days of their dating, Leila formed an even stronger friendship bond with her then brother-in-law-to-be. He was a bit of a recluse. In many ways, he reminded Leila of Kaobi and she was ecstatic that her sister had found something so 'dependable' in someone – Leila seldom used the word 'love'. It always felt a bit too heavy, convenient and overused. When he asked her to be best man, Leila thought it hilarious. It was a black, white and silver ceremony – extremely picturesque in a modern way and Leila smiled when she looked at herself in the mirror that morning. She wore a tuxedo (why ever not?!). It had a rich gloss to it and she had the trousers made to fit snugly against her skin. Her killer black and white heeled brogues were the most expensive shoes she had ever bought, and they stood out iridescently – rightfully so too. But for her quiff, she slicked her hair back.

'I'm going to be the bestest best man ever!' she had said to Charlie that morning.

'I know. It had to be you. Who else can pull off a tuxedo and still be so effeminate?' he had smiled in return as Leila slotted in their corsages.

'By the way, you look like some super bad-ass chick from a James Bond movie.'

'As long as I get to kiss Sean Connery, I'm good,' she said. They both giggled.

It was a glitzy wedding – really posh too. They had champagne glasses with stems consisting of Swarovski crystals. The rooms sparkled. The tables consisted of a combination of white candles, silver glitter and Swarovski studs with matching Swarovski studded upholstery. When she welcomed the groom to her family, she reaffirmed her love for the immediate family, stating honestly that people would come and go but families were stuck together – it was love by default. She commented on how she was happy to be 'stuck with' this family and welcomed Charlie to their inner circle. She meant every word. Leila referred to her family as an oak tree with many branches and she thanked God for the new branch – him. She prayed that he would stay firmly attached and bear beautiful leaves, a couple or more brightly blossoming flowers and hang on strong enough to feed into the stem – the soul – and become a permanent part of the intricate cult that Leila and family permit a select few. Leila looked out of the window. It was a full moon.

'Mr Moon,' she began, still on the microphone, pointing.

'Did you order that?'

'I did, Leila. Only the best for your sister. Besides, when you and Akash tug so hard at our heart strings, it's no surprise that we are creating magic here tonight! How am I doing on my first day as a branch on the Cranston-Jasper Oak tree?'

'A full moon? Damn good!' she responded and the live band drum rolled at her declaration. It was second cheesiest moment Leila had ever experienced (first, being her first kiss with Kaobi on the beach, but a moment that would follow her to her grave. In her heart, it was in a shelf marked 'favourites'!)

The room cheered loudly. Mr Moon gave the thumbs up!

Akash kissed Leila and she still saw forever in his eyes. Her eyes were drawn to the left of the room where the wrinkly old fortune-teller was peeping at her through a red chiffon veil. Leila was unperturbed by her that night. Leila stared for a few seconds and then smiled. The ageless woman smiled back.

This is your life, and it's ending one minute at a time.
- Chuck Palahniuk, Fight Club

Chapter Eighty

Stitches on Life's Fabric

From the first breath of life until the last, we form various psychological relations with people. These ties fluctuate between one-on-one to less individual categories, running concurrently. Our relationships range from interaction with parents and family (nuclear or extended), friends and most intricate of them all, romantic involvements. In a guide to understanding the nature of these relationships, think thus: in order to accomplish social survival, the phenomenon called life demands as essential, interpersonal, co-dependent and/or interdependent relationships. Without some sort of correlation or the other, life would not exist! The dynamics of these relationships and what we opt to do with them effectively define who we are.

In my ever-changing perception, I think of life as a huge fabric. I think of the relationships we have amongst each other as stitches. Stitches – big or small, pretty or not, dull or colourful, interesting – stitches nonetheless. These stitches make one life distinct from any other; these stitches determine our uniqueness!

As a starting point to an insight into the different psychological make-ups of these relationships, think about the moment a baby takes its first breath. Commonly if born into an ordinary nuclear family, this is followed shortly by skin-to-skin contact with its mother, a cuddle with its father and perhaps its first attempt at suckling for food. In an old Chinese language, the bond between a mother and child is often contrasted against the connection between the ten fingers and the heart. Put your hand on your heart – unarguably, there is the physical distance in-between; however, if you cut off the hand, it hurts like hell! Indeed romance fails us and so do friendships, but the relationship between parent and child, less noisy than all the others, remains indelible and indestructible, the strongest relationship on Earth, so much so that no bond has proved to be stronger. The love between a man and a woman instantly becomes more intense by experiencing the birth of their child. The love the child has for its mother naturally extends to its father, because in effect, its father is an extension of its mother. In one miraculous moment, a family relationship of passionate devotion is born! As the family grows, the love extends to other siblings and the child's family becomes its first experience of any social obligation in life. From this relationship one begins to understand the concept of attitudes and behaviours. In learning the complexities of siblings' behaviours, the child understands that while some types of behaviour are acceptable to him/her, others simply are not. The child learns to manipulate these attitudes to adapt to his/her own needs. The family relationship is paradoxical. It requires the most intense love on the family's side, yet this very love must help the child grow away from the family and become fully independent. And it begins!

As a direct consequence of 'cutting the apron strings', we form 'friendships'. Some of these friendships are as a result of behaviours learnt whilst part of our family unit, and others are formed based on our own little peculiarities. 'Friends are the family we choose for ourselves' – while this quote is, at best, really cheesy, it bears some semblance with the truth because the prototypes which friendships take in our lives are similar to big tree – a huge, successful oak tree for example. It has many branches. It started out as a seedling. Along the way it became a little tree and developed a few branches. Unfortunately, along the trail of its growth, some of these branches broke off. During the process of metamorphosing from seedling to tree, new branches formed at random stages; there was no protocol for the formation of these new branches. Apparently, the essence of true friendship is to make allowances for another's little lapses. When a little rot becomes a huge life threatening disease, it is then probably less destructive to wither it out permanently, hence the reason why the branch got lost. Alternatively, there was a natural disaster, a huge storm or wild fire which by no fault or interference caused the branch to fall of its own volition. The former refers to cases where friendships are intentionally terminated for lack of compatibility, while the latter, to situations where both parties grow up to understand life differently and consequently no longer speak the same language. The new branch being formed randomly along the way is much akin to the saying that some of life's truest happiness is found in friendships we make along the way. Much of the vitality in a friendship lies in the honouring of differences, not simply in the enjoyment of the similarities. While you never find an orange growing off an apple tree, it is rare, but not a total impossibility to find a white rose amongst red roses. This indeed is rare but rare in this case is most beautiful. Whether formed from childhood, or in old age, by and by, no distance of place or lapse of time can lessen the friendship of those who are thoroughly persuaded of each other's worth.

Perhaps learning to be a good friend is the requisite a,b,c in the genesis of a romantic interest. After all, according to Jeremy Taylor, love is friendship set on fire! Often mind-set developed in our prelapsarian days establishes the foundation of our personalities. Traits similar or dissimilar in another person will often form the object of desirability. The unity of two people in love is the direct experimentation by these two people of the social skills required to survive in life. Elizabeth Ashley said, 'in a great romance, each person plays the part the other really likes'. A direct corollary of this hopefully is a romance which ends up being a lifetime commitment. Sometimes, this is attainable, but the nature of life is such that in love there are no guarantees. Should the former be the case, boy meets girl, both fall deeply in love with each other, and life permitting, they start their own family. And thus the cycle of relationships being a birth to death experience starts all over again, i.e. the first breath of life is taken, and so on and so forth.

Relationships, therefore, are a fundamental trend of life, which we learn more about as we grow older and wiser. In doing so, however, the deep-seated issues that come to light are skills that if applied correctly, could potentially lead to a lifetime of happiness. This bears its axis on the ability to create a balance in our relationships, skills that do not come easy at all. The vital elements are acceptance, forgiveness, compromise and greatest of all, love!

If we can love without season or ceasing, it reflects in the active relationships we create with other people. At the end of life, we look back at our fabric of life and realise that these stitches determine how we lived! For when the stitches were rough and ugly, we took it with a metaphorical smile and moved on. The result was that the stitches subsequent to that were schooled to be absolutely beautiful. We cannot dictate the way the world reacts to us, but we certainly can dictate the way we react to the world. It is therefore up to you to make your stitches beautiful!

Here's wishing you beautiful stitches while creating your fabric of life, good luck!

Leila x

Chapter Eighty-Two

'Speaking of relationships, Mum, or should I say thinking…' Dahlia interrupted Leila's thoughts.

'How do you do that?' Leila asked.

'Do what?' she asked.

'Intercept my thoughts. Read my mind!' Leila said puzzled.

'You are thinking of the Mr and Mrs Moon love story, aren't ya?' she asked chewing.

'Spit the gum out. Yes I am, amongst other things.'

'Can I guess?'

'No. How do you know? I don't like the way you look when you chew gum. It changes the pronunciation of your words.'

Dahlia did as she was told. 'You are too posh for your own good Mother!'

'It's just not ladylike.'

Dahlia rolled her eyes, adjusting her cardigan.

'Happy birthday, sweetheart. I love you to infinity and beyond.'

'I'm eighteen. I am an adult now Mum!'

'Indeed. You are never too old for my cuddles,' Leila said squeezing her tight, and then added, 'or my pancakes!' Dahlia beamed as they both made their way to the kitchen.

'I had a weird dream, Mum. Basically, what happened was…' but then the phone rang.

Leila put the phone down and looked at Dahlia mournfully. 'My grandmother died this morning,' she said.

'I'm sorry, Mum, but Greatgran was really, really old. It was bound to happen.'

'That doesn't help, Dahlia. I still grew up loving her as one of the most amazing people I know.'

'I know it must hurt, Mum. Even I am hurting and I didn't know her as well as you did'.

With old age, Leila's grandma featured sparingly in Leila and Dahlia's lives, not because of any love lost either way, but simply because her speech was heavily impaired, so phone calls were rarer, visits were less often because she was no longer as agile or mobile as she was previously, she could no longer bake, make pies or knit. And with Dahlia and Leila all the way out of London, it took a couple of weeks of planning to make a visit possible. One moment stood out in Leila's mind. It was the moment she had spoken to her about being pregnant with Dahlia. The advice, the wisdom, the love.

'I love you forever, grandma,' Leila whispered and with that, the calls came pouring in - Leila's family, friends, well-wishers, people trying to organise a quick funeral.

'It is what she would have wanted!' Leila thought if she heard that line one more time, she would scream.

Leila was on the phone to her mother when Dahlia shot through the door, hysterically.

'Oh Mum, oh Mum, we've lost Gucci. The gardener just found her. She's dead!'

'Dahlia, one second. I am just on the phone to your nana. I will deal with that shortly!'

'Deal with that? Mum! It's Gucci. How can you be so insensitive?'

'Dahlia, I just lost my grandmother, in case you hadn't noticed. You barely flinched when I told you about your greatgran, and here you are screaming down the house for Gucci. How do you think that makes me feel'?

'You are so selfish, Mum. Yes Greatgran died, but I grew up with Gucci. She was my companion most of the time. I played with her, sang with her all those mornings you could not be bothered to do much with me,' Dahlia spat!

'How can you say that'? Leila put the phone down.

'It's true, Mum. She was my best friend!'

'You are allowed to grieve, Dahlia. You are not allowed to insult me. I did a damn good job bringing you up, part of the time on my own.'

'Admit it. Half the time, you wished I wasn't there. You wished that so you could keep going off with Aunty Olga, getting drunk and getting stupid tattoos!' she barked, pointing at Leila foot. 'You just had to get a Conure, why didn't you get a Macaw or an African Grey? It would have lived longer.'

'Dahlia, how spoilt are you? How can you speak to me that way? And how can you ask me stupid questions?'

'Stupid? Your tattoo is stupid. I hate it by the way. I hate that tattoo, and I DO know what it means, even if you think I don't.'

Leila froze. She did not say a word. There they stood face-to-face, maintaining eye contact. Both were the exact same height with an uncanny resemblance. It was like looking at the same person in two generations. They had the same colour hair, the same shaped legs, and even their hearts measured the same hypersensitivity.

'I'm sorry. I didn't mean that, Mum. I didn't…' She reached out to Leila. As soon as she took Leila's hand, Leila collapsed into an untidy heap on the floor, sprawling most maladroitly, resembling a starfish. Dahlia had not seen that coming. She did not think Leila saw it coming either. She was therefore rooted to the spot for a few seconds before a reaction kicked in.

'What the…' Dahlia shrieked and raced for the phone. She called emergency first to get an ambulance.

'Dad, I haven't got a clue about resuscitating her. I don't know, Dad. I DON'T KNOW if she's breathing. Come home now!' she screamed.

'Aunty Olga…!'

And so they spent the morning in hospital. Leila sat with her mother as endless tests were conducted in quick succession. They poked and prodded, drew unforgivable amounts of her mother's blood; Dahlia felt sick to the stomach. Dahlia sat holding her hand all through.

'Leave her alone'! She said to one of the nurses in a weeping whisper.

'We just need to do some tests to make sure your mum is alright.' Dahlia nodded.

'It's probably just an anxiety attack!' Dahlia said, still nodding, not sure if she was trying to convince the nurses (whose job it was to care for her professionally, and not emotionally. Their mental distance was pretty apparent) or herself. For if it were some panic attack (which her mum had suffered one or two of), then what threw her into panic mode? The mention of the tattoo? Leila had some explaining to do. Dahlia took a deep breath and then examined her mother's face. She knew every wrinkle, every contour; she recognised every smile, every expression. She knew her mother inside and out and was able to read her thoughts – easily. This unnerved Leila. Dahlia smiled. Her mother was a weird, posh woman who got on her last nerve but Dahlia doted on her every word, obeyed her without question and cherished her cuddles. The bond was unshakable. Her dad came a very close second. He was literally wrapped round her finger and Dahlia knew this. There was nothing she asked for that she did not get financially (especially financially), emotionally and mentally, that she did not get in a heartbeat. Sometimes Dahlia felt like Akash was in direct competition with Leila for her love, but was always quick to dismiss this thought.

Leila stirred. Dahlia's trail of thoughts was lost as she turned to her.

'Mum,' she whispered.

Her mother groaned, opened her eyes, smiled weakly at Dahlia and then shut them again. She grimaced.

'Are you in pain?' Leila nodded. 'Where?' Leila still had Dahlia's hand in hers so she simply slid both hands down from in-between her bra-less breasts where they rested to her tummy. Dahlia caressed gently. Leila fell asleep.

She sat there still staring at Leila, wondering what her secret was. She knew her mother had stories. She wondered about her relationship with her dad. She knew they loved each other, but she was old enough to notice the vacant looks Leila gave him sometimes. Maybe people grew up and stopped loving each other in the romantic sense and then families became intertwined by rebirth, etc and then it became platonic in its capacity as 'family love'. Well, that's what Nana had implied the other night. She was sceptical about this version. It did not sound complete. There was something else. One day she would find out. Her mum was asleep. Dahlia's thoughts drifted back to her dream the other night. Suddenly she started to sweat. She had actually dreamt of her grandmother's death. She had not seen Gucci's demise though. The dream had been made up of little flashes, which were all only moments-long at a time. The most vivid story of her dream was her mother's tattoo. This was no surprise though, as the picture on her mother's ankle had been the subject of many a recurring dream. They usually were more prominent around birthdays for some reason. The picture was of a tangled webbing of some sort, there was Arabic writing enclosed within it. Following one of such frequent dreams, which had this time involved a revolving crown, and the fact that Google had informed her that her name, 'Adaobi', pronounced her some sort of Nigerian Princess, she had fantasies of sovereignty. She had observed her mother's reaction at the sight of the 'Princess Dahlia Adaobi' tag on her bedroom door. Dahlia had tried so hard but that was one moment when she was unable to decipher her thoughts. Every time Dahlia asked Leila about the name, Leila went all stuttery, vague and seemed to lose concentration and balance. The mention of her tattoo brought about the same reaction. Dahlia smiled. Yes, her mother was a strange one indeed – very secretive. Still, she was the love of her life.

When the nurse berated Dahlia for using her phone, she excused herself and went outside where she bumped into Akash on his way in. He was in floods of tears and looked like he had been crying for weeks!

'What's the matter, Dad? She's ok. She's stable.'

'What did they say?' he asked, reaching out to Dahlia.

'Nothing yet, they are doing some tests. She's not unconscious, just asleep so please get a grip, Dad,' she said gently. In Dahlia's arms, Akash wept some more. Every bone in his body told him what the problem was. It was just something he had expected to happen at some point, he just did not know when. It had been twelve years, but it was rearing its ugly head. He hated to be so pessimistic, but he knew – the cancer was back!

When they got into the room, they met the doctor on his way out. Akash shook his hand grimly as he looked on at Leila, trying to decode her expression. Akash took her hand in his.

'I don't think I can fight it this time,' she said weakly. Akash burst into tears again.

'Will someone tell me what is going on in here?' Dahlia asked, frustrated.

'Sweetheart, I think you need to sit down,' Leila said making room for her beside Akash, on the bed.

Leila told her about her history of cancer. She told her of how she thought she had beaten the disease forever. It had been twelve years and her annual tests had been negative thus far, and even though she was never able to bear any more kids, her body had been doing fine. She told Dahlia how it very nearly killed her, how she had put up the biggest fight of her life and overcome it.

'But this time, sweetie, I don't know if I have enough fight in me!'

Dahlia looked at them both one after the other.

'So you need chemo? How much damage has been done? What did the doctor say?'

'It's come back pretty aggressively. The doctor said he cannot be sure. It's up to me to opt for chemo or not.'

'How long have you got?'

'I don't know, Dahlia. It could be anytime.'

'I cannot believe you two!' Dahlia said, her tone – quite annoyed.

'So you have sentenced yourself to death because it's too hard to fight? And you, Dad, you ought to be ashamed of yourself. You should be lifting her up, not drowning in sorrow and allowing her to prophesy her own death. The doctor has even offered chemo. This is 2014, not the dark ages. Don't make me swear at you. What are you two like? Mum, what kind of lazy attitude is this? You want to die? You want to leave me? And Dad? You two are unbelievable. I will leave you to wallow in your self pity because I will not… no, hang on.' She paused and rephrased: 'I will NEVER take part in this premature pre-funeral!' She spat it out in fury, and with that, she stormed out of the room.

She met Olga outside.

'Glamour Puss!' Olga greeted, looking at her from head to toe. She looked at her hair, worn in a bun with a few loose tendrils here and there, the simple low button cut Moschino shirt, the skinny jeans with legs shaped exactly like her mother's and her patent leather Louboutins. She had received a text from Leila, and knew exactly what to do. Dahlia walked straight into her arms.

'Is your dad with her?' Olga asked. Dahlia nodded.

'Coffee?' Dahlia nodded again.

'My mother is one of the strongest women I know. Nothing ever gets her down. She fights with fucking barbarian zest, you know, Aunty Olga? Sorry for swearing.' Olga nodded and dismissed the apology.

'I cannot believe that she would give up just like that. And Dad, I cannot understand how he could allow her do this…and even join in on the pity party. For fucksake, the doctor has not said she has days to live or anything drastic like that.'

'Dahlia, sweetie, your dad is just scared. Your mother is the love of his life and he doesn't want to lose her. Your dad is sometimes really bad at handling things like this. He hides by resigning himself to the fact. In his mind, if he accepts it then he will not be disappointed.'

'How silly is that though?' Dahlia asked. They sat in silence for a while before they went back in.

'Mullato! What's this I hear about you letting cancer tell you what to do?' and then the lecture began. It lasted 45 minutes with Dahlia chipping in occasionally. By the forty-ninth minute, the following conversation ensued between Leila and Akash with Dahlia and Olga observing.

'Leila, I am sorry I have adopted this defeatist attitude. It is down to nothing but fear of losing you. The first time, I did not handle it well. I even ran away. Watching what it was doing to you was too much for me to deal with. I admit this. This time, I will fight with you. I will give you everything you need. I will be by your side and aid your restoration. You know my mantra – Man jeetai jagjeet – he who conquers the mind, conquers the world!' Leila smiled. She had not heard that in a long while.

'There is nothing to be sorry for, Kash. Thank you for your support. I will fight again,' she said simply and she held Dahlia's hands. Dahlia and Olga both smiled. The mood was sombre. Further conversation would have been an added strain. Everything that needed to be said was said. Leila lay in her bed, Akash sat on the chair to her left side, Olga on her right and Dahlia in her bed.

'I will fight again,' Leila said. Those were the last words spoken that evening. Emotional exhaustion took its toll and they all fell asleep.

The world breaks everyone, and afterward,
some are strong at the broken places.
– Ernest Hemingway

Chapter Eighty-Four

When they got home from the hospital that day, they had a little funeral for Gucci outside by the beach. Akash bought a little brown box where she was laid in. All three of them got busy digging up a grave for her. She was put in slowly and covered up with a wooden cross to mark the location of the grave. Naturally, it had to be around the most suitably earthed spot.

'It has to be in the corner over there…no, Leila. It will get water logged and it needs to have direct sunlight,' she heard Kaobi's voice. Leila smiled. Once upon a time, Leila and Kaobi actively created destiny around there. They sang Amazing Grace because, in Dahlia's words – 'that's what they do at funerals'. Leila was taken back to Kaobi's funeral; she sang with passion, and she wept. Dahlia seemed pleased. She would have been shocked if she could read her mother's thoughts at that moment.

They marked her tomb – 'Gucci Parrot – companionship through melody. We will hear your song in our hearts forever'. They went in and had a glass of chardonnay each. On Leila's prompt, they listened to Stevie Wonder's 'signed, sealed, delivered' and R Kelly's 'Step'. These were Gucci's favourite songs. They giggled as they reminisced about the hilarious bird. It was a nice funeral. Dahlia was grateful for this. It was all she had wanted – a befitting send off for her BFF!

Meanwhile, if there was ever love, it was glorified in the three years that came after that. Akash proved his love through and through. Leila could not have asked for more.

It was the 25th of April 2017 – sixteen years after the day this date became significant, it was their wedding anniversary.

But Ruth said, "Do not urge me to leave you or to return from following you. For where you go I will go, and where you lodge I will lodge. Your people shall be my people, and your God my God. Where you die I will die, and there will I be buried. May the LORD do so to me and more also if anything but death parts me from you."
Ruth 1:16-17

Mujhe baar baar mat kaho ki mein tumhen chor doon yaan tumharaa peecha naa karun. Tum jahaan jayogi, mein wahin jaungaa, jahaan tum rahogi, mein wahin rahungaa. Tumhaare apne mere apne honge, tumharaa bhagwaan mera bhagwaan hoga. Jahaan tum marogi, wahin mein tumhaare saath marungaa aur wahin dafan hoongaa. Mein dua kartaa hoon ki bhagwaan aisaa karen aur hum dono ko maut bhi judaa naa kar saken (I pray that God does this and we stay together until our last breath)

She looked up from his bare chest where her head laid and they smiled at each other. She re-curled herself in his arms.

'Is this it? If so, do I fly or fall?' she asked herself. Then she looked at him and said:

'*Mere husband, mere pati – My husband.*' His eyes shone with delight. He licked his lips and slicked his hair. Leila grinned. He had a bald patch in the middle of his head and he still slicked his hair. She still found him sexy.

'*Meri biwi, meri patni, meri jaan, meri dilruba – My wife, my love, my sweetheart*' he said back.

She had gone through life learning many variations of love and had come to realise one thing: there is nothing overly romantic about love. You read about it in books and watch movies, and this puts so much pressure on the world about its interpretation. Love is love. It is classless and individual. It is not hectic, overbearing or sexual. It is pure and accepting. She was content. She was not head over heels for Akash. No, she knew better. Besides, she was unable to forget the strength of her feelings for Kaobi. Nothing could ever take that away, but for this lifetime, she would dedicate herself to Akash. She had made peace with the idea and enjoyed his masculinity, and loved him for who he was. He had got her for life. She had him till death.

Akash stroked her hair as he thought how much God must love him to give him this opportunity again. He wished she adored him the way she used to. He longed to be her alpha male, the one who could tell her what to do, to see the burning desire for him in her fiery eyes, but he was satisfied that he had her. And Leila was loyal, hesitant...but loyal. He had her till death.

'Give me you. All of you. Bring your frailties and bad habits. Bring your culture and religion and values. I will bring mine. Together let's make love until we die,' he whispered

'I accept you. I accept your love. I give you my dedication and loyalty...until we die. That is guaranteed,' she said. They both smiled.

"...I would rather have eyes that cannot see; ears that cannot hear; lips that cannot speak, than a heart that cannot love."
- Robert Tizon

The Penultimate Chapter

Fly or fall

It began to bother her when she awoke from such dreams, recounting that whenever her feet were separated from the ground, she fell or flew, but knew not which. For weeks on end, she wondered.

And every morning she sat in front of her mirror, and when she lashed on her mascara, she secretly begged her eyes for answers. Why was she in limbo?

So if the dream was the story of her life thus far:

She knew that if she tried with all her might, one day, she would fly and in her mind's eye, many a time she took off. She would look to her left, and to her right and there would be clouds, the sky, chirping birds and, occasionally, a rainbow. Then she would see pink elephants, and she would smile. Well, you never know if you never dream.

So flap, flap, flap…off she went.

A storm!

Even the weather lady gets it wrong sometimes, so she, being neither psychic nor qualified in crystal ball reading had not foreseen a storm so big, a storm that clipped brave, resilient, but naturally sensitive wings. And she even lost feathers. They fell in gold, they fell in silver, they fell amidst pieces of broken heart, broken dreams, teardrops that she had frozen. The fiercer the storm, the harder she flapped, but even superwoman would have struggled with this one. Then she fell. When she fell, everything went quiet – no sun, no moon, no clouds, and no rainbows – just her falling, and her feathers paving the way under and parallel to her. Even her pink elephant came crashing down in all its glory; it could easily have rivalled humpty dumpty's unfortunate demise.

So that morning, she fell in slow motion and parallel to the sky. But on her way down, she encountered magic, transfixed in eyes that appeared slowly in a mirror before her. These eyes belonged not to her, but possessed the most curious qualities. In their sparkle, she found her buried smile, her lost treasure, pink elephant! She remembered her strength and she rocked from side to side until she jolted. Feather by feather, her wings were restored until she flew again. She had found her miracle!

The mirror in the sky had been temporary, if not fantasy. It had no place in her future. Therefore, she sulked and mourned, but eventually understood that it did not always come easy, but she was grateful that her broken wings were unbroken. She accepted that sometimes even her mind would not conjure up pink elephant. Therefore, for every other second, she relished in the memory of when her eyes met the eyes in that mirror, and how the inner strength within the archives of her soul was unleashed.

Yesterday she fell, today she flew, tomorrow? Well, she knew not if she would fall or fly, regardless, somewhere along the way, she had experienced magic in a little 'big' miracle. In that moment with the mirror, she built indestructible wings. For that reason, whether she fell or flew was inconsequential, and would not alter her dreams. The point is she created her own little fairy tale and lived happily ever after.

Leila x

PS

Leila's Note: ...you fall, you fly – that's life. There is often a little miracle in every day. Grab your miracle and dream your tomorrow into reality. According to flying or falling chick above, you never know if you never dream! Off to find my pink elephant ;)

The Final Chapter!

'It's the magic of England. Autumn is bittersweet and much too short...every tree is different, every shade of red and orange and yellow and, finally, brown is different – the purity of the air, the effervescent sky, the magic of seeing the world falling around you and raking it all together – jumping and crunching and scattering. We have had some awesome moments together here on this beach. But the way it looks today…' She paused and closed her eyes.

'The way it looks today – this particular shade – the feeling of darkness even in light. Or is that all in my own mind? Perhaps my sight of the world is fading?'

'Stop it, Mum.'

'Don't worry. It is the inside that counts. You bring sunshine to me. My heart at this moment is one pretty, blindingly colourful rainbow.'

'This is so much to take in, Mum,' Dahlia said kneeling beside her mother's rocking chair, caressing her thighs, her feet…her tattoo. Leila smiled intermittently.

'I know, flower. Look in that bag. The title deed is in there. I officially hand this house over to you. Patricia has drawn up all the paperwork. Everything has been done. I trust you to take care of it. Happy twenty-first birthday my Princess. I know it was a week ago, but we never found the right time. I needed to be alone with you. It had to be done properly.' Dahlia was trembling.

'Does Dad know all this?'

'About the house? Of course.'

'How does he feel about everything else?'

'Sweetheart, there is no such thing as black and white. Your father and I have dealt with everything the best way we knew. He is not your biological father, but he has loved you from the day you were born. Of that, I am one hundred percent sure.'

'And Kaobi? What about my real family?'

Leila smiled. 'I cannot believe this day has come.' She brought out a piece of paper. 'These are the last numbers I have. This is the address I have. It's all up to you. Do what you want to do with the information and whatever you decide I will be behind you always. Don't forget that. If in doubt, just listen hard. You will always hear my voice. I have breathed wisdom into you and I will guide you. I will never let you go through life on your own.'

'So that's what the tattoo is all about – about your destiny!!'

Leila breathed heavily, choking on tears. She nodded.

'Indeed. Dahlia, there is one thing that I have pondered over for a long time. Coincidences. Do they exist? Everything has played out so far according to what that woman...the wrinkly old fortune-teller with the scrawny fingers told me. Remember the Macbeth story? Sometimes it's in the laws of attraction. I don't know if my life has played out this way because it is how it was destined to, or if I attracted this destiny myself...you know, subconsciously. Where do we draw the line between coincidence and destiny?'

'And the wrinkly old fortune-teller with the scrawny fingers?' Dahlia asked.

Leila pointed. She sat solemnly in the corner; she was humming lowly; her eyes never departed from Leila's.

'I see no-one though,' Dahlia said.

'I know,' Leila smiled and shut her eyes.

'Please don't close your eyes. It's scary when you do that.'

'There is nothing to be afraid of. Your heart and mine are one. I am always with you.'

'Your dress, Mum, it's beautiful. I have never seen it before. Is it new?'

'It's called a bubu. Your grandmother gave it to me on the day I took you to see her. It makes me feel so close to Kaobi.'

'You never let him go really, did you?'

'He's embedded in my history, flower. He gave me you. How can I forget him?'

'Don't go, Mum.' Dahlia could sense what was happening. Please don't leave me yet. I have questions.'

'Ask then.'

"Does the walker choose the path, or the path the walker?"
– Garth Nix, Sabriel

Epilogue

Her bright red rocking chair.

'Mum? Dahlia called out. Leila opened her eyes. She continued, 'in life there are no guarantees. There could be dust or rain, gold or gain, cold moments of pain. You just never know. It is only certain that you will laugh, you will cry, you will die. The only thing I can say to you is that I have tried always to be the best I can be. I have been brought up with values and I have lived according to the rules. Life has ensured that these rules were not always the easiest to adhere to, and I am fallible like every other mere mortal. But I have met the most wonderful people in my life and the memory bank in my heart is rich. I have the best family; my friends are amazing. I have seen a lot of disappointment as well. People will let you down, Dahlia. Take it all for what it is, keep what is worth keeping and with a breath of comfort, blow the rest away. Live and let live. Everybody has his or her own story. Give space in your heart to understand and accept flaws, but not to the extent that you lose yourself.

Leila wiped the tears from Dahlia's eyes and smiled weakly.

You, sweetheart – you are my most prized person, the love and joy of my life, my pride; you are also my destiny – past and future. You hold my legacy. You are my re-incarnation. You are me. I look at you and I see myself. I will be watching to see what you do because I am curious to see how it will all turn out.

'My journal is in there. It has my favourite articles from my weekly blog. The final one is about the pink elephant. I wonder what my end is. Do I fly or fall?'

Dahlia took a long, piercing look at her mother.

'Mum, you fly.'

'Kiss me,' Leila said. 'I will always…always be with you.'

Dahlia kissed her slowly on her lips and allowed her mother's eyes to tell her everything else she was too tired to say. Time stood still to respect the moment. From the corner of her eye, Dahlia saw Akash making his way across to them.

Leila shut her eyes…

An invisible thread connects those who are destined to
meet, regardless of time, place and circumstance.
The thread may stretch or tangle, but it will never break!
– An ancient Chinese Proverb

THE END!